# WILD
# DOG
# CARIBBEAN

# WILD
# DOG
# CARIBBEAN

A NOVEL

DAVID J. MUMFORD

iUniverse®

# WILD DOG CARIBBEAN
## A Novel

iUniverse books may be ordered through booksellers or by contacting:

iUniverse
1663 Liberty Drive
Bloomington, IN 47403
www.iuniverse.com
1-800-Authors (1-800-288-4677)

ISBN: 978-1-4917-4447-5 (sc)
ISBN: 978-1-4917-4434-5 (e)

Library of Congress Control Number: 2014915354

Printed in the United States of America.

iUniverse rev. date: 09/23/2014

This book is dedicated to Ro.
For what other reason?

# PREFACE

*Wild Dog Caribbean* is the first of a series of novels written in my youth, a rather turbulent period of life filled with confusion, instability and uncertainty. In the intense, seemingly all-evasive search for meaning and purpose of life, the vastness and scope of the quest was undertaken with a dedicated, serious and unrelenting determination to find answers, truth, and enlightenment. Now that the decades have passed and anxiety and instability have coalesced into some sort of inevitable, mellowed acceptance of destiny, this intense pursuit of wisdom and knowledge that once totally possessed my being has segued into a much lighter viewpoint that some people would label youthful folly. In many respects, the mistakes and blind buffoonery of the young wandering days offer a mirror to the lighthearted, comic drama of my remaining time on Earth. I hope you enjoy reading *Wild Dog Caribbean* as much as I enjoyed living it.

—David J. Mumford
*August 5, 2014*

# PART 1

# CHAPTER 1

## *In the Beginning*

t was early September, 1973. Buster Murdock, at midday, arrived at the Nassau International Airport and was waiting for his baggage. There was lots of chaotic noise. A seemingly endless stream of announcements over the loudspeaker accompanied thousands of people, scurrying like ants running every which way. A small Bahamian band in the corner was playing the song, "Seven Hundred Islands in the Sun." The blind man, Jake, was playing the electric guitar with a huge grin on his black face—bright white teeth protruding out between his thick lips. The old man seemed to be enjoying himself. *But God*, Buster thought, *I'm sure glad I can see.*

His baggage finally came whirling around to him. The lean, white American of average height picked up his backpack, cased guitar and suitcase, and after a brief stop at customs, he headed towards the Bahamian Ministry of

3

Education booth set up near the bar. Tripping and falling all over his luggage, he finally made it to the smiling, young, chocolate-colored lady in the booth.

"Hi! I'm here!" he said, setting down his possessions. He ran his fingers through his dark brown, swept-back hair—hair that dropped over his ears and showed signs of becoming long.

"Name please?" she asked.

"Buster—Buster Murdock!"

"State?"

"Florida—Daytona Beach, Florida."

"Hmmm, Mr. Murdock, I don't seem to find your name on the list," she said, thumbing through the list of expected teacher arrivals.

"What do you mean I'm not on the list?"

"I mean, you're not on the list! Who told you to come down here to Nassau?"

"Work Force Employment Agency in Miami," he said nervously. "I mean, I paid a three hundred dollar fee and they told me I got the teaching job here, and my hotel room was paid for and everything!"

"What employment agency?"

"Work Force Employment Agency!"

"Hmmm, this agency is not on our list. As far as we're concerned, this agency does not exist!"

"You mean they took me for three hundred bucks?

"I know nothing of employment agencies, sir."

"Jesus!" Buster said. "The last thing that happens to me in my own country and I get taken—well those bastards!"

"Pardon me?" the girl asked.

"Oh, nothing, nothing," he said, as he stroked his heavy, black beard.

"Are you a qualified teacher, Mr. Murdock?"

"Yes, Ma'am—I have a Masters Degree in English. I just got it from the University of Florida," he said proudly.

"I'll tell you something, Mr. Murdock: since you are here now, you go to this hotel, the Pilot House. Tell them you are with the Bahamian Ministry of Education. Get settled in and tomorrow you go to the Ministry and they will try and place you."

"I have a job, then?"

"They will tell you—thank you!" She looked at the line forming behind Buster. "Next!"

He grabbed his luggage and caught a fifteen-dollar taxi ride into the city, not knowing what to expect from the funky, Bahamian way of doing things.

The taxi stopped and Buster stumbled out onto a red carpet, landing on a pair of patent leather shoes. The doorman stood perfectly erect at attention in a tuxedo uniform.

"Pilot House?" Buster looked up at the doorman. The huge black man just nodded his head. Buster got up and walked into the air-conditioned main lobby and set his things down. Standing below the chandelier in his t-shirt, dirty dungarees and tennis shoes, he gazed about. "Jesus!" he said to himself. "I don't know about this place."

A young, strikingly beautiful brown girl walked up to Buster and absolutely stupefied him with her glamor. "May I help you?" she asked in a perfect British accent.

"Uh…," he muttered with his jaw open. He had never seen such an exotic looking negro woman before—so refined, such a smooth complexion. "Uh, yes! The people at the airport sent me here. I'm a teacher from the States." He spoke with a slight, southern drawl.

"Oh yes, right this way." She led him to the office—Buster

staggering behind, wishing he had worn something else besides blue jeans.

"Name, please?"

"Murdock—Buster Murdock!"

She thumbed through the pages of a legal pad. "Hmmm, you do not seem to be on the list. Have you registered at the Ministry of Education?"

"Well, Ma'am, I'm supposed to be, but now I'm not quite sure if I'm supposed to be. I think I may have to straighten a few things out first. This employment agency, Work Force Plus, said I was all set up with hotel room and everything until I got settled in."

"OK—we will put you in this provisional room until you do. Meanwhile, because you are not on the Ministry's list at the present time, we must collect room money in advance—a two-day minimum. That will be sixty dollars!"

His jaw dropped again. "Uh, sixty dollars?" he whimpered. Just coming out of the university, sixty dollars seemed like six thousand to him. "But the Ministry will reimburse me, right?"

"That will be between you and the Ministry," she said.

He signed a few travelers' checks and handed them over to the beautiful lady. "I can see right now," he said, "these things aren't gonna last very long."

"That is for sure!" she said. "Be careful with your money, Mr. Murdock. Nassau is an expensive town."

"Yeah, well, thanks for the warning, Ma'am! Have a nice day!" He picked up his things and went to his room.

That afternoon the Ministry was closed for a "Goombay Summer Holiday," a native tradition. So, in order to straighten things out, he would have to wait until the next morning. Meanwhile, he decided to take a walk around downtown Nassau. He felt a bit strange. He had never been in a foreign country by himself. He had been in Mexico and Jamaica before, but they were on vacations with friends and only for a short time. But this time was different, because he knew that he was going to stay—at least until Christmas— three and-a-half months. He was going to work and give teaching a chance. So, Nassau was different. He was amazed at the colonial flavor it had. He walked down the famous Bay Street and smiled at the different colored buildings—mostly pink and cream colored. *Pink*, he thought, *of all colors, pink*. Lots of black and silver Rolls Royces passed him, showing him that there was definitely money in this city. And he looked at all the different shops: watch shops (tax free), liquor shops (tax free), dive shops, boat shops, motorcycle shops, souvenir shops, straw hat shops. He was impressed— shops, shops, shops, and everything in a different style than in the United States. It was a treat for Buster's eyes to see different things. That was one of the reasons he left in the first place. He needed a change of scenery. Somehow, all the towns in the United States seemed to be boringly similar. He just had to get out.

Then, suddenly, he stopped on a street corner. His heart seemed to drop to his feet. Right in front of him was a sign: "Kentucky Fried Chicken—Finger Lickin' Good." "Fuck!" He yelled. He hurried across the street to escape from this American, capitalistic blasphemy, but he ran right into another sign: "Burger King—Home of the Whopper." Nassau suddenly lost its English colonial flavor. "Fuck!" Buster yelled again. "Let me outta here! Don't these people ever stop?" He had traveled hundreds of miles and it took him a lot of money to get out of the American Scene Magazine, only to find these "Parasites," as he called them.

He took a turn and walked up Frederick Street, passing the town cemetery and noticing the eclectic colored cottages and their quirky sizes and shapes. Then he walked down to the docks and to Woodes Rogers Walk where all the fishing boats came in.

After only a few hours of rambling around, he suddenly felt as if a train had rolled over his body. A tremendous fatigue fell over him. "Go to bed, Buster," he moaned to himself. "Go to bed—all this is really neat, but it won't go away. It'll still be here tomorrow." So in the early evening, he listlessly drifted back to the Pilot House and soundly slept until the next Bahamian morning.

The most unorganized institution on the face of the earth was the Bahamian Ministry of Education. The building itself looked good—there was no doubt. It looked marvelous, in fact, and Buster was commenting to himself how pretty it was as he walked through its iron gates. It was a large pink mansion on the top of a hill overlooking Nassau and the Caribbean Sea. The grounds were beautifully kept and trimmed. The grass was golf-course green and there were palm trees scattered all throughout the area.

But the inside was another story. Buster walked into the main entrance and asked an old, black desk clerk directions: "Uh, good morning, I'm a teacher coming from the States and I need to talk to somebody about an assignment."

"Yes, room 5-A," he answered.

Buster walked into room 5-A, a small, drab cubicle that looked like a doctor's waiting room. There were about fifty other people waiting to see a particular person hidden behind a closed door. "Pardon me, is this for new teachers?" he asked a middle-aged white man sitting next to the entrance.

"No, I believe, and certainly hope," the man said in a heavy English accent, "that this is for outgoing teachers."

"What do you mean, outgoing?" Buster asked.

"Just what I said, mate—outgoing. We're going out, ya know, mate? Like home, mate! The Buggers are shippin' us out"

"Why?"

"C'mon now mate, you've heard about it, right? They're shippin' us micks home on the first boat outta here. They just got their independence and they want all us Brits to go home—the bleedin' buggerits!"

"But they'll be short of teachers, won't they?"

"Short? Huh, that ain't the word for it, mate. They just won't have any! They'd rather not have any teachers than have us in there. It's the principle of the thing, I suppose."

"Why that's the dumbest thing I've ever heard!" Buster said.

"Dumb? Huh! American, are you?"

"Yeah, American."

"Why, you're dumb to even come here. These black fools don't want anything white here. But, I suppose being American'll help a bit. They just don't like us Brits around—Independence, ya know—the bleedin' black fools. The whole country's gonna sink."

"Jesus, I had no idea the situation was so bad. I had heard they needed teachers, but …. Anyway, where're the in-coming teachers?"

"Beats me! Try 5-B across the hall—sounds good, anyway."

"Thanks, man—good luck to you!"

"Luck knickers!" the Brit chuckled. "You're the one that's gonna be needin' it, mate."

Buster walked to room 5-B, his nerves a little shattered. *What a crude conversation that was,* he thought. *And him calling me 'Mate.' Jesus! I'm no fucking 'Mate!'* He walked into the room and nobody was there. He knocked on a door that had a sign reading "Mrs. Miller."

"Come in," a gentle female voice sounded. Buster walked in timidly.

"Hello, I'm a new teacher from the States and I'm looking for the right person to place me."

"Yes, come in and have a seat," she said in another English accented voice. She was practically hidden behind the mountains of papers stacked on her desk. She was a mid-thirtyish black woman—light complexion—beautiful, but a little on the plump side.

"Name, please?" she asked.

"Murdock, Ma'am, Buster Murdock!"

She thumbed through the pages of a notebook. "Hmmm!" she said, puzzled. "I don't seem to find your name on the list. Who told you to come down here to the Bahamas?"

Buster was getting kind of bored with the same question all the time. "Work Force Plus Employment Agency in Miami," he yawned.

"What employment agency?"

"Work Force Plus Employment Agency, Ma'am."

"Hmmm, I've never heard of it. And they told you to come down here, Mr. Murdock?"

"That's right! They told me everything was set up—that you had a job for me and that I had a hotel provided for, plus transportation and all that."

"Hmmm, they must have gotten the word from somebody else—But don't worry Mr. Murdock, we'll get it straightened out."

Buster was getting worried that maybe his trip down to the Bahamas was in vain. All that money especially—down the drain.

"Are you a qualified teacher, Mr. Murdock?"

"Yes, Ma'am. I have a Masters Degree from the University of Florida."

"Do you have documents, please?"

Fortunately, Buster had brought a miniature, wallet-size diploma with him. "Yes, Ma'am, right here!"

"Very good. Hmmm, in English, right?"

"Yes Ma'am."

Mrs. Miller smiled. She liked this young American's Southern gentleman style of courtesy. "OK. Fill out this application form while I do a few things, and I'll be back in a few moments."

She left the room, leaving Buster to fill out the form in the midst of stacks and stacks of papers and brown folders. She came back about fifteen minutes later with a few brown folders in her hand. "OK, Mr. Murdock?" she asked.

"Yes, Ma'am," he said, handing the application to her.

"Very good." She placed the form on top of one of the stacks on her desk. "We will take a look at these and we will have your assignment ready for you on Monday."

"Monday?" Buster said. That's five days from now. Can't it be any sooner—like tomorrow?"

"Mr. Murdock, please take it easy. We have to process the application and that takes a little time. And, of course, we want to place you in the proper school, right?"

"Right!"

"And Friday is Goombay Holiday and nobody works."

"Oh, I see. Well, uh, the hotel—what about the hotel? Do I get reimbursed for the hotel room?"

"Where are you staying now?" she asked.

"The Pilot House," he said.

"Yes, well, that's where the teachers usually stay that we've hired inside the States. But since we are hiring you directly down here, reimbursement would be impossible. I suggest you find a place somewhat cheaper."

Buster's heart sank. He could only think of the sixty dollars he had shelled out. "Well, OK, Monday, then."

"Monday, Mr. Murdock. And welcome to the Bahamas!"

"Thanks, Mrs. Miller!"

Buster walked out the door feeling taken on one hand but relieved that at least he got a job. "Welcome to the Bahamas," he muttered to himself. "Welcome!"

Buster stayed one more night at the Pilot House then moved out to something more his own style. He woke up one early, sultry morning swatting mosquitoes in a four-dollar-a-day room at the Delancey Guest House on the other side of town. Now, the Delancey Guest House was quite international. At least so proved the walls of Buster's room, because underneath all the squashed mosquito bodies on the walls was graffiti from all over the world: Fuck You (of course), Chinga tu Madre, Merde—1954, and hundreds of other symbols from Chinese to Arabic. Even though the Delancey Guest House looked like a seventeenth century, green colored haunted house, and the walls were so paper thin that Buster could hear couples in all languages trying to win the international marathon prize in copulation, there was one nice thing about it other than the price of the room, and that was its location. It was up on top of a hill—greenery all around—overlooking Nassau and only ten minutes walk to the beach. He could not complain, really. It was a nice place to stay, temporarily anyway. Meanwhile he could look for apartments, get to know the city better, go swimming, etcetera. It would be an overall, general plan of relaxation before beginning work—something which he was not all that enthused about, but knew he had to do.

It was on a Friday, the second day of the Delancey Guest House stay, when Buster was walking down Bay Street and ran into an old university acquaintance of his, Jim Parkson. Buster knew he would be down here but did not know exactly where or when. It was, in fact, Parkson who informed Buster about the Bahamas: that the country had just got their independence and that they were kicking out the Brits and that they would be needing teachers.

"Parkson!" Buster exclaimed. "'Bout time I ran into you. How the fuck are you?"

"Murdock! Wow, man, I really didn't think you'd make the move down here."

"Well, I thought I'd give it a try, you know what I mean?—being in a different country and all—besides, job crisis in the States—nothing going on up there, you know?"

"Yeah, man, I know! Told you, didn't I? Let's go for a drink!"

"Far out! It's hot as hell out here."

They stepped into a patio bar next to the sea.

"Let's celebrate, my friend!" Parkson said. "I'm really glad to see you!"

"Yeah," Buster said. "It's nice to see somebody I know, too—almost a relief, it is."

"What'll it be, man?"

"Beer sounds good."

"Beer, nonsense!" Parkson said. "We're celebrating, remember? Hey, I discovered a really far-out drink here you'll really like." He looked around for the waiter. "Hey waiter—waiter—two Harvey Wallbangers, please!"

"Harvey Wallbanger?" Buster asked.

"It's great—you'll love it! It's a combination of orange juice, vodka and Galiano liqueur."

"Sounds good." Buster looked at his friend rather untrustingly. Parkson had long, blond, unkempt hair with a scraggly, patchy beard that one could see through to the chin and face. He had a big nose and a slender face, and when he talked, he placed his lips to the side and murmured from there. His voice was a quiet one and at times he was hard to understand mainly because of his soft voice.

"So Murdock," he said, obviously glad to see a familiar face. "When did you get here?"

"Oh, I got here a couple days ago," Buster answered. "I found out that nothing was set up for me down here."

"You didn't go to Work Force Plus employment Agency, did you?"

"Well, yeah, wasn't that the one you told me to go to?"

"No man, no man! That was the one I told you not to go to. They're fly-by-night crooks at that place—everybody knows that!"

"Yeah, everybody but me, and they wiped me clean for three hundred bucks. I could swear you mentioned that one to me, God—dammit! Did you go to an agency?"

"No, I already knew that the Brits were leaving quickly. I made a few phone calls myself down here, and they told me just to come down."

"How long have you been down here?"

"A month now. I've got me a car and everything now. I sorta know the ropes around this place. The school I'm at is not bad, and my apartment is nice. Did you know this place has got over two hundred and fifty teachers short? They'd rather be without teachers than have the British here."

"Yeah, well thanks for telling me," Buster said.

"What a number the English must have done on these people!"

The Harvey Wallbangers came—tall frosted glasses containing a yellow, tropical mixture. The black waiter set them on the table.

"That will be eight dollars please, mann," he said.

"Eight dollars?" Buster wildly exclaimed.

"Uh, yeah," Parkson said. "Things are kind of expensive around here. Wait'll you see the price of hamburger—four bucks a pound. They gotta import everything, man, everything. But this one's on me. Take it easy. You just gotta get used to it, that's all!"

He gave the waiter a ten-dollar Bahamian bill—a light green note with tropical fish and multi-colored coral fans on the front. He collected the change and the two Americans lifted their glasses for their first Bahamian toast.

"Well, here's to the Bahamas," Parkson said.

"To the Bahamas," Buster said. "May we have luck." They both took a sip on the straws.

"By the way, Murdock, where are you staying?"

"Delancey Guest House for the moment."

"Delancey Guest House? God, what a dump!"

"Thanks a lot, fucker! You're full of encouragement. I suppose you live in a mansion."

"Mansion no, but it's a real nice and pleasant place right near Fort Charlotte, five minutes from the beach. It's an efficiency, but there's room enough for two. Why not come and live there—we'll share the rent—that way, maybe we could beat some of these prices around here."

"Jesus, live with you Parkson? I dunno, man. I'm used to living with women!"

"Be practical, Murdock! It's gonna be at least a couple months before you settle down here and get to know people—and I'm talking mostly about the money-wise thing now. Rents are outrageous. Mine is $350.00 bucks a month, and it's nothing special."

"Jesus! Well, you got a point there, Parkson," Buster said. He stared into his iced drink and was reluctant to give any form of answer. He did not know Parkson very well, but well enough to know that back at the university he was called "Jinx" because of his luck. It was Jinx because Parkson was one of those people who always had bad luck wherever he went, and at times this bad luck would wear off on the people around him. It was bad luck in the sense that whatever he did or wherever he went, something wrong would happen to him. For example, one time he took a trip from Florida to New York City for a couple of weeks. One day he got lost in the subway and it took him two whole days before he saw light again. He went to Yankee Stadium to see the only live ball game in his life, and it got rained out. He went up the Empire State Building and the first time in the building's history, the elevator got stuck for three hours. Even in Florida he was infamous. Thousands of things always went wrong with him. Once he went inner-tubing down the Chattahoochee River just outside of Gainesville, and out of fifty people in the group, his inner tube was the only one that went flat, and he had to walk the rest of the way along the banks of the river. He went to Disney World once and got mugged in the Haunted House.

It was things like this that made Buster leery of having

anything to do with Parkson. Being in a foreign country, that's all he needed, bad luck.

There was a silence in the bar as Buster gazed out at the turquoise colored Caribbean Sea. *God-damn, he's got a point there*, he thought. *I mean, Jesus, economically speaking, it makes sense. And it would be good to know somebody here at first—especially somebody with a car—a big advantage in getting around the island.*

"Well," Buster said, "I'd have to see the place first, you know what I mean?"

"Yeah, sure, man. I'll tell you what—I'm having some people over tonight for a sort of Goombay celebration. I'll come over and pick you up at Delancey's Flop House—uh, excuse me, Guest House—around eight, and we'll take it from there, OK?"

"Good enough!"

They took the last sips of their Harvey Wallbangers and left the bar.

"OK, so I'll see you tonight, OK Murdock?"

"OK, great!"

And they parted smiling. Buster had a good feeling inside of him. It was nice to know that he was not on the island alone. As many faults as Jim Parkson had, at least he was somebody—somebody known that was going through the same experience as he in a foreign land, and that made a big difference to Buster's state of mind.

At the party there was such a mixture of people: Buster had never seen so many people from different places all conglomerated in one place. At the university he always went to parties with a Cuban here or a Puerto Rican there, but nothing like a few Germans, a French couple, a young Chinaman with a Fu-Man-Chu mustache, two Arabs and three Japanese-American girls from Memphis, Tennessee, gathered in a circle drinking Bacardi Rum straight and passing around marijuana joints. Jinx was one that needed people around him, to say the least. If he did not have people around him, he got fidgety.

"Hey Parkson," Buster said, "Where did you get all these people?"

"Well, most of them are just passers-by visiting Nassau on their way to other places on cheap flights. Nassau is kinda like a nucleus for international flights." Parkson paused, then added, "Hey man, pass that bottle!"

"Jesus!" Buster exclaimed. "What a motley lookin' bunch." He looked the apartment over. "This place is kind of small for two people, don't you think, Parkson?"

"Yeah, but maybe we could go looking for a larger one once we get settled."

"Yeah, well I suppose you're right. Hey, I've been thinking, and uh, I've decided to take you up on that deal, OK?"

"Hey, that's great, Murdock!"

"Will tomorrow be a good enough time to move in?"

"Whenever you want, Brother."

"Brother, hey man, don't get too personal! I'll see you later, I'm gonna check out all these foreigners. Jesus, Parkson! What a motley lookin' bunch."

Most of the travelers were decked out in worn-out blue jeans, desert-boot type shoes, long hair, and every one of them was dirty and in dire need of a hot bath.

Buster walked over to the tall blond boy in the corner. "Don't Bogart that joint, my friend!" Buster said, remembering his university, hippie days in the late sixties.

"Excuse me?" he asked, handing the joint to Buster.

"Don't Bogart that joint, my friend!"

"What means Bog—Bogart?" His English had a heavy foreign accent.

"Forget it, Mack! What's your name?"

"Folker—Folker Schnell."

"Ah, German are you?" Buster said. "I know a little German. Let's see, schnell, schnell, that means fast, right?"

"Yes—Folker Fast!" He smiled.

"Hey, man, that's great. My grandfather is German, you know!"

"Oh, yes? That's funny, because most Americans I've talked to like to tell me that their grandparents are German!"

"What are you, a wise ass or something?"

"Excuse me? Wise ass?"

"Forget it, Fast!"

"Goombay—Goombay!" Someone yelled. The drums could be heard in the distance. The party moved from the room and everybody walked towards the center of town.

Goombay was the summer festival in Nassau, very similar to Carnival in Rio. Everybody took to the streets with drums, Coke cans, bottles, anything to make noise and rhythm.

The closer the party got to town, the louder the drum sound became until it seemed to pound the hearts of everybody. Excitement was in the air because none of the foreigners had really experienced anything like this before. The sound attracted them like magnets. When they finally reached the procession, the group automatically dispersed into the thousands of black Bahamians keeping a tremendous African beat while dancing towards one direction, down Bay Street. The African drums were especially effective. The main line of drummers was in front but other drummers were interspersed throughout the crowd. The drum sound was so deep and powerful that it sent vibrations through everybody and one could not help but move to the rhythm. Even the young Chinaman could not help moving up and down. There were large fires on the curb intermittently where the drummers stopped to stretch the drum skins. Smoke mixed in with the odor of fish from the docks and that special smell from human, Negro sweat. It was just one huge mass of black people dancing and moving to the rhythm following the drummers down the street in a chaotic noise of singing, chanting, screaming, whistle blowing, drums, cans, sticks, and foot shuffling. It was a Goombay, Goombay—Goombay Summer night in Nassau.

On Monday morning Buster stood in Mrs. Miller's office trying to catch a glimpse of her every now and then through the stacks of paper.

"OK, Mr. Murdock," she said, "We have placed you for the time being in Donald Davis Junior High School on Atkinson Road. We feel that this school is in desperate need of a good English teacher and we hope you will be of great service to us there.

"Junior High School, Ma'am?" he said.

"Yes, is there something wrong?"

"No, uh, well… I was sort of thinking in terms of at least high school. Uh, me and little kids, well, I don't know, Ma'am!" Buster's training at the university was in Higher Education.

"Well, that's what we have decided for now. Do the best you can and see what happens. If you don't like it, you may put in for a transfer after a few months. Sign here, please." She handed him a contract. "Your contract is for one year with seven hundred and fifty dollars a month. Is that sufficient for you Mr. Murdock?"

*Jesus!* he thought. *Seven hundred and fifty dollars a month?* He gulped. He had never had that kind of money before. It was always a one dollar and seventy-five cent an hour pizza-parlor job near the university for him.

He squirmed in his seat and cleared his throat: "Uh, seven hundred and fifty dollars a month—uh, is that tax free, Ma'am?"

"Oh, definitely!"

"Seven hundred and fifty dollars—well, uh, that's not too bad, I suppose. Yes, Ma'am, that'll be fine—I'll give it a try." He did a good job in keeping a calm look on his face, although his heart was beating rapidly.

"Very good, then, Mr. Murdock!" she said. "You will start immediately. They are expecting you right away."

They shook hands and he walked out the door feeling a bit queasy. "Kids?" he said to himself. "Me, with kids? But Jesus, seven hundred and fifty bucks a month—that's a lot of pizzas!"

Buster caught a taxi to the school. It was a fairly modern cement block structure with three wings and a large patio in the center. The school was located in the interior of the island in one of the poorest sections of town. When Buster first caught a glimpse of it, he was disappointed. Being in Nassau, he had expected to be in a nice neighborhood by the seaside with nice daily walks on the beach on the way to work. This was quite the contrary. Broken down shacks surrounded the school and dirt roads sufficed for transportation. Public water fountains lined with conch shells were the only means of water for many of the residents and privies were scattered behind each shack. Such squalor with such richness just a few minutes away amazed him.

He entered the office and asked for the headmaster. A tall, dark figure came from a side door. "Yes, are you the new teacher?" the man asked.

"Yes, sir. The Ministry just sent me. I'm Buster Murdock."

"Right. I'm Percy Trahn." His eyes seemed to go back and forth and everywhere except into those of Buster's. "Yes, Mr. Murdock, just go upstairs directly above us to the teachers' room and we'll be with you as soon as we can."

Buster went upstairs. Class was in session and voices of teachers and children filtered out of the rooms. Two young boys went zooming past him, running after another of their classmates. *Uh oh*, he thought, *here we fucking go—kids*! If there was one thing Buster did not like, it was children running around in a school. Having children around him just was not his idea of an exciting, knowledge-seeking adventure.

He nervously walked into the teachers' room. There were only two teachers sitting down, casually conversing. All the others were in class.

"Hi! A new teacher?" a red-headed, freckled young man said in a British accent.

"That's right." Buster said.

"Poor wretched soul," he said, turning to the fat lady next to him. "Bloody Bugger don't know what he got himself into." He looked back at Buster. "Have a seat, man!"

"What do you mean by that remark?" Buster asked, sitting down.

"I can't tell you, ol' boy, you'll find out soon enough," he said.

"Yeah, I suppose I will," Buster said. He looked around

the room. It was a large room with flapper windows on all sides—lots of air coming in. There was a ditto machine in the corner, a sink and counter in the back with a coffee pot and cups, a large table in the middle of the room and ten sofa chairs next to it scattered in a semi-circle.

"American?" asked the fat lady with a Spanish accent.

"Yes, Ma'am, from Florida."

"Blimey!" said the red-head. "They're coming in by the hoards. That's the fourth one in three days."

"Yeah, I heard something about that," Buster said.

"That's right," the Brit said. "Don't make sense, really. They get rid of us and so the Americans invade. That's like taking one bad apple out of the barrel and puttin' in another. Fuckin' Bahamians—they do everything bum-side backwards."

"You sound a bit bitter," Buster said.

"Listen Mate, I've been here six years—two, three-year contracts. Not only I, but all of England have given this country everything it's got. And now that they've got their independence, they're bootin' us out like a cat that's entered the wrong house. That's gratitude for you!"

"Just how are they booting you out?" Buster asked.

"By the pants, Mate! Everybody. Why even in this school, five of us Brits are goin' within the month, and they are already about ten teachers short here. Classes already have so many kids that they are comin' out the windows. And it's gonna get worse, Mate. The year hasn't really started yet—this is only the first part of September. Just you wait!"

"Well, that's kind of a slap in the face for just getting here," Buster said.

"Larry Shortings is my name. I'm from Birmingham."

"Nice to meet you—Buster Murdock's mine."

A bell rang and total pandemonium erupted. An uproarious, mass scream of the children jutted out of all the classrooms and the teachers started coming into the room for their break.

After a round of introductions to the teachers, the headmaster, Percy Trahn, entered. "Mr. Murdock, here is your schedule. The day is pretty much under way now, so you will start tomorrow morning. Meanwhile, my assistant, Mr. Johnson, here, will walk you around and introduce you to the school, OK?"

"Fine, Mr. Trahn," Buster said. "Mr. Johnson, how do you do?"

"Yes, Mr. Murdock, won't you come with me, please?" he said. He was a small, light colored Bahamian with a faultless British accent.

Mr. Johnson took the new teacher all around the school: to the gymnasium, shop, pre-fabricated buildings. He also introduced Buster to the over-all, general school procedure. It was very similar to an American junior high school with seven periods and a home room. The main subjects were English, Bahamian History, Mathematics, Religion, Shop, and Physical Education. One hour, called Project Hour, was set aside for special projects that each individual teacher would work on with the students; projects such as skits, arts and crafts, music, etcetera.

After the introduction, it was rather late and Buster was unusually tired. Everything was so new to him and all these novelties seemed to have hit him all at once in one day. All he wanted to do was go home. He thanked Mr. Johnson, then quickly grabbed a taxi back to his new abode with Parkson at Fort Charlotte. He collapsed on the bed and fell deeply to sleep—totally oblivious to his new world.

Parkson came in about five o'clock in the afternoon practically bursting down the door. "Hey Murdock!" he yelled. "Let's go swimming!"

Buster jumped out of bed. "What? Say? What the hell?"

"Let's go swimmin', man! I just got a new dive watch—tax free—and wanna try it out!"

"Jesus, man!" Buster said sleepily. "Give me a break, will you? You gotta bust down the damn door like that?"

"God, man, what's eatin' you? Alls I asked ya was to go swimmin'!"

"Yeah, yeah, right—OK—uh, let me get it together and I'll be right with you." He blankly looked around the room.

Buster got a towel and put on his trunks and sneakers—all set to go swimming. Parkson was already out on the street waiting for him, waiting to brave the challenge of Nassau Bay with his goggles and snorkel already on his head and a pair of extra large swim fins hanging from his arm.

"Jesus Christ, Parkson, where are you going?"

"Gotta be prepared, man!"

They walked towards the beach. Buster noticed that Parkson had put his bathing suit on backwards, but he did not say anything, for he was still too sleepy to talk.

When they arrived at the beach, Buster ran immediately to the water and flopped in. "Ah, this is great, Parkson!" he yelled. "Just what the doctor ordered!"

Parkson was still fiddling with his flippers, trying to get them on his feet. "Yeah, yeah!" he said. "I'm comin'!"

Buster was doing all kinds of strokes in the not-so-clear, but creamy, light green water. He started with the butterfly stroke, then switched to the backstroke, then the breast and finally into the crawl.

At last, Parkson entered the water. He looked like one

of the frogmen from Jules Verne's book, *Twenty Thousand Leagues Under the Sea*, ready to brave something. His brand new Japanese dive watch, guaranteed waterproof to a depth of six hundred and sixty feet, glistened in the sun. "I'm coming now," he said in his snorkel. "I'm coming!" He fell into the water and flip-flopped around in a circle like a captured fish that had been thrown back into the water. He then awkwardly flip-flopped out towards the coral reef.

Meanwhile, Buster had had enough. He went up to the beach to lie in the sun and dry off. The afternoon sun beat down on his closed eyes. He felt the wonderful rays permeate his skin throughout his entire body as they evaporated the drops of water still swimming around in his beard. "Jesus, this is nice," he said out loud. "I've got to do this every day after work—wash my troubles away!" He let out a big sigh and yelled, "Jesus, this is just fantastic! Bahamas, Bahamas, Bahamas—Great!"

Parkson for quite a while stayed in the water, with every two or three minutes checking out the time. The coral reef was filled with tiny, tropical fish and majestic purple coral fans. Once in a while, he would see a coke can float by or a cellophane wrapper. The filth came from the port with Nassau's shipping traffic leaving most of the oil and garbage that floated in front of Parkson's goggles.

The sun was gradually getting lower in the West and it was getting harder and harder to see the bottom. He checked the time—underwater, of course, and decided to get out. The brave adventurer swam to shore and waddled up to Buster. "Whew!" he said, drying off. "Now that's what I call diving in clear water. Ya know, in Florida the water is so sandy half the time that you can hardly see a thing."

"Yeah!" Buster said. "Hey, what's that on your back?"

"I don't know, what? Let's see!" He reached behind and grabbed at a wet, slippery substance. "Well, I'll be God-damned, it's a Wonder Bread wrapper!"

"Nice clean water, right?" Buster said.

"Well, yeah, it really is. You can see bottom and everything. Great watch, too. It's really handy to tell time underwater, ya know?"

"OK, OK, and out of water, too." Buster said. "What time is it? I'm hungry!"

"Uh, well, let's see. It's uh, six thirty. Let's split!"

"OK, split man, split! That's heavy English for you! And you have a college education?"

"Of course, man—how do you think I've made it this far?"

"Well, Parkson, I won't answer that!"

And they "Split" back to their apartment near Fort Charlotte.

After showering, they both prepared what was left in the empty refrigerator and settled down to a hamburger, scrambled eggs and rum.

"What time is it, Parkson?" Buster asked, gorging down a pickle.

Parkson turned his wrist in front of his face and gazed down at his new treasure. "It's uh, it's …. Well, I'll be God-damned, it's six thirty!" And tiny beads of water had formed underneath the crystal.

Parkson was definitely jinxed, indeed. Upon realizing this, Buster from then on called Parkson by his deserved name, Jinx.

The following day was Buster's first full day of working in the Bahamas. Jinx gave him a ride, for his school, where he taught high school math, was only a mile down the road.

Buster really was not looking forward to his first day: first and above all, kids—he had never worked with children before and did not care for them all that much, either; second of all, he would rather be at the beach. It was a beautiful day—a little on the hot side. As he got out of Jinx's car and walked towards the school building, he thought of how he was going to approach his first class: *OK, Murdock ol' buddy, you gotta be a man! All I gotta do is go in there and tell them my name. Then, I'm gonna teach those little people a little English, by God!*

He walked directly to the teachers' room. Very quickly he met a couple of young female teachers in their early thirties, both from England. The bell rang and first period began. It was nine o'clock. All the teachers, including Buster, dispersed and headed towards their respective homerooms.

Then one of the female teachers stopped him and said: "What, lad? You're not taking a stick with you?"

"Stick?" he asked. "What on earth for?

"Why, you've got to beat the little whimpers!"

"Beat them? I haven't even met them yet!"

Beating was completely out of the question for the young, peace-loving American. The subject of beating was not even mentioned at the University of Florida. Child psychology was the best—he even took a few courses in it. Beat them? Buster could not even conceive of the idea. He would not even know how to begin doing it. *Beat them?* he thought. *Crazy! Absolutely nuts!*

"Well, you will!" the lady said. "You're committing suicide if ya don't, ya know!"

"I'll take my chances, Ma'am. Thank you."

The thin, English lady walked off to her homeroom with a gigantic two-inch wide yardstick. She was definitely prepared.

*Beat them?* Buster thought again. *The woman's insane!* He walked into the home-room expecting to see mild-mannered children all in rows with their hands folded on their desks waiting for "Teacher" to arrive: but there they were in all their massive, chaotic glory. Buster found a room full of eighth graders crawling under the desks, striding the windows, writing on the blackboard, hanging from the lights, screaming, yelling, boys kicking the girls, girls scratching the boys, etcetera, etcetera.

Buster just stood there completely awed. "Jesus Christ!" he whimpered to himself.

Now at the University of Florida in Gainesville, it was all lesson plans, and the children should do this, and they should not do that and they learn best when... and they learn least when... and the best books to use were ... and if there were any discipline problems, simply call the parents and that usually did it. It was also very handy to divide the children into small groups at times and do special projects, put on little skits, sing songs, and above all, be a teacher—a person responsible for the education of the young with an extremely heavy influence on their little lives. A teacher was a father, a mother, a brother, a sister and companion—be gentle but firm and pat them on the head once in a while and always give words of encouragement.

"Hey, you! Buster ordered, "Get down from that light!"

"Yes, Mr. Teacher, mann!" a little boy answered.

"And you girls get away from that blackboard!"

"Oh, but we wanna draw some more, teacher!"

"And that group in the corner—put those desks back in order!"

They ignored him.

"I said put those desks back in order!"

"Yes, mann!" they finally responded.

"And be quiet everyone!" He took a seat at the teacher's desk and opened his roll book in front of him. "Be quiet, I said!"

They did not comply.

"Please be quiet, OK?"

Still the same uproar.

Then, finally losing patience, he raised his voice: "Shut up, Jesus!"

There was a slight resemblance of quiet.

"Now my name is Mr. Murdock and …"

The class erupted again, this time in an uncontrollable, uproarious laughter. They were not used to hearing American last names and this one just struck them as being funny.

"Uh, be quiet please—please be quiet—Shut Up, Jesus!"

The laughter subsided somewhat.

"Now I'm going to call roll and I want you to answer by saying 'Here' and by raising your hand so I'll know who you are. Shhh, please be quiet!" He started calling roll: "Sandra."

"Here."

"Ronnie."

"Here."

"Neville."

"Here."

"Hey you—you in the blue shirt—get away from that window! Salina."

"Here."

"Hey you, little girl—leave your friend alone!"

"Wooooooooo!!" The whole class erupted and started laughing and beating on the desks.

"Quiet, please—Uh, please be quiet—ya'll wanna be quiet, please?"

The roll took an entire hour to call, finally ending at the pleasing sound of the bell. Buster was more than ready for the ten-minute break between classes. Nerves frayed, he entered the teachers' room.

"What's the matter, mate?" Larry Shortings said approaching Buster. "You look a bit worn!"

"Thanks, man," Buster said. "You don't look too good yourself! Jesus, I don't believe it—I just don't believe it! I've just had the absolute worst class in my life—ever!"

"Why, you ain't even started yet, my friend." Shortings said.

"Damn, I'm no disciplinarian. I can't discipline even myself let alone freaking kids, for Christ's sakes!"

"You'll have to learn that, if you're gonna stay here, mate! Discipline is the Golden Rule!"

"Well, hell, I was just taught to be gentle and firm and they'll go your way!"

"That' must've been in the States—my, you do look a bit green behind the ears. These little, black monkeys don't pay any attention to words. You've simply got to hit them!"

"Hit them?" Buster said still surprised. "Jesus, I'm a peace, love and happiness kind of guy, man. I can't hit anybody."

"You either hit them, Murdock, beat the living shit out of them, or you won't survive." Shortings put it frankly.

"Isn't it against the law?"

"What law? They expect it! If you don't hit them they won't respect you and they'll walk right over you. Here! Take my stick!" He handed Buster a gigantic yardstick. "I'll get another in the office—they got plenty of 'em."

"No, that's OK," Buster said. "I can't, I just can't hit anybody, that's all. I'll take my chances."

The bell rang for second period. This time it was a group of seventh graders—much quieter than the first group. It was their first time in junior high school, coming from the ranks of different elementary schools, so they were very nervous and shy. They were no problem and were easy to control.

Third period was the opposite, however. This was a group of ninth graders—fourteen year olds—experienced in the art of harassing teachers. They were the old-timers and knew the ropes. They seemed to be much more difficult to handle, much bigger kids physically than all the others.

Buster entered the class: "Hey, you—get down from that light! You, get away from that window!" And it was the first class all over again. *Jesus!* he thought. *I have a feeling it's gonna be a long year here—Christ, why me?*

Relieved by the bell once again, it was now twelve o'clock, time for lunch. Most of the teachers ate a home-made lunch in the teachers' room while the kids were free to run around the campus with their own lunch pails or stand in line for conch fritters, deep-vat fried pieces of breaded conch meat, chicken legs and Coca Cola that were sold by a catering service in the central patio of the school. Buster went down for some chicken legs and a Coke and brought them up to the teachers' room. He sat next to two new, young teachers, Dean Totton, a short and stocky physical education coach from Canada, and Ted Edinthaler, a large but somewhat flabby American from Fort Lauderdale, Florida who took on the geography and shop classes.

"Do you guys believe this?" Buster asked them, slumped in a lounge chair. "I mean, do you really believe this? This is a zoo, fellas, I mean a real zoo!"

"No kiddin'," Dean said. "I've been here a week and I'm ready to go back to Canada."

"Yeah man," Ted commented. "I still find it hard to believe how they hit kids here. I mean outright smack and whack 'em with all their might!"

"I know. I refuse to do that!" Buster said. "I'll quit before I hit anybody. Jesus, that's insane!"

"You should see it in P.E.," Dean said. "Almost total uncontrol! To get them to play baseball? All hell breaks loose, eh! Everyone wants to either pitch or bat, eh? And if they don't get their way, they scream and yell and do all kinds of ugly things."

"I don't know man," Buster said. "I just can't handle this discipline madness—I just can't handle it!"

The lunch hour zoomed by like it was only five minutes and it was back to class. The bell rang and they all got up to go.

"Only one good consolation," Ted said, "only two more periods and it's going home time—the beach, drinks, smokes, air, space!"

"It won't come soon enough," Buster said, and he drifted into a seventh grade class watching all the other teachers go their own ways armed with two-pound yardsticks.

This seventh grade class after lunch was another breeze: pleasant, shy children not really knowing what was coming off. But Buster's last class of the day happened to be a group of wild, savage ninth graders out in the wooden, prefabricated building off from the main building wings. The class was so bad it made Buster feel nauseous, which in turn, left a horrible feeling of emptiness inside: a feeling that possibly all that higher education at the University of Florida would almost have to be completely thrown out the window if he was to deal with these people. He spent another entire hour just calling the roll. It was all he could do to keep the spitballs out of his ears.

After class at three o'clock, Buster went to the office to talk to Headmaster Trahn. "Excuse me, Mr. Trahn, but when do the children get their books?" he asked.

"Books, Mr. Murdock?" He said surprisingly. "Oh, yes, books! Well, we'll work on that next week sometime. Right now, we're still busy with schedule organizing. Next week, Mr. Murdock, next week!"

*Right*! Buster thought. *Next week we'll get organized*!

He walked out of the office and ran into Ted Edinthaler. "Hey Ted, let's go for a drink. I need one and bad—you know what I mean?"

"Hey, I think I know what you mean! You're not the only one."

They walked to the parking lot, hopped on Ted's new Honda Fifty and went to the Pilot House for badly needed drinks. Two stiff Harvey Wallbangers each and a cool sea breeze on the Pilot House's shaded patio bar made the new teachers forget where they had just come from and what they had to do in the weeks to come.

# CHAPTER 2

## *Wild Dogs & Swollen Hands*

It was well into the second week of school when Buster got his own motorcycle. A direct one thousand dollar loan from the Bank of Canada got him a purple Yamaha two hundred and fifty cubic centimeter beauty from the Nassau Bike Center. Ted Edinthaler, Dean Totton and Jinx were all there at the christening party, a wild and raving rum and champagne bash that gave the name of "Naomi" to Buster's precious new baby. Naming it "Naomi" was the least the boys could do for the remembrance of the exotic black woman Dean had hired for the occasion.

Buster was mighty proud of his new purple machine. He had always wanted one. An old, run-down Vespa in high school in Daytona Beach, and a sloppy mo-ped in undergraduate school in Gainesville, just had no comparison to this sleek, brand new two hundred and fifty cc Yamaha with chrome fenders that sparkled in the sun. He started making daily tours of New Providence Island, always driving the English way—on the left hand side of the road. The tours made him forget the nightmare he was experiencing at "Davis" and it got him out of the city madness of Nassau. Even though Nassau was small and funky, it was still a city.

But Nassau had its good points, too. Buster really liked the small shops and Woodes Rogers Walk, and the straw market and horse-drawn carriages for the tourists. He also liked the big luxury liners as well. They were fun to go on. More than once he had gotten a special teacher's pass to go on board. He walked around the decks and dreamed of having enough money to afford a cruise.

But then again, it was good to get out of the city and get to the beaches—far away from the school and even away from Jinx, whose weird idiosyncrasies were starting to really get on Buster's nerves. Naomi, in essence, was his beautiful escape machine.

The only problem with Naomi was that Buster was terribly paranoid about getting her stolen. Crime was a definite problem in Nassau and motorcycles were the easiest and most perfect target. He was so paranoid, in fact, that he became obsessed with the thought. No insurance company on the island would even consider taking the risk of theft insurance on any kind of motorcycle. He, therefore, procured three large, heavy-duty marine chains and three heavy-duty Yale storm locks to put on her for safekeeping—plus the front wheel locked by a key in the middle of the handlebars. He would lock her up in front of the police station in Nassau to walk around town, and he would still feel uneasy. Sometimes, he would lock her up to a tree near the beach and go skin diving. Every time he would make a dive down to the bottom to take a close look at some coral or a colorful psychedelic fish, the flash would occur to him that while he was hallucinating on the ocean floor, some Bahamian just might be cutting the chains on Naomi to high-tail her away. He just could not bear the thought of one thousand dollars slipping away from him like that. That only meant a lot of extra English classes he would have to teach.

Naomi also came in very handy in carrying her master back and forth to work. This made it very convenient and he now did not have to depend on Jinx for rides.

After the second week of school, the kids finally got their books: small, beat-up readers only to be passed out, shared and then to be collected at the end of class. It was a pitiful sight for Buster because some of these children were fourteen years old and they did not know how to read. They were on the equivalent level of American third graders, if that. They did not know how to even take care of books: virtually manhandling them and grabbing at pages, tearing them out. It was a mountainous problem and Buster at one time wanted to take the problem to the parents. But then he found that most of the parents were illiterate, poverty stricken and not geared for educating their children at all. It was all the parents could do to stay above water. Some parents were beggars, others sold beads to the tourists, others were maids, fishermen, conch shell divers, and many were unemployed rummies. Educating their children was completely out of their realm—they did not even know what it was. So Buster could hardly blame the children.

What bothered him the most was the discipline. For two full weeks he had refused to carry a stick in the classroom, but then he broke down one day. He was pushed to the limit by one, uncontrollable ninth grade class. He hauled off and slugged one wise guy in the solar plexus who had told his teacher to "Fuck off!" The rather big-for-his age fourteen year old bent over double and Buster threw him over his back and carried him down the stairs to Trahn's office. He dumped the misbehaved adolescent on the headmaster's desk.

"Here!" he said as the headmaster was writing some notes on the desk. "You take care of this one! I've had it with these guys!" Buster grabbed the nearest gigantic yardstick and marched back into the classroom.

"OK!" he yelled. "Anybody else want it, just try me again!" and he waved the stick in the air. The room was better ever since.

These days were very trying for Buster. The hot, humid air stuck to the skins of everybody like warm Vaseline, and the September afternoons were getting so miserably hot that everybody's temper was running short. It hurt Buster immensely to hit the kids, but now he realized it was necessary at times, considering the circumstances—but he hated it with a passion. There were many times when he thought of just quitting—giving up and going back to the States.

The only real relief was after school. That was when life on New Providence really began and became quite pleasant. His afternoon rides on Naomi and daily swimming at the beaches were soothing to his head. Almost nightly rum bashes with Dean Totton, Ted Edinthaler and sometimes Jinx were the cure to everything. Dean had such great humor that he had everybody on the floor laughing in fits with some of the things he'd say. Sometimes Buster laughed so hard that the joke transcended itself into an insane, therapeutic release from such emotionally draining days that the children constantly dumped on everybody.

Jinx was beginning to become an outright burden for Buster and for many people around him. Something was always happening to him. One night during a party he stepped outside for a breath of fresh air and came back ten minutes later with his long, blond, stringy hair all messed up, his pants all muddy and his shirt half-way torn off of him.

"What happened now, Jinx?" Buster asked, saying those famous words that became familiar to everyone—they became known as the "What happened now, Jinx?" words.

"I almost got mugged!"

"Jesus!"

Jinx's popularity was spreading throughout the island. It was ridiculous, and Buster was at times fearful of this bad luck wearing off on him.

One Saturday night Jinx and Buster held a party: lots of rum and hashish to go around for everybody. It was a rollicking party with some young women teachers from the States and lots of Bahamian women, too. The party was loud until around three o'clock in the morning when complaints from the neighbors started coming in. Then things settled down; but Jinx had passed out many hours before. The next morning Jinx got up as the sun was rising over the sea. He walked out to the front patio with a cup of coffee and noticed the myriads of colors the new sun was casting on all the tropical plants around him. Then he peered across the street and noticed that his car was not where he had left it. He walked out on the street and still no car. He ran from one end of the street to the other and no car. Then in a frantic break, he threw his coffee cup down and ran into the apartment where bodies were strewn all over.

"Murdock—Murdock!" he yelled, shaking him in the bed.

"Yeah, yeah—who?"

"Hey Murdock, man, did you take my car last night?"

"Car? No—why? What happened now, Jinx?"

"Somebody stole my car—it's gone!"

"Oh, Jesus!" And Buster rolled over back to sleep.

And it was very true. Somebody had hot-wired Jinx's car, took a joy ride to the other side of the island and left it with no gas in the middle of a dumping ground.

After this, Jinx had had enough of crime in the area and was determined to move out to another part of the island. He frantically went apartment hunting shortly after he got his stripped car back and found a large place in the interior of the island, several miles away from Nassau, but just a few short miles from the Bacardi Rum Factory. The place was called Rockydale. It was a new, cement-block apartment complex with five apartments on each of the two floors. Next to it and drowned in tropical flora was the owner's house—complete with chickens, horses, goats and parrots. The cement-block structure was a far cry from the beautiful, quaint Fort Charlotte efficiency apartment; but it was said that crime was at a minimum, and that was what Jinx was most worried about.

Buster wanted to stay in Fort Charlotte alone, but paying that much rent would cut deeply into his funds— especially after just buying Naomi. So he decided to move into the big, spacious Rockydale complex with Jinx and give his luckless buddy one more try. At least they would have separate bedrooms and they could both keep their distances.

It was the beginning of October when Buster got an attack of homesickness. So he called his girlfriend back in the States, Patricia Shannon, and asked her of the possibilities of coming down for a visit. There was no problem. She was not working at the time and had to get out of Gainesville for a while. Gainesville, that small university town in the middle of Florida, was pleasant, but at times a wave of claustrophobic sensations struck that made people restless.

The only hesitation was when to come down. Buster had missed her and wanted her immediately. She, too, was anxious, but she hadn't had her period yet and wanted to wait until it happened. That way she could start the birth control pills again and be all recycled, "Or something like that," as Buster put it. Sometimes female things just completely baffled him. But after not meeting any "good" girls on New Providence yet, he was mostly just horny. It had only been a month since he saw her last, but he thought of her a lot, and that was his mistake.

"Get your ass down here, now!" he said over the phone. And that was that. On Friday, October fifth, after only one week at Rockydale, Patty came down to join Buster in the large room with the king-size bed—pushing poor Jinx into the smaller, sunless room right next to the owner's parrot cage hanging from the tree just outside the window.

Now Patty was a sexy little lady: short but well built, long brunette hair that reached the small of her back, and an unusually well-formed face with high cheek bones, good lips and perfect teeth. Buster always checked the teeth first on a lady— it was his motto, like kicking tires on a used car.

So they were together again. The one-month separation was the longest they had been apart for an entire year. Buster liked the separation, really. He thought of those nice parties with Dean Totton and Ted Edinthaler. Although he had not scored on a nice Bahamian girl yet, he had recognized the possibilities: beautiful, smooth, brown-complexioned

Bahamian women in their long African gowns. But then again, Patty was a sure fire.

Patty arrived on the island on Friday afternoon, and the whole weekend they made love like rabbits, coming out of the room only to go to the bathroom or the kitchen to do the absolute necessities of life. It was such a pleasure for Buster not to even think about those monstrous kids at school or even of Jinx, that poor misguided soul of a roommate who could not seem to even keep his shoes on straight. It was such a pleasure to be with Patty: so soft, so absolutely wonderful to touch and divine to sleep with—she fit his body like a glove.

"But Buster, I wanna see the island," she complained Sunday afternoon in a light southern accent common to Central Floridians.

"You'll see it, don't worry, Baby—Plenty of time!" he said, and it was back to their familiar horizontal positions.

On Monday, Buster called into work sick. "You see, I have this terrible sore throat," he said in a whisper to the secretary, "and can barely talk! I probably won't be able to make it for a couple days!"

So he and Patty hopped on Naomi and started their tour around New Providence Island. It was a beautiful, cloudless, autumn day. Naomi performed wonderfully for the two lovers. Patty on the back would squeeze her legs hard around her man's hips and wrap her arms around his bare chest. It was the first time Buster had orgasms on Naomi and it was marvelous. How great it was to feel so alive and content.

They stayed away from Nassau and just traveled mostly the circumference of the island, stopping every-now-and-then for a dip in the sea and love sessions in the bushes. For lunch, they stopped at a chicken shack and had conch fritters and fried gizzards—good for male potency, as rumor had it. Then it was back on Naomi to explore unknown beaches.

At every new beach Patty would whip out a Thai stick from her leather bag, and they would sit in the sand and get piously stoned on the high potency marijuana before taking their walks down the beach: it seemed righteous and fitting to do so. They sat in their cloud of magic smoke while watching the light green waves with perfectly formed white crests come crashing in. They hallucinated finely on rainbows from the ocean spray that flashed directly in front of their eyes, as if each wave had especially made a rainbow for just the two of them. After each stick they would walk the beach for what seemed days and days, but in reality it was only a matter of fifteen minutes or a half an hour: sometimes holding hands, sometimes stopping to embrace, sometimes breaking into a run. Other moments Buster would walk ahead and be alone for a few minutes, catching his own thoughts and contemplating by himself but with that good feeling, that secure feeling that he would not have to be alone for long and shortly he could rejoin that beauty of nature, his woman. It was truly paradise.

But paradise was a state of mind, and when Wednesday rolled around, Buster was forced to take his mind out of the clouds and waves and gear it back to work again. He winced at the mere thought: it made his heart beat faster, but he knew it had to be.

While Patty went sightseeing in Nassau on Wednesday, Buster went back to work armed with his yardstick, but with all good intentions of not using it and to be a peaceful, loving teacher for the rest of the week. But again he proved to be wrong, and the kids had him yelling at them before the first hour was over. It was hard on his head. It started throbbing. Children's high-pitched voices pierced his ears like rooster crows in early morning, and the four walls and floor of the classroom seemed to be moving and swaying in a big circle. Each class hour seemed to last five and his only relief was the ten-minute break between classes where he would slump down into one of the lounge chairs and hold his throbbing temples.

He could not wait for the workday to be over. Every moment he thought of Patty and the heaven they passed together for four straight days. It seemed that was the only thing keeping him on his feet. The day finally came to an end after a long, last period with the ninth graders where he was forced to hit a couple young ones on their fannies. He detested hitting and it made him nauseous; but then, it was the last straw, and he convinced himself that maybe it was a necessity.

He hopped on Naomi and went to pick up Patty at the straw market, their meeting place for the day.

"HI!" she said in great spirits. "Have a nice day?"

Buster looked at her with glassy, bloodshot eyes. "Get on and shut up!"

They went straight to Rockydale. Buster was so exhausted he did not even make it to the bedroom. He flipped off his shoes and fell limply onto the sofa—out cold to the world. Patty went to the bedroom, got a pillow and placed it underneath his head. He slept soundly for three hours.

Buster woke up to the gentle voices of Patty and Jinx having a casual conversation about life on New Providence. Jinx, too, was tired from a long day at his school, but he managed to sit in an upright position.

"Good morning, Murdock," he said. "How the fuck are ya?"

"Uhhhhh," he groaned. "I'll survive, I guess. Ohhh, Jesus, those kids, I just can't handle them. How've you been, Jinx? I haven't seen you for a while?"

"OK, I guess. It was a bitch of a day for me, too!" Jinx looked like a Zombie.

"Look at this nut! Patty said to Buster. "He bought a new pair of sandals today but two right feet!"

"What?" Buster said, looking over at Jinx. "What the hell you do that for?"

"Well," he said embarrassingly, "Uh, it's just what I've always wanted—uh, two sandals for the same foot!"

"Didn't you try them on before you bought them?" Patty asked.

"No, they were size nine—they looked all right."

"Jesus Christ!" Buster said. "What a Bahamian!"

That evening the trio went down to the ship, *Emerald Seas*, one of the large, white luxury liners out of Miami. They ate dinner on board and had a look around the boat. Jinx had obtained special teachers' passes—four for the occasion—but his date stood him up; so it was just the three of them. Jinx was a nice guy when things permitted him to be one: considerate, soft-spoken and gentle.

The ship was huge with several large eating rooms, game rooms, piano lounges and dance floors. It hardly seemed possible that all this steel and half-marble interior could float. On the top deck the three Americans leaned over the railing and looked down at the dwarfed dock below them. Ten stories of ship miniaturized the people walking on the dock. Also, ten stories of ship gave them a great view of central Nassau all lit up: the pink and cream colored buildings cast against an artificial city-light hue made the town surrealistic in appearance.

"Nassau sure is pretty like this, isn't it?" Patty said.

There was pleasant silence filled with contemplation. A light, salt-smelling sea breeze brushed their hair.

"Sure is," Buster answered, breaking this silence. "It kind of makes you forget about all the ugly things."

And the evening drifted away like a tide dropping lower and lower.

The ugly things Buster referred to were not only the crimes in Nassau and the children at school, but Rockydale itself also had its problems as well. Both Jinx and Buster had moved to the interior of the island to avoid crime and the hustle bustle of downtown Nassau, just a ten-minute walk away. However, the boys found, after a few nights of sleeping—or not sleeping—that Rockydale was located on the main interior highway that connected one point of the island to the other. This meant that big semi-trucks and noisy land rovers roared passed their bedroom windows all the way up to the small hours of the morning and actually shook the foundation of the cheaply constructed cement building.

When the traffic stopped, the dogs began. In the back of Rockydale there was a large bush forest that looked peaceful enough during the day and half the night; but beginning in the early morning, it revealed that it housed not hundreds but literally thousands of wild dogs that began barking around three o'clock and did not stop until the sun cast its full light over the bush. The barking noise would start with a single, isolated yelp and grow into a virtual mass chorus of scraggly mutts without homes communicating their misery to one another. There were so many dogs that every morning the barking sounded like there were twenty kennels right outside the Rockydale windows.

Buster, being a light sleeper, was so disgusted with this that he could have outright murdered Jinx for having left "Peaceful" Fort Charlotte. At least Fort Charlotte was relatively quiet—crime or no crime. But Jinx could sleep through anything and even the loud "Wracking" sound of the landlord's parrot's "Good Morning" greeting could not wake him up.

All this noise bothered Patty, too, but she did not say anything. Her mother had taught her a good southern expression of courtesy: "If you can't say something nice, don't say it at all." So Patty kept quiet, but she did not get much sleep either.

After coming home from the Emerald Seas visit, both Buster and Patty passed a sleepless night feeling the vibrations of the traffic and listening to the "Audible hallucination," as Buster put it, of the wild dogs. That morning Buster went to work in a bad, grumpy state of mind.

But the school did not help his outlook on life, whatsoever. It was chaos from the very beginning. Buster arrived a few minutes late and the first thing he saw was one of the few black Bahamian male teachers whacking a child's hands with a thick yardstick—both hands at the same time right across the knuckles, three times. The young boy, not more than twelve years old, if that, wailed like a woman who had just lost her husband. Petrified, the rest of the class sat in total silence. It was not a very pleasant sight to see at nine o'clock in the morning. It was going to be a hot day. Buster's clothes were already sticking to his body.

The first class, the eighth grade, was not too bad. It was the normal discipline technique of Buster shouting about fifty "Be Quiets" before they finally settled down and started reading aloud *Robin Hood and His Band of Merry*

*Men*. These books were the only ones available and most of them were torn and with pages missing. Robin Hood was also a story these kids found almost impossible to relate to: forests, bows and arrows, medieval castles, deer, gold, and white princesses. It was a monumental task for any teacher. Education? Some of these children had never gone more than fifty yards from their own conch shell-lined, community water fountain.

But at least Buster realized this: he had good insight. So he mustered up what energy he had for such an early morning occasion and tried to make the class somewhat exciting. Throwing everything away that was crammed down his throat in Education classes at the University of Florida, he stood on top of his desk pretending to shoot bows and arrows, or mimed sword fights, or exaggerated romantic lines, or ran around the room looking for gold. All weapons or medieval artifacts, of course, had to be drawn on the blackboard.

It was the third period, the ninth grade, that gave Buster a bad time this day, and he felt it coming from the very second he entered the room. The kids seemed to be unusually out of hand. The more "Be Quiets" and "Shut Ups" Buster yelled, the more out of hand they got: forty little black children with eighty eyes all impressing on Buster's mind; forty sets of mostly white teeth protruding out of forty thick pairs of lips going up and down, back and forth. Finally, nerves shot, he erupted. He started flailing his stick in the air. Everybody that got in the way got hit. He looked like a cowboy swinging a lasso at a herd of cattle. Things quieted down with the exception of one big, tall girl in pigtails called "Big Sandra." He told her in a raised voice to change chairs. She hesitated at first; but then, mumbling something to herself, she scornfully moved.

When the bell finally rang and there was a mass exit to the door, the pig-tailed girl ran out the door and shouted through the flapper windows, "Fuck you, mann!" looking right at her teacher. The whole class heard this and roared with laughter. Buster broke into a run, chasing her down the corridor. He signaled to her and gave her the look that said if she did not come she was going to really get it. She did not come.

Now thinking only of what he was going to do with the little girl, if anything, he walked to the teachers' room for lunch, but with a destroyed appetite. He sat down, slumped in his chair in a contemplative manner.

Larry Shortings, that red haired, British mathematics teacher, came up and sat next to the forlorn American. He was in a cheery mood. "What's up mate—why the gloomy look?"

"Oh, nothing" Buster said.

"C'mon, let's have it out—somethin's eating you!" he said.

"Well hell!" Buster said, finally giving in. "I just had a little girl say something to me that's bothering me—that's all!"

"Beat the shit out of the little, black monkey!"

"Jesus Christ, man, how can you say something like that?"

"Easy! Just work here six years and you'll discover what worthless creatures these little, bleedin' bastards are."

Buster looked at him in disbelief, his temper mounting. "Dammit, you're really screwed up, man! Your white, freckled skin is about to make me sick!"

"Easy now, Mate!"

"Don't call me Mate, for Christ's sakes—I'm not your Mate!"

"Oh, my goodness!"

"Oh my goodness, my ass! Jesus, now I got a better idea of where all this racist madness comes from and where the U.S. got it from in the first place!"

"You can certainly tell you're green around the ears, Bub."

"Bub? Jesus, you're disgusting!"

"Must be the heat!" the Brit said, loosening his tie and rising. "Hope you cheer up—Cheerio!" He left the room.

Buster popped a greasy conch fritter in his mouth. He felt it slither down his digestive tract and land like a bomb in his stomach. "Cheerio?" he said to himself. "Fuck!" The next half-hour he contemplated on what to do.

The bell rang and all one thousand, five hundred kids skirmished to their respective classrooms. Buster went to the ninth grade class to get Big Sandra. He walked into the prefabricated building and there was instant hush. All the kids had a feeling of what Mr. Teacher was up to. Buster pointed to her. "You, to the front, please!"

Very reluctantly she walked with her teacher to the office. There the headmaster was, Percy Trahn, sitting on his throne with his bamboo cane on the desk in front of him.

"Here's the girl I told you about Mr. Trahn," Buster said.

The tall, lean, black-as-a-pipe stem Trahn stood up and went into his famous Donald Duck routine: "Now you know you're not supposed to talk back girl!" he yelled. "Let me see your hand!"

Buster was going to leave, but when Big Sandra started to break down, he thought maybe he had better stay and see what he got the girl into. Her cry at first was a little whimper—then it wound up into a full-fledged, eerie wail.

"Oh Lordy, Lordy, Lordy!" she screamed. "Not my hands—No, No!"

"C'mon, c'mon girl," the headmaster said. "Hold out your hand!" He held the cane high in the air, ready to come down like a guillotine. Tears as big as fingernails streamed down Sandra's face. "Tell Mr. Murdock you're sorry!"

Buster was red with guilt and felt nauseous.

"I'm, I'm, I'm sorry, Mr. Mur—Murdock! She lifted her hand but jerked it back again to her side.

"C'mon, c'mon," Trahn said. "Stop your foolishness! Your hand, your hand!"

"Oh Lordy, Lordy, Lordy!" she screamed. Then she started into a language that only God could understand—it was as if she were talking in tongues like in Baptist revivals.

"C'mon, c'mon!"

Sandra's language melted back into decipherable English: "Our Father who art in heaven!"

Then the meeting of human flesh and bamboo occurred with a deafening

WHACK!!

Big Sandra's loud screech made Buster's ears immediately start to ring. With his head lowered and hearing more whacks and screeches, he walked back to his afternoon class leaving Sandra and Percy Trahn to their little games, determined never again to take anybody back to that madman's office.

After school, Buster, emotionally exhausted and barely able to think, met Patty at the Pilot House patio bar.

"Hi!" she said smiling, already sitting at a table. "Have a nice day?"

"Right!" he said. His hands flopped to his sides and he just glared at her.

"I sure could use a lemonade," she said, holding her throat. "I'm dry as a desert!"

"Good!" He grabbed a wicker chair and sat down.

"And after the drinks, let's go get some African designed fabric I saw early this afternoon," she said.

"Right!—fabric!"

"Then let's go buy some of those dynamite tiny little sea-shells so I can make a necklace."

"Sea-shells!"

"And then we can pass by the Conch Shack and take home some conch fritters for dinner."

"Shack Cunt!"

After Patty's lemonade and Buster's three gin and tonics, a Harvey Wallbanger and a joint, the couple went home to bed for a nap.

That night Buster stayed home and sulked the entire evening over the incident at school. Finally, he brought himself to the kitchen table and wrote the following letter to the Ministry of Education:

October 11, 1973

Permanent Secretary
UFS Head Teacher
Ministry of Education & Culture
Nassau, Bahamas

Dear Permanent Secretary:

Holding a Masters Degree in English from the University of Florida, I believe that the knowledge I have can be better applied for service to the Bahamian people at a higher level of instruction. Therefore, I request that I be transferred from Donald Davis Junior High School to the Bahamas

College or the Government High School in Nassau, New Providence, Bahamas.

Your consideration would be greatly appreciated.

Sincerely,
Signed, Buster Murdock.

The next day Buster dreaded the thought of going back to Davis, but he knew he had to. There was no other way around it. He had already gotten sick the first two days of the week. But he could not sulk again too much, for it was a Friday and a special one at that: it was October twelfth, Columbus Day. At the school there would be a grand celebration for the discovery of the New World with only half a day of class and the rest of the day would be a party for the kids and a student-faculty softball game.

The morning classes dragged by so slowly that it felt like Columbus would never make it to America. The children were so anxious for the party that they could not sit still for even a second. All little black bodies perpetually squirmed in their chairs as if they had flapping fish in their underwear. To keep them quiet was totally futile, so Buster just let them go and did the best he could to keep the room fixtures intact.

When the party began after lunch, each teacher was assigned to pass out ice cream to their home-room students and to sing songs, play records and dance. The assignment sounded easy enough for Buster: simply pass out the ice cream and then watch as the kids do their own thing. But passing out the ice cream turned into a nightmare. In the office Buster obtained the box filled with vanilla bars, nutty-buddies, creamsicles and banana popsicles. He barely passed through his eighth grade homeroom door when all forty children literally attacked him.

"Jesus!" he yelled. "What's going on here?" The cardboard box tumbled in his hands as the children grappled for it, pumping their teacher with bony little elbows and knees in all parts of his white, sweaty body.

"Oh God!" Buster desperately yelled. "Get away you guys! Get away!" His voice could barely be heard over the children's screaming and yelling. "OK, everybody away—away!" He shooed them like flies. "Nobody gets anything until all is quiet! Everybody form a line or you won't get anything!"

But just after he said that he realized that forming a line and making them be quiet would be absolutely hopeless—he would be there until Christmas time. He squeezed his way to the teacher's desk and stood on top of it, towering over the mass of black, bushy heads, and caressing the brown box filled with Columbus Day treasures. He gave a loud whistle with his fingers.

"OK, Everybody shut up!"

There was pandemonium.

"I said be quiet!"

Still, no way. But he had to get rid of the ice cream because it was quickly melting all over him.

Giving up the idea of the line formation bit, he started handing out the bars one by one to a sea of outstretched, black hands. It was like one of Buster's hallucinations again. Ten thousand arms and hands seemed to be reaching out to him with millions of white eyes popping out of black heads and with hundreds of thousands of wide-open mouths with large sets of white teeth hungrily projecting onto the screen of his own surrealistic movie.

Then suddenly the ice cream box was somehow knocked out of his hands and all the bars fell to the floor. There was a mass scramble of little people diving to the floor while Buster just stood on the desk looking at his empty hands.

Dean Totton was having his problems, too. In charge of the softball game, he had to select, out of hundreds of kids, only nine players to defend their title against the faculty. There was outright rebellion amongst the ranks of the non-selected, and the game never did get under way. But at least it was an excuse for the majority of the students to get away from the main building, go to the ball field, weasel their way to the fringes of the field, and then finally make their escape to liberty and to the freedom of the Christopher Columbus weekend.

The beginning of the weekend brought the ending of Patricia Shannon's visit on New Providence. One full week was hardly enough to get out of Buster's bed and see a little of the island. However, she had to start work soon at the local Gainesville leather craft shop and had to leave a more extensive tour of the Bahamas until maybe another time. They were on the way to the airport in Jinx's car the day after Columbus Day when they both realized that paradise was over.

"See you at Christmas, right Patty?" Buster said.

"You better come up!" she replied.

"Be sure to tell my friends, hi!" he said, one hand on the wheel and the other on her leg.

"Be sure to write me!" she said, one hand on her purse, the other on his leg.

"Sure! In between Harvey Wallbangers!"

"Ha! You couldn't afford the postage! Speaking of letters, just in passing I thought I better tell you: Rick Ruft is back from Vermont."

"What?" The car swerved off the road and almost hit a scavenger dog. He braked hard and the car came to an abrupt halt—the engine stalled out. "Jesus, Jinx has good brakes! I mean, uh, what?"

"Take it easy, Buster," she said, surprised at Buster's car maneuver. "Are you trying to get us killed? All I said was that Rick Ruft's back in town!"

"Oh, is that all you said?"

"Yes, he's working temporarily at Kelley's restaurant."

"Now's a fine time to tell me. That fucking hippie? What the hell's he doing back?"

"Buster, don't get so upset! He's just my 'ex'—don't worry! He said he needed a Florida tan, that's all."

"Oh, is that all?"

"And besides, he's my then—you're my now."

"Yeah—right! That's what I'm afraid of. Asshole! A Florida tan my ass!"

"Well, he was surprised to hear you were down here, that's for sure. After reading your letter he …"

"What? He read my letters? Well that God-damn …. What did you let him read my letters for?"

"Buster, he opened one without me knowing—I didn't know."

"Well that …." He thought of all the Patty Poohs and Patchy Babies, and I love yous he spilled on the pages of his letters to her.

"Anyway, he just wanted to see how much you cared for me, that's all."

"Oh, is that all? Christ, well that no good, long-haired …."

"Buster, we're gonna miss the plane!"

"Bad thing for you, right?" he said scornfully. "Why, he's probably waiting at that God-damned hic town, Gainesville

Airport with his arms wide open!" He madly turned the key and started the engine.

"Buster, don't be so narrow minded, for crying out loud! We all know you're an international traveler now."

He looked at her in angry disbelief and said: "Well you just go get bent!"

He peeled out—onto the asphalt once again and not another word was said all the way to the airport. For Buster, there was a terribly uncomfortable silence and his stomach ached with an empty feeling inside.

As they stood in the waiting room just before the last call for her flight, Patty softly and rather apologetically said: "See you at Christmas, right Buster Baby?"

"Fuck, I dunno, will you?"

"Oh, don't be that way! Everything is OK! Believe me!"

"Yeah, I believed you once before, remember?"

"Trust in me!" She gave him a long wet kiss. "Smile!"

He smirked. She gave him one last small peck on the nose then grabbed her small, leather carrying bag and boarded the plane.

School was now well into the second week of October when discipline problems for Buster, as usual, propped up. It was an afternoon seventh grade class, which had been relatively good compared to the other classes, but in the past two weeks conduct control had gotten progressively worse. Even though the weather was getting a bit cooler, tempers still soared easily amongst everybody. Finally, in this particular class, Buster blew up again. But this time, the madder he got, the louder the students became and the more they laughed.

Now, while most of the teachers continued to severely beat and flog their students, after the office incident with

Big Sandra, Buster refused to hit anybody—no matter what the circumstances. Nevertheless, he still carried one of those enormous yardsticks as a sort of deterrent. But this one afternoon, the deterrent did not work and it failed to quiet the students down. So Buster got frustrated and whirled the useless stick out the door. All the kids laughed. Therefore, he decided to keep them after school. It was a good tactic, for they seemed to loathe this worse than anything else. After the last bell of the day, all the children sat with their arms crossed and literally scowled; their only determination was to get out of that hellish, four-walled classroom and out into the afternoon salt air.

Fifteen minutes later there was a beautiful silence in the room. "Now this is the way I want it to be from here on out," Buster said, "and this is the way it must be if we're even going to start learning English in here. OK, You can go now!"

They all charged out the door. When the last little girl finally squeezed her way out the door, a small group of boys all yelled in unison, "Honky," and "Honky," and "Honky" again. Then they tore off running.

That did it for Buster. The next day he was going to totally annihilate a group of little twelve-year old black Bahamian boys.

That night it was on Buster's mind—it bothered him. First he got slack from white Brits and now slack from black Bahamians. It pained him because he was not used to this black-white conflict and had never really been exposed to it before. He was from a liberal, educated family that had traveled and moved around a lot. He was taught that no color or race or whatever should judge a person. Some of his best friends from grade school on up were blacks, Puerto Ricans and Cubans. He even had a black girlfriend in undergraduate school. The relationship lasted well over a year-and-a-half until she had to move back to Brazil. She was, to Buster, the sweetest, most understanding, most gentle girl he had ever had and was proud of admitting that fact to everybody. The concept of equality was never thought about because it was always there.

He thought a lot of what he was going to do with the kids, but he did not lose much sleep over it.

The next day he asked little Ronnie Baylor, one of the culprits with a perpetual smile on his face, to come to the blackboard. The class was silent and had a feeling that something was up.

"Ronnie," Buster said authoritatively, "Spell 'Honky' on the board for me please!"

H-A-U-N-K-Y, he wrote.

Buster erased it. "Ronnie, spell 'Honky' on the board for me please!"

H-A-U-K-N-I-E.

Buster erased it. "Ronnie, spell 'Honky' on the board for me please!"

H-O-N-K-E-E.

He erased it and looked sternly into the silent, bulging little white eyes that showed nothing but confusion as to what was going on. "And he can't even spell it," Buster said to the class. "Ronnie, spell 'Nigger' on the board for me please!"

N-E-G-E-R

Buster erased it. "Ronnie, spell 'Nigger' on the board for me please!"

N-E-G-I-R

He erased it. "Ronnie, spell 'Nigger' on the board for me please!"

N-I-G-R-E-R.

He erased it, and once again faced the class: "And he can't even spell it! If he can't spell it, then I don't think this little man knows what he's talking about. Calling people names in the first place is a mark of ignorance..." and he stopped short and thought a moment.

Buster indulged in a fifteen-minute soliloquy on equal rights and even cited memorized quotes from Martin Luther King. He was quite surprised at his own quality of oratory. Half the class were spellbound, the rest were fast asleep.

After waking up the drifters, he wrote on the board: Write a full page on how Brotherhood can be attained in the Bahamas. Those who do not turn in the paper tomorrow will have to stay after school and write it. So do it tonight!

"OK!" he said. "You can go now!"

Hurricane Gilda came the next day and school was cancelled for the rest of the week.

Hurricane Gilda seemed to come out of nowhere. Watchful eyes from the Nassau weather bureau had been zeroing in for a few weeks on a tropical depression as far down as the Virgin Islands, but it did not hit hurricane proportions until just southeast of Cuba: the alerts came only a few days before it was to hit smack on New Providence. When the warnings finally did come out, the whole island turned into a beehive of frantic activity: all schools closed; hotels and shop windows were boarded up; food stores and hardware stores kept extra hours for provisions; and yachters strapped down everything they owned in rough moorings to save their very lives. The wind mercilessly pounded the island, sending debris flying every which way, virtually stopping cars and bending over double palm trees that seemed to bow down in remittance and total surrender to such power.

Meanwhile, Jinx and Buster were cozily snug in their living room at Rockydale, listening to a special four hour Beatle concert on the radio and cleaning out a pound of marijuana Jinx obtained the night before. "Gotta store your acorns," he kept saying.

What a pleasure it was for Buster not having to go into that school. It was really starting to wear thin on him. But as he sat listening to McCartney's song, *Get Back*, mixed with the grueling thunder of the wind, he could not help but worry about Rick Ruft's visit down to Florida. It ate away at his mind, and Patty's words kept haunting him.

He remembered the last time Ruft came down to Florida for one of those "Tans". Not only did he get a good tan, but he also got a good part of Patty as well: Patty lying and cheating her way through the whole affair, making love to Ruft in the morning and to Buster at night. She was kept busy, to say the least, and got caught only when she got her times mixed up one day. Buster went over to her place one lovely spring morning and got the pollen shocked out of him upon seeing his girl in bed nude with this disgusting looking, long haired, bean-pole of a young man in his birthday suit. But Buster was terribly lost in love with Patty and found it difficult to even think about leaving her.

Buster's bad thoughts about Ruft kept whirling around the marijuana smoke that perpetually hovered over both his and Jinx's heads. These thoughts ate at him and ate at him—gnawed at his heart. But the words of Beatle George Harrison soothingly filtered the darkness: "Beware of thoughts that linger. Winding up inside your head." Buster shifted his thought patterns, realizing that heavy gloom should not be a part of this day off. His new thoughts swirled him to sunny, white sandy beaches with palm trees gently blowing in the sea breeze.

Hurricane Gilda passed without too much property damage to the island, considering other hurricanes, but there were several deaths. A few Bahamians had died in upturned cars or cars squashed from falling palm trees, and a couple of islanders were electrocuted from downed power lines. But the biggest catastrophe was that of a Haitian refugee boat, an ancient wooden schooner very similar to a Chinese Junk. The boat was dastardly overloaded with not only people but with all their worldly possessions. In the high seas right inside the Nassau Harbor, the boat went down. All fifty refugees, coming from Papa Doc's terror and squalor of Port-Au-Prince, drowned. Half shark-eaten bodies washed up on shore like dead fish in a red tide. BASR (Bahamas Air and Sea Rescue unit) worked long, arduous and frightening overtime hours hauling out of the water other bodies—wet, rubbery and soaked like teriyaki steak. Hurricane Gilda left no mercy.

Drifting into the first days of November produced cool and pleasant days in Nassau. Hot tempers seemed to have faded away with the hotter months and people were in good spirits. There were lots of funky parties during the week that soothed the ruthless days of Buster's roll of sometimes teacher and most of the time disciplinarian. His island fling with Patty seemed like ages ago. He was getting more into the Bahamian culture and meeting a lot of nice, good people. There were plenty of pleasant and sometimes exotic girls of all colors coming in and out of his realms of possibilities for new affairs. His friendship with Dean Totton and Ted Edinthaler solidified, and it was only on rare occasions when they were not seen together doing something of mischief during their free hours of recuperation from the school. It was like a bond of mutual understanding of going through the mutual sufferings of nightmares at Donald Davis Junior High School.

Dean Totton had been an athlete for a long time; but he was not the typical, stereotyped jock of ass-patting, go get 'em type American footballers. He considered himself not an athlete but rather a "Health Educator" where one gets into the science of the body as affected by each sport. He had many close friends in Canada who were well-known athletes in the country. He told Buster one night at a party that he was friends with Canada's World Health Authority. This authority wrestled in the Munich Olympics. He had brought back to Dean an ounce of opiated smoking mixture that was processed in Germany. "Absolutely Deadly," Dean said. "Thank God for World Health Authorities!"

Dean was used to rough and tough sports and knocking his kids down at Davis whenever they gave him trouble— so the discipline problem really did not bother him. Ted Edinthaler was also doing alright, approaching a "Numbed-out" point of view, as he called it. The shop teacher's mitre box was his salvation. He just casually threatened to saw off hands if any little kid gave him problems.

But Buster had much more of an emotional involvement to his situation. He just could not figure out how English could be taught: how it could be integrated practically into the lives of these children, of which many would leave in a few short years and become just like their parents. It also ached his heart every time he saw one of the teachers whack somebody's little knuckles or clip somebody on the ears.

This trauma reached a final straw one afternoon when Buster went to the office to place a book order. The door was closed—unusual—and Buster sensed something wrong. He opened the door and found a large ninth grade boy sitting in a chair in the corner with his head bowed down and his body shaking in near convulsion. His pain was so great, he was beyond crying. His head had large welts that looked like bleeding barnacles. The side of his face swelled out like a puffed blowfish, and his hands were so swollen it was hard to see his fingers.

"And tell that ambulance to get here fast before his mother comes!" Trahn finished saying to his secretary. He looked over and saw Buster standing in the door. "Yes? What do you want, Mr. Murdock?" he snapped sharply.

Buster was totally repulsed. He looked at Trahn, the secretary, the boy, then he quietly said, "Oh, nothing, sir—nothing!" He slowly backed out of the office, closed the door and broke into a run towards his motorcycle.

He hopped on Naomi and sped towards the Ministry of Education. "I quit!" he yelled. "I fucking quit! I can't stand it—poor Bastards—no more—no more—no more! I fucking quit!"

He rode up to the mansion thinking that these people could take their island beauty, their palm trees and pink palaces and "Stuff 'em!" He marched into Mrs. Miller's office without even knocking.

Mrs. Miller looked up between her stacks of bureaucratic garbage. "Oh, Mr. Murdock," she said surprised. "You're just the man I want to see!"

"Yes Ma'am," he said breathing heavily, "And I have a few things to tell everybody here, too!" He came only to quit. He was not even thinking of telling about the boy—that was their business.

"Yes?" she said. "Well, here's good news for you." She

took a folder from the top of one of the stacks. "We have decided to transfer you to the San Salvador Teachers' College on the out-island of San Salvador."

"Yeah?" He was speechless.

"That is, if you'll approve of working on an out-island."

"Approve?" he said. A flash went back to an old dream of a paradise island: long white beaches, palm trees and sun. This seemed too good to be true.

"You must take into consideration that the island is not Nassau, and the social life as well as work is considerably different. However, there is a housing allotment and a slight increase in pay."

"Well, Mrs. Miller, I must say that I'm certainly ready for a change." He started calming down.

"So you will accept, then?"

"By all means, Mrs. Miller! By all means!"

"Let me say again, Mr. Murdock, that not too many people want out-islands for assignments. Out-island living is very different than life as foreigners are accustomed to."

"Oh, well, that doesn't matter—I adapt easily."

"Good! Well then, we'll have your contract and plans ready for you tomorrow and you'll leave for the island next week."

"What do I do about Davis?"

"Friday will be your last day. We'll inform the headmaster in due time, but meanwhile, don't mention anything to him, OK?"

"Don't worry, Ma'am! Don't you worry!"

"Good! Well then, Mr. Murdock, did you have something to bring up?"

"Me, bring up?" He thought, then flashed back to the incident at school. "Oh no, no Ma'am!" he stuttered. "Uh,

I'll probably have a million and one questions for you, but I'll have to let all this soak in first, OK?"

"Well, just call me if you have any questions," she said smiling.

"See you tomorrow, Ma'am!" Buster virtually ran out the door. He hopped on Naomi, revved her up and sped off down the hill yelling, "I don't believe it," so loud that all of Miami could hear him.

Buster's Nassau epic was quickly and unexpectedly drawing to a close. He could hardly believe it was possible that a transfer had come so quickly, but after his briefing at the Ministry, it all started to become clear. He was to ship Naomi on the out-island mailboat, *The San Salvador Express*, at government expense and his plane ticket on Bahamas Air was given to him the very same day of his briefing with a few of the so-called "High Officials" on the top floor of the Ministry.

San Salvador Teachers' College was, according to them, one of the highest, most prestigious centers of higher education in the country, second only to the Bahamas College in Nassau. It was to be an honor to work there, and Buster was made to promise to give his utmost in helping this country through the difficult times of transition to independence. He promised—anything, anything except Donald Davis Junior High School.

The night before Buster left for San Salvador, all his Nassau friends threw a going away party for him, naturally. Everybody brought a bottle of rum to Rockydale and Jinx was generous with the cokes and marijuana—although Jinx himself could not participate. He was flat on his back with a broken nose that one of his sixteen year old students gave to him in a fit of raging frustration over simple algebraic multiplications. There he lay on the sofa, immobile, with a large white bandage on his face with a few spots of dried blood on the bottom side, wanting to talk so badly; but it ached with a tremendous throb every time he muttered even a simple "Yes" or 'No." Buster knew he was going to be relieved, getting away from Jinx. He often thought that Jinx's bad luck might wear off on him, little by little, and that was all he needed.

There were a lot of Bahamians at the party and Buster kept battering them with a non-stop barrage of questions about life on the out-islands. Most of the answers were so negative that it made him sort of skeptical about leaving New Providence, the "Civilized Island." One wise ace said that he hoped Buster was good at the ancient art of jerking off—there was absolutely nothing to do. Another Bahamian asked if Buster liked to make boats. Another said that San Salvador was good if one was on a nature trip. Another commented: " The island is only good if you have a chick with you." Other such remarks were: "Take your own liquor and lots of food with you; you can collect shells on the beach; you'll be the only white person there, do you like sheep? You can count the stars." All these cracks made Buster pretty nervous, but he thought, *What the hell*? He knew that he had to sacrifice a few things for peace and quiet. He would take his chances.

But one thing was for sure! It was "Goodbye" to Rockydale and all those cars and trucks and packs of wild dogs. It was "Goodbye" to Jinx—God help him in everything he does or does not do, or anything that happens to him; and above all, it was "Goodbye" to Percy Trahn and his Donald Duck excuse of a school. It was "Hello" to paradise for Buster Murdock.

# CHAPTER 3

## The New World

All the way over on the un-crowded, two-hour plane ride, Buster was thinking of paradise. *Yes, San Salvador Island*, he thought, *a true Bahamian out-island*. He learned at the party that it was called "Out" because it was away from the capital, New Providence. *Peace—quiet, sandy beaches that would stretch for miles, sun, a pretty Bahamian girl in a grass skirt by his side—playing in the sand and rushing down to the water, splashing, kissing, falling down, laughing, loving, eating roast pig by the fireside, native chants ....*

"Fasten your seat belt, please, sir," the ugly forty-year old black stewardess said. "We'll be landing soon."

Buster snapped out of his dream, "Huh? What?"

"Fasten your seat belt, please, sir!"

When the plane landed on the large airstrip, it came to a halt in front of a wooden conning tower with a sign reading, "Welcome to San Salvador, Stepping Stone to America."

Buster no sooner got off the plane carrying his guitar when five people from the college came up to greet him.

"Mr. Murdock?" a short, plump milk chocolate colored man asked.

"Yes, sir!"

"Mr. Ginnis, Principal! Nice to have you on San Salvador." He kept a long smile like a Chinaman.

"Nice meeting you, sir!"

Then another chocolate-colored man—teddy bear like body—presented himself: "You must be Mr. Murdock!"

"Yes, sir!"

"Osborne Stubbs here, Vice Principal. Nice to meet you." He extended his hand for a shake.

"Nice meeting you, sir."

"It's a nice island," he said with a smile from ear to ear, his huge, white teeth protruding out like that of a horse. "Not much to do—not much entertainment... Oh, I see you brought your own. Well, all the better for you, sir—Excuse, please."

"Mr. Murdock? Jones here! I am to see you to your flat," a dark, black man said with no teeth.

"Nice meeting you, sir." Buster wriggled and squirmed his toes. The half-pound of marijuana he had stuffed in his shoes began to feel uncomfortable. He picked out his luggage from the pile thrown on the asphalt and limped towards Jone's car.

Then finally a thin, anemic looking white man dressed in safari shorts and sandals approached him. "Mr. Murdock?" he said, his index finger in the air.

"Yes?"

"Petah Kentard here," he said in a very deep English accent. "I'm so glad you came, we've been expecting you. I'm the head of the English department and we've been needing somebody like you for about five years."

"Oh yeah?" he felt important.

"Are you set up for dinnah yet?"

"Jesus, I just got here!"

"Oh my word! Well then, you will have dinnah at our place tonight."

"Sounds good enough, I suppose!"

"It's settled, then—around sevenish? See you then—cheerio!"

"Cheerio!" Buster said. *Sevenish*? he thought. *Jesus*! The British accent just did not hit right with Buster. It sounded so put on, so unbelievably formal. Even in Nassau he could not get used to it—it sounded right out of the movies and when real live people talked it came over somewhat false. He was used to down-home country, American, southern accents; and once in awhile a Bronx accent would come slipping down—But an English one?—almost never.

He got in the car that Jones was waiting in and they sped down the road away from the airport.

"Jones," he said, "I understand you're taking me to an apartment."

"Yes, sir!"

"Well, make it a good one!"

"Ha, ha—Yes, sir!" he laughed, his big wide mouth looked like a tunnel.

To get to the apartment Jones had to drive right through the campus. It was an old United States Air Force Pan Am tracking station converted into the Bahamas Teachers' College. There were old, aluminum quonset huts and grayish-green, one-story office buildings all clustered together on a large, flat point of the island. The turquoise sea seemed to surround the entire campus: it was visible from all buildings.

The road weaved in and out of low, one-story porch-screened buildings, then finally the car came to a stop in front of an old, elongated flat building that looked like a World War II barracks.

Out to greet the car was a tall, slender, young white man. "Hi, I'm John Dailey," he said in another English accent.

Buster got out of the car and extended his hand. "Nice meeting you, John, I'm Buster Murdock."

"Well, come, come on in!" Dailey said. "I've been expecting you."

His apartment was all cleaned up. The place was huge. It was airy and spacious with large windows and a view overlooking the ocean: the turquoise colored water was in his back yard. The apartment had a big stereo set-up, lots of books on shelves, a large bar, a huge kitchen with windows looking right into the sea, two large bedrooms and a den with a piano.

"Jesus!" Buster said, impressed. "This is, uh, well this is really nice!"

"Yes, it is 'tisn't it?" Dailey said matter-of-factly. "It used to be the Principal's place 'til he moved up the hill."

"This is really hard to believe!" Buster gawked. "Jesus, this is paradise!"

"Yes, well you'll find out that …"

Dailey was cut off. Just then Peter Kentard drove up in his cream-colored Volkswagen with his wife and two children. They piled out of the car and walked into the apartment.

"Hi there!" Peter yelled. "Like for you to meet my wife, Robin, and my daughter, Susanna and son, Howard."

"Hi, ya'll—nice meeting you!" Buster said.

"Mummy, Mummy," chuckled the daughter, "He talks funny!"

"Shhh, you hush-up now!" Robin said, a tall, monstrously built woman. "I told Petah that it wasn't very polite of him to ask you for dinnah so soon, Ha, ha, ha, ha…."

"Ha, ha …." Buster smirked.

"Ha, ha, ha …. But we are looking forward to you coming over. You are coming with him, are you not Mr. Dailey?"

"No, Ma'am," he answered, "I've already an engagement."

"Oh, so sorry! Well then, Mr. Murdock, around sevenish then?"

"Right, around—around sevenish." He shifted in his shoes and grimaced.

"Oh Dear," Robin said, "Is there something wrong with your feet, Mr. Murdock?"

"My feet? Oh, no, no—my feet, no Ma'am. Just a long flight is all."

"Oh yes—Good Heavens, poor dear! Well, cheerio!" And Robin, the silent Peter and the kids piled back into the Volkswagen and puttered away.

"Well, those are the Kentards," Dailey said. "You'll be seeing quite a lot of them."

"They certainly are British, aren't they?"

"We all are!" Dailey said. "You're the first American here in years. But we won't be here for long. I think you know the story by now, right?"

"Yeah, I've been informed a little."

"Well, let me get my things on and I'll show you around the place a bit."

"John ol' buddy, I think I'll take a little rest first—it was a long flight."

"Oh yes, of course—how silly of me not to think of that! Well then, I'll just step out if you don't mind and see you after dinner."

"Sure, after dinner!"

Dailey stepped out and Buster walked around the apartment. He could not believe it—right on the ocean—and to think of all that time spent at Rockydale: the dumps, the pits, a nightmare. This was a dream. He walked into his room. The desk overlooked the ocean. The whole place was quiet, conducive to thinking—a writer's paradise. He took off his shoes: something he had wanted to do since he had put them on early in the morning. He hid the half-pound of marijuana under the mattress and laid down to fall into a nice, restful slumber. "Ahhh—Peace," he sighed.

He was just getting back into his dream of the Bahamian girl on the sandy beach when: ZAP!! BANG!! I Love you Bayeebeeee! Hard acid rock came blasting from the room next door. It was so loud it sounded like the record was on full blast in his very own room.

"Ayyyy!" he yelled, practically hitting the ceiling. He shot out of bed and banged on the walls several times. He sleepily walked outside as the music continued. He was so surprised that his heart pounded as if he had taken a few laps around a track. He plopped himself into a hammock stretched between two pine trees on the side of the barracks. He mumbled to himself over and over again: "Jesus, I knew it was too good to be true. Fucking noise, noise everywhere! I knew it was too good to be true." Disappointed, but now too tired to think about it, he gently rocked himself to sleep in the swinging hammock.

Sevenish and Buster arrived at the Kentard's cottage door. "Oh, Mr. Murdock," Robin said in her high, breaking voice, "Come in, come in."

"Oh, what a nice house! Beautiful view," Buster exclaimed. It was a small cottage right on the beach with two bedrooms, spacious kitchen and living room. It was almost brand new and was kept so extremely clean—almost to the point of sterility.

"Yes, we like it," she said.

Peter came from the kitchen: "Hello, Mr. Murdock. Can I get you a gingah?"

"A what?"

"A gingah—you know, I believe you Americans call it a—Canada Dry, is it?"

"Oh yeah, a ginger ale. Yes, please—and leave out the rum!" Peter glanced back and gave him a dirty look as if rum was not even intended to be added in the first place.

The dinner was a nightmare. The Kentard's children were outside playing, so they were not the problem. The problem was when Robin delicately placed one piece of baked chicken leg on everyone's plate, three small, round boiled potatoes and four measly Brussels sprouts. Buster was so hungry that he proceeded to pick up the chicken leg and devour it, Kentucky Fried Chicken, Finger Lickin' Good style. And there Robin and Peter stayed, upright in their chairs with napkins tucked into their shirt collars, aristocratically beginning to work on the meager portion of chicken with knife and fork. Buster could have eaten about ten plates instead of one, and when he asked for seconds, Robin was very surprised. There were no seconds.

Their conversation was unbelievably boring. That is to say, Buster thought it was a big put-on at first: so formal and British accent dry. It consisted of what the American thought to be that "Lousy, fucking English gibberish—mumbling constantly about absolutely nothing." Seemingly nothing—but the entire conversation was based around college talk: very serious— not a smile was cracked. The British couple did not want to know what or where Buster was from, nor what he did in the past. They were only concerned about what his use would be at the college. Buster was sick. Too much serious talk over the dinner table completely ruined his meager meal. How he wanted to go back to his new room, light up a joint, listen to the sea and fall asleep—calling it a day. Just moving from one culture into another was enough for him. Too much was too much.

"Well, thank you for the meal. I think I'll …"

Then Peter interrupted: "Shall we now go to the video tape room for a small initiation?"

"I think that's a good idea!" the robust Robin said, wiping green Brussels sprout stains from the corners of her mouth.

"Well, I, uh," Buster stuttered, "I thought I'd, uh …" He caught both Robin and Peter staring at him. "…well, sure! To the video tape worm—uh, room! Excuse me!"

They walked away from the family residential area at the end of the campus (which consisted of four small cottages on the beach side, a sandy road, then four other small cottages on the bush side) and onto the adjoining campus, which began with four long, student dormitories—two beach side, two road side. As they walked through the area, Peter explained to Buster a little about the island and college history and functions. Buster listened attentively: "The college was originally a United States Air Force Tracking Station built in 1954 for use mainly in following missiles and satellites launched from Cape Canaveral, Florida. However, this system became rather archaic over the years, and as a result, closed down. In 1967 the Bahamian Government bought the installation and converted it into the "Bahamas Teachers' College."

"And the students, Peter—what about the students?" Buster asked.

"Yes, of course. The Ministry of Education in Nassau selects the students. They must undergo a series of difficult exams and interviews, and once chosen, they are under a five-year contract. Their three-year education here at the college is fully paid for, including room, board and transportation. They are divided into first, second and third year courses of study. When they graduate they have a two year obligation to teach on an out-island designated by the Ministry."

"How many students are there?" Buster asked.

"There are approximately 150 students in total, and actually, only about 650 people are on the entire island of San Salvador."

"Only 650 people on the entire island?" Buster asked, surprised.

"That's right! The island is very small—only seven miles long and about 4 to 5 miles wide at the very most. The people are interspersed around the island."

"How many teachers are there all together?"

"Lecturers, Mr. Murdock," Robin injected. "We are called lecturers here at the college."

"Oh, well, excuse me—lecturers!"

"Well let's see," Peter continued, "there are about 15 at the moment, but we hope to be getting more soon."

They walked passed the cafeteria building, then reached the classroom buildings, all United States Air Force structures. They were long, one-story annex-types approximately twenty years old. On one end of a classroom building was the special videotape room. It was small but well equipped with Sony video tape recording equipment and egg cartons on the walls for acoustics. Robin sat down and Peter started plugging things in and setting up the camera, explaining to Buster as he went along. Buster, very sleepy-eyed, nodded his head in understanding everything.

"Now Mr. Murdock," Peter said, "I want you to sit right over there and we will put you on camera."

A ZAP and a RRRRR and Buster's image appeared on screen.

"Ha! He exclaimed. "Look at that! It's me! Buster Murdock the First!" He went into a Soupy Sales routine making faces, putting his fingers in his mouth and stretching his lips, waving, "Hi Mom, Hi Mom!"

Peter stood with disbelief, wondering what kind of blundering imbecile the Ministry of Education had sent to work in his English department. Robin sat upright, eyebrows raised not even with the slightest hint of a smile.

"Ha, ha,—ha ... ha..." Buster calmed down and stopped his antics. "Uh, well ... I guess I got carried away. Sorry!"

It seemed as if the videotape machine was the most serious thing in the world for this English couple. It was as if their lives depended upon it. And as Buster later found out, with nothing to do on the island, this machine actually was the biggest toy in their lives.

After the tape room, all Buster wanted to do was to flop down on his bed and go to sleep. Such a long, long day for him, it was beginning to affect his thinking. He had been up since dawn and it was now eleven o'clock. Nothing could register in his head anymore. His mind just could not take in anything else.

"Well folks," he said casually, "I think I'll ..."

"Now Mr. Murdock," Peter interrupted, "I would like to go back to our place and talk."

"Talk?"

"A little business, you know—find out what you can do."

"Yes!" Robin said. "We must figure out this schedule once and for all—now that you're here."

"Well, I thought I'd uh, … well, you see, I'm very …" Buster looked at them both, "… very … anxious to see what I'm going to be doing here." He was mad at himself: *Why didn't I say tired?* he thought. *God-dammit. Coward! I gotta get some sleep, man, this is crazy! Where am I? Who are these people?*

"Shall we go?" Peter asked.

"Can't wait!" Buster said.

They went back to the Kentard's place. Buster looked up and discovered a sky carpeted with stars. *Jesus Christ!* he thought. *That's beautiful! And Jesus, help me get away from these people tonight—please?*

They reached the cottage and once again sat down for discussion. This time there was no ginger, no nothing—just straight business.

"Now," Peter said, "We have one big problem here and that is that I understand you are a specialist in English Language Writing and Literature. Am I correct, Mr. Murdock?"

"Specialist? Uh, yes, that's right—uh, Specialist!"

"But what we asked for specifically from the Ministry, Mr. Murdock, was an English Course Methodologist."

"A Methodologist?" a tired, slouching Buster asked. "What the hell is that?"

"Mr. Murdock!" Robin perked up, shocked. "Good gracious, watch your language—Please!"

"What did I say?"

"Well, ahem," Peter cleared his throat. "Apparently, the Ministry has boo-booed again and sent you."

*Boo-booed?* thought Buster. *Jesus Christ, is this guy for real? I'm so tired—look, you sickly looking weasel, let me get some sleep, will you?*

"But would you be willing to take over some Methodology?" Robin asked.

"You mean to tell me," Buster said losing his patience, "that they sent the wrong person and I don't even belong here?"

"No, no, Peter said. "We certainly could use another person in English, but we are definitely lacking in this area."

"Well ..." Buster said, catching his normal "Jesus." He raised his voice: "I barely know what this jargon word means much less teach it. And I don't think it's fair at all to the people I would be teaching it to." He shifted positions in his chair and raised his voice even more. He was exhausted and his patience had run out. "Now if you are going to stick me with something I know very little about, then I might as well get on the first plane out of here!"

"Oh no, no, no, no, no! Peter said.

"Oh no, no, no, no, no!" Robin said along with him.

"We'll see what we can do," Peter said, trying to calm down his guest. "I just suppose then that we'll have to wait until Mr. Patrick Cramble comes and see what he can do."

"Patrick Cramble?" Buster asked.

"Yes!" Peter said. "Another badly needed English Specialist. In the meantime we'll be working out your schedule and put you in the Literature and Drama courses. Will that be suitable for you, Mr. Murdock?"

"Yes, Pete! That's what I'm 'Specialized' in." He thought, *Thank God! Now I get to go home!*

"Very well, then," Peter said nervously. The saying of his shortened name sounded so crude. "So, I'll see you over here tomorrow around eightish and we'll get things sorted out then."

"Eight o'clock? In the morning?" Buster had hoped for at least a day's rest.

"Bright and early Mr. Murdock!" Robin said.

"Right! Bright and early!" He rose from his chair, Peter accompanying him to the door.

"Good night, Mr. Murdock," Peter said. "We all hope to have a good year heah."

"Right, Pete—good year!"

"Sweet dreams, Mr. Murdock!" Robin said, giving a little wave.

"Right, Rob, sweet dreams!"

Buster walked back to John Dailey's place. Dailey was sitting in a lounge chair with a drink in his hand waiting for him.

"How did it go?" he asked. "That's kind of rotten, Kentard making you stay up like this on your first day."

"Jesus, I think my brain is fried to the gray matter."

"Can I offer you a drink?" Dailey asked.

"Sure!" Buster said immediately. "Boy, do I need one now—uh, rum and 'gingah' please."

He downed the drink, and without saying hardly a word to Dailey, he retired to his bed. He dreamed, oddly enough, of the British Redcoats charging up a hill to confiscate his marijuana, yelling in perfect, teetotaling English accents: Peter Kentard getting all the action on video tape.

Buster's first class at the college was an advanced writing class given to eighteen second year students—all young women. From the very first moment he walked in the class, he was absolutely astounded. There was complete silence as he walked in and thirty-six white eyes popped out of their chocolate-colored orbs, waiting in anxious anticipation to see what this new teacher looked like and how he performed. After so many years of studying under old, British fogies and spinsters, they certainly did not expect to see a young, bearded American with a smile walk in casually and say, "Good Mornin', how are ya'll?" All the girls mumbled a reply, then looked at each other as if their Savior had just approached them.

"This is section 2-F, is that right?" he asked.

"Yes, sir, yes, sir, yes, sir, yes, sir ..." They all said in unison.

"Yes, sir?" Buster replied. He had never been responded to in that manner and was not quite sure how to take it. He still felt too young for that "Sir" business, he was only twenty-four years old. "Wow, uh, listen, my name is Murdock—uh, Buster Murdock." He wrote it on the board. "Just call me Buster, or Murdock, or whatever, but I don't know about this 'Sir' stuff." The girls chuckled.

"Where are you from Mister Murdock?" a girl in the back asked.

That 'Mister' flashed thoughts through Buster's mind. *Jesus!* he thought. *That's right out of slave days—Mister and Sir.*

"I'm an American from Florida," he said. "I suppose you can all tell by my accent." He started to imitate Peter Kentard's accent: "Uh, Mistah Petah Kentard told me this was a good group, but he didn't tell me it was all women. I think we're all gonna have a good time, heah."

Everybody let out a big laugh. It was like a laugh of relief more than anything. To have a teacher so young and a bit on the informal side was such a welcomed relief for them: they were not used to it at all. Throughout their whole lives they had been pinned up and whacked down by stiff-collared teachers feeding them dry, English ABC's from aging, yellow-white pages of eighteenth century English textbooks.

"Well, this is a writing class, so the first day, Petah Kentard wants me to see how you write. Please get out a sheet of paper and in your best English write me a theme telling briefly of your life. For example: age, what island you're from, your family, likes and dislikes, etcetera, etcetera. And remember, you're talking to me in this theme and to nobody else. You have the whole hour. Good luck!"

The sound of shuffling papers and pens drifted through the classroom as Buster took a seat at the teacher's desk. There was no talking whatsoever. He opened the desk drawer and found a paperback book. *Oh good*, he thought. *This'll give me something to do*. He looked at the title: *Scandal in the Staircase—Bournemouth England*. He supposed, *Hmmm … nice intellectual book*. He started thumbing through the book giving a glance upward once-in-awhile to the eighteen hands frantically pushing pens. *Incredible*! he observed. *What a difference from the monkeys at Davis in Nassau—Jesus, what a difference*! His eyes drifted out the flapper windows to the turquoise sea right across the small campus road. The sea looked as if it were a part of the windows—the current running through the flappers. The cool, gentle sea breeze rushed through the windows caressing the entire class with a gentle trade wind tranquility. *Jesus, this is a breeze*, he thought, still disbelieving. *I have a feeling I'm gonna like it here*." He was thrilled, actually. This was just the kind of Peace he had been looking for. It was a dream he had had for so many years that was finally becoming a reality. In the States, it had been all those cars and people running around—all that air pollution and noise. Even in Nassau this chaos was spirit killing. But, San Salvador? This was what he had been looking for. It was this very moment—with the sound of the waves lightly thrashing the shore, the sea-breeze, the mature students in their silence working—when Buster had that ever-so-slight feeling of being helped by a force bigger than he. *Thank you, Jesus!* he thought. *I'm blessed.*

A few days later Naomi came on the mailboat. It was like a grand reunion with an old friend. There she was, strapped on the deck of the *San Salvador Express*, looking as if she were smiling and ready to be ridden on. Buster walked down by the dock to get a closer look at her, but there was a large crowd of natives unloading the boat, a boat that looked like a 1940, over-sized tugboat. Many other people were just standing around the dock waiting to get their own goods off the vessel.

Bahamian mailboats were the bloodstream of not only Bahamian communication to the outside world, but also for the Bahamian out-islands' existence. The mailboats were the means of trade to the capital, Nassau. Out islanders packed their agricultural goods, whatever they may be, citrus, livestock, straw goods, even fish, and sent them either to stopovers on islands en route to Nassau or to the capital itself. The mailboats were also the only means to obtain necessary food staples, rice, vegetables, frozen meat, from Nassau, which in turn received their goods from other parts of the world, mainly from England, the United States and, strangely enough, Holland and Germany. Most food on the islands was imported and it all had to go through Nassau first, then distributed to the out- islands through these vital mailboats. The mail was also carried on the boats, but recent changes in airplane schedules reduced the load.

The *San Salvador Express* arrived on the island of San Salvador via Cat Island and Rum Cay, short stopovers en route, usually every Wednesday. It then left the following day. It had no time to waste. The voyage was a three-day affair from Nassau to San Salvador, but in high seas it took longer and sometimes the Caribbean acted up so much that the old boat did not even make it to the most easterly located of all the Bahamian islands, San Salvador. In those cases, San Salvadorians did without for a couple weeks and sometimes even had to end up rationing rice. However, those times were few because the good ol' *San Salvador Express* was quite dependable with a good, experienced crew.

After Buster stood witnessing the excitement of the dock—Bahamian men and women laughing, yelling, arguing, men in small trucks from Cockburn Town, the main village, coming to pick up their goods they had ordered for the week, muscle-bound crew members helping to take off everything and anything and placing them on shore, refrigerators, ducks in their cages, pigs, tied up goats—the crowd thinned out somewhat and he made his move towards Naomi. Two burley, black-as-night crew members lifted the precious, purple machine off the boat and carefully set it on the dock. Buster, the only white human being around, hopped on his pride of the Caribbean, waved and thanked both the captain and the crew members for taking care of his "Gal," and purred away from the dock and onto firm San Salvador soil. He was ready to break in Naomi and introduce both her and himself to San Salvador Island.

There was only one road around the seven-mile long, five-mile wide island. Buster took the clockwise, westerly route starting from the dock in Cockburn Town. Naomi functioned seemingly even better on this small island than in Nassau. Buster thought that it must have been the air. The first building outside Cockburn Town was the post office and telephone-telegraph shack. Buster passed by and waved to an old black man who was sitting out front. The next building he whizzed by was only a half a mile down the road. It was the only island hotel called "The Riding Rock Inn"—a corporate enterprise owned by a business conglomerate from Fort Lauderdale. Right across the road was a small chicken shack. Then only a half a mile away from the "Riding Rock" was the old Air Force base, already familiar to Buster as the San Salvador Teachers' College. The main road by-passed the entrance to the college and Buster just waved and said, "See you later!" For the next six-and-a-half miles, there was nothing but scrub brush and beach. But Buster had to be careful of the pot holes in the asphalt road, for at times they got as big as kettle drum heads. Often he had to go slow and swerve around them as if he were on an obstacle course. The first building he came to was on the beach side. It was an abandoned, stone building sunk deep into palm trees. A small sign was tacked on one of the trees that read, "Polaris by the Sea." He wanted to stop and explore a bit, but this being his first excursion around, he thought it best just to make it around the island first. He waved and said, "See you later!" Only a half a mile from the Polaris was the old United States Navy base. It was a cluster of Quonset huts and old barracks. The main landmark was a tall, red and white painted water tower. Buster found out later that the base was an anti-submarine look-out station used in tracking down any suspicious submarines during World War II. This base, like the Air Force Tracking Station, was bought by the Ministry of Education and used as a high school for the island. Another half a mile down the road and on the northern tip of the island, Buster passed by a sign which read, "U.S. Coast Guard Loran Station—Authorized Persons Only." He looked up and on top of a hill was a two-building military base with an American flag flying over the larger of the two structures. *Jesus*! Buster mused. *You can't escape Americans for nothin'! They're all over the place*! Extending out from the base was a chain of large white, limestone Cays that had a striking resemblance to the White Cliffs of Dover. These white cliffs contrasted beautifully with the calm, green water surrounding them. It was another couple of miles when he came upon a small Bahamian village, The United Estates. There was a white stoned Baptist church up on the hill and just up and behind the church was the island lighthouse. Buster again passed it all by and would do his exploring later—plenty of time. He passed by the local Ministry of Education elementary school which was just an elongated cracker box. After this, there was nothing but beach for several miles: a white, sandy beach with turquoise water sweeping its shores. Buster was now on the windward side of the island, the Atlantic side, and rough waves pounded the offshore reefs with thousands of white crests. It was quite an impressive contrast from the lake-like Caribbean side where the college was located. All down this Atlantic side there was a lot more foliage and more hills. Palm trees and high scrub brush lined the "Highway." This was a great "Highway" observed Buster, and even though sometimes the asphalt disappeared into sand and rocks from washouts, there was no traffic—absolutely nothing. The only thing he had to watch out for at one time was a lost Billy goat that crossed the road with a couple of burps and turd droppings. Then coming across from the Atlantic side heading southwest very near Cockburn Town, he came upon a large white marble cross surrounded by a big, semi-circle of flag posts with their flags of different countries waving in the air. He drove up and read a sign at the foot of the cross: "First steps of Christopher Columbus in the New World." "Far out!" Buster said aloud. "I've made history!"

After a thirty-five mile addition to Naomi's odometer, Buster was getting quite tired. He hurried past Cockburn Town and once again passed the telephone shack, the Riding Rock Inn, and finally went into the main entrance of the college with its sign, "San Salvador Teachers' College—Bahamian Ministry of Education—Authorized Personnel Only—Visitors Must Have Pass From Main Administration Building." He drove up to John Dailey's place, turned off Naomi and felt real good: it was a feeling of having done something, been somewhere and learned a little. He liked the island—an interesting little thing. *I think I'm gonna like this place*, he thought again. *Just what I'm looking for*! He let out a big smile, patted Naomi on her gas tank, then went inside for a rest and dinner.

It was a week later when Patrick Cramble arrived on the island. The name had been thrown around before—Patrick Cramble—and Buster knew that this guy was not only supposed to take over the Methodology courses, but he was also supposed to live with him. John Dailey's beach room, he came to find out, was only temporary and that he was soon to move to the "flat" on the roadside. The news was a bit disheartening to Buster, but he sportingly yielded: the apartment was only fifty yards from the beach—a minute walk. Buster prayed and prayed hard that his new roommate was going to be at least half-way decent. Anything would be better than Jinx, really. He did not want to be hassled with all the bad luck, the problems and the this-and-that of incompetency.

Buster wondered what this man, Patrick Cramble, would be like; for having a good roommate was important for his well-being and comfortable living. If he had it his way, he would much rather prefer living by himself; but as the Ministry put it, they must make use of all space on campus. Rumors had it that "Mister Cramble" was from Canada; but those were only San Salvadorian rumors, and island rumors traveled fast. Rumor also had it that he was an "English Specialist." Would Mr. Cramble be a stiff-collared, briefcase carrying, imbecilic teacher? Or would he be a freak—a long hair, maybe—somebody that he would be able to communicate with, smoke a little marijuana with once in a while? Hopefully, Cramble would be that and would have something on the ball as far as humanness, coolness, togetherness and get-alongness. After all, Buster was going to have to live with this man for the remainder of the school year.

Buster was to meet Cramble at dinnertime in the teachers' room of the student cafeteria. He waited and waited, but no one appeared. After a half an hour, he poured some coffee and was putting the teaspoons of sugar in the cup when Patrick Cramble, accompanied by Osborne Stubbs, made his appearance. Buster's heart sank down to his feet and his teaspoon completely missed his cup—sugar falling all over the table. It was that feeling of instant dislike from just the first glimpse of this guy.

Patrick Cramble was very fat, his chino pants hung down as if he were carrying a load, and he waddled into the room brushing back a little flip of his thin, shaggy-dog, blond hair.

"Mr. Murdock," Osborne Stubbs said, smiling like a horse, "This is Mr. Patrick Cramble."

"Yeah, nice meeting you," Buster said in a low voice. He stood up.

"Hello," Cramble effeminately said. He looked at Buster cross-eyed.

Buster grabbed his hand to shake it like a lumberjack, but what he actually touched was something as sleazy and damp as a year-old washrag.

The three sat down for dinner. The fat, female kitchen servants brought in bowls of Bahamian peas and rice and trays of pork chops. There was a quiet moment: the kind of quietness that surrounds people who have just met for the first time. Then the conversation suddenly began. Questions seemed to suddenly come pouring out.

"How long have you been here, Mr. Murdock?" Cramble asked.

"My name is Buster, please," he said, shoveling some peas and rice into his mouth. "I was in Nassau for two months, then I just got here a little over a week ago."

"Were you teaching in Nassau?"

"Yes—I taught at Donald Davis Junior High School. It was rather rough—the kids, you know. Kinda funky, though, you know, everybody called it Donald Duck School—Ha, ha, ha, ha …"

There was complete silence.

"Uh, anyway," Buster said picking up the conversation, "Where are you from?"

"Baltimore."

"Hey—Apple core!"

"What?"

"Uh, never mind! Baltimore, eh?"

"That's right—and you?"

"Florida. Pass the salt please! Buster grunted. Stubbs passed the salt.

"Do you have any transportation?" Cramble asked.

"Yeah, I have a motorcycle—it just came in on the last mailboat run."

"A motorbike?"

"No, a motorcycle!"

"A motorcycle?"

"That's what I said, dammit!" Buster started losing his patience. He threw his pork chop on the plate.

"Oh," Cramble murmured effeminately. He jammed some peas into his baby face. Several fell back down on his plate. Then he said: "You don't need a motorcycle on such a small island—a scooter is big enough!"

"Speak for yourself, man! You don't even know this island yet, how can you say that? It all depends on what you prefer—you got that?"

"Oh, well…."

Another silence prevailed. Meanwhile, Osborne Stubbs did not say a word. He was busy looking at the fat kitchen servants.

"Where did you teach in Nassau, Mr. Murdock? Cramble asked.

Buster's heart sank deeper. His thoughts flashed: *Am I going to have to live with this incompetent, Baby Huey milksop for a whole year? This guy looks worse than Jinx. But how can that be? Nothing could be worse than Jinx. Calm down now Buster ol' boy, calm down. Give this dude a chance.* "But I already told you where I taught, didn't I, Cramble?"

"You did?"

"I did!"

"Yes, I do believe he did," Stubbs finally added to the conversation.

"Oh!" Cramble shoved some peas onto his spoon with his thumbs.

Dinner over, Stubbs stayed behind with the lady servants while the two Americans walked over to John Dailey's place. Buster wanted John to get a glimpse of this new character. It was dark, but the moon was very bright. The stars were out but somewhat dimmed by the light of the moon. There was a comfortable, evening sea breeze.

"Where did you teach in Florida?" Cramble asked Buster.

"I taught part-time at Santa Fe Community College in Gainesville. Where did you teach?"

"I taught remedial education for five years in a mental institution right outside the city."

"You mean an asylum?" Buster politely asked, avoiding the words, Nut House.

"Yes. I was in the psych ward, teaching psychotics. Those people were literally insane." He looked directly at Buster. As dark as it was, Buster could see Cramble's crossed eyes. Cramble continued: "Yes, ha, ha, ha... I taught in an insane asylum." He looked up at the moon.

Buster started shaking in his pants. *Jesus Christ, that's just what I need*, he concluded silently. *Fuck! A perfect island paradise totally ruined by this—this Nut! Cramble really is worse than Jinx. But that's impossible—worse than Jinx? Why this guy, of all people? Why me? Why did this have to happen, Lord?* Buster was really in a state of disbelief.

They reached John Dailey's apartment.

"Evening John," Buster said. "What's happening?"

"Oh, just relaxing a bit," Dailey said.

"John, this is Patrick Cramble, Patrick, this is John Dailey."

"Mr. Cramble! Dailey said, shaking Cramble's hand—another sick handshake.

"Yes, Mr. Dailey!" Cramble said.

"Listen gentlemen," Buster said, "I must take a ride on my cycle now, so if you will excuse me."

"Yes—of course," Dailey said.

"See you later then!"

Buster just had to get away from Cramble. There was a certain uneasiness, a disquietude that the man emitted to him. He got on Naomi and took off. Anywhere—just anywhere, it did not matter. He rode about five miles to a desolate beach, thinking the whole way that all this was not happening. All this formal English and dumb, artificial formality was too much for him. He stopped, parked alongside the road, and walked down to the beach. It was quiet—all but the crashing waves. He plopped in the sand, gazed up at the heavens and at the top of his voice he yelled: "Shit, Fuck, Cunt, Cocksuck, Motherfuck, Lick, Dick, Bastard, Pervert, Bitch, I can't, I can't, I can't !!!" A lone bird shrieked and ruffled in the bush behind him.

# CHAPTER 4

## *Alone on an Island*

Classes were going well. Buster only taught fifteen hours a week—then the rest of the time was his. The classes were easy to teach, tapping the resources stored in his brain throughout six years of a formal American university education. There were also no discipline problems whatsoever, and this was the biggest relief for him. The students were mature, young adults who were on San Salvador for only one reason, to learn to become teachers themselves. The process for these students to get to the island was difficult. Entrance exams and careful screening to get accepted to the college were, just as Peter Kentard had said, quite competitive. Those who ended up in the actual classroom were really choice. But they were perhaps, as Buster thought, too mature and choice, because the majority of them expected to be spoon-fed: information belched out by the teacher and noted down by the student, only to be regurgitated back on tests.

It was often so quiet in the classroom that Buster wanted somebody even just to drop a notebook or something to kill the monotony. It was like pulling teeth at times to get them to talk or even answer direct questions. To ask personal opinion was out of the question. Buster could not figure out if it was his newness, a general Bahamian shyness, a British tradition, or what, but he knew from the very beginning that one of his biggest problems would be to loosen up his students and get class participation.

At any rate, it was a beautiful change from Davis—that zoo of a school he babysat in. On San Sal he felt he was actually teaching; and what a pleasure it was to write on the blackboard and glance out the windows every once in a while and see the turquoise Caribbean. His subject matters consisted of Literature, Expository Writing, Speech and Drama. In the Speech and Drama class, he was free to do what he wanted with the students, but in Literature and Writing, Peter Kentard wished for him to carry out assignments and projects that Robin had already started until the term was over at Christmas time. Then in January he would be able to make out plans and course proposals of his own. But in the meantime, he would have to stick with short theme assignments and some absurd medieval English legends of Robin's choosing. But there was no complaint on Buster's part. Fifteen hours? What a dream!

Finally, Buster and Patrick Cramble started settling into their new apartment. They moved in on the same day without exchanging a word. It was a large petitioned apartment at the end of one of the students' dormitories: the last old, elongated barrack on the roadside just before the cottage residences began some one hundred yards further up the campus road. It was hard for Buster to make the move:

first of all, to move from Dailey's beachside room into a room with a view of the island's interior scrub bush and the campus electricity house, a building containing a large diesel generator that lit not only the campus but also the Riding Rock Hotel, was a big let-down. Second of all, to move in with some "Kook from a Baltimore mental institution," as he put it, was hardly his idea of a romantic relationship. But, "God-dammit!" he said to himself while moving. "The island is so nice, I absolutely refuse to let these fucking trivial things bother me." Trivial they were, maybe, but they were still in the back of his mind eating him away: why couldn't he wake up to the gentle pounding of the waves instead of a gnawing, growling sound of a diesel generator, and why couldn't he live with someone only half-way weird rather than this strange, Baby Huey nincompoop from Baltimore? These were only a few things that he would have to come to terms with and resolve within himself if he was to find happiness on the island.

Buster's first two weeks on San Sal had passed and depression started entering in. Everything was taken so seriously: not only in the classroom and with other teachers, especially the Kentards, but even on the tennis court it was a life or death matter. It seemed that there was no room to smile anymore. Austin Riley and John Collins, two relatively young, stiff-collared English physical education coaches at the college who had been on the island several years, challenged "The American" as they referred to Buster and "The Australian," a tourist at the Riding Rock, to a game of doubles. The Englishmen took the game so seriously at the hotel court that there was no fun in it after the first game—not set—game! The Australian was a bit more relaxed, laughing at his own mistakes occasionally, but Riley and

Collins played as if their entire lives depended on it. They refused to let a pair of colonial twits beat them.

Buster found it so absurd, he burst out laughing and started to crack jokes. But every time he did, the Elizabethan Englishmen would frown and keep stiff upper lips. The irony of the whole thing was that the coaches could not afford to take it seriously; really, they were not that good of tennis players. They would miss the ball many times and hit it over the fence often. When this occurred, they would go into a routine of frustration and yell out some English profanity: "Oh, Christopher Robin!" or the ball would go into the net, "Oh, Shuttle Bottom!" or the ball would go in the opposite direction where they wanted it to go, "Oh, Haggish Features!" or the ball would go over the fence, "Oh, Bloody Hell," or the double fault, "Oh Buggerit!" or the old thrown racket number and a loud, "Knickers!"

The language was so incredibly unbelievable for Buster. He was always used to a simple "Fuck, Bastard, or Cunt!" But after seeing all this, it was just "Jesus!" and a chuckle after every English swear word his opponents cried out. If the tennis game was that important to them, he would let them win.

But it was not just the tennis games that were getting Buster down, it was everything. He was going through sort of a new culture shock. Just when he started getting used to Nassau and feeling comfortable with friends, places and customs, he felt thrown onto the island of San Salvador with a whole new set of readjustments to go through. First of all, getting adjusted to the people was the major obstacle: getting used to a different set of Bahamian people and then trying to fit in with the staff members—the overwhelming majority of them British ex-patriots, firm lipped, serious with extremely dry jokes (but only when the rare occasion for a so-called joke occurred). The second major obstacle to overcome was the nothingness of it all—no place to really cruise and enjoy the sights, no nightlife to speak of. There was beach and that was all. The old country drive into the Florida interior, with all its variation and wildlife, seemed lifetimes away from him.

There was nobody that he could go and visit—nobody to get stoned with. At least in Nassau there were the parties, the friends, the girls, the whole social gamut which detracted his attention away from the misery of his zoo keeping at Donald Duck School and made his life quite enjoyable on the island of New Providence. He remembered laughing with Dean Totton and Ted Edinthaler—laughing so hard his stomach ached and had to stop to catch his breath. The antics and jokes of his friends kept him rolling with laughter in his chair for hours. He missed getting stoned with them and riding their motorcycles around Nassau and going cruising down by the luxury liners—all of this a healthy catharsis from the day's wild experiences at school. And the girls—ah, the girls! They were fine: beautiful, international, intelligent and fun to be with. But on San Salvador, there were really no women to speak of—just the backward Bahamian out-island girl students who came from the bush—no possibilities at all. Strangely enough, he felt a distant longing for Donald Davis Junior High School, as bad as it was. At least there, he could apply his whole self, both body and mind: emotionally yelling, making faces, running up and down the aisles, throwing students up against the blackboard, cracking jokes that people genuinely laughed at, running into the staff room shouting at his friends, "Hey brothers and sisters, what's happening?" while flashing peace signs. Now on the island of San Salvador, he had to watch everything he said. He cracked jokes at smile-less faces, he had to put up with the life or death seriousness of the English department head, Peter Kentard, and his wife, and now, the seemingly nothingness of it all.

He felt a genuine loneliness creep in—an emptiness with a feeling of having made mistakes. He longed for home and wanted to be with Patty. He wanted to be with real Americans—to talk with them with real smiles.

He had received no mail yet and it had already been a couple of weeks. Even after letters to Dean, Ted and to Patty (notifying her of the change of address more than anything), there was still no reply. It was on one of those lonely nights when in his room with the windows wide open and the sound of the diesel generator of the electric house filtrating through his room, he broke down and wrote Jinx—of all people.

The following night, Buster's depression worsened and his convictions about Patrick Cramble's craziness were confirmed. Buster was in the kitchen making some coffee when Cramble ran in screaming: "Hey, Hey, Buster, you know that mouse I saw the other night?"

"Yeah," Buster said. He remembered that Cramble had pointed out a mouse scurrying across the living room; but Buster, trying his damnedest, sure did not see it.

"Well," Cramble continued, breathing heavily, "I just saw it again tonight and it went right into your room. I didn't chase him. It wasn't my fault, he just went in." He looked worried and scared.

"Oh really?" Buster said, pouring some coffee. *Jesus Christ*! he thought. *A mouse is a mouse is a mouse and that's it—no big deal.* "Well, Patrick, if he comes and eats me up in the middle of the night, I'll let you know, OK?"

Cramble's face cringed with concern. His fat, nearly mongoloid face wrinkled and he shook his head. "Oh, I just don't know, I just don't know!" he said and waddled back towards his room.

Buster went into the hallway to go to his room and get a book when he ran right into Cramble staring down at the floor.

"See, there he goes again!" he cried.

"There goes what, Patrick?"

"The mouse, see?" He pointed.

"No, I don't see!" Buster said. He thought the whole thing was getting downright creepy and strange. "Oh, OK, Patrick, OK, there he goes!" he said just to get this case off his back. He started walking towards his room door.

"Hey!" Cramble yelled. "Don't chase him back into my room!"

"I couldn't help it, Patrick," Buster said. "He was moving too fast."

Buster entered his bedroom and slammed the door. "God-damn!" he said aloud. "God-damn, God-damn is that motherfucker ever weird! He ought to go back and teach at that mental institution where he belongs. God-damn, let me outta here—let me outta here! This is right out of Alfred Hitchcock!"

Buster also had to put up with seemingly mongoloid idiosyncrasies. They would both be sitting in the living room reading or doing something when out of the clear blue sky Cramble would say, "Hmmm, I've gotta teach Math Method tomorrow. I better get ready!" Then he would go into his room and put on a white corpsman's smock. Or he would sometimes break the silence and say: "Hey, there goes that mouse again!" Buster would look but see nothing.

What bothered Buster the most was that this character did not know how to flush the toilet. Quite often Buster would walk in and see a huge, long trunk filled with corn or white maggots, or something very similar, floating in the bowl. It grossed him out completely. *Jesus!* he thought. *A Methodology Specialist? Fuck! This dude has got to get his own methods straightened out first.*

But then there were times when Buster thought that this guy maybe was not that bad—and sometimes he felt he was actually communicating with the man. Cramble was single and he was single; Cramble was an American and he was an American; they lived on the same island and in the same apartment. All this was at least something in common. They talked about these things and mentioned that all these things were a bit odd, and how different they both were from the predominantly married staff members who ran around in cliques.

One night Cramble mentioned the word "Marijuana" and cited an incident where a teacher he once knew was caught smoking the stuff with his classmates. The principal of the school suspended him for three days, but the Teachers' Union butted in and came to the rescue, narrowing the sentence down to a mere half-day suspension.

*Hmmm, that's interesting,* Buster pondered. This was his opportunity to feel his new roommate out. Just maybe he would have somebody to smoke with. "Uh, Cramble, have you ever smoked marijuana?"

"I have on occasion," he replied, "But I don't much care for it. Besides, there are enough vices in this world without marijuana. And besides, what would the students think?"

So that answered Buster's question, and it was back to the drawing board.

One morning Buster woke up with a feeling that maybe his depression was subsiding. "Good Morning—Good Morning," he sang, "The best to you each morning—A brand new day is dawning, Wish I knew where I was going—Good Morning, Good Morning to you…." It was truly a fantastic morning: a sunny cool, crisp, mid-November morning. He had a cup of coffee and played his guitar. With great vibes, he was feeling good and was prepared for a new day.

His first class was not until eleven o'clock, so he took a ride on Naomi into Cockburn Town and mailed a few letters to friends in the States that he had written the night before. Cockburn Town was just a village, really. It was only a few minutes' ride from the college. Even though it was the largest Bahamian settlement on the island, not more than one hundred people lived in it. It consisted of one main street, half dirt-half asphalt, with several side streets made of hard sand. Scattered throughout the small area of the town, on the side streets, were little, matchbox-like wooden houses with lots of tropical foliage around them. Most of the homes had electricity supplied by privately owned, gas-powered generators mounted inside small shacks in the backyard. On the main street there was the dry-good store, a bar, a tiny laundry-mat and a small clothes and fabric store. At the end of the street, near the ocean, was the island gas station: two antique gas pumps that supplied fuel for island transportation. The post office, Episcopal and Catholic churches and town pier were all outside the central area on the main road leading from the town to the college.

On Buster's way back from the village he passed the college administration building and saw Robin Kentard getting out of her Volkswagen. *Hmm*, he thought. *I think*

*I'll drive over and say good morning and ask her about coat hangers—yeah, I do need some coat hangers.*

Robin grabbed her books and slammed the car door just as Buster pulled up. "Good morning, Mrs. Kentard, how are you today?"

"Fine, Mr. Murdock, just fine, thank you."

"Say, would you happen to have some extra …"

"Mr. Murdock," she interrupted in a desperate tone, "Section 2M2 must be changed to a different time. I'll have to go over the Master Time Table and let you know about the change. Do you have them next period?"

"Yes, Ma'am, but do you have any …"

"Well, I'll go in there with you and check with them on the change as well."

"Yes, Ma'am. Uh, as I was going to ask you, would you happen to …"

"So, I'll go and ask Mr. Ginnis for the schedule and I'll see you in class."

"Uh, well, you do that," he said. And as she marched inside the administration building he said to himself, "And forget about the fucking coat hangers, and hang 'em around your damn neck, wench! Way to ruin my morning, you dedicated, sensitive-less, female I don't-know-what. And stick that timetable up your stiff-collared you-know-what! Good morning!"

Buster had only been two-and-a-half weeks on the island when he became fully aware that the passage of time was completely different from any place else he had ever been. In the States, and even in Nassau, there were things to do that occupied his time: television, friends, sandlot football games, drive-in movies. But on San Salvador, there was nothing and time seemed to drag on and on and on: two-and-a-half weeks and he already felt like he had been on the island for two full years. He had time like he had never had before. Just teaching three hours a day, one hour in the morning and two at midday gave him all the time in the world to do nothing. He did not know what to do. Swimming and diving both in the early morning and after the midday classes was grand: crystal clear water, colorful tropical fish; actually, the most spectacular waters he had ever been in. It was much cleaner than in Nassau: there was no cleaner nor clearer water in the world. However, he only had one coat of skin, which he did not want to wrinkle up and wither away. Also, many times he had to get out of the water early because of abundant schools of large barracuda—barracuda that never looked very friendly to Buster. So after his swimming, sessions he would go and read seemingly thousands of books that he checked out of the college library. This passed the time somewhat, but then again, he only had two eyes.

After this time passage awareness, there occurred a series of incidences that led Buster to a deep depression. They were seemingly trivial things, but the fact that Buster had all this time to dwell on them made them much worse.

First, Naomi broke down and the brand new, two hundred cubic centimeter Yamaha became crippled with only one cylinder working. The only mechanic on the island, Bert Storr, needed to send off to Nassau for a new set of piston rings—So Naomi would be limping on half power for at least two weeks—it might as well have been an eternity. John Dailey told Buster that it was typical of the Nassau Bike Center to make their bikes run only up to the two month warranty and then shortly thereafter break down so they could rake in more money. According to Dailey, the Nassau Bike Center had the biggest racket in the country.

The next thing that really bothered Buster was his roommate, Patrick Cramble. The scampering mouse hallucinations subsided a bit, but lately Cramble had been complaining of black Bahamian worms squirming in his spaghetti—"Nigger Worms" he called them. He also gave Buster the impression that he was still working in the insane asylum in Baltimore, for he kept referring to classrooms as wards and the students as patients.

Buster's own depression was not helped much by Cramble's sufferings of culture shock. The patients, as he told Buster one night while eating spaghetti, were not taking a very good liking to him. His rapport was not good. *Actually,* thought Buster, *it really wasn't his fault—these students had probably never laid eyes on a semi-mongoloid white person before.* The patients were not cooperating in Cramble's therapy wards and that bothered him a great deal. Cramble said that he had it rough, coming in the latter part of the term — especially when the Bahamians were not used to change— they did not like new teachers one bit. Cramble only thought of himself. He did not think about Buster's situation at all; for Buster had come in at the middle as well, but he seemed to get along with the students just fine. Patrick Cramble was simply out of his element. He did not know how to swim, he never went to the beach and he did not like the sun—it hurt his white, tender baby-skin. He stated that he was ready to take the next plane home. But Buster managed to convince his roommate that he was merely going through a period of adjustment and that things would get better. Right!

Another night Buster just had to get stoned. He rolled several joints and went down to the campus beach. At the time, it was a very righteous scene, but he paid for it afterwards. He really got ripped. He smoked four numbers one right after the other. The stoned feeling came on to him very fast, like a locomotive on a track traveling up the backside of his head. His mind started to expand so rapidly that it seemed to go out of his head, melt into the universe and unite into total harmony with the elements. The half-moon was suspended like a light bulb hanging down from a ceiling. Stars were all over the place, spilling down onto the horizon line. Falling stars dropped like flies, waves gently patted the shore and the wind whisked through his ears. He felt like he was on a spaceship traveling through a timeless odyssey of infinity. There he lay in the sand—truly flying through space: a lone man on the face of the planet, the earth his ship and the moon controlling the flow of his blood. Flying, flying, whizzing through the universe….

But after several hours, he got cold and went back to that seemingly small, enclosed four-walled bedroom of his. When he woke up the next morning, realizing he was at San Salvador Teachers' College, reality hit him like an exploding star. He became so depressed that he walked around for several days in a listless, spaced-out manner with only the asphalt telling him that he was on Mother Earth with other mortal men.

His depression became deeper. If only there was somebody just to ask him if he was OK—that would help him out a little. But there was nobody—nobody cared. He walked around as if he were in physical pain, but he knew only his heart was low. Even his bones ached as if he had rheumatism or the like.

One day he felt so bad he reported to the administration building that he was sick and unable to give classes. The principal, Mr. Ginnis, excused him. He hopped on Naomi and rode to the nearest vacant beach outside of the campus.

The whole day he just sat in the sand, peering out into the horizon and reflecting. What was he doing on this island? There must be a reason or he wouldn't be on it. The horizon, that straightest line in the world, produced a type of movie screen where Buster saw himself giving guitar concerts or playing in a tavern in New England, or recording his own songs. He also saw himself flashing on the horizon screen, pounding away on his typewriter, working on some novel of great significance in Greenwich Village. Then the movie on the horizon would fade away and he would suddenly realize that all he was really doing was sitting on the beach and earning a living by teaching "Fucking" English to people he was not even quite sure understood him. And even to write a novel? What a joke! There was little or no motivation for writing on the island. The only inspiration came from nature—but it seemed that even as limitless and indescribable as the sky and sea really were, man's description of them got dull, boring, redundant and meaningless. Looking at a sunset with a sky appearing to be on fire and then slowly and silently being extinguished by the waves keeping time was quite amazing and righteous—for sure! But in the end, it all amounted to, so what? After it was all over, he would still be on the beach looking at the horizon, getting badly bitten by sand fleas and those God-awful, fist-size mosquitoes—his ass getting sore from sitting on limestone rock, his back aching and his stomach growling with hunger. Then it would be time to go back to the God-forsaken four-walled room of his, only to find it filled with the noise from the electric station, and a kitchen with empty cupboards with the exception of a bag of white rice containing very little nutritional value. And to top it off, he would encounter a God-awful, ugly as sin, hallucinating roommate with whom he could not communicate. So then it would be a trip down to Cockburn Town on a crippled motorcycle only to find the food store closed. So then it would be back to the apartment: hunger pains increasing, room gnawing with electricity making, and it all boiled down to white rice and who gave a damn about a fiery red sky at sunset? There was God right in front of him—but so what?

He went to bed and cried himself to sleep. "Fuck!" he whimpered softly, fluffing the pillow. "Alone again—but for years and years—Christ!"

This was the lowest point in Buster's depression, but it subsided shortly after. One Sunday morning a few days later, he was talked into going to the Anglican Church by one of his students, Anne Villeneuve. She just happened to be the big, robust wife of the preacher, Father Villeneuve. Buster could not refuse.

He got up early to try and psych himself up for the ordeal. He hadn't been to church in years and he tried to refresh his memory. He pulled his pants on: "God!" he said aloud. "Please fix my motorcycle!" He slipped on his socks and best sandals: "Dear Lord, let there be a warm woman in my bed next week." He threw on his new Dashiki, a loose, African-patterned shirt he had bought in the Nassau straw market: "Heavenly Father, let there be a juicy red steak on my plate this evening." He looked into the mirror and combed his hair and beard. He noticed the hair on his head was getting longer. The weight made it straighter and it was hanging down and curling around his neck. His full beard was getting thicker and darker, now completely hiding the skin of his face: "And Dear God, when I go home for Christmas, may my mother like my beard!"

Buster felt good this morning—stronger than other days. Light headed, he let out a rebel yell that made Patrick Cramble jump out of bed: "Onward Christian Soldiers, Fuckers!!" He threw open the door and burst outside. "Let there be light!" he yelled. His arms went up in the air as if to greet the Almighty. And Buster saw that it was good. A few minutes later, an old, gray Air Force mini-bus filled with students stopped by and off they went to church.

The church was right alongside Cockburn Town. It was a typical, small town's church: white, barn-shaped with a small steeple and wooden steps leading to the main entrance. Buster walked in along with the others. He was impressed. It was more than he thought. The inside was all dark brown, stained wood, filled with pews and wooden, crucified Jesuses tacked on the walls. The altar was draped with white clerical silk and adorned with beautiful flowers. Alongside the altar was an ancient pedal organ. As ancient as it was, Buster was surprised that they even had one.

He entered a pew, knelt and said the Lord's Prayer, something that had been instilled in him at birth and one of the few things he hadn't forgotten in all those years. But it was not a quiet Lord's prayer. Roosters started crowing and goats brayed right outside the arched, windowless, window sills. Babies were crying and old men were in the back hacking and coughing away.

Buster sat back in the pew, waiting for the show to begin. He looked around and noticed that he was the only white person in the church. A strange feeling overcame him. In the United States, anywhere he went, not only in church, the situation had been the other way around: one or two blacks here and there peppered a crowd. But now? It was very strange. He noticed some familiar faces: above all, Mr.

Ginnis and Osborne Stubbs. And just to his side was Miss San Salvador, the island beauty queen. Buster had met her a few days before in the food store. She was extremely friendly with a beautiful smile on her light-complexioned, chocolate-colored face. In the pew she glanced over to Buster and gave him recognition by smiling and a little wave. Buster smiled, too, and went into a wild fantasy. "Oh, Jesus!" he said to himself, squirming in the pew. "Incredible!" He swallowed.

The show began with the ringing of a bell. Everybody stood up. The organ began—terribly out of tune—the organist moving from side to side pumping away the air through the tubes. Father Villeneuve entered the altar area. He was a lean, six foot four inch, domineering black man who towered over the entire congregation. He sported a small, brillo pad Van Dyke beard that set back his eyes deeply into his emaciated cheeks. Buster was amazed: he was a spitting image of a black Abe Lincoln.

After several songs and prayers, the sermon began. Father Villeneuve took the pulpit and commanded it forcefully like an evangelistic savior, deeply and hypnotically peering into his flock as if the souls of everyone were on trial. He had a great preacher's voice with an educated British accent: high, yet rich with a lot of support. He had a strong, energetic tone to his voice, coordinating it effectively with terrific, flying gestures. Countless of times Buster had heard the same sermon topic—the topic of how the faith of Jesus and only this faith could save the world—but he had never heard it so effectively and dynamically delivered. He was captivated by Father Villeneuve's mere presence. Buster, at that moment, truly believed.

The sermon was the absolute best part of the service, but the communion went on and on and on. Nobody knew how to sing, either. It was all out of tune and babies were crying. The roosters penetrated Buster's ears and his knees ached badly. Now he remembered why he had stopped going to church. His only savior was Miss San Salvador. *Jesus, Miss San Salvador*, Buster thought. *Her legs, her legs! How gloriously crossed they are. And her tits, Oh my God her boobs! How they divinely roll over onto the next pew as she prays. Oh my God, what beauty. Jesus, the humanity!* He trembled in the pew and bit the prayer book to restrain himself.

When the affair was all over, everybody streamed out of the church and stood outside, shaking the preacher's hand and talking—just like a deep Georgia church social. Everybody was well dressed: the men in suits and women in formal dresses.

Buster went over and talked to Anne Villeneuve to say how much he enjoyed the service. But as she was inviting him back next week, he very politely reminded her that he would come from time to time, but was not a regular church goer.

The gray bus made several trips back and forth, carrying students to the college—back to their dormitories and Sunday afternoon lives. As Buster reached home, he threw open his bedroom door as if finally in liberation. "Praise the Lord!" he yelled out. He tore off his clothes and violently, but religiously, shucked his sacred tool to the visions of Miss San Salvador. "Oh, Jesus Christ!" he panted. "Thank you!"

## HYMNS

| 5 | 549 |
|-----|-----|
| 362 | 8 |
| 338 | 86 |

Then finally came Thanksgiving. The U.S. Coast Guard leader, Greg White, had invited all the college lecturers and administrators to an American Thanksgiving Dinner at the base. It was at this dinner where Buster started meeting people of his own race and kind. Appetizers were first. People stood mingling around a large, sheet-covered pool table filled with American goodies, something Buster hadn't seen since he left the States: Fritos, Ritz Crackers, Seven-Up, Jack Daniel's, potato salad, cranberry sauce, olives, etcetera.

R.B. Baker, a tall, dark-haired, twenty-two year old enlisted man with a scrimpy beard (unusual for Coast Guard regulations), looked at Buster and both their eyes met. R.B. had a look in his eyes that gave the young college lecturer the impression that they had known each other for years. It seemed like one of those instant friendship type things. *Thank God*! Buster thought. *Maybe here's a friend*. But there were a lot of people in the Coast Guard recreation room and eating area, and to really talk to any one particular person was too hard to do.

Buster met a lot of other sailors as well. He met George Lindbry, the cook and a fellow Yamaha owner—a one hundred cubic centimeter machine. The bike, however, was broken and George was waiting for parts to come in on the military supply plane that flew to the island once a week from Fort Lauderdale.

Buster also met the captain of the base, a young twenty-four year old graduate from the University of Maryland. Greg White was tall, well built, blond and sported a well-kept, light red beard. He was soft-spoken and his mannerisms gave Buster the first impression that it would be difficult for this type of guy to lead other men. Even though he was physically large, he did not seem to be the authority type. But, he was in the position as Captain and had his job to do. He also had an image to keep: that of a striking young commanding officer, entertaining important people on the island (maintaining island diplomacy and good relations) with a strikingly elegant woman by his side. And a strikingly, elegant woman he had indeed. Her name was Barbara—Barbara Oskalowski, a Canadian with a tall, slender, extremely well-shaped figure, light skin and long, silky blond hair traveling down to the small of her back. She was absolutely beautiful and drove all the Coast Guard sailors on the base, all fifteen of them, berserk—many times to cold showers or bedroom whacking jobs. She happened to be the only single white girl living on the island. She lived and taught at the island high school just down the road. Although this school was easy access for the sailors on the Coast Guard base, she was known to be the "Captain's girl" and therefore off-limits to any horny swab jockey who even thought of taking a trip to the old, converted U.S. Navy base. And there she stood: drink in hand, socializing with the captain's guests, always by his side. *Or was it the captain always by her side?* Buster thought. He glanced at the couple now and then between appetizers of olives and potato chips and noticed that there was a strange interaction between the couple. Every corner of the room she went to talk to somebody, the captain followed—and it was not the other way around. *Hmmm*, Buster thought. *Weird, strange, weird—but nothing—no significance.*

Buster did some more mingling and his spirit started to fly—meeting people, real people that he could at least communicate on some sort of similar wave length—for they had a few things, American things in common. Also, none of the boys on base had ever been near a mental institution.

He found out information about the base. Its main purpose was maintaining the Loran navigating beam that sent out a bleep that helped thousands of boats in the Caribbean chart their courses. The base had been on the island since 1955 and had a lease with the Bahamian government until the year 2000. The fifteen man crew changed constantly: sailors coming and going throughout a year's duty. The chain of command consisted of only one commissioned officer, one non-commissioned officer and the rest were enlisted men. It was a self-subsisting base, depending only on supplies coming in on the Air Force cargo plane from Fort Lauderdale once a week. Every man had his own particular duty: from cooking to sophisticated electronic beams to swabbing the decks and cleaning the barracks. Fourteen men lived in the petitioned barracks— two and three men to a room, with the captain living in separate quarters apart from the main building. This made it perfect for him with his steady girl, but it left fourteen others in agony, for the boss prohibited women in the barracks. It was down to the very last enlisted man that thought this rule was totally unfair—especially at times when everyone knew Miss Oskalowski was inside.

The Thanksgiving party grew larger and larger with people coming in gradually from the college. Patrick Cramble waddled in, but he did not mix with the crowd. He stood off to one side, alone, checking out the mouse situation. The Bahamian administrators had no problem mixing with the Americans. Even Father Villeneuve came with his wife— both entering the rec room with wide, happy smiles. But the English stood off to one corner, talking mostly amongst themselves, drinking ice tea. Austin Riley and John Collins and their wives, Betty and Caroline, chatted away with the

Kentards or with the Bachrans, a typical, aging, ex-patriot English couple that taught Education courses at the college. The only time the English talked to anybody else was when the captain and his girl, or more accurately, his girl and the captain, came up to them to find out how things were going. They would answer usually with a dry, "Splendid, splendid, yes indeed, splendid." But for them to talk to any Bahamians or even to petty, American enlisted men, was to lower themselves too drastically for their teetotaling comfort: politely nice, yes, but they kept their distance.

There was one couple that Buster liked immediately, Berry and Ethlyn Silversmith. Berry was a thirty-five year old Englishman who was the only white student at the college. He was married to the young and beautiful, black headmistress of the island high school, Ethlyn. They were always seen together and had large, happy smiles of contentment on their faces. They were very friendly and liked Buster as well.

Suddenly, a big, deep clang sound rang out and six large, steaming, Butter-Ball turkeys were set down on the banquet table just begging to be carved and gorged down by any nationality. The captain raised his hand and demanded a few moments of silence while he said an American Thanksgiving prayer. When it was over, even Father Villeneuve smiled with approval. The long table was now set with a smorgasbord-type of arrangement, and everybody helped themselves. The English, with a spoonful of everything and a small piece of turkey daintily placed on their plates, could not believe their eyes when they saw the American men pile onto their plates mountains of mashed potatoes and cranberry sauce and piles of light and dark meat covered with mounds of stuffing and gravy. There was rock music in the background coming from speakers hung in the corners, and good old, American twangy accents floated about the festivity. Although there were no football games to watch on television, nor bespectacled grandmothers knitting by the fireside, not only Buster but all the other Americans truly felt at home on this small island, thousands of miles away from their families and friends.

After the pumpkin pie with good ol', down-home whipped cream, Buster walked outside, away from the noise and stuffy-people air. He found R.B. Baker sitting on the bench near the flagpole, smoking a cigarette.

"God-damn!" Buster said. "I'm so stuffed, I won't have to eat until Christmas!"

"Yeah, me too!" R.B. said. "It was great, right? Lindbry is a good cook. Hey man, look at that view! Isn't it beautiful?"

They both sat silently for several minutes, gazing out onto the deep, blue, white-capped ocean with that limestone, white-cliffed island chain extending out towards the North. The warm wind was stiff and the sound of the American flag snapped like someone rapidly shaking out sheets. The flag rope pounded the aluminum pole.

"Jesus!" Buster said, breaking the human silence. "I better put my motorcycle over there in the corner so the wind doesn't decide to carry it away."

"That's a Yamaha 200, right?" R.B. asked.

"Yeah, sure is. You know anything about 'em?"

"Oh, I know a little." He was elusive.

"Well, maybe you could help me—it doesn't seem to be working right. The plugs keep getting oil in them. One of the natives, Bert Storr, said it was the piston rings. He fixed the right side, but the left side went out this time. Can't figure the damn thing out!"

"Bert Storr, eh?" R.B. said with a smile. "Christ, the God almighty engine mechanics on this island. He's a Bahamian, right?"

"Yeah…"

"Do you believe him?" His piercing eyes swelled out of his beard and landed right on Buster's perplexed face.

"Well hell, what do I know!" Buster exclaimed. "I can't even put together model airplanes! The only thing I know is that my bike isn't fixed yet!"

"Well, to tell you the truth," R.B. said, "I used to work in a Yamaha shop in Massachusetts."

"Yeah?" Buster said. His face lit up. "Well, I'll be a bird's turd! You're the man I wanna see!"

"Sounds like you're just not riding it right. Let's take a look at it."

"Not riding it right?" Buster said. "Jesus, how could I not be riding it right? I mean, my ass can only sit on the seat a certain way, and my feet can only be placed on the pedals, right?"

"Yeah, but you gotta have your head screwed on, facing forward, man!" R.B. smiled.

They walked over to the bike.

"By the way," Buster said, "This is Naomi. Naomi, this is R.B.! Uh, by the way, what does R.B. stand for?"

"Robert Burgess—but just call me R.B., Naomi—Nice to meet you!"

It seemed as though both men had been on the island too long.

R.B. toyed with the plugs. He started going into detail as to how two stroke engines worked and he went into the this-and-that of Yamahas. All of this information went completely over Buster's head—but Buster thought this guy sure knew what he was talking about.

"Yeah, here it is," R.B. said, examining the oil in the plugs. "You're riding it wrong. I bet you've been babying it too much."

"Well, I have been taking it easy—not revving it past 6 rpm's on the dial," Buster said shyly—"6" meaning six thousand rpm's.

"6 rpm's?" R.B. was surprised. "Fuck, man, no wonder your plugs are like this! This is a two-stroke engine, man. It has a high, whining sound—not a low purr like a Honda or a clump-clump like a Harley Davidson. Fuck, you should just rev the piss out of this thing—shift on at least the shifting points, 7.5 rpm's, and take it past the red line around 8—10 rpm's at least once every time you get on the thing." R.B. started Naomi up and revved it so high that Buster feared the pistons were going to seize up.

"God, man, take it easy! Buster said.

"That's the way she's supposed to sound!"

"Jesus! So I've been riding it wrong?" Buster yelled. The loud, high shining sound whip-cracked in the wind. "And all this bullshit about piston rings, eh?"

"Yeah, man!" R.B. started to explain in a loud voice, practically shouting. "You're running it at such a low RPM that you're not giving it a chance to burn up the oil that's going down into the cylinder, therefore letting the oil drip into your plugs and clogging 'em up so much there's no spark—thereby crippling your engine."

"Oh!"

"Watch this!"

R.B. hopped on Naomi and took it for a spin—ruthlessly winding Holy Hell out of the machine.

*Oh, Jesus, my poor bike!* Buster thought. *R.B. is gonna burn it up and drive it into the fucking ocean.*

But no. R.B. came up the hill with a huge smile on his face.

"Fixed! He said satisfactorily. "You're on your way. Just do what I tell you and she'll treat you right."

"Jesus, R.B. this is just great! Thanks for everything. Naomi is well again!"

"Sure, man. Hey, whatayasay we go to the Riding Rock bar one of these nights for a few drinks?"

"Sounds terrific!"

"Well, the Coasties," as the sailors referred to themselves, "are restricted from the campus right now."

"Restricted?" Buster asked.

"Yeah, fuck, it's a long story—tell ya later. And I got the duty and other things here for another week, so let's say around next Wednesday about 9:00!"

"Great! Don't think I'll be doing anything then."

"So long, and take care of that thing—be good to it and she'll treat you like a king."

Buster whizzed off with the wind and caught the road back to the college. His spirit was so high he sang at the top of his lungs all the way back. What a feeling it was to be down and lonely so long and then just in an instant—a breath of air—things took a one hundred-and-eighty degree turn for the better. There was nothing like the possibility of having a friend on the island to warm thoughts and comfort the pain of longing for home and a low heart.

After the Thanksgiving holiday, it was all downhill for Buster as far as school was concerned. There were only one-and-a-half more weeks of class, then began a half-week study period for the students, followed by exam week, then Christmas vacation. The term was all over for practical purposes, with the exception of tying up loose ends in the classroom. Buster was still carrying out Peter Kentard's desire of keeping with the assignments Robin had given to the students. They were terribly boring for him and he could not quite see what some of the homework had to do with education. But, he thought, after Christmas he could start with his own stuff.

One of the assignments Robin had given the students for Thanksgiving recess was to write a creative anecdote on the topic, "A funny thing happened on the way to the dance." The first day back to class, Buster collected the stories and graded them; but they were so bad that the highest grade was a "B" and very few got those. Most students had misunderstood the assignment and wrote on a funny thing that happened <u>at</u> the dance—but he could not flunk them all for that.

The funniest paper was written by the preacher's wife, Anne Villeneuve. Buster read it in disbelief, and it gave him a slightly better idea of the mentality of some of the students:

Wow! Dance Time Again
By Anne Villeneuve

I took my dress out of the closet, put it on the bed. Got my shoes, put them on the floor in front of the bed and then I stepped into the shower. I shampooed my hair and I stood there for a minute, letting the warm water run all over my body. It felt good, mann!

Stepping out of the shower, I wrapped a large towel around me and then, I went to the mirror. I pushed my hair in a pony tail with a ribbon. I dabbed a little perfume and powder on, then, I slipped my dress over my head. Sitting down on the bed, I slipped my feet into my shoes.

I was wearing pink and white. My dress was white: my ribbon, earrings and shoes were pink.

After I was dressed, I had a second look at myself in the mirror.

Stepping out of the porch door, I remembered I didn't have the one dollar which was admittance fee. I had to turn back. The old people use to say, "Never turn back my child! It is bad luck!" But I had to go back for the money.

I got it and the walk would take about half hour to the club.

As I stepped outside I was struck in the face with complete darkness and a voice.

"Hi there Anne! Going to the dance?"

"Who are you?" I cried.

"Oh! Come on, mann! You know who I am!"

"No I don't! Please tell quickly!"

"I am Buster Hannah!"

"Oh, my God! I thought you was someone else! Mann, you almost frighten the hell out of me!"

"Ha, ha! Heeee! You don't say!"

"What are you doing here?"

"Waiting for you!"

"Really!"

"Yum!"

"Why?"

"I like you!"

"Really!"

"Yum!"

We walked in silence for a while, then I felt this thing touching me. I jumped. It happened again, then I realized it was Buster trying to get his arm around me.

I said, "Stop it Buster, and now!"

"Anne, you know you like this!"

"Stop it! Now!"

He pulled me a little closer to him.

"Buster, stop!"

"Give me a kiss!"

I break loose and started to run then, down I went, face to the ground. Buster couldn't see me because it was too dark then, he too tripped. He landed right on top of me.

I was frighten, crying and laughing at the same time.

Buster helped me up. I brushed off my dress, touched my hair, but my knees were scraped. They were bleeding. Buster ran to the nearest block, with his hanki and brought it back, then he rest the cool cloth on my bruises.

"Buster, I mind slap you for this!"

"Anne, I didn't mean it and I'm sorry!"

I felt sorry for him and I told him it was alright.

We went to the dance. I had a few dances, but I had to leave because my knees were stiff.

*Jesus Christ*! Buster thought while reading through this. *What would the old man think? Poor ol' (young) Father Villeneuve preaching the Gospel to his lost sheep and his wife writing and thinking like this? She must be having orgasms in the back of the classroom, while me, Mr. Teacher, writes on the blackboard.* Buster dropped the paper on his desk and gazed out the window to the vacant lot and the electricity house. He reflected: *Wasn't it Jesus who said that if ye so much as have one thought of desiring another person—thou hast committed adultery—or something like that? Jesus Christ! What would the old man think?*

With Naomi purring away like a kitten, Buster drove up to the Riding Rock Inn. He passed in front of the swimming pool, glided past the restaurant and main lobby and parked by the wooden staircase that led to the bar. R.B. Baker's Honda Fifty was leaning against one of the posts. The whole Riding Rock Inn was made of wood: a sort of modern, one-story cottage-type structure located right on the beach. Off to the side and separated from the bar and restaurant were eight sidewalk-linked cottages. Buster had learned that the Riding Rock was a business venture of a Fort Lauderdale real-estate cooperation. They not only made money off diving clubs from Florida that came down once-in-awhile, but also, and mainly, from prospective clients who came down from Miami, Atlanta and New York to buy land on the island. The real estate people also pushed onto their clients condominiums at the colony of cottages that the corporation was in the process of building on the southeast point of the island. The corporation had its own Cessna twin engine plane that flew in supplies and clients three times a week from Fort Lauderdale, and it also had several cars and trucks to whiz clients around the island to help push the condominiums and land sales. Some of the tourists flew down to the island on special Mackey Airline charter flights that made runs from Miami periodically. Also for the tourists, the hotel rented out small Honda Fifty scooters all lined up in a small shack off to the side of the swimming pool. Buster also found out that the Riding Rock had no electricity of its own and that it tapped its juice from an underground line from the college electricity house only three-quarters of a mile away.

Buster entered the bar and met R.B. sitting at a table in the corner, relaxing, smoking a cigarette. R.B. was the only other person in the bar. It was dimly lit with candles on the tables. A giant ship helm wheel hung from the ceiling with small, dim, yellow lights on the hand spokes.

"Hey, R.B., what's happening?" Buster said, taking a seat.

"Well, here we are, right?" R.B. said. "Glad to see you made it! What'll it be?"

"Jesus, I don't know—what are you having?"

"Heineken—seeing as how that rot-gut, horse-piss Budweiser cost the same around here," R.B. said in a Massachusetts –type accent.

"Yeah, I know what you mean—I'll take the same."

"Jimbo—Two Heinekens, please!" he said to the young, black, well-dressed bar tender. "Ever been here before?" he said, reverting back to Buster.

"Yeah—but there never seems to be any people here." Buster said.

"Just you wait, man! They start flowing in just before Christmas and it doesn't stop until May or so. Friday the Finger Fuckers come in and the place will be different a little bit."

"Finger Fuckers?"

"Well, yeah," R.B. chuckled. "Actually, they're called the Finger Lakers down here because it's a group of American Archeology students from small colleges up around the Finger Lake area in up-state New York. About twenty-five in all, I guess—usually. All the Coasties call 'em Finger Fuckers because more than half the group is usually girls— and that—for horny swab-jockies like me—means hope and light. Ya know what I mean, man?"

"Jesus, sounds great—also for horny college teachers, too. Ya know what I mean, man?"

They looked at each other. They understood and laughed. The cold beers came.

"Hey, whatayasay we go outside to the patio?" R.B. suggested.

"Fine!"

They picked up their beers and walked onto an adjoining, long wooden patio that extended over the ocean. There was a magnificent view of not only water, but also billions of stars stretching from the horizon line all the way up and to the back of the building.

"Jesus!" Buster exclaimed. "This is absolutely incredible!" The sound of waves crashed on the rocks below. They both sat down at the umbrella table—umbrella folded down.

"Isn't it though," R.B. said. "This is really righteous. This is why people come to the Bahamas. The beauty is really incomparable. Let's do a doobie!" He whipped out a flat metal cigarette box and selected a marijuana joint. He lit up.

"Well, God-damn!" Buster said with a huge smile. "It's about time. R.B., Brother, you're a Godsend!"

"Hey, thanks, I needed that! It's about time I'm appreciated around here." Now R.B. was not the old, run-of-the-mill Coast Guard enlisted man. He was an electronics whiz and extremely intelligent. He had been attending Phillips Andover Academy in Andover, Massachusetts, a Harvard prep school, when he got expelled for snorting cocaine in the bathroom. He enlisted in the Coast Guard because, as R.B. put it, it reduced his sentence from the law and provided a chance to put to good use his electronics hobby.

"Hey, R.B., what's this about you guys being restricted from the college?"

Buster asked.

R.B. took a long, extended toke on the doobie. "Well," he said, letting out slowly and passing the joint, "It's really absurd. Ron Evens, the only black Coastie, one night went over to one of the girls' dorms at the college. He and his girlfriend, one of the students, had just had a fight and she locked herself in her room with three other girls. She was really pissed off at him for something or other. Evens was pretty drunk and determined to talk to her. So he went around the back and tried crawling through the window. But his girl tried to close the window on him. Evens kept saying, 'Wait, Wait,' but the other girls in the room thought he was saying, 'Rape, Rape.' So they came over to help Evens' chick. They finally slammed it on his head, busting it—glass flying all over the place. Evens then fell to the ground, half unconscious. The girls later said that Evens had threatened to throw a bomb in the room—which was bizarre, because there's nothing to make a bomb with here on the island; and anyway, Evens is such an easy-going guy that making a bomb would be totally out of his character and smarts. And it wasn't 'Bomb' he yelled out, either, it was 'Mom' he kept moaning 'cause his head hurt so much."

"Jesus!" Buster said, passing the joint back to R.B. "What a nightmare!"

R.B. took a long drag on the joint. "Anyway," he continued, "The whole thing made so much noise, it woke up everybody on the block. All the girls ran out and started beating up on Evens there lying on the ground—poor bastard. Then Father Villeneuve appeared and broke it up, saving Evens' life. As a result, this upset the people at the college so much that the captain here had to have a big summit meeting on the island with all the so-called

'Officials.' The captain did his diplomatic best. I really give him credit. It was all agreed upon for a two-month prohibition of the college grounds for the Coasties—it ends after Christmas, by the way."

"God, sorry to hear about that," Buster said taking the joint. "What a hassle!"

"Yeah, fuck! Evens felt so bad afterwards—mostly for what he did to the guys, 'cause a lot of guys at times just like to go over and just talk to the girls—you know what I mean? Not laying eyes on tits and cunts and not hearing soft voices at least once a day can be a real bitch for the boys here."

"I can imagine! I'm lucky, I guess, because at least I can sit down in the class and stare at little black beavers every once in a while. Hey, do you want this roach?"

"Nah—just throw it into the water." R.B. whipped out another joint from his flat, cigarette case and lit it up with his Zippo.

The two young men sat in silence—a silence of communication—passing back and forth the joint and gazing out at the stars. They did not have to look up at the stars because the blanket of twinkling objects started at the horizon line. It was an ultra-clear night. Constellations were so clear and marked; they were easy to identify. And the falling stars did not seem to fall, but rather shoot like bullets across the firmament: from left to right, or from right to left, leaving trails billions of miles long. Others even seemed to shoot upwards.

The two friends became so stoned, that they rarely spoke to each other the three hours they sat on the patio. R.B. broke the silence one time mentioning to Buster that it sure would be a nice place for a romance—perfect. Buster wholeheartedly agreed. The problem was to get a girl and that it always seemed that a guy either had the place and not the girl or the girl and not the place—but seldom two at the same time. R.B. agreed to that seemingly deep, profound thought with a mere response of a "Yeah, Fuck!"

Finally, the bartender came out and informed the boys of closing time. They staggered down to their bikes.

"Hey, Murdock!" R.B. said. "Since I can't come onto the college, why don't you just come on over to the base—we got a different movie every night for the gang, plus beer and eats. Tomorrow night I think there's a James Bond on. It starts at 7:30."

"Hey, that sounds great, man! Uh, but what about that sign that says, 'Authorized Personnel Only'? Am I allowed on base?"

"Whataya mean, are you allowed on base? What a dumb ass question! Anybody can come on base—it's a democracy, isn't it? That sign's just to keep the goats away!"

"Fantastic, man! It'd sure make a difference around here—movies, you know?"

"God, do I! They're one of our few forms of entertainment on this fucking island. If it weren't for them we'd go bananas."

They both started up their bikes and hopped on.

"And don't forget the Finger Fuckers Friday!" R.B. yelled. "5:00 at the airport!"

"Aye Aye, Sir!" Buster shouted.

They both spun off down the road towards their homes on the island.

Buster was in real high spirits for the next few days. R.B. had given him hope on the island. There was nothing like a friend. It made the island livable, knowing there was one handy. Even the thought of Patrick Cramble did not bother him so much. The James Bond thriller was the best movie he had seen in months—in fact, the only movie he had seen in months. Buster was feeling good.

But his next depression came the following day when he went to the airport to greet the Finger Lakers. He thought only he and R.B. would be the only ones checking the whole thing out—but he was terribly mistaken. As he approached the airport tower, he saw a large crowd. However, it was not the Finger Lakers: it was all the horny Coasties and a few of the older college students just waiting like vultures for their prey to step down from the big silver bird that was two hours late upon arriving.

"Fuck!" Buster yelled aloud. "Fat chance I've got for all this!" His heart sank and he almost cried.

He was even more disheartened when the plane finally did arrive. Out stepped twenty young, American college boys and only eight girls. Every girl wore dirty blue jeans, had fat asses hanging down to their feet and were blanketed by those God-awful pimples on their faces. *Fuck!* Buster reflected. *Leave it to fucking American girls to wear those God-damned, fucking blue jeans all the time. Why in the hell couldn't they wear dresses once in a while, for Christ's sakes? Especially the fat ones, Jesus! There's nothing worse than fat, pimpled girls in dirty, hanging dungarees and God-damned, fucking sagging asses—turn me right off*!" He left the airport disgusted, leaving the Coasties, in all their horny anticipation, gaping at the girls, eyes out of their heads, drooling like dogs waiting for food.

He suddenly felt a dry loneliness creeping over him once again. He went back to his room, stared at the wall, then went to his desk and wrote Patty:

It was a meaningless, schmaltzy letter, but he wanted to send it anyway; there was something healing in cathartic writing. He sealed the letter in an envelope and left it on his desk for the next morning's mail. He went to the bathroom—first flushed Cramble's corned log—"Fuck!" he said aloud. Then he went to the kitchen and prepared his scrumptious dinner—dinner a la Buster.

# CHAPTER 5

## *Back to America*

It was finally study week at the college—a four day break for the students to cram: to read and study what they should have read and studied throughout the entire term. For all practical purposes, the term was completely over for Buster. Now it was only a matter of waiting out the two-and-a-half weeks before he could leave the island. Peter Kentard made up all the exams, supposedly standardized, multiple choice questions on Literature, Education and Methodology. Buster would only have to administer them and then hand them over to Peter and Robin for grading.

But that was the killer part of it: there was nothing to do and the waiting game of two-and-a-half weeks passed Buster's life at the pace more like that of two-and-a-half years. There had been still no communication with the outside world. Swimming was out of the question because of a cold snap that swept the islands. So, it was daily bouts with loneliness within the four walls of his warm room and trips to the Coast Guard base for movies and a game of pool every-now-and-then in the Coast Guard rec-room. There was the Riding Rock bar, but that just seemed to depress him even more: drinking, hunched over the bar, thinking of home and Patty.

It was after study week when Buster received his only letters from Patty. He was ecstatic this morning when he picked up the envelopes at the administration building where the mail was sorted for the teachers. The two envelopes were postmarked differently, but they had arrived together—they were forwarded by Jinx. Buster stuffed them in his pocket, let out a big rebel yell and ran home to read them alone in the privacy of his apartment. He read them as postmarked. The first letter must have been written in a fit of depression, for it was full of melancholy statements of how much she missed him, how much she loved him, and how much she wanted to spend the rest of her life with him.

But the second letter left him stone cold. It was full of stories about what she and "former squeeze" Rick Ruft did on weekends. And then there was this new boy wonder named Ollie that started to slip through the lines periodically. Buster dropped the letter on the floor. He did not know what to think. "Jesus Christ!" he said aloud. "There's that God-damned Rick Ruft again. Ha! Couldn't make love to anyone else—Bullshit! Absolute bullshit! This cunt's lying and I know it. I can see it right between the lines. And God-dammit! Ollie? Who the fuck is Ollie? Sounds like some fucking foreigner who probably can't even speak fucking English. Jesus Christ, help me! Patty writes, 'He had me in a trance last night and I forgot who I was and ....' Oh, Jesus—stop! My poor fucking head! She did it with him, I know she did, right between the fucking sheets, I just know it. The cunt, she's capable of anything. 'And forgot where I was and what I was supposed to be doing.' Oh my God, it's as plain as day. God-dammit!"

Buster shot out of his chair, hopped on Naomi and hit the main road to Cockburn Town, going eighty five miles an hour—Naomi floored. "Fuck, Fuck!" he kept saying as the wind hit his eyes, bringing tears down his cheek. He stopped at the telephone-telegraph shack to make an emergency call to Florida. He rushed into the office, "How's the telephone working these days?"

The old fat man behind the counter slowly said, "It not work, mann."

"Christ! Buster said, putting his hands to his head. "Well, how's the telegraph, then?"

"Good, mann—just fill out pink paper and da mann come tonight to tap it out."

Buster impatiently grabbed the pink telegraph message paper and feverishly wrote: "Dear Patty, I can read between the lines. Beg of you—Please, for the Love of God—Jesus Christ, keep your pants on! Coming up shortly. Buster."

"When will this get there, sir?" he asked the old man.

"Tomorrow morning, mann."

"Thanks!" Buster paid the man and walked out of the shack. "Fucking, fucking, fucking cunt!" he said to himself. The rest of the day he walked around in a worried daze.

He was depressed again. For several days he swam in a drunken rum stupor with worried thoughts of Patty winding up inside his head. There was nothing to do and that made matters worse. There was nothing to distract him, no work to help pass the days. Why did he have to wait for all the students to leave and then attend the Ministry's college party for the staff at the end of the term? He was doing nothing—he could go! He brought this up with the principal, Mr. Ginnis; but his reply was that it was a matter of diplomacy more than anything and that it would look bad if a lecturer left before the students. So, Buster was destined to help monitor exams a few hours a week and battle with himself the rest of the time.

One early evening Buster was sitting at his desk trying to wade through a term paper one of his students gave to him for revision before turning it into the "Vultures," the Kentards. All of a sudden he heard a putter-putter sound of a Honda Fifty outside the door. He recognized it immediately as being R.B.'s machine. R.B., a tall lanky figure, burst through the door, his eyes bursting out of his crimpy beard like two, over-sized light bulbs sunk into dark, fixed sockets.

"Hey, Murdock!" he said loudly, "Got anything to drink?"

"R.B.! Hey, man, what are you doing here on campus?" Buster said.

"Shh, just don't say anything and everything'll be cool! Got anything to drink?"

"Well, it's good to see you!" He threw the term paper aside. "Uh, let's see, drink? Yeah, I think I got some beer in the fridge or some coffee."

"Good! Get yourself a beer. I have something for you."

"Oh, yeah? What is it?"

"Get yourself a beer, man!"

Buster went to the kitchen, popped a can of Heineken and returned to the bedroom. He found R.B. slouched in the chair as if his body was a part of this piece of furniture. His eyes were so wide open, it looked like his mind was hovering around his head.

"Looks like you're up to something, R.B.," Buster said. "What's happening?"

R.B. reached into his Coast Guard weather jacket and pulled out a plastic, bronze colored vial and held it up to the light. "Downs, Brother Murdock, Downs!" he gloriously said, eyes opening even wider. "MX Sedatives. They just came in on the supply plane this morning—'bout time, God-dammit! I ordered them from a medic friend of mine two months ago." R.B. was really doped up. It seemed like his motor nerves were not functioning properly, his body was so limp. "I've been going since 1:00, after lunch."

"Hey, man," Buster said excitedly, "I've taken downs lots of times—Quaaludes and shit—but what do these MX things do to you?"

"They make ya feel new, my brother—absolutely new. Here, take one—and a belated Happy Thanksgiving to you!!"

"Well, Jesus—this is just what the doctor ordered. I gotta feel new around here—can't stand it any longer." Buster held the capsule in his hand for a moment, then popped it into his mouth. He chased it down with a few gulps of beer.

"Let's do a doobie!" R.B. said. He whipped out his flat, metal cigarette case. He selected one of his prime joints, took out his Zippo from his coat pocket and lit up.

"God-dammit, R.B.!" Buster exlaimed, sitting at his desk. He looked at that term paper and then at some of his English grammar books stacked to one side. "Fuck! I'm awful damn glad you stopped by tonight. I was goin' nuts around here. I mean, really nuts!"

"Don't feel alone, man," he said, holding in the smoke.

"Yeah, I suppose so," Buster continued. "But lately I've had this chick back home that's sort of been fucking up my head. I just got some really strange letters the other day and…"

R.B. interrupted: "Hey, don't talk to me about cunts tonight, OK? They're all just a bunch of cunts! If you don't think about 'em, you're all right."

"Yeah, OK!" Buster took the joint from R.B.'s dangling hand.

"I mean, who doesn't around here have a chick back home running around, screwing their heads off? While we're down here—us poor saps are pulling our cords because this group of Finger Fuckers are downright putrid losers and the captain's girl, Barbara, always has to wear those God-damn silk mini-skirts—Fucking A!"

"Yeah, you're right," Buster said, Bogarting the joint. "Best not to even think about it."

"And anyway," R.B. slurred, "Who fucking needs it? You and I got the best dope in the entire Bahamas now—what more do you want?"

"Yeah, that's the spirit! Let's do another pill!"

"Good fucking idea—where did you get that idea, Murdock?"

They both simultaneously popped another capsule each and washed it down with the Heineken.

"Ah…" R.B. said. "That's God-damn good beer. Why can't Americans make beer like this? Busch Bavarian is an absolute disgrace to all taste buds and stomachs of the human race!!"

"Here's to the human race!" Buster held up the Heineken can.

"Yeah, to the fucking human race!" R.B. said.

"Hey, Brother R.B., let's go get some more beer at the Riding Rock!"

"Good fucking idea! Hey Murdock, where did you get that idea?"

"Comes natural."

They staggered out the door to their bikes.

"Hey, take it easy on the way," R.B. warned. "I almost spilled twice on the way here from the base. Try to make sure you keep feeling the handle bars!"

They safely made the short hop to the Riding Rock and entered the bar. This time there were a lot of people: tourists from Lauderdale and some of those Finger Lake girls. Good vibes were in the air and it seemed to both R.B. and Buster that everybody was smiling. They ordered their Heinekens and went out to the patio to sit down at the umbrella table. It was another beautiful night, but a bit chilly.

"Hey R.B.," Buster said, "Uh, I'm starting to feel numb—like I can't feel anything."

"That's good—it's good for you!!"

"Yeah, like Wheaties."

"And good for you, too!"

Then a few Finger Lake girls came out to the patio with several young men from Fort Lauderdale. They joined the two stonies. The duo looked normal except that limp-like slouch in their chairs gave them away. They both started talking to the group. R.B. talked electronics to a transistor circuit distributor from Miami and Buster was locked deep in college football ratings with a University of Miami graduate. They avoided the girls —it was useless with all those men swarming around them. And besides, they were determined to stick to their mutual pact of not thinking about "Cunts."

The conversation was good for them both. It took their minds off of being on an island. R.B.'s mind was distracted from that God-awful, fifteen man military base with following orders all the time, and Buster's mind was finally off of those God-awful letters from Patty. He could not trust those words and they also reminded him of what he was missing.

But when Buster started noticing a marked slur in his speech, he became a little worried about being coherent. He turned to R.B., "Hey, Buddy—didn't we have something to do back at my place?"

R.B. was still talking, but his speech was really turning into an indecipherable babble. The man he was talking to seemed bored and uninterested—especially talking to a drunken, doped-up Coastie. "We did?" he spurted out.

"Yeah, don't you remember?" Buster kicked him underneath the table.

"Oh yeah, that's right—uh, we did."

They both stood up and shuffled into the bar, leaving the Florida group looking at each other in amazement.

"Damn!" the Miami circuit man said to the group. "Looks like those guys have had one too many—they're really wired!"

They both hopped on their bikes and safely made it back to the college to Buster's place. They slumped back down in their chairs once again, lighting up another doobie and sipping on the cans of Heinekens they took out from the bar. Their minds were amazingly clear as they passed the joint back and forth and looked at each other in cosmic understanding. But their bodies did not respond: they were limp. Also their speech was practically gone. They both let out big laughs upon realizing this, both thinking how absurd at times verbal communication can really be.

"Hey Murdock!" R.B. grunted after finishing his beer. "I gotta go, man. I got duty tomorrow morning at 0-6-hundred."

"Yeah, I gotta get up myself tomorrow sometime after twelve," Buster mumbled. "I've got some heavy shell collecting to do—fuck! But hey, man, I could go for a cruise—I'll go with you—at least part of the way.

"Far out!" R.B. belched.

It was late and all was quiet outside until they both got on their bikes and revved up. The sound of the motorcycles split the silence of the campus, and without a doubt, made sleeping students stir in their beds. They wheeled through the campus, Buster taking the lead. But it was a very weird sensation for both of them. Their bodies were not feeling anything—it was just mind on road. They swerved out of the campus entrance and caught the road towards the Coast Guard station, swerving left and right going around curves. Buster started going fast, leaving R.B. puttering behind on his Honda Fifty cc. He felt no fear of the speed at which he was going. He rounded curves at seventy miles an hour, making daredevil downshifts and saving hairpin curves by scuffing his foot on the road. It was strange for him because he did not feel this speed. He looked at the needle on the speedometer and it read sixty, seventy and sometimes eighty miles an hour at the turns. Usually when he made the turns, the speedometer read thirty-five to forty miles an hour, and even at these speeds his heart would skip a beat. But this time—it was only mind on road.

Then it happened. The most radical curve on the island came up: he was going seventy-five miles an hour, Naomi screaming with all her two-stroke might. Buster saw the curve and knew what he had to do: put his foot down and lean hard to the right. But the curve came up so rapidly that he became confused. He downshifted once—the bike skidded and the curve came closer. He downshifted a second time—the bike skidded again. It was then that he realized he could not make the turn. He glanced at the speedometer, but could not see the reading. He looked up and saw the bushes coming right at him. He finally gave in to the reality of things: he was going to dump. As fast as he was going and as fast as all this was happening, he still had a split second flash of how he was going to land when he hit. Then—Impact—Smack! The bike screamed like an elephant being shot by a hunter. Buster flew off, doing a complete flip over the handlebars. The ruffle of bushes snapped and popped in his ears. The bushes softened his landing and he stopped in a pile of dried bush surrounding a hard limestone rock. He lay on his back: his mind was blank for a second, but he realized it was blank. Then the vision of his bike began to register in his head, but he could not move. He stared straight up at the stars and saw visions of white whales swimming between constellations. His body was twisted like he had been in a ski fall and Naomi was on her side, lying like a wounded horse. He had hit his head on something and could feel a great tingling sensation on the side of it—but strangely enough, it did not hurt. He began laughing hard—out loud as hard as he could.

Then R.B. rounded the curve and saw the twisted wreck. He got off his scooter and ran over to Naomi. "Wow man, what are you trying to do?" He yelled. "Is the bike OK?"

Buster finally rolled over on his side and tried to get up. "Jesus, the bike, I don't know!" he moaned. He finally stood up and got out of the bushes. But instead of checking out the bike, he started walking down the road as if walking in his sleep. He was feeling no pain, but his body was shaking like a Quaker.

"Hey Murdock, where are you going?" R.B. shouted.

R.B. ran up to him and grabbed him by the shoulders. "Buster, man, you OK?"

Buster's body was now shaking uncontrollably. "Jesus, I dunno!" he said, dazed. "I coulda gotten hurt—you know what I mean? I mean, killed! You know what I mean? I mean, that coulda been my death right there! You know what I mean? I mean …"

"Hey, Buster, snap out of it, man!" R.B. embraced him to try and stop his shaking. "Do you hurt, man?"

"Feeling no pain! But why is my body shaking?"

"You only have about a thousand cc's of adrenalin pumping through your body right now, that's all. Here—C'mon man, let's go over and check your bike out." He had one arm wrapped around Buster. "You'll be OK, man—here, sit down here for a minute!" R.B. went over to Naomi. The headlight was still on but the motor had stopped after that giant shriek it made. He picked it out of the bushes and placed it back on the road. "Wow, man! Absolutely nothing happened to it—it's perfect! I mean, the son-of-a-bitch is perfect!"

"Good," Buster said with his head in his hands—uninterested in the condition of his bike. "I mean, I coulda been killed, you know?"

"OK, OK! But you're alive, right? So cool it!" R.B. yelled. "A good biker always dumps every once in a while. Just chock this one up as experience, that's all!"

Buster's shaking subsided. R.B. started Naomi up again—she purred. "Fantastic!" he said, "Just like nothing happened. Everything's OK, now, man."

"R.B., I'm scared to get back on the fucker now!"

"No man, no man," R.B. said convincingly. "To overcome that fear, you gotta just get back on it and drive away!"

"Right!"

"Just take it easy—keep it cool, no reason for speeding—and surely no reason to be afraid of it. Just respect it, man. C'mon, ready to go?"

"OK—I'll be heading for home." Buster cautiously mounted the bike. "Hope I make it back!"

"Don't worry, man. Just remember, respect it!"

"Thanks, R.B." Buster said. He managed to crack a smile.

"Take it easy now!" R.B. slapped him on the shoulder. "See you later."

They both took off in separate directions. Buster drove home at a snail's pace thinking of the accident. It was certainly a close one and he was grateful to somebody for being able to walk away from it alive.

He coasted into the college and parked outside his apartment. He noticed it was a beautiful night, then went inside. Feeling no pain, he slithered into bed and had a terrific night's sleep. It was truly the best night's sleep he had had on the island.

The next morning Buster woke up feeling groggy, stiff as a board with bruises all over him and not quite sure where he was. He felt a heavy pain on the right side of his hip. He looked down and discovered a deep blue mark from the hipbone all the way down to his kneecap and about six inches wide. He lightly touched it and grimaced with pain.

He went to the kitchen to make some coffee. He turned on the small transistor table radio Cramble had just received on order from Nassau. There were some squeaks and squawks and finally a station from Miami distantly came in. The news was blasting away: Israel and Egypt are still having it out, the oil situation in the U.S. is grim, giant truck blockade against fifty-five mile an hour speed limit, the Watergate situation is dubious, President Nixon's finances in question, seven killed in Chicago fire, North Vietnam still fighting, food prices still up, Baltimore beat Miami in football, and fifty-five degrees in the Silver City. More international news: Another white man was killed on the island of St. Croix in the West Indies. That makes twelve white men this year that have lost their lives for probably political reasons on this predominantly, black inhabited island paradise. "Jesus!" Buster said aloud. "Isn't there anything pleasant on the news these days?" He whacked the radio silent and the sound of boiling water took its place. He stretched. "Oh Jesus!" he said, aching in every bone.

Time dragged terribly and the Ministry's staff party still seemed centuries away. But at last the students started leaving for their homes on other islands. This was a good sign, because it meant that Christmas was just around the corner. Special Bahamas-Air flights flew in to sweep the students off to Nassau where smaller flights were waiting to take them to their respective out-islands. The students were from islands scattered all over the archipelago: Grand Bahama, Great Abaco, Andros, Eleuthera, Cat, Great Exuma, Long, Crooked and Acklins, Mayaguana and even some from New Providence. Most of the lecturers at the college always went to the airport to bid farewell and Christmas wishes. When the planes came in, it was the event of the week.

Buster was taking all of this in stride, for he did not know the students that well yet for hugs and kisses. But, he did go down and watch; it gave him something to do. Standing by the conning tower, he overheard one group of pretty female students talk about him. One girl said how she wished Mr. Murdock could be under her Christmas tree.

They all let out a big giggle. Buster glanced out of the corner of his eye and tried hard not to smile, but his stomach was slightly convulsing. It made him feel real good and put him in a good mood the rest of the day. How he would have loved to be under her Christmas tree, too—she was beautiful.

The days passed and Buster's only good consolation and moments of relief was his thoughts of going home for Christmas. He decided one morning to write to Patty one more time: possibly the letter would reach Gainesville before he got there.

As slow as the days passed for Buster, the last six days on the island before the Christmas vacation swept by as fast as a shooting star. R.B. came over on one of his days off and they both ate some blotter acid that R.B. received in a letter from one of his friends in Massachusetts. But the LSD was not very strong and their trip did not culminate to much of anything. Most of the time they just sat on the west point of the island hallucinating on a large whale that had washed up on the rocks and was decomposing. They had named it Johan and were pleased at the fact that they were not inside the whale's stomach. Both men's hearts were light because Buster knew he would see Patty only in a matter of a few short days, and R.B. was happy expecting his orders back to the continent very soon.

In the middle of the week, one of Buster's female students, Eula Mae, came over unexpectedly, insisting that she cook dinner for him. It was a pleasant surprise. He had not had a female cook for him in ages. It was almost a relief as her lean, perfumed black body entered the apartment and headed towards the kitchen.

But Buster was not quite sure how to handle the situation. Professional ethics in teaching told him that a teacher should keep his hands off the students and look down the road for leg satisfaction. But, what could he do, he thought, when it was knocking at the front door?

She was beautiful in the kitchen—what a sight to see. She had short, cropped hair, a beautiful complexion, a little round behind that protruded out from the small of her back. What a treat for the eyes in the kitchen—what a grand difference between looking at her and looking at Patrick Cramble's fat, mongoloid ass hanging down to the floor.

The only problem was the conversation. It was uncomfortable and Eula Mae only spoke when spoken to.

"How many brothers and sisters do you have, Eula Mae?" Buster asked.

"Ten—all on Eleuthra."

"How does your family celebrate Christmas, Eula Mae?"

"We have tree, mann, then presents, the church, the party, mann."

"Uh, how old are you, Eula Mae?"

"Twenty three, mann."

*What an intellectual conversation*! Buster thought. But she was beautiful, anyway. Her nice little cheeks on her rump jiggled as she stirred the peas and rice. And wearing tight shorts, her long, beautifully shaped legs were a slap in the face to the young lecturer.

*Jesus, chocolate—chocolate*! he fantasized. *Drool, drool, Good God, I've been on this island too long.*

But he kept his professional standards and was quite astonished at his own behavior and control. The Kentards, he thought, would be proud of him.

The long-awaited last night on the island finally came. Buster had packed weeks earlier, so the only thing he had to do was attend that flaming Ministry staff party held at the island commissioner's house just outside of Cockburn Town. The party was all shake hands and smiles, rum punch and conch fritters. The men wore sport coats and ties, except Buster who wore a Dashiki and a shell necklace, and the women donned long flowered dresses. The Bahamian music consisted of only three, forty-five rpm records: "Got a Letter from Miami," "Independence Bahamas," and "Brown Girl in the Ring." The funky beat, heavy on the bass side, filled the air: "Got a letter, from Miami / In that letter was a dollar / Took that dollar / Bought some powder / Put that powder on my collar." People jiggled on the makeshift living room dance floor. There was silence between records—then: "Independence Bahamas / Independence Bahamas / Seven hundred islands in the sun!!" And everybody got nationalistic and joined in singing. For Buster the party was OK for a while, but the playing over and over again of the same records started giving him a headache. Also, the same questions over and over again from Ministry officials from Nassau almost made him fall asleep standing: "How do you like the island, Mr. Murdock? How do you like the college, the native people, the English people, and how does it compare to Nassau?" etc., etc. The only things that kept him awake were the greasy conch fritters that oozed down his esophagus and bounced around in his stomach. He was in intestinal pain.

The only Englishman Buster talked to at the party, in fact, the only one he could really talk to on the island at all, was John Dailey. But still Dailey kept his distance all the time. Dailey said that he was going to Nassau for the holidays and visit a girlfriend—"Recharge the batteries," as he said. And Patrick Cramble was sitting over in a corner, hands in his lap, playing wall flower, but Buster did not bother intruding on his privacy.

After the seemingly fiftieth play of "Brown Girl in the Ring,"—"Brown girl in the ring—sha la la la la / Brown girl in the ring—sha la la la la la la. Brown girl in the ring—sha la la la la / She looks like a sugar in a plum—Bum, Bum!!", Buster could not stand it any longer and had to leave. His excuse to leave, as he told Mr. Ginnis, was that he had to go home and pack and get ready for home.

He hopped on Naomi and drove down the cement driveway heading back towards the college. He was relieved it was over, but dismayed that all that waiting for weeks was for only this party. He got about half-way down the road when he saw a single headlight coming his way. Closer, closer, then he recognized R.B., his unmistakable whites of the eyes, popping out of his head.

"Hey, Murdock!" he yelled over the roar of the engines. "What's happening?" They both came to a stop in the middle of the road.

"Just got outta that damned party I told you about. Fuck! What are you doing?"

"Just cruisin', man. Hey, let's do a doobie!"

"God, I thought you'd never ask!"

They revved up their bikes and cruised down the airport strip: the large, concrete open area reserved during the day for spotted air traffic, but at night, open territory for stoned motorcyclists. They stopped in the middle of the strip and R.B. whipped out his trusty metal cigarette case. Once again the stars were falling all over them. R.B. popped open his Zippo and flicked the fire.

"Hey, man!" he said to Buster who was staring up, spellbound at the stars. "Finger Fuckers are having a big bash at the Quonset hut at the ol' Navy base—wanna head on over and check it out?"

"Good idea—it's my last night and the night's young." He looked at his watch. It was midnight.

"We better go now, then, so we don't miss anything."

They rode down to the Navy base side by side, passing the joint on straightaways between curves. When they reached the Quonset hut, hard acid rock was coming out of all sides of the aluminum structure. The stoned duo walked in and were confronted by a scene right out of a 1950 teen-center dance—but everybody was water-faced drunk. It was rather late, for it seemed that everybody had paired off: the ugly girls were falling all over the men. Some pairs were making out in dark corners and others were dancing in hard, close embraces to hard acid rock provided by the battery powered record player. A few natives from the United Estates village were by the bar plucking away at a guitar and pounding violently on a goatskin drum. It was chaos: acid music echoing against the aluminum walls, pimpled young college men yelling and ugly, pizza-faced girls screaming, drum beating, bottles breaking ….

"Looks like we came a little late, Murdock!" R.B. said, peering into the whole mess.

"Jesus, I'll say! But what the hell? I just don't care anymore, you know R.B.? These chicks are so fucking ugly—I think I'd rather be with sheep! And the guys—why they're just too 'Cool' for me!"

"You got a point there!"

"And all this noise, Jesus, you wouldn't think this would happen on a peaceful island like this, would you?"

"Well, I believe it. Leave it up to fucking Americans, man—they know how to come into a place and bombard anything!"

"Let's get outta here!" Buster said impatiently.

They hopped on their bikes and drove away from that madhouse to a small dune on the beach about a mile down the road. They did another doobie and talked about families and Christmas. Then they emotionally parted with a brotherly embrace—vibrations zapping through their hearts telling them that they were true friends.

The following morning, Buster went home for Christmas. The journey was a half-day stop in Nassau, then a change of planes to Miami later in the day. Buster took a trip into Nassau first to take money out of the Bank of Canada, then do some Christmas shopping. He bought his three younger brothers straw hats and wooden carved voo-doo heads sold at the straw market. He bought a long, flowered, Bahamian dress for his mother, and a deep blue and red paisley Dashiki blouse for Patty. He was pleased with the presents and knew that everybody would like them. They were different and very non-American.

On the plane to Miami all he could think about were the things he had missed after being away from his country for almost four months. *Jesus!* he thought. *Give me a McDonald's hamburger—and a fucking chocolate milk shake. Give me real live, honest to God French fries and hot apple pie. How I long for a candy bar—just a measly candy bar is all I want—my kingdom for a Milky Way! My kingdom for a pimple! And good ol' Country Music—enough of this "Got a letter from Miami" bullshit! And Jesus, give me my Patty! My God, how I've been fantasizing on you lately. I've been balling you in every conceivable position for weeks. Ah, yes, get me off these islands for a while—please! Give me some good wine, women and song; give me a city with pollution and cut-throat aggressiveness for a few days; give me the energy crisis with fifty-five mile-an-hour speed limits—you sons of bitches! Give me a Nixon!*

The plane landed in Miami and Buster quietly and ceremoniously said loudly: "Thank you, God—the U.S.A." He rapidly went through customs with no problems with the exception of a close scrutiny for drugs in the wooden voo-doo heads he bought. Then he ran to National Airlines for his connection to Daytona Beach.

One of his younger brothers, Tom, was waiting to pick him up. After a long, brotherly embrace, they were on their way home in the family's red Volkswagen convertible. Buster stared out the window and saw old, familiar landmarks: hotels, boutiques, old dance halls and bars that were such a vivid memory of his not-so-long-ago past. High school memories seemed to stick like glue in his mind, whereas many memories of college sort of just faded away.

They arrived home, the car coming to a stop in the driveway. Buster took out his two small suitcases and headed towards the doorway, his heart beating with anticipation. There was a large, white sheet hanging from the awning on the entranceway that read: America Welcomes Brother Buster home from the Bahamas / Merry Christmas and a Happy New Year. Buster dropped his suitcases. He choked and tried to hold back tears. Suddenly the door flung open and out ran his beautiful mother. With a large, white smile on her face from one ear to the other, she gave him a huge hug, zapping cosmic love vibrations throughout his entire body. His other younger brothers followed giving him strong pats on the back, yelling "Hey-Hey,"

Laughing and hanging onto his shoulders. It had been a long time—they were so glad to see him. So moved, Buster could not help it. He had missed them much more than he thought. Being able to hold back tears no longer, he broke down and cried.

Buster was so dog tired after his arrival, the long flights back and emotional reception at home, that he flopped in bed and slept soundly the rest of the late afternoon and night. He had wanted to call Patty in Gainesville, but he just couldn't drag himself from his room.

The next morning he woke up early feeling great: he was back home again. He walked outside and picked up the folded newspaper that was thrown on the lawn. He slipped off the rubber band, opened it up and read the headlines: "Energy Crisis Mounts." "Fuck!" he said, and folded it back again. He looked up at the cloudless sky, the bright, Florida sun penetrated his face. "Wonderful," he said. "Wonderful! Just fantastic."

He walked inside to the smell of bacon and pancakes that his mother was fixing in the kitchen. "Ah, now's the time to call Patty," he said to himself. He picked up the phone in the living room and dialed—no problem remembering the number. But, there was no answer. "Jesus!" he said. "Maybe she's stepped out or something. I'll call back after breakfast."

He walked into the dining room and the round oak table was all set with a large platter piled with Oscar Meyer bacon strips and along side this, another large platter with stacks of Aunt Jemima pancakes. It was as pretty as a picture: all the plates set for the family on the round table. Glasses of orange juice were by each plate and yellow butter and Log Cabin syrup were on the Lazy Susan. The sun blazed through the large tinted dining room window, spliced, in rays by the large rubber tree plant just outside the glass. *Ah, it was great to be home*, Buster thought.

The brothers, ages ten, fourteen and eighteen, came in one by one to the dining room and adjoining living room area. Brother Tom turned on the stereo system. The speakers wailed out Chet Atkins' version of "Yakety Sax," and everybody started dancing—including Mother Murdock, who made the mistake of entering the living room. Buster grabbed her by the arm and did square dance swings, do-sa-do's and allemande lefts and rights with her while the younger brothers stood on their heads and did somersaults. When the song ended with its final guitar licks and runs, everybody let out a big, "Hey!" and clapped their hands. Then it was time for breakfast.

Apart from the absolutely delicious American food, the good ol' American conversation was fantastic, too. Mother Murdock told of all the local happenings and who got married and this and that, and his brothers injected happenings at their respective schools. It was really a great feeling for Buster to listen to Americans again. There was something about unmarred, American English with a slight Florida southern accent that sounded like soft music to his ears.

He was anxious to call Patty again. He downed the remaining few gulps of orange juice left in his glass and went to the telephone. He dialed, a ring tone, then once again, no answer. "Fuck!" he said to himself. "I wonder where she is?" He would now call after lunch.

Meanwhile, he and Brother Tom took a walk down to the beach. Buster thought that even with all the hotel garbage and boardwalk madness, it still had not ruined the beach—it just seemed a part of it after all these years. The waves were big and the crashing and pounding sound of Atlantic crests was a delight after being on the relatively calm, Caribbean side of San Salvador. The two brothers watched a couple of surfers in wet suits catch the same wave and go up and down on it as if they were juggling with themselves. The Murdocks took a walk on the boardwalk. The smell of salt water taffy and hot dogs and the sounds of the cling clang of flipper machines sent nostalgic flashes through Buster's head to when he was a small boy and spent days upon days running around and skateboarding on the asphalt boardwalk, weaving in and out amongst the groups of retired tourists and visiting college students from the North.

Brother Tom and Buster spent the rest of the day on the boardwalk—eating hot dogs, cotton candy, pizzas, shooting airplanes or toy ducks passing by in closed boxes, table bowling, playing the flipper machines and taking rides on basher—bumper cars and twirling tea cups. It was so grand that Buster was lost in a nostalgic merry-go-round, forgetting completely San Salvador and even Patty.

But the early afternoon drew to a close. With their pockets empty of money, it was time for the brothers to go back home. As soon as Buster arrived at the house, he picked up the phone. "She's gotta be here now," he said to himself. "Jesus, dinner time, she's always home." He dialed again and once again, no answer. "Jesus!" he said. "That's strange!" A weird sensation melted over his body. "I wonder where the fuck she is—maybe at her mother's house in nearby Bradenton—but I don't have the number. And besides, she's expecting me. I'll call late tonight."

He called late that night, but still no answer. So the next day, it was off to Gainesville in the red Volkswagen convertible, worried stiff as to where she was or if anything had happened.

It was a long, boring drive to Gainesville, approximately three hours; but the A.M. radio made the traveling easier. He had not heard good songs and American disc jockeys for months. What a pleasure it was not to have to listen to that Bahamian, funky beat. But his mind was spinning around, wondering where on earth Patty could be. *Maybe she went to St. Augustine for a few days*, he thought. *How we both love that little, Spanish colonial town. But Jesus! Who would she go with? Or maybe she went to White Springs by the Sewanee River? Or maybe she went tubing down the Chattahoochee River? Who knows? Maybe she just took a sleeping pill or two and was really out of it?*

It was in the afternoon when he finally reached Gainesville. He passed the old University of Florida and once again his mind sped back to when he was a student. He remembered all those hell-raising football games: *Go Gators! What absolute, asshole madness! And all those concerts: Stephen Stills, the Beach Boys and the Rock and Roll Revival—Far out!* His mind flashed back to classes and some of his old professors: the worst being that "Asshole," three-piece-suit wearing Education professor, Dr. Al Schmidt, whose only goal in his totally, non-creative mind was to become a totally, non-creative college president. But then the best professors flashed into his mind: that chain-smoking Poetry professor, Dr. Jon Cardi, and his cocaine-snorting novel instructor, Harry Rues, and then the absolute best, but most eccentric Writing teacher, James Nicky, who would come to class most of the time completely inebriated, reeking of Southern Comfort whiskey and angry at the world. But every once in a while he would appear sober and be marvelously brilliant: demonstrating his genius in poetry and literature and keeping everybody hypnotized upon reading his own melodic passages. The English language never sounded so sweet.

Finally, Buster left the university behind and entered the

west side of town, the student ghetto where Patty would be hopefully awaiting him, ready to ball his eyes out. He pulled up to her house, an old, wooden, antebellum style mansion that had been converted into apartments for university students. He got out of the car, stretched his legs and walked up to the front porch. He was somewhat disappointed that she had not come bursting out of the screen door and thrown herself upon him. But, oh well... he thought, there would be plenty of time for that. He knocked on the door and a long-haired, spacey-eyed young woman in a long dress opened the door.

"Uh... hello! Is Patty here?" he asked, surprised. *Who the fuck was this girl?* he thought.

"Patty? Oh, yes, Patty—the girl with the long brown hair?" she said.

"Right!"

"Uh, she's not here!"

"Well, where the hell is she?"

"Are you Buster Murdock?"

"Right!"

"She left this envelope for you." She went to a small table by the door. "Here!"

Buster tore it open and read silently:

Dear Mr. Buster Murdock,

I have gone to Amsterdam, Holland with Ollie for Xmas. I love you! Signed, Patty

His face turned pale—he suddenly felt faint. He looked at the glassy-eyed girl.

There was a long, painfully enduring pause. The thought

flashed before his eyes: *Why is it that death and Dear John letters are always so final?*

"Well, I suppose that takes care of that!" he managed to mutter. "Did she leave any other word?"

"No, just this note," she said.

"Jesus Christ! Well, just for the record, who are you ?"

"I'm just visiting, staying here for the holidays—friend of a friend of a friend."

"Oh, I see, one of those. Well, thanks!"

"Sure," she said. "Uh, sorry, hey!"

"Yeah, right!" He hung his head. "Well, what can you do? Qué será, será—right?"

Buster got back in the car and slowly left the mansion behind. He was in shock. He did not know what to do or say or anything. He could not even cry, it was just so hard to think. But he did feel hunger. He pulled up to a Krystal hamburger restaurant and mechanically walked in. He ordered two hamburgers, lots of onions, a bowl of chili, French fries and a large Coke. He sat down in a booth with the food in front of him on a tray. He looked around: *Goddamn sterile, fucking joint,* he thought. The Krystal restaurant was a small chrome box with windows, white tables and stainless-steel counters. He stared at the square-shaped hamburgers. "Gut bombs!" he said quietly—"fucking gut bombs." He downed them both and started in on the spicy chili. He then took a swig of Coke and stared into the cup. Suddenly he broke out into a loud laughter, spraying Coke all up his face and into his nose. People in the other booths turned around and gave him a stare. He gave a little wave at them and stopped laughing. But he could not stop chuckling. Tears welled up in his eyes. Shoveling chili beans into his mouth, he kept thinking about Patty. "Jesus

Christ—that's funny," he babbled to himself. "The fucking cunt's off now sitting on some asshole, blue-eyed Dutch boy's face, freezing her tits off in the fucking Dutch winter. And that cocksucking Ruft dude. Ha, ha, ha, ha! What a waste of a human being. That whore deserves everything she fucking gets. I've had it with these people here in this damn, student hic-town. To Hell with them all!!!"

He finished his beans and downed his Coke. He got in his car feeling, for some reason, not sad, but relieved. It was as if a big weight had been lifted off his shoulders. All that time down on San Salvador thinking about her and wondering what she was doing and worrying if she was waiting for him—it all seemed totally absurd to him now. As he caught the main highway back to Daytona, he smiled. *At least I know it's all over*, he thought—*no more bullshit!*

He turned up the radio full blast and with the top down on the V.W. he sang along with the songs and farted out chili beans and gut bombs all the way back home—nostalgically dedicating each glorious, anal blast to his long lost friends and professors he once had back in Gainesville, Florida, U.S.A.

# PART 2

# CHAPTER 6

## *Back to the Island*

So for Buster Murdock, it was back to Daytona Beach for Christmas and New Years. Thank God for the love of his family. He knew that he would always have that. Being back home with his family members made him realize that no matter what happened to him or how many girls shafted him, the most beautiful woman in the world, his mother, the woman with the most love, most compassion, would never leave him. It was not that he had an Oedipus complex or anything like that—it was just that comforting feeling of her motherly love that consoled him.

At first Buster thought that the finale with Patty would bring him down; but after a few nights of dancing and singing at the Tradewinds Tavern and one night of heavy cocaine snorting with old, home-town friends that never left, he was back on the right path—Patty seemingly light years away.

But on the plane back to the Bahamas, he felt skeptical. Once again he was leaving things behind that had surrounded him all his life—American things—and going back down to a culture he still was not quite sure of and did not understand. He was going back to being in a minority, surrounded by blacks and living on a paradise island with six hundred and fifty people—not too much to do. What bothered him most of all, however, was the thought of going down to a place with little or no possibilities of female companionship. He thought of the women students: some of them exotically beautiful. *But Jesus!* he thought. *It's hard to talk to hollow heads—almost all of them having no experience outside island living and being so distant.* Indeed, they were complete worlds away from Buster's American background. But then there were the Finger Lakers. *But Fuck!* he thought. *Conch shells have smoother complexions and sheep have better bodies.* Of course, he realized, beauty was only skin deep: but talking to a bunch of immature, pimply faced, giddy American college girls was a total bore to him and not what he had in mind for overseas affairs.

*Ok,* he thought on the plane. *I might as well put all this aside and forget about women until the summer, six months away. After all, a man only longs for women if he thinks about them, right Buster ol' boy? I got my own friends—but Jesus, R.B. is going to be leaving soon. And the Englishmen—Good Lord! They speak the same language and everything, but man, what a difference in cultures and ways of communicating. OK, Murdock, forget friends! I'll just hide out in my apartment. I'll let my hair grow down to my ass and put my mind into my work. That's it—all work: become creative in teaching, reading and writing. I'll become totally absorbed in my work and myself. Women—out of the fucking question!* Buster was prepared.

He stumbled into his apartment on San Salvador with two suitcases, mostly filled with books and cassette tapes for his new cassette player he got for Christmas. He set the suitcases down in the screened corridor entrance way and met Patrick Cramble who had been to Nassau for the holidays. There he was, in the corner, setting a pair of mousetraps. He looked up at Buster.

"I'm gonna get these little buggers!" he said effeminately, and turned back to his business.

*Jesus!* Buster thought. *He's started already. What a pleasant thing to come back to.*

He entered his room. It was musty with that not lived in look and smell of vacation vacancy. He opened the windows and the electric house noise rushed in with the salty, cool sea breeze. He went into the bathroom to relieve himself and : "Fuck!" he yelled. "This damn log in the bowl. Doesn't this guy have any consideration for others? Shit!" He flushed— "God-damn!" He went back to his room, took out his new cassette player and put on Beethoven's Seventh. He started arranging his room with the new things he had brought back from the States. It was going to be a long winter, he thought. He might as well make the place as comfortable as possible.

The first day back at work was on a Wednesday. There was a teachers' meeting and department conference in the administration building. Classes would not start until the following Monday, after the students returned on special flights over the weekend.

The general teachers' meeting was mostly political with Mr. Ginnis addressing the staff and welcoming back everyone to San Salvador Teachers' College. His roly-poly, teddy bear manner in speech delivery was quite amusing and Buster could not help but let out a laugh at first. The

Englishmen surrounding Buster gave him a big stare down. The meeting, at any rate, was fairly entertaining and Buster enjoyed himself. He felt important being at a meeting of such "High Caliber."

But the English department conference got off on the wrong foot. There were five people in all: the big, tall, ageing British ex-patriot called Mister Bachran, Bach for short, Patrick Cramble, Buster, and of course, the Kentards, the department heads. They all entered a small conference room, Buster by Peter Kentard's side.

"Good morning, Mr. Murdock," Peter said.

"Uh... Good morning, Pete—I mean, Mr. Kentard." Buster said.

"How are you today, sir?" Peter asked.

"I'm just hunky dory, thanks! How 'bout yourself?"

"Oh, my goodness! Very well, thank you! We have lots of work to do," Peter said rapidly. "We should get down to it!"

"Uh, yeah, well, uh..." Buster was surprised. It was the first day back at the ranch and there was not even a slight interest in vacation passing or anything personal of the like. Buster was expecting to hear at least a "Did you have a nice Christmas?", or a greeting of, "How were the holidays?", or a kindly, "How's the family back home?", or something human like that.

However, it was just a cold salutation of business: "The major project today is to distribute teaching duties," Peter said. "Mrs. Kentard and I have made a tentative schedule and hope you will be in agreement with our decisions."

"Yeah, right, well...uh..." Buster answered. *Jesus Christ!* he thought. *I bet they spent their whole Christmas holiday worrying about who's going to do what and when and.... Jesus, what a fucking miserable existence!*

"Shall we have a seat, everyone?" Robin said in her high, cracking voice.

The whole group sat down at the round table. One of the fat kitchen ladies brought in a tray of tea and cups, and they were passed around the table.

"I hate tea!" Buster whispered to Cramble. Cramble tried to ignore him and did not say anything.

Peter Kentard started with special duties, but his wife shortly butted in and took over the meeting.

*Poor henpecked bastard*, Buster thought. He looked around him and observed in detail just exactly who he was with. *English teachers*, he contemplated, *fucking English teachers: that miserable lot of lost souls that for reasons of lack of initiative, creativity and bravery, intellectually pursue the only thing they were raised with, their fucking mother tongue. But I'm one of these creatures! Why? It must be lack of bravery or something. Why can't I be a ship's captain on the high seas, or a jet plane pilot dropping bombs, or a big game hunter killing elephants, or an astronaut, or something exciting for Christ's sakes. But a fucking English teacher confined in a four-walled cubicle with a fucking blackboard and chalk, looking at black students pick their fucking black noses? Jesus!*

And Mr. Murdock," Mrs. Kentard's voice interrupted his thoughts, "Mr. Murdock—are you listening?"

"With my utmost attention, Ma'am."

"Because you have the Speech and Drama classes, we have decided to turn over to you the video tape equipment. It will now be your responsibility and we hope you will take advantage of this privilege."

"Yes, Ma'am. Uh, thank you, Ma'am!"

"You will also be teaching Contemporary Literature and Expository Writing to sections 1-C, 1-F and 2M2."

"Yes, Ma'am. Uh, thank you, Ma'am."

And the meeting went on and on, taking much longer than Buster had ever thought it would. He kept looking out the window at the beautiful ocean, longing to go out and take a swim. He almost fell asleep several times. Robin's voice was so monotone and boring. She gave English Methodology courses to Cramble and Education Theory and History to Bachran. Peter, or rather Mr. Kentard, of course, would have his duties in the library along with sharing the senior English classes with his wife. All this could have been said in fifteen short minutes, but it took over three, long, painstaking hours. When it was all over, Buster burst out into the fresh air, hopped on Naomi and sped to the Riding Rock for a stiff rum and Coke and a joint he had kept guarded in his sock.

After a nice, relaxing two hours on the Riding Rock patio overlooking the ocean, Buster decided to go into Cockburn Town and check out the billiard table at Zebedee Jones' bar. He hopped on Naomi and went to the center of the village and pulled up to the stone structure located right across from the Jake Jones' dry goods store. Standing outside the door of the bar was Zebedee Jones, a giant of a man. He stood six feet six inches tall—lean but with shoulders as square as a bull's and forearms as large as Buster's thighs. He was famous in all of the Bahamas as being one of the strongest men the islands had to offer. Nobody dared to challenge him in a fight. Whenever there were disagreements in his bar, he would merely put himself between the arguers, stretch out his arms and separate the two, or three or more men and diplomatically with his deep, soft voice, restore peace. Fortunately, Zebedee was not the fighting type. His grandiose, white smile was as big as his body and his disposition was tranquil, easy going and peaceful. He was also very intelligent. He ran the dry goods store on the island for his aging father, Jake, and was always trading with Nassau merchants.

"Howdy, "Zebedee," Buster said. "What's happening?"

"Hello, Buster," he said smiling. "I see you're back from the States!" Zebedee had known this, for he had met Buster just before Christmas.

"That's right," Buster said, putting Naomi on her stand. "It was really nice to see the family again. How were things here?"

"Fantastic, mann. Christmas is one of my favorite times of the year. Lots of joy and good weather, mann. Hey, mann, R.B.'s in the back!"

"Oh Great! Thanks, Pal. How are the kids?"

"Just fine—livelier than ever, mann."

Buster went inside. As he walked towards the bar, he saw R.B. playing billiards in the game room. "R.B.!" Buster yelled. "Hey, you bastard—how the hell've you been?"

"Murdock! You son of a bitch!" R.B. yelled back. "'Bout time you got back!" They embraced.

"Hey, man," Buster said, "You shaved your beard off!" R.B. was now sporting a large Fu Man Chu mustache that draped down to his chin.

"Yeah, Captain told me to clean up a bit."

"Well, your stash looks good."

"Thanks! Hey speaking of stash, some great shit came in from Lauderdale yesterday. Wanna try some?"

"Speak no further, my good man!"

The two Americans walked out to their motorcycles and sped northeast to the Christopher Columbus monument. They sat underneath the marble white cross, passing doobies the rest of the afternoon and philosophizing on the discovery of the New World. They imagined what it must have been like for Columbus' crew to set sight on land after being at sea for so long—what a feeling that must have been. No wonder, they thought, Columbus called the island San Salvador— Saint Savior—for it saved the entire voyage for the sea-weary adventurers. Buster felt good, and R.B. equally as well. It was great to be back on the island.

Most of the students came back to San Salvador on Saturday on three special

Bahamas Air flights out of Nassau. As it was the diplomatic, obligatory tradition, the college lecturers all went out to greet them on the separate flights spaced four hours apart throughout the day. There they were, future teachers of the Bahamas, stepping down from the plane ladders, ready for another crack at progressing in their college careers. The mountain of luggage was virtually thrown out the belly of the planes, and on all three flights there was a chaotic grab-bag affair with students jumping all over each other trying to get at the center pile. Students were taken back to the college in the college, all-purpose truck, an old, open-air, hay-ride truck used for everything and anything. It made several runs back and forth from the airport to the college and it did not stop until the last student was back to his respective dorm. The noise of the students shifted from the airport to the college, and the campus was in a sort of quiet uproar. The students were really glad to see each other again. Back pattings and yellings and stereos blasting away spiced a happy reunion of sorts to let off steam from being so polite and playing the San Salvador Teachers' College student role to family and friends back on their home islands.

Classes began that Monday with no change from the last

term. Everybody stayed in his or her same sections and in the same classrooms. Buster decided in his Literature classes to completely throw away the British Isles and start using something these people could relate to. He chose from the book storage room in the administration building a series of books written by Caribbean writers. One series was *A Day in the Sun*, a novel that took place in Port-Au-Prince, Haiti, and another was *Off Shore Winds* by a Jamaican writer, which had the setting on the outskirts of Kingston. Maybe these books were not the best literature in the world, but at least they were by black writers writing about black island cultures with their everyday life and problems with characters that at least some of the students could half-way identify with. No more of that Robin Hood and his band of merry men in Sherwood Forest, or Samuel Johnson's English dinner parties. If Buster used those types of stories, no matter how dynamic he would be, everybody would be sleeping on their folded arms on top of their desks.

His Expository Writing class would be no problem whatsoever. He would just use the old, University of Florida Freshman Composition method of beginnings, main bodies and conclusions. For his students to captivate that idea would take the whole term—as it did the Florida students.

And finally for his two Speech and Drama classes, he would start out by having his students memorize a favorite passage from whatever or wherever—whether it be from a newspaper, the Bible, or any other material—and give a five minute delivery to the class with the videotape machine whirring for post-speech criticism and comments. He himself delivered his memorized "Desiderata" speech for a demonstration, using good gestures and a clear, strong projected voice.

So for Buster, the whole thing of teaching was an absolute cinch. There was nothing to it for him- it came natural. With only fifteen hours a week in a classroom right smack on a turquoise ocean, being paid one thousand dollars a month plus housing, who could ask for more? It was paradise.

It took Buster all of five days to get adjusted to his new routine. Then came Friday night, and being satisfied with his work, he was ready for the first Rip of the Winter at Zebedee Jones' Harlem Square Bar.

Buster smoked a joint listening to Straus' *Blue Danube* on his new cassette player, then headed toward Cockburn Town. Slowly pulling up to the center of the small village to Zebedee's bar, Buster took Naomi weaving in and out of the parked cars on the dirt road—all the old Fords, Chevies, English Minis and Vauxhall Vivas were parked on the side, but blocking a good part of the road. The white Coast Guard van was parked on the side of the stone building, and the stoned college lecturer pulled up alongside of it to park Naomi. As he was doing so, he hit a large rock that he did not see. Naomi quickly dropped to its side, throwing Buster off and underneath the Coast Guard van. "Jesus Christ!" Buster yelled to himself. "That joint did a lot more to me than I thought—fuck!"

He got up and brushed himself off. The loud, funky-beat, live music was flowing out of the open windows. The music mixed with the loud yahooing and hee-hawing of human voices. He walked up to the lighted entrance and entered the bar to the tune of Johnny Nash's song, "I Can See Clearly Now." He saw a mob of people in the recreation room bobbing up and down to the music. Smoke and the heat of human bodies immediately penetrated all the regions of Buster's skin. He walked up to the bar and saw Zebedee's giant figure towering over the entire scene. The bar counter was unusually crowded. Lots of men and women of all ages and from all over the island were standing around drinking to the service of Zebedee, who seemed to be the nucleus of everything.

Zebedee spotted Buster and let out a big smile. "Hello, Buster, mann!" He extended his gigantic hand and dwarfed Buster's white fingers in a gargantuan handshake. "How are you?"

"Fantastic," Buster said, almost shouting because there was so much noise. "Hey, this is great, Zebedee! This is the best thing on the island yet."

"Yes, mann, lots of the good vibrations. You know what I mean?" He let out a laugh and his body swayed with the live, twangy music.

"Yeah, I know what you mean! How about one of your fabulous rum and Cokes?"

"Made, mann, made!" He went to the ice cabinet and started to make the drink.

Meanwhile, Buster stood squeezed amongst all the black bodies at the bar, checking the whole scene out. He watched the dancers through all the smoke that lingered in the room. He immediately noticed a tall, lean white figure wobbling up and down in the middle of the crowd—it was R.B. with a cigarette dangling from his mouth and thin black hair dropping down over his eyes. His eyes were glued to the swinging vaginal region of one of the ugly Finger Lakers. Buster smiled, then let out a chuckle. *Great!* he thought. *Just great!*

Zebedee brought over the rum and Coke. "I put it on your tab, mann, OK? He said.

"Great, Zeb! A lot easier, right?" Buster felt important. He had never had a tab before in a bar—it was always the money right away. He had a feeling he was going to like the Harlem Square Bar. There was a lot of local atmosphere—much more so than the Riding Rock Inn that geared solely to American tourists. Zebedee's bar was local and for the people. *Culture, man*, Buster thought. *Culture*!

Suddenly, he felt a tap on his shoulder. He swerved around and a bright, white face flashed in front of his eyes. It was such a surprise—deep blue eyes and long, blond hair and rosy lips hit him like an unexpected camera flash in complete darkness. He had to blink a couple of times to clear his eyes.

"Hi!" A female voice penetrated Buster's ears. It was the sweet voice of a smiling Barbara Oskalowski.

"Uh… hello," Buster blurted out, taking a sip on his new drink.

"I see you made it here," she said.

"Uh, yeah, all in once piece, too, I think. I just fell off Naomi."

"Naomi?"

"Yeah, she's my motorcycle."

"Oh dear, are you all right?"

"Sure, man, no problem—I didn't even feel it!" Buster's head was spinning from the joint he smoked. "Uh … let's see, your name is uh … Jesus, I'm sorry, I've forgotten your name!"

"Barbara—Barbara Oskalowski."

"Oska who?"

"Oskalowski! It's Polish—I'm Polish Canadian. Many people here just call me 'Babs'—it's a lot easier I've found out."

"Oh yeah? That's interesting. I'm really sorry I forgot your name, you know."

"Oh, that's OK."

"We only met that one time at that Coast Guard Thanksgiving dinner, remember?"

"Yes, I do indeed. That was very nice. I didn't know you Americans ate so well!"

"Well, that's why we have such strong bodies."

"Oh, dear!"

Buster let out a smile and put on a suave and debonair appearance. He caught himself staring at her. She was beautiful, so tender like. He had not seen anything like that up close in ages.

Then the thought came to him and he expressed himself directly and to the point: "By the way, Babs ... Babs, right?"

"Yes, that's right."

"Uh, where's the captain tonight?"

"Oh, he's not here," she said.

"Got the duty or something?"

"No—in fact, I don't know where he is, really, and I don't much care!" She sounded scornful.

"Oh yeah?" Buster's eyes lit up like light bulbs. "What happened? You guys have one of those lover's quarrels or something?"

"Oh, no! We are finished!"

"Finished? Since when?"

"Just before Christmas. I couldn't stand him anymore!"

"Wow, that's news! You guys looked so perfect together, you know what I mean? At least from the outside—both tall, blue eyed, attending social events, always together..."

"Yes, well, that was it—it was strictly social. He put me on display and he used me to be his glamorous girl for a glamorous Coast Guard captain. I resented it after awhile."

"Wow! Well, I really didn't know, man. That's great! Uh, no—I mean, that's uh, bad—sorry 'bout that!"

"Oh, don't be in the least! I'm free now. Let's dance!"

"Great!" Buster set his drink down in the corner.

The two struggled through the crowd, went up close to the band from Nassau and started jiggling to the old tune, "Got a Letter from Miami." R.B. came bopping up and slapped Buster on the back and gave a little wave to Babs. Everybody was smiling and bobbing up and down with their feet shuffling and arms waving in the air.

For the rest of the evening, Babs and Buster danced the night away, stopping only to order more drinks at the bar. Once-in-awhile Buster would step outside with R.B. for a doobie behind the Coast Guard van. When they came back inside, they would once again resume dancing with their chosen partners. For Buster, hardly any talking was done with Babs. This night it was only body movements and "Yahoos."

Buster was so awed by the phenomenon of dancing with such a beautiful woman that he forgot everything else. He forgot his gentlemanly manners and ignored his partner much of the time. He was really not interested in making up trivial conversation to try and impress the girl he was with, not that he was able to, being stoned as he was. Nor was he interested in inventing clever schemes to conquer this treasure of the opposite sex. He seemed to be only interested in music and dancing—just an overall, general letting off steam and being loose and light-headed. When the music stopped and it was time to go home, Buster was so drunk and stoned that all he was able to say to Babs was: "Hey look, uh … see you later!" He hopped on Naomi, leaving the entanglement of cars behind in the dirt road, and crawled home to sleep all Saturday with no dreams whatsoever.

When Buster awoke late Saturday afternoon, it was cold

and heavy rain was coming through the opened windows. The first winter storm had come. Early Saturday morning, huge, billowing clouds had come blowing in from the Northeast and quickly engulfed the entire island with a blanket of seemingly gray brain matter. A cold, strong wind came ripping down along with them, battering the wooden island shacks as if they were tiny match boxes and shaking the heads of palm trees as if they were mop heads—their trunks bowing back and forth as if begging for mercy. And the sea—there was nothing more beautiful than the sea like this: totally covered with whitecaps as far as the horizon line—the wind ramming tops of waves and trying to blow rolling crests back to where they came from. The jagged coastline on the east, Atlantic side, was pounded mercilessly by mountainous ten to fifteen foot waves, slamming into the limestone rock and spraying skyward up to over fifty feet. On the west, Caribbean side, the sea was calmer, but the angry six to ten foot waves rolled in and looked like they were trying to grab the shoreline and take it back out with them. The current was unbelievably swift and seemed to be running as fast as the wind was blowing. When the rains came, they burst in sheets: hard petitions of water sweeping over the land area like that of an immense, hard spray of the nozzle of a hose.

The storm was good for a change. It brought in a roughness of weather that made it much more exciting than dull, sunny, tranquil days all the time. The crispness of the air brought in a clarity of mind to human beings and a different way of looking at things. The change also introduced the feeling of hope—hope that there was something else in life than monotony and that monotony had to end—even sunny days.

But clarity of mind for Buster was somewhat difficult to obtain upon first awakening. After such a night of raising hell at the Rip, his mind was spaced-out and hung over. But he was able to realize that rain was coming through the open windows and that the whole side of his room was wet, including his bed, his own head, and the video tape equipment he had brought to his room on Friday afternoon for experimentation. He got out of bed shivering. He rapidly closed the windows and threw on some warm clothes. He went into the kitchen to make some coffee, and while waiting for the water to boil, he did some jumping jacks and burpees to get his poisoned blood circulating again.

Buster dragged his body back to his room, carrying the steaming hot cup of coffee in his hand like a career navy chief on board ship. The room was cold, but not uncomfortable. His bones felt a pleasant chill—something he had not experienced in a long time—especially after a long, hot summer in Florida, then an even longer and seemingly hotter autumn down further South in Nassau. Feeling chill was quite a sensation.

He took a seat at his desk with the iridescent lamp hanging over from the bookshelf, the light illuminating the writing area. He sat with his head braced up by his left arm, pen in his right hand, his eyes closed, mind conscious of the wind howling through the door and cracks of the windows—but not conscious of much else.

He lit up a Dunhill cigarette that Barbara had given him at the Rip and that he had slipped into his shirt pocket for reserve. He watched the white smoke rise. As it slowly rose, thoughts came to him burning through his hungover mind like the tobacco in the cigarette. He thought of Barbara and the great time they had had dancing at the Rip. At least he found out that she was free—or so she said. After Patty and many other relationships with girls, he knew that being free was relative.

Buster mistrusted that word free and especially the girls who said it. Free? He wondered how long that freedom would last for this Babs girl—or was it Barbara—or Oska somebody? He could not remember her name. *Ha*! he thought. *A free girl is hard to find. More than likely she still has emotional hang-ups on the captain.* Buster had yet to ever meet a girl that did not have at least one man that was still attached in one way or another. It was his experience that after starting a relationship, the girl, without fail, always brought in another guy to the scene—telling of past affairs with him and how hard it was to break away, and why they had separated, and all their differences. And almost without fail, this guy or the other would sooner or later always appear at a most inopportune time and either want the girl back or go out to dinner and maybe then some, and etcetera, etcetera.

Buster did not want this anymore. His emotional state could not take it. He was exhausted fighting for women. He philosophized: *Why is it that there are more women in the world than men, with men always seeming to be fighting for women? That's ass backwards! It should be the other way around.* He took a long, deep drag on the cigarette.

So he mistrusted Barbara when she said, "Free." Buster could imagine that no sooner would he start to get emotionally involved with her, when the captain, sporting his tall body, blond hair, blue eyes and well-trimmed beard, would one day show his face and another unpleasant showdown would take place.

"Forget Barbara!" he said aloud. "I'd rather be alone,

enjoy my independence and my own self with my own shit surrounding me without any interruptions. Also, Buster ol' boy, remember the pact you made on the airplane back down here—get totally involved with work!"

But then, God was he lonely for those beautiful thoughts that come around when falling in love with a woman. A sudden loneliness for Patty came over him. His heart felt as empty as a floating bottle in the middle of the sea. A sudden barrage of thoughts about Patty entered his mind. *Jesus Christ*! he thought. *How could she have done such a thing? How could she be so deceitful, unfaithful like that? How could it be that we spent such a fantastic time together on the beaches of New Providence—always looking into my eyes and softly saying, 'I love you, I love you,' and then taking off with God-knows-who without even a hint that she was leaving me?*

Buster could not understand it. Both depression and bitterness struck him like a baseball bat on the head. He decided to write her a piece of his mind. With a bottle of rum on his desk, he wrote three long pages of whining, love-sick gunk.

But then he realized he was losing his train of thought and was getting off the track. Plus, he did not like the wording of the letter or anything. It showed his weaknesses too much. The wording sounded like a little baby whimpering to suckle its mother's breasts. He scratched a big "X on the paragraphs and crunched up the papers.

"The hell with it! Fuck that girl!" he yelled.

He crumpled up the entire letter and took a big swig of rum. He suddenly stood up feeling the alcohol ignite his esophagus and stomach. He grabbed the three balled-up papers and went into the bathroom. "Here, Patrick Cramble!" he said ceremoniously. "These words belong to what you disgustingly leave behind! And with these papers follow the complete end of all my thoughts of this girl—forever and ever—Amen!" Buster threw them in the bowl and flushed. The papers whirled round and round and then quickly disappeared along with the ever-so-familiar corned, Cramble trunk.

Buster was exhausted. After so many words and emotional feelings winding badly up inside his head, he could think no more. He flopped down on his bed and stared up at the ceiling. The corners of the room were spinning around from the rum that boiled inside his stomach. After several hours of blank staring and listening to the wind roar outside, his eyelids fell, and that's all he saw of that Saturday.

He woke up Sunday morning, the wind still howling and the rain coming down harder than ever. He got up and walked through the bare, gray, ghostly living room to the kitchen. He was ravenously hungry, but there was nothing much to eat. He opened the refrigerator and discovered it was empty with the exception of a half a dozen eggs and several slices of bacon hidden in one corner. "Jesus," he said softly, hoping that Cramble would not hear. "Sorry Cramble, but I've just got to have these." And he cooked himself a glorious bacon and egg breakfast, topped off with grits, coffee and rum. Delicious! He was feeling good. His mind was much clearer than the day before and in much higher spirits. He went back to his room, turned on Beethoven's Fifth and read the rest of the morning and most of the afternoon. It was a very quiet, stormy day—a good day to stay home.

In the late afternoon, Buster started playing around with the videotape machine. He had brought the equipment over from the studio Friday afternoon because he wanted to use the weekend to become more familiar with the machines. It was a brand new Sony set-up with a tape recording unit, the camera on a tripod and the television screen all joined by large, black cables. It was a simple process, really, of merely putting on the magnetic tape like a reel-to-reel tape recorder, aiming the camera and the image would then appear on the screen simultaneously.

Buster connected everything and played a few folk songs on his guitar for testing. He then played it back. "Jesus," he said viewing the screen. "How did I ever get so handsome? And that's the best popular music I've ever listened to on television. He went up to the television to focus the image a little better. Suddenly, he heard a loud roar of a truck engine mixed in with the sound of the rain outside. He looked out the door window and there was R.B. in the white Coast Guard van—cigarette dangling from his mouth.

Upon seeing Buster peeking through the window, R.B.'s eyes widened and a big smile lit his face. He jumped out of the van and ran through the rain to the apartment. "Hey, Murdock, what's happening?"

"Hey, R.B.,—great to see you, man. What the hell did you do with the weather?"

"Oh, I decided to change it for a while—tired of the same ol' sun all the time. You know what I mean?"

"Yeah, sure do! Hey, you're just in time for the concert—have a seat."

"Hey! Where'd you get this set-up?" R.B. asked, scrutinizing the equipment.

"Do you believe it? I'm in charge of this stuff now—Responsibility, you see! Me! Responsible!"

"Hey, that is funny!" R.B. reached in his coat pocket and whipped out his metal cigarette case. "Doobie, anyone?"

"I thought you'd never ask!"

"These are spiked with hash, man. They're dynamite! Try them and see!" He laughed and lit up. "They're good for you, too."

"So, what's new, R.B.? I haven't talked to you in a long time. You were so busy with that Finger Fucker the other night…."

"Yeah, I got my dipper wet, too!"

"Yeah?"

"Yeah! Hope I don't get the scuz, though. I had to keep my eyes closed the whole time. She was so God-damned awful ugly."

"Jesus, so that's how you did it—you kept your eyes closed!"

"The only way, my Brother!" R.B. passed the joint. "Besides, it was my last fling on the island. They ship me off Thursday—I put in a request for early leave and they gave it to me. 'Bout time those bastards up there did something for me."

"Hey, that's great!" Buster said. "But God, I hate to see you go so soon. Jesus, you're the only friend I got here." He passed the joint.

"Well, I sure ain't gonna stay here for you, that's for sure. There'll be others. Hey! How'd you do with Oskalowski the other night?"

"Well, she dances all right, I suppose—but really, I was too drunk and stoned to do or even think about anything serious. I'm not quite sure I even remember what happened."

"Everyone knows now she's free. The captain up at the base is taking some bad gas. He's really up in the air. The other day he told everybody to take the day off—something you never hear in the military. And if they heard about this in Fort Lauderdale, they'd fry his ass."

"Jesus, poor guy. I know how he feels."

"Ah, he's just a tall, candy ass! Anyhow, if you wanna do anything with Babs, you better step on it 'cause guys in the barracks are already talking about their plans with her—horny bastards!"

"Well, fuck! There goes my chances. You see, R.B., I'm at a point now where I could give a big flying fuck! I don't care anymore! Let them do what they want, but I'm through fighting for fucking women. I refuse to fight!"

"Who says anything about fighting, man? The next time you see her, just put a lip-lock on her with your down-to-earth approach that you have, and she'll be all over you."

"Fat chance!"

"Hey, man—you'd be surprised how fast she'll cling, running scared from those horny jock straps at the Coast Guard, drooling all over her."

"Fuck, I'll just stick with the sheep—forget it! How 'bout another toke?"

"Yeah, man," and the sailor took a long draw from the joint.

Buster played back his songs while they both watched his guitar antics on the screen.

Buster took a long puff on the joint. "Wow!" he said. "This stuff is good!" His head lifted to another dimension.

"Told ya."

Buster adjusted the roach and they both snorted for several minutes.

"Whew!" Buster sighed. "This is fantastic! Got any more of that hash?"

"Yeah, I'll lay you on my stash when I leave—the least I can do for a friend!"

"R.B., you're great, man!" Buster reached for the rum

bottle left on his desk the day before. "Here's to your new duty!" He tipped his elbow and the bottle made a bubbling sound.

"I'll drink to that, too," R.B. said. He took a big swig. "Yeeeeehawwwwww! Knit, knit, knit!" He flapped his arms like a chicken and fell back onto the bed.

The tape ran its due course and the machine shut off automatically. Doped, rummed up, and oblivious to the world, they both passed out, sprawled on the bed, fully clothed with shoes still on their feet. The thought never occurred to them that it was their last night together on the island.

Back to a normal week of class, Buster was in high spirits. It seemed that the weekend had done something to his mental state: shown him hope—that maybe it was possible to have good times on the island. He taught well and dynamically, even though for two days the classrooms were flooded from all the rain from the storm. But the storm had subsided, classrooms were drying out and the video tape machine was back in its original place, the studio. Buster had quickly erased his concert from the other night for fear that Father Villeneuve or Peter Kentard might drop in and watch it.

The Tuesday Nassau mail plane brought in two new teachers on the island, a married couple named Dave and Anne Troff. They were young, twenty-six year old teachers from Manchester, England; but their minds seemed to be more on the level of forty-year-old, tea drinking croquet players. They were very formal people and Buster's first impression of them was just a mere, "Jesus, not more!" David Troff was to teach Mathematics and Physical Sciences and Anne was to go and teach first and second grade at the elementary school in Cockburn Town. As far as their residence, they were placed by special request from the ministry in the last empty cottage on campus—road side, right across from the Ginnis' house.

Also, this was the week that R.B. left San Salvador. It seemed that he departed so fast on Thursday that Buster was not even sure R.B. had passed by the apartment to bid his farewell and dump off his drug stash. But it was that six-by-four inch, hand-carved brown wooden box that proved to be the only evidence of him doing so. He remembered the embrace R.B. gave him and a simple, "Keep it cool, Murdock! Here you are and it's good for you, too!" R.B. proudly handed the small box to him and rode away on his Honda Fifty back to the base to collect his things and then to fly off the island on the military plane, back to the land of the free.

Buster went inside his room and opened the box. It was shear beauty right before his eyes: a full ounce of cleaned Columbian Gold marijuana stuffed in a baggie surrounded by large chunks of hashish wrapped in aluminum foil. Spread out evenly in the box were pills of all kinds: Quaaludes, black widows, orange sunshine LSD, and weirdly enough, a few orange one-a-day multiple vitamin tablets and some Excedrin aspirin. "R.B.!" Buster shouted, "I love you!" Buster was certain that his friend had cosmically received the thought. With R.B.'s collection plus the stash of his own, Buster was all set for the winter and even the spring. Finally, he broke down and wept for the loss of his good friend.

It was Thursday afternoon, after classes, that Miss Canadian Imperial came traipsing down the steps of the Bahamas Air special afternoon flight. She was quite popular and the college staff was obligated to greet her at the airport.

She was on the island for the weekend, however, not for diplomatic reasons, but merely as a personal guest of Father Villeneuve's. Both he and his wife, Anne, had been close friends of the beauty queen for many years.

When Buster saw her from the distance, she was strikingly beautiful: long, black, straight (but stiff) hair, smooth black complexion, pleasant, negro features. Buster's imagination went wild: *How I'd love to have those nice thick lips just eat me up, and those lovely feminine arms wrap around me and embrace me for hours upon hours, making me feel like a real man—hmmm, chocolate upon whipped cream, Lord! I gotta get outta here before I wet my own dipper*! He got on Naomi and sped off back to his apartment with still more fantasies speeding through his brain.

He ran into his apartment and rolled a Columbian doobie. *Maybe this*, he thought, *will erase some of my fantasies*! But no—they only increased after the joint:

Buster's tool sprang up like a rubber doggie bone. He rapidly tore off his pants, flopped on the bed, and violently started to shuck away, his sweet imagination taking all-out control: moaning, groaning, forgetting all cultures, religions, races, places and seeing only Ms. Canadian Imperial female flesh enveloping his total being.

Suddenly there was a hard knock on the door. Buster quickly stopped and pretended not to hear it. But then another knock, and another persisted. "Oh, Jesus Christ!" he said quietly. His heart was pounding, but his dipper was slowly drooping down and losing its hardness. "OK, OK, I'll answer the fucking door," he said. "It sounds important. Fuck!"

"Uh … Yes," he shouted. "Who is it?"

"It's Barbara!"

*Barbara?* he thought. *Who in the hell do I know by the name of Barbara?*

"Barbara Oskalowski!" her voice clarified.

*Oskalowski?* he said again silently. *Oskalowski? Who the hell?*

"Ah, yes! Babs Oskalowski! He finally said shouting, still panting from what he was doing. "Uh … Can you, uh … wait just a second? Uh … I'll be right out!"

"If you're busy, I can come back!" she said.

"Oh, no! No! Stay right where you are—I'll be right out! Uh, can you go into the living room?"

"Yes, sure," she said. She went to the living room and sat down.

Buster ran and grabbed his pants on the floor and rapidly pulled them on, his sword now completely dwindled. He pulled on a T-shirt then quickly lit up some incense to rid the smell of his doobie. Finally, capturing some composure, he walked out of his room and debonairly entered the living room.

"Good afternoon, Barbara. What a pleasant surprise!"

# CHAPTER 7

## *The Start of Something New*

A nd it started up with Barbara Oskalowski. That afternoon as they sat in the living room, Buster slumped exhaustingly in a chair practically on the other side of the room. He was riding high on his joint and kept losing his train of thought, hallucinating on Barbara's barrage of trivial words coming out of her beautifully formed, pink mouth. He was not quite sure at times that she was even there; and other times, he knew he was hallucinating badly and envisioned the only single, white female resident on the island as a cartoon caricature right before his very eyes. The conversation on his part was very little: he hardly said a thing. Barbara had asked him if he wanted to go to the Coast Guard movie with her that evening, but he was so much in the air that he politely said that he was very tired and had some exams to grade—but maybe on Friday night. She responded quickly as if she had everything organized in her head, and said that Friday was the Rip and that it was dance time. Well, then maybe he would see her there at the Rip and have a dance or two. And it was only after Barbara left and an entire hour later when Buster got the munchies and dug into some left-over Kraft's macaroni and tuna fish casserole, masticating profusely, that it suddenly dawned on him that this "Chick" wanted something that he had, and that he was such a "Dumb-ass-fool" for not paying much attention to her earlier. Upon realizing this, he was really perturbed at himself, and it bothered him. Why was he so dense all the time when it came to women? Why could he not have picked up on her intentions at the very beginning? Now maybe it was too late and he would lose his chance. "What a dumb fuck!" he said aloud. He threw the empty casserole pan in the kitchen sink to let it soak and went into his room to brood. He smoked another joint and for two hours he marveled at the pictures of a new book, *The Seed* by Ram Das, that Brother Tom had given him for Christmas. He forgot "Dumb-ass" women for the day and threw his mind towards the big ice cream cone in the sky.

It was Friday night Rip time. Buster pulled up to Zebedee's bar and parked Naomi right next to Barbara's old Vauxhall Viva. Live, twangy music once again came flowing out of the windows. This time Buster did not fall over, or anything—he had not smoked or drunk a thing because he did not want to appear to Barbara as a "Fucking babbling idiot," as he said to himself. Tonight it was going to be straight city all the way and turn on the intellectual and cultural charm. He was dressed in blue jeans, tennis shoes and a bright red velour shirt with thick blue stripes running around his chest. Around his neck he put a Bahamian bead necklace. He looked quite the exotic adventurer: his hair getting longer and longer and beard getting thicker and starting to flow down past his throat. He flung open the door and entered the smoke filled bar—the smell of negro body odor rammed up his nose. As he walked further inside, his eyes immediately zeroed in on Barbara, the only white person dancing with some black college students. Babs was tall and overlooked the heads of the dancers. She appeared as if she had kept her eyes glued to the entrance way waiting for Buster. He let out a smile and gave a small wave. She did the same, then did a couple twirls and dips—her head going up and down, keeping time with the funky beat.

Buster walked over to the crowded bar and saw Zebedee feverishly jamming cups into the ice machine, then filling them on the bar with Matuselem, the best brand of dark rum in the Caribbean.

"Zebedee!" Buster yelled, his voice merely blending in with the noise of all the people talking and hollering and the music blaring—"Zebedee!" he yelled again.

Zebedee caught him out of the corner of his eye, then let out a big white grin: "Oh, Hey Murdock, mann! How are you, mann?" His voice was so warm and gentle—it was such a contrast coming out of such a large man.

"Just great! It's a real ripper tonight, eh?"

"Yes mann, as always. What'll you have?"

"This time, I think I'll try one of those Matuselem darks with 7-Up, OK?"

"You got it!" He immediately brought down one of the rum bottles from the shelf.

There was an end to a song and Babs came up to Buster. "Hi, handsome!" she said.

"Hey, what's happening?" he turned away. Even though he was burning with desire inside, he tried to look disinterested. He was experienced enough to know about "Chicks" somewhat. His philosophy was that no matter how much he desired or loved a girl—one must not show it in the beginning—especially in the beginning. The more interest and affection a man showed towards a woman, the less she would chase after him, and vice versa. That was one of his mistakes he made with Patty, he had concluded. He had shown too much affection for her and she ran like a scared rabbit. So this time he would have a different approach. He knew there were a lot of drooling Coasties after this white "Dame" and Babs knew it too—that's why she did not want them. Also for Babs, there was some sort of mystic intrigue about this college English teacher. She knew that in order to have a position such as his, he had to be well educated and well paid, and apart from this, he was a long-haired American—a combination that was totally unknown in her conservative Canadian background. She had never known nor associated with a long haired man before, was not quite sure of its significance, and above all, she had never really intimately known a man from the United States. Of course, there was Captain Greg White, but according to Babs, he did not really count: that affair could hardly have been called intimate. Buster was intrigue for Babs, and she was bound and determined to get to know him.

"How 'bout a dance?" she said in a strong, Canadian accent: "'bout" sounding like "a boot."

"No, I just got my drink—but thanks! You go right ahead!"

"Oh well, I think I'll sit this one out then myself. What are you drinking?"

"Kool Aid."

She laughed. "Oh, don't be silly!"

"Would you like one?"

"Yes, please. I'm dreadfully thirsty!"

"Dreadfully? Jesus, I haven't heard that word in a long time. Zebedee! Another Kool Aid, please!"

Zebedee acknowledged and smiled.

"What part of Canada are you from, Babs?" Buster asked.

"Kapaskasing," she said.

"Where?"

"Kapaskasing. It's a small lumber town in the North. My father is a lumberjack."

"A lumberjack, eh? Jesus, I read somewhere that bank tellers and lumberjacks have the lowest IQ's of all the professions." Zebedee brought over the drink. "Thanks Zeb—my bill, OK?"

"No problem, mann!" Zebedee said.

"Well, that's not true!" Babs looked a little hurt. "My father is a very intelligent, hard working man."

"Is he Canadian or Polack?"

"That's Polish, please! My father is Polish. My parents came over during the war and have been in Canada ever since."

'Do you speak Polish?"

"I'm bilingual—Polish is my first language."

"Oh yeah? Hey, did you hear the one about why Polacks have a low suicide rate?"

"Be careful, I'm sensitive!"

"'Cause it's hard to kill yourself jumping out of basement windows—Ha, ha, ha, ha …."

"Very original—you're horrible!" She slammed her drink down on the bar and started walking towards the door.

"Jesus, what did I say?" Buster thought. He rushed and

grabbed her by the arm. "Hey, sorry about that, OK? It won't happen again—it was just a joke!"

"Well, it was in bad taste, and I must say, I'm quite surprised at that coming out of an instructor of higher learning."

She turned away again, but Buster hurried around to block her path.

"OK, OK! Look—so I blew it!" he said, arms in the air. "I told you it won't happen again. I didn't know you were so sensitive. And furthermore, I do consider myself an educated, well-cultured man—and if you don't accept my apologies, well then—Never mind!" He left her standing, and he walked back to the bar. "Zebedee, another drink, please!"

The music struck up again to Johnny Nash's song, "I Can See Clearly Now." Everybody was shuffling their feet, hooting and hollering. Buster clutched his drink, lost in a world of thought at the bar: *Fuck women! I hate 'em! They're so God-damn sensitive, they'll cry over anything; but when it comes to fucking up and playing with the minds of men and their feelings, why, they're stone cold, insensitive whores—all of 'em. All this lovey-dovey madness, and you hurt my feelings by saying that bullshit is all fucking theater. Fuck 'em. Pardon my French, Murdock, but fuck it!*

"Mr. Murdock—hello—what's going on?" Dave Troff, the new Math lecturer slapped Buster on the back.

"Well, Troff, this is where the action is," Buster said. "You might as well get used to it here on the island—it's a long way to June." He tipped his glass.

"Blimey! A bloody racket, this is!"

"Where's the wife?"

"She's in the crowd dancing—don't you see her?

There—there she is!" A little pink skin stood out in the blackness that dominated the bobbing crowd.

"Why aren't you dancing?" Buster asked.

"Hmph! Don't take to it much meself. I take more to this!" He held up his glass filled to the top with straight Bacardi rum.

"Jesus, be careful with that or they'll have to drag you outta here."

"Naah, not me, mate—it's in my system now, you know? I drink more than a half a bottle every day and it doesn't phase me in the least. I've got to keep the blood circulating, you know?"

"Well, I drink a half a bottle of rum and I'm on the floor."

"You've just got to know how to take it!"

"Actually, I'd rather just have a nice hit of acid."

"Acid? You mean that LSD?" Troff became fidgety.

"Yeah—it's healthier than alcohol ever will be!"

"Naah!" Troff responded instantly. "There are too many problems in this world without that! I'd rather keep my own head. Well … ol' chap, I must be making my social rounds—Cheerio!"

Buster took a sip of his drink and thought, *Cheerio? Boy, did he really get nervous! Wish the straight asshole wouldn't call me chap. Christ, if he keeps drinking like that, he ain't gonna have no head no how sometime real soon like!* He felt a light tap on his shoulder and turned around.

"Hi handsome!" There she was again, Babs, in all her blond, blue-eyed beauty.

"Oh, now it's you again!" He took a large gulp from his drink.

"I'm sorry. I suppose I over-reacted." She said.

"Uh, just a little, maybe?"

"How 'bout a dance this time?"

"Yeah, sure. Why not?"

They both went to the dance floor and melted in with the rest of the crowd going up and down, back and forth. With the exception of Anne Troff, they were the only whites dancing. The Finger Lakers had gone back to New York earlier that afternoon.

The two North Americans danced and drank the rest of the evening away, Buster being careful not to say too much to this straight, white girl that he did not really know. He was especially careful not to mention the word Polish again or any of its derivatives. They enjoyed themselves. Buster really loved to watch Babs' movements while fast dancing. She drove his imagination to good distances: that wonderful pelvis in motion and incarcerated breasts in her bra trying to sway back and forth on her chest. *Not bad*, he thought, *Not bad*! Barbara, too, liked the way Buster moved—especially in the slow dances. They fit together. Even though she was on the tall side, their pelvises meshed and she could feel the nice hardness of his pant-imprisoned wang pressing up against the lower extremities of her stomach.

Everything was going fantastically well at the dance; everybody was in high spirits. But when midnight rolled around and a fat, mongoloid figure entered the bar, there was an instant, fearful hush. Even the student musicians stopped playing and there was a terrible silence filled with bad vibrations. Students started filtering out of the place in large groups. Only the local islanders remained. All of the faces of the students were long and drawn and shades of anger came out of their eyes.

What happened was that earlier in the week, the

student body was informed by Mr. Ginnis that the new assistant warden of the campus was Mr. Patrick Cramble, and that he was to be under the direct orders of Father Villeneuve, the morals keeper on campus. And because Father Villeneuve wanted everybody to be good, upright Christians, he had placed a curfew on the campus: all students were to be back in their hostels by 12:30 and lights out at 1:00 on Friday and Saturday nights. On weekdays, the curfew was 11:00 at night, lights out by 12:00. Mr. "Do-Goodie" himself, Patrick Cramble, enforced these orders to the very second.

This scene outright enraged Buster. *Why did these students have to go?* he asked himself. *They were fucking adults, not little children. They didn't need anybody to tell them what time to go to bed. Some of the students were older than Cramble himself, yet he was telling them that now was the time to go home and tuck in for the night? Ridiculous!*

Buster walked over to Cramble who was standing in the corner invigilating, taking notes. "Hey, uh, Cramble," he said, "Hey, uh … you're not taking this assistant warden business seriously now, are you?"

"I most certainly am," he said effeminately. "Why shouldn't I be?"

"Well, look, it's Friday night! There's nothing for them to do tomorrow! Besides, they were really enjoying themselves until you came along playing Dragnet."

"Hey listen, you. You tend to your own knitting and I'll tend to mine!"

"What? Knitting? Jesus, that's good vocabulary, Cramble! Well let me remind you, though, you're in a very unpopular position, and you're asking for trouble."

"I'll take my chances, you!"

Buster turned away and joined Babs at the bar. "Wow!" he said to her. "That guy is really sick. I mean sick!"

"Who is he?" she asked.

"Well, Miss Barbara, that poor excuse of a man is Mr. Patrick Cramble. I'm sorry to say and truly hate to admit that that flaming, mal-formed, animalistic asshole happens to be a fellow American and my deranged roommate."

"He does look a bit strange, doesn't he?"

"That's not the word for it—and he's making me sick right now just by being in my line of sight. He's embarrassing! Let's get out of here!"

"How 'bout a spin in my car?" Babs said, once again pronouncing about like "A-boot."

"Fine! Let's pass by the college and I'll drop off Naomi."

"I'll be right behind you."

They walked out of the bar, passing right by Cramble. Buster ignored him completely. They went to their vehicles and headed for the college. Buster was still perturbed at Cramble and found it hard to believe that he was actually playing policeman. But he did not let it bother him too much, for his concentration energies were rapidly swinging over to that lovely lady following right in back of him. *I think I got her now,* he thought. *All I have to do now is put a dynamite lip-lock on her and it'll be all over—Just like R.B. said. But keep your cool, Murdock. Don't rush in like a horny rooster! Let her do the work. I think I'm just going to sit back and let it all happen.*

They pulled up to the apartment. Buster put Naomi on her stand and got in the shot-gun seat of Barbara's Vauxhall Viva. She jammed it in first gear, but let the clutch out too fast. The car jerked and screeched several times before it smoothed out to an unsteady glide.

"Whoa!" Buster said. "Women drivers!"

"No, I just got this car for Christmas," she explained. "It must be fourth-hand on the island, and I'm still not used to the gears. That's all."

"Oh, I see! By the way, where are we going?" Buster asked.

"Well, I thought maybe just a little spin to the west end. I know a nice place. It's a nice change from the noise at the Rip."

"You're the driver."

There was a silence as the car moved down the main island road. They both felt uncomfortable. The silence was too uncomfortable for Buster, so he decided to break it. "Babs, what ever brought you down to this God-awful, end-of-the earth place?"

"That's funny. I was going to ask you the same thing," she said, both hands on the wheel, eyes cautiously on the road. "Well, let's see. I just graduated from the University of Toronto in Physics and they offered me a full scholarship to graduate school. But I was so tired of being a student and sick of Toronto that I just had to do something for a change. One day last June at the student union building there was an announcement on the bulletin board posted by the Bahamian Ministry of Education, a poster advertising teaching positions in the Bahamas. It was really just what I wanted—a total change of everything—at least for a while: change of climate, culture, scenery, situations, you know?"

"Yeah, I suppose so. Boy, what a change, too, right? What did your family think about all this?"

"Oh, they flipped! Especially my boyfriend, Brad."

"Oh, you have a boyfriend back home?"

"Yes, I do. He asked me to marry him just before I left."

*Jesus Christ*! Buster thought, looking out the window.

*Here we go again! Why did every fucking girl have to have a boyfriend back home? Back-home boyfriends always ruin everything. Can't women be independent once in a while and leave their fucking back-home boyfriends behind"*

"And what happened?" he asked her.

"Oh, I love him very much," she said nonchalantly, "and I accepted. But first I told him that I had to come down here to be on my own and enjoy my youth a little bit—one year would be sufficient. Also, I would be able to work down here and save money enough so when I return, we could move into a nice apartment and be monetarily comfortable while I go to graduate school. By then he would be out of school, too, and start selling stocks and bonds."

"Stocks and bonds?"

"Yes, stocks and bonds."

"Would you still have the scholarship when you go back?"

"Oh, yes. I obtained a one-year waiver."

"Wow! You seem to have everything planned out in your life!"

"Well, so far, things are going according to plans. What about you?"

"Me? Well, as you have seen these past couple of days, I'm a college teacher—myself just out of graduate school at the University of Florida since August. But now, I suppose I've converted into a dope-blowing adventurer ready to see the world. As far as this gig goes here, well, anything can happen after June. I haven't the slightest idea, and really, I could care less at the moment. That's my future!"

"Oh, dear, dope blowing? Oh dear, do you smoke drugs?"

"No, I smoke marijuana and hashish. Does that scare you?"

"Well, I must say, I've never met anybody who has, but it sounds interesting."

"Interesting?"

"You seem to be quite normal, too."

"Normal?"

"Yes! Well, what I mean is, you don't seem to be like what the anti-drug people say: marijuana smokers turn into mindless paraplegics and listless zombies."

"Yeah, man, you don't know me yet! I'm actually a zombied-out paraplegic." He went into a curled fingered hand and side mouthed tongue-in-cheek routine.

"Oh, don't be silly! Oh, this is the turn off." She braked and turned down a sandy road, heading towards the beach.

"Barbara, just where are we going?" he emphasized.

"I would like to show you a real nice beach—it's my own private beach and nobody knows it but me!"

"Oh, that's nice!" he said. Then flashes of confusion hit him: *Hey, this chick's up to something, Murdock. Be smart now, Buster ol' boy—don't blow it! Keep cool—act as if you're not interested, and don't say Polack!*

The car came to a stop right at the end of a beautiful, sprawling beach. It was lit by a three-quarter moon, the light casting a gray hue on the beach and boulders and making a road of light on the sea.

*Oh my God!* Buster thought. *What do I do now? She has stopped the car. What the fuck do I do now?*

"Welcome to my beach," she said and slid over to Buster's side of the car. "Oh, don't get the wrong idea, Buster. It's just that my door here won't open from the inside, so we have to use yours."

"Oh, I see," he said, his heart beating wildly. "Well then, we get out, right?"

"Uh huh!" she said, learning more towards him.

"Hey, uh, Babs," he said suddenly, putting his arm

quickly around her, "Well, uh… if you really want to know the truth, uh, I don't know what to do!"

"What do you mean?" Her shoulders started to cuddle.

"Well, uh, what I mean is, uh … well, it's been so long since I've had a sheep in my arms that …"

"Sheep?"

"Huh?"

"You said sheep!"

"Did I say sheep?"

"Yes you did." She looked at him closely.

Buster cringed and thought: *Oh, Jesus! God-dammit, Murdock, don't fucking blow it! Don't open your dumb-ass mouth anymore, for Christ's sakes! Lip lock!*

He slowly placed his lips on hers, and she rapidly opened up his mouth with her tongue. She then started crawling all over him.

*Wow!* he thought, surprised. *This is totally unexpected— especially coming from a conservative, engaged Canadian.* He felt her tongue encircle his palate. *Jesus, I've never done it in a Vauxhall Viva before. Volkswagens in drive-in movies, OK, but this has definitely got to be a first. Oh Jesus!* He felt her hand move on top of the bulk outside his pants. *Ahhhhhh!* He slipped his hand underneath her dress to a glorious warm bush. Then all of a sudden, she stopped cold and withdrew her tongue back into her own territory behind her rosy lips.

"OK, that's enough for tonight!" she said curtly.

"What?"

"I said, that's enough for tonight—we don't want to take this too seriously now, do we?" She sat upright like a rigid schoolteacher.

"But we just started!"

"And we just ended! There'll be other times."

"Oh there will, will there?" he said perturbed, his dork sagging like a wilted hot dog, his balls aching and moving up and down like roller coasters.

"Well, I hope so, don't you think? I just don't want you to think bad of me—especially the first night!"

"Oh, it's one of those, then!" he said. "OK, it's your game, baby. I could give a big flying fuck! Let me outta here, I need some fresh air."

He opened the door and started walking down the beach alone. He was in pain. It hadn't been since early high school that he had had a serious case of the blue-balls. "Fucking fickle women," he mumbled. "They don't know what they want—especially this one—engaged and everything. Jesus, give me a break! Why is it that women always think they can maneuver us men? Damn!"

Barbara ran up to him and coupled her arm with his. Walking and looking at Buster in the moonlight, she softly asked, "Are you mad?"

"About what?"

"About cutting you off like that. I feel sort of bad now!"

"No, forget it!"

"It's just that I don't want you to think wrongly of me—especially being the first night."

"Hey, forget it, OK? I'd like to go home now."

"Right—Home—OK."

They went back to the car and climbed in the one door that opened. There was total silence driving back to the college, but this time it was not an uncomfortable silence like the anticipation that prevailed on the way to the beach. Buster was tired and his rum drinks at the Rip were taking on their after-effects: he was blank and could not think. Barbara also was tired but hoping that she hadn't hurt

Buster's feelings. She thought that maybe what she did was dumb after all and hoped he would understand and not immediately discard her. She was also thinking about that "Dreadful" drive back to the Navy base. She was not looking forward to that at all.

They finally reached the college. Barbara swerved her car up to Buster's door, stopping but leaving the engine running. He opened the door and stepped out.

"Buster?" she said, trying to make up to him. "How 'bout a movie at the Coast Guard station tomorrow night?" "'bout" sounding like "a boot."

"Uh … let's see, tomorrow is Saturday, right? Or today is Saturday—that's right. Uh … listen, I've got campus duty—which means I gotta stay on the campus tomorrow night. But if you'd like, why not come over here for dinner. That is, if you trust my cooking. Afterwards, I'll give you a grand tour of the college."

"Oh, that sounds wonderful!"

"OK, I'll see you tomorrow about 5:00 then." He leaned into the car and gentlemanly-like kissed her on the lips. She warmly responded.

He slammed the door shut, waved goodbye and walked into his apartment. *Jesus Christ*! he thought. *Fucking women—always trying to be pure with their bodies, but in reality having more sex desires and fantasies than men. This purity bit is all theater and this chick is no different.* So now Buster could understand Barbara's reactions. He felt good and knew inside that a couple more nights and a couple more lip-locks and he would have her.

Buster had campus duty Saturday night. Every college instructor had their own night once a month to make the rounds on campus, making sure the doors and windows were closed and locked and the lights were turned off: also making sure that none of the students were up to any mischief. This was Father Villeneuve's idea—keeping Christian security on campus.

It started out to be a normal evening on campus. Barbara came over and had dinner with Buster; the Polish Canadian beauty surviving the American cuisine of fried hamburger, white rice and tomato sauce, with rum and Coke to drink. After several drinks and an interesting conversation about ordinary likes and dislikes of everyday life, they started to walk around the campus. They first approached the dormitory area with everything seemingly to be all quiet. Then they passed the classroom area, which seemed to be all right as well, with the exception of a few lights left on. Barbara thought it absolutely ludicrous to be making duty rounds. It was something school patrols did in her elementary school. But Buster kind of liked it. It made him feel important.

They rounded the corner of a classroom building when Buster spotted lights on in the Arts and Crafts building. There were some people standing outside. It looked rather fishy, so they walked over. There were several students standing outside by the door and on the steps. A very eerie sound of moans and groans came oozing out of the opened windows. Buster felt bad vibrations, and Barbara grabbed his arm. They walked up the steps and encountered three senior students blocking the door.

"Good Evening, Mr. Murdock," a tall student muttered. "What are you doing here?"

Buster recognized him as Frederick Darey. "Hello, Frederick! I'm on duty and gotta check the place out. I might ask you the same thing, buddy. What's going on here?"

"Revival, sir." He said smirking. "Come on in!"

Buster walked into the entranceway and peered into the room, his heart beating madly. He saw the room filled with his own students sitting at desks, moaning and groaning wildly. Everybody was crying and shaking their heads. One girl was standing alongside her desk wailing away, talking to the spirit in a loud, penetrating voice.

"Yes, Sir, Dear Jesus," she wailed. "Oh Lord, God! Yes, Sir—Yes, Sir!"

Carol Monson, a self-confessed preacher and senior student in charge of all this was standing in front of the group, his head bowed down into his cupped hands.

"Yes, Sir, Dear Jesus!" the girl continued. "Oh Lord—God—Yes, Sir—Yes, Sir!"

There were a few other male students standing in the corner of the room with the look of fear in their eyes as if they were not quite sure what was happening.

Buster was scared, too. With all his years living in the South, he had never been to a Baptist revival before. He had heard that they were filled with moaning and groaning, but did not realize they would be so frightening.

He turned back to Frederick Darey. "Frederick, what is all this bullshit?"

"Talking to Lord Jesus, sir!" he answered.

"Well, how come you're not in all this madness?"

"I just got out, sir!"

The wailing of the girl student continued. "Yes, sir, Dear Jesus—Oh Lord, Oh Lord!" Then her voice, trembling more than ever, let out a gigantic scream that split the moans and groans in half. She ran out of the room screaming at the top of her lungs, running madly back to her dormitory.

Buster turned to Barbara: "Uh … well, I do believe it's

time to go now!" He pushed his way through the door. "Let's go Barbara. Hey, Frederick, take care of that girl, will ya? Go see if she's all right!"

"Yes, sir!"

"And when this madness is all over, turn out the lights, will ya?"

"Yes, Mr. Murdock!"

Barbara and Buster both hurried down the stairs. "Let's get the Motherfuck out of here!" he said. "Jesus, I'm gonna have nightmares, now, I know!" They walked towards the beach, Barbara on Buster's arm, the screaming and yelling of the girl still coming out of her dormitory.

But Barbara seemed to be relatively composed throughout all of this. "You seem to be taking this OK," Buster said, still shaking a little.

"Well, I've seen this before," she said softly. "They have these up at the high school every once in a while. Berry Silversmith explained to me that these islanders are very superstitious still, and their belief in the Spirit is one of the only things they have to keep them going on these islands. With little or no modern conveniences—no television, no newspapers and hardly any books, their range of comprehension is limited only to their feelings—feelings that must come out in the form of physical expression to the Spirit; this Spirit formed by the common, emotional energies generated at these meetings."

"Jesus Christ, whatever happened to the old Communion with wine and a little wafer?"

"Well, maybe that's what's wrong with the religion we have. It lacks these spiritual feelings. How many times has that wafer and wine really moved you?"

"Jesus, it only gave me sore knees!"

"See? That's what I'm saying. I think that what they're doing here, as primitive as it seems to us, is good for them. They need it—maybe we do, too!"

"Yeah, maybe you're right. Whew! Anyway, sort of a harrowing experience, being the first time and all."

"Easy now! Shall we walk on the beach?" she suggested.

"Sure!"

They took their shoes off and walked down the moonlit, sandy beach, leaving the only footsteps on the entire sandy shoreline. They reached about half-way down the beach and sat down, looking out to sea—the road of moonlight rippling on the water.

"Beautiful," Buster said softly, "It's just beautiful out tonight."

"It sure is," Barbara said. "It makes it worth being down on an island in the middle of nowhere, eh?"

"Oh, is that where we are? On an island?" He looked at her, her silhouetted lips begging for a kiss. Buster conformed, placing a hard lip-lock on her. Then they fell to the sand. Barbara quickly unfastened his belt and wrapped her hand around his tool, going up and down in a gentle, slow motion.

*What the hell?* Buster thought. *Might as well not take these things too fast. Little by little! Let her get her jollies off. Above all, Murdock, don't attack her like a horny Coastie! I'd scare her away. Let her imagination fly for a while. Oh God that feels good!*

*I wonder if he's liking this?* Barbara thought. *I hope I don't hurt him doing this too hard. I wonder what Brad will think? Oh dear, Buster's kiss is strong and wet. Oh my, this thing takes up my whole hand. The hell with Brad! He's up there and I'm down here. I hope Buster will be satisfied with just this tonight. I don't want him to think I'm easy and would do it with just anyone. Oh, my! What happened?*

Her hand filled with a warm, slimy substance. "Eeeeww!" she said to Buster, withdrawing her hand from his pants. "You should have told me you were coming!"

"Well, you didn't ask! Here—take this!" He sat up and handed her a handkerchief.

She wiped her hand, wiped Buster's apparatus a little, then buried the cloth in the sand. "You don't mind do you?"

"Hell, what's a hankie?"

"How do you feel?" she asked.

"Oh, very good, thanks," he answered. "How are you doing?"

"Oh, marvelously well!" They embraced and fell back in the sand. They lay for several minutes until they noticed the breeze taking on a chill.

"Shall we go?" she suggested.

"Sure!"

They got up to walk back to the apartment. Before they left the beach, Buster took one last look back at the moonlit sand. Only their footprints marked the beach: footprints that lead to the indentation of their bodies imprinted on the smooth surface of sand.

"Hmm," he said softly to her, "I ought to have campus duty more often."

And it got carried away after that beach scene. Barbara lost all her inhibitions and fears of making love with Buster. She had no regrets whatsoever for cheating on Brad, either. As she had thought down on the beach over and over again—he was up there and she was down on San Salvador. Her philosophy was that she was young and on a year's adventure—out of the norm. Why not try a bit of everything, especially enjoy her body? She thought, why the hell not? She let it loose and started taking birth control pills that she had bought in Nassau just in case. She started seeing Buster about every other night, going over to his place or Buster biking over to hers. She always wanted to be with him: security, she thought. Lying in bed with a strong man that she liked and knew she was going to see often had a comfortable feeling behind it. And she knew that even though this would not last, at least she would have Brad to go back to in the summer. Nothing gained, nothing lost.

As for Buster, well, easy come, easy go, he thought. He could not take this thing too seriously because it was all happening so fast that he was not quite sure it was true or if he was just hallucinating. Why was this happening to him, anyway? He thought. Seemingly ten million hungry guys on the island and the only single white girl happens to pick him out. It was hard for him to comprehend. He was not quite sure how long it was going to last. Maybe it would last a couple of days or a couple of weeks, then she would tire of him and go onto a Coastie or a tourist or somebody. *But what the fuck?* he philosophized. *Take it as it comes, Murdock ol' boy, easy, easy—no emotional problems—Better than fucking sheep for now, anyhow!*

Buster was curious as to why Babs left the Coast Guard captain—or why he had left her, or whatever. It all came clear to him one evening when he outright asked Babs. She frankly explained that there were three main reasons: First, and most important, Greg White was a premature ejaculator. The few times they tried it, four to be exact, he always left her high and dry while he spurted out on her breasts and military sheets. He would then roll over, say "Thank you, Ma'am," and fall asleep. Secondly, he was not his own man. He kept following her around like a little puppy dog, kissing her ass, trying to do everything to please her and doing everything she said. She found great difficulty in trying to comprehend how he could be a leader of men. And finally, he used her as a social puppet: taking her to dry Bahamian and English parties, trying to play like he had it made with a beautiful, blonde chick by his side—a successful, well educated Coast Guard captain sucking on gin and tonics and keeping the image. She could not stand it: "Absolutely dreadful!" she said. White had no spark, no adventurous spirit to him. It was everything according to society his whole life. She could not stand it. There were too many guys like him in Canada. On her year abroad she needed somebody different. She needed somebody to dominate her, somebody to tell her what to do and not the other way around. It was probably her Old World, Catholic background coming out in her, but it was so true. As far as she was concerned, a man that was so prissy as to follow her around was no man at all. Security and domination was what she needed. And even though Buster did not know this at first, he could not give a "Big flying fuck" either. He had his own problems.

One of these problems was his roommate, Patrick Cramble. He was becoming a big, royal pain in the ass. Tranquil island living was destroyed by this Baby Huey mental case that resided in the room next to him. Cramble had decided to conduct his student conferences on Remedial Reading Methodology and Elementary School learning habits (which was totally absurd because Cramble had never even been close to a Bahamian elementary school building let alone Bahamian children) in the comforts of his own room. This meant a steady barrage of students coming in and out of the apartment all hours of the day and night: opening and closing the front door of the apartment, traipsing by

Buster's room door, talking, laughing and singing. Every group that finished and walked out of Cramble's room had to pass by Buster's door on the way out. Buster could hear them commenting on how weird, how very strange-weird that "White dude" was.

Buster several times had politely mentioned this disturbance to Cramble, but the shaggy dog fat man always turned away, completely ignoring him. It came to a peak one night when Buster was reading Alexander Solzhenitsyn's novel, *The First Circle*, a book that required much concentration and time out for philosophical reflection. But his reading was constantly interrupted by talking, laughing students passing by his room. This tore at Buster's spirit. It seemed to take him by the heart and squeeze adrenalin out of his aorta. He thought, *Christ, if I can't have peace and tranquility on a small, fucking island in the Bahamas, why in the hell am I down here in the first place? After all, isn't that what islands are supposed to be about, peace and tranquility?* He could not take it any longer. He shot out of his reading chair, threw the paperback book on his desk and barged into Cramble's room. There Cramble was, sitting at his desk, officially consulting three innocent male students sitting with their hands in their laps. Two other students were standing, waiting outside the door.

"Hey, Cramble—Hey, man, this just can't be!" Buster blurted out.

"What do you mean?"

Buster raised his voice. "I mean like there are ten million students coming in and out of my house, man, and they're bothering me! You got what I mean, man? I've told you this before—but now it's just gone too far. I need quiet around here!"

Cramble turned to his students. "Step outside for a moment, will you please?" They got up and left the room, closing the door behind them. Then he turned to Buster. "Now you listen here, you," he said in a raised but still effeminate, soft voice. "I'll do what I want in my own room!"

"No you won't!" Buster responded immediately, his arms beginning to flail in the air. "This is my house, God-dammit! It's not a fucking classroom building. Take these students elsewhere! This is not Grand Central Station, you know!"

"Now listen here, you. You're not going to tell me what to do!"

"The hell I'm not!" he yelled, his eyes coming out of his head in anger. He went up closer to Cramble's large, but droopy, fat body. "And if you don't get them outta here, I'm gonna slap your flabby face silly. Then I'm gonna proceed to knock your fucking mongoloid block off! Ya got that?"

"Oh, dear me!" Cramble said, withdrawing, putting his hand up to his mouth in total surprise. "Well, well…. We'll just see what Mr. Ginnis has to say about this!"

"What?"

"Yes! I'm going to tell Mr. Ginnis!"

"Jesus Christ! Did you really say that?"

"I most certainly did!"

"Well, I'm really scared, you know? You go right ahead and do that, OK? And don't forget to tell him that I live here, too—Asshole!"

Buster stormed out of the room. The corridor had filled with students waiting for conferences. Some of them had their ears up against the walls listening in.

"Mr. Cramble is sick!" Buster announced to them. "He will be unavailable for consultation for the rest of the evening. Everybody go home! Good night!"

The scurry of footsteps sounded like a flock of sheep going out of the apartment. Buster got on Naomi and went to the Riding Rock for a stiff drink, thinking all the time only one word: "Asshole!"

Another small problem that was becoming bigger was Father Villeneuve, the almighty standard of morals keeper and Religion lecturer on campus. Buster's first impression of this black, Abraham Lincoln looking priest was that of divine admiration—especially in the way the man conducted services and delivered the sermons at church: dynamically and overpoweringly. But slowly Buster was beginning to discover that Father Villeneuve, possessing the word of God, was actually controlling the actions of the Bahamian college administration. Because he had this powerful possession of direct contact with God, everybody listened to what he said. He made the rules and whatever he said was final: Osborne Stubbs and Mr. Ginnis being two of the biggest believers and followers of Father Villeneuve's word.

But it was not this that bothered Buster so much as to the hypocrisy of the man that he was slowly discovering. When he talked to the seemingly liberal-minded preacher, the man of God was all smiles and back slapping, always wearing a silver cross around his neck to remind everybody of his spiritual powers. But then he would turn around and walk away, leaving Buster with a feeling of uneasiness and mistrust about the man: such as, he wondered what this guy was really up to—like a politician looking for a vote.

These convictions were strengthened when one afternoon Father Villeneuve came over to Buster's place and started talking nonchalantly about pre-marital sex: how he was all for it and that one had to try things out before taking big steps etc., etc. But Buster felt uneasy in the conversation and was wondering the whole time what this guy was trying to get at.

"But one must not go around broadcasting pre-marital activities like it was common place and acceptable to older generation Christian believers," the preacher said.

"Of course not, Father—you're absolutely right!" Buster said.

"And therefore, maybe you better not have that white school teacher at the Navy base leave her car in front here overnight."

"What?" Buster could not believe what he had just heard.

"Yes, Buster, my child, you are still new here and do not know fully yet that people around here have bad thoughts and rumors spread quickly."

"Well, so what, Father? Let them fly! I could give a big flying ... uh," he caught himself just in time. "Uh ... what I mean is ... I don't care what people think, and besides, you said yourself that expressing love is not bad."

"Yes my son, but the students here are very delicate and we must watch over them very carefully. When they see this lady's car they get wrong ideas. It's a bad influence on them."

"Jesus Christ!"

"Pardon me?"

"Uh, no, I mean ... uh ... well—OK, Father. No car in front, OK?"

"That is the spirit Buster, my son."

*I wish he wouldn't call me his fucking son*! Buster thought. *I'm not his son—he's only a couple of years older that I am. Jesus*!

"Now we would not want to rock the boat here on the island, would we my son?" Villeneuve said, putting his arm around Buster.

"Oh, no, Father —of course not! No rocking the boat!"

After this conversation, Buster went over to the Navy base to inform Barbara. She was sitting in her living room with both Berry and Ethlyn Silversmith. Buster blurted out exactly what the preacher man said. Babs was embarrassed and turned red, but Berry burst out laughing.

"He's the bloody one to talk—the stupid twit!" Berry said, trying to catch his breath. He brushed back his 1957 pompadour with his hand. "Why it 'twas just two years ago before he got married that I walked in on him and Anne fucking away in the back bedroom of Osborne Stubbs' cottage. Stubbs had sent me from his office over to his place to pick up some bleedin' administration folders in his room—not knowing, or at least forgetting, that the divine couple was at his place. That's one of the reasons why the two had to get married. I took advantage of the occasion and told a few people. Before I knew it, rumors spread around so fast that a big scandal developed on the island. Father Villeneuve ever since then not only hates me, but fears me as well. So he leaves me alone."

"Jesus Christ!" Buster said. "Now I don't feel so bad."

"He was stupid in saying that to you, the bloody hypocrite!" Berry continued. The girls started to laugh at the whole matter. "If he knew that you always come up here and that you know me, I think he would have thought twice about approaching you like that—the bleedin' bastard."

After Berry's explanation, things started to clear away and become lighter in Buster's mind. They all had a good snort of Matuselem Rum found in Babs' cupboard and toasted to the "White" schoolteachers' health and sexual activities.

# CHAPTER 8

## *The Season for Love & High Seas*

I t was in the early part of February when more bad weather came. One early evening while Buster was playing a little solo basketball at the Navy base, he looked out to sea and flashed on three gigantic waterspouts contrasting against the horizon line. He was amazed, because it was only seven minutes before that he had looked out at the same place and they were not there—he had seen only a few black clouds forming. The spouts were awesome: three jet-black funnels right in a row, all three the same size and shape—wide at the top forming from high, black clouds, then snaking down to the water line, ready to tap out of existence anything and everything that was sucked up into their paths. Buster stopped dribbling the basketball and just stared, repeating "Jesus" over and over again. He had never seen anything like this before. He had heard of waterspouts in the Bahamas, but three in a row like this was beyond his imagination. He had also read a book on the Bermuda Triangle. He had read that the island of San Salvador was right-smack-dab in the middle of the triangle. He remembered chapter after chapter of boats strangely disappearing and entire flight squadrons being picked out of nowhere with no explanation whatsoever left behind from the disappearance. But with phenomena like this happening right before his eyes—especially the rapidity of their appearance—the Bermuda Triangle was no longer a mystery to him. The power of these potential tornadoes was immeasurable, and the wrath of God could come down to all living creatures that had the misfortune of getting in their way.

But the chances of them hitting San Salvador were remote. They were too far away and the chance-ratio of hitting a small land dot in the middle of the ocean was one in two million. Buster, however, said a prayer out loud, anyway, thanking the Lord that he was on firm ground and not out floating in a boat.

It was only a half an hour after sighting these monsters when high winds and sheets of rain hit the island, ripping through the Navy base, breaking windows and wooden shutters. The storm came so suddenly that it was unthinkable that Buster return to the college on Naomi. It was a very good excuse to stay at Babs' small efficiency apartment and have spaghetti and wine and play strip poker for dessert.

The high winds and heavy rains lasted well over a week-and-a-half. Because the classrooms at the college kept flooding, classes were held only sporadically: which meant therefore, not much to do—lots of idle time for nothing— idle time to be whittled away, cooped up in the house. This brought on another depression for Buster. He hated being imprisoned inside, not being able to enjoy the benefits of the island. After all, that is what he came down to the Bahamas for: to do lots of swimming, diving and sailing. But all winter long, he had done none of this. His time had been more occupied with getting stoned, beginning romances and taking care of work tasks. Maybe the spring would be better, he thought. And that's all he could think of while he was inside his room, the wind and rain pounding his closed windows.

During this period, the only really constructive thing he could do was read. He had gone to the campus library, Peter Kentard's pride and joy, and checked out volumes of books from obscure novels to travel and geography books. He also read a potpourri of tomes he had brought down from the States for Christmas. He devoured the books like they were his last grasp at sanity on the island. The texts fed his mind, keeping it from drifting too far into the depths of mindless mediocrity and longing to be someplace else. The list was quite extensive with some popular titles he had always wanted to read but never seemed to have the time. Now was the time: *The Magic Mountain*, *War and Peace*, *Anna Karenina*, *Doctor Zhivago*, *Crime and Punishment*, *Fathers and Sons*, *Gulliver's Travels*, *A Tale of Two Cities*, *The Adventures of Don Quixote*, *The Count of Monte Cristo*, *The Three Musketeers*, *Faust Part One*, *Faust Part Two*, *Moby Dick*, *Uncle Tom's Cabin*, *Gone with the Wind*, *The Seed*, *The Politics of Ecstasy*, *The Teachings of Don Juan (A Yaqui Way of Knowledge)*, *On the Road*, *Naked Lunch*—and the list started degenerating from the Beats on down.

Receiving letters was now a lost cause. Just to think about not getting letters sunk Buster back more deeply into depression. But he did write a few letters to old friends and family when he got a sudden urge to talk to somebody.

In his writing he built things up on the island with his imagination. This made things look better for him. After writing, he felt better—even though thinking that maybe these letters would never arrive.

The Cramble controversy ended as quickly as it had started. The students no longer came over to the house. Evidently, Buster's words were strong enough to scare the oversized pants off of Cramble, but they still did not stop him from leaving gigantic logs in the bathroom bowl. And while the relationship of courtesy was slowly dwindling between the roommates, Cramble's popularity amongst the students was on the rapid descent downhill. He had busted up a couple more Rips, which the students did not like at all. They detested a teacher telling them what to do like that—especially a white one. They were adults themselves. Some were even married with children on other islands. Who was this "Nit-Wit, scatter-brained, fat-ass white man" telling them what time to go to bed? It was absurd! One Saturday morning Cramble got out of bed, walked outside and found both tires on his Honda Fifty scooter flat with two fat, rusty nails in each tire. He got them patched up the same day; but when he busted up the Rip the following week, the same thing happened again—two nice big, beautiful flat tires. It took him quite a while before it dawned on him that these flat tires were possibly a direct consequence of his playing Elliot Ness. But this would not stop him, "By God!" The divine law must be carried out and it was Cramble's divine duty to see that it was good!

Barbara helped a great deal in relieving Buster's combat against loneliness, and vice versa. Barbara several times wrote to Brad up in Canada and she received a few love letters herself. But there was nothing like a smooth, masculine voice close to her ears and a warm, muscular body close to her body to accompany her on cold, rainy days and nights. Buster also was comforted with the female touch in his life, but he still told himself not to take the relationship too seriously because it could end at any time.

The biggest problem, he felt, was communication with Barbara. Their backgrounds were so different that even though they spoke the same language, they were total worlds apart in cultures. Buster, now having long hair crawling down to his shoulders with his beady eyes sunk back behind his long beard, frightened Barbara, the conservative Canadian who was used to super short hair neatly trimmed around the ears. She did not even smoke marijuana, and that really bothered Buster. How could he relate to her on the same mental plane, he thought, if she stayed straight all the time? It was difficult to comprehend for him. Many times he longed for R.B.'s companionship—now there was communication, he thought.

Babs was afraid of smoking marijuana and even at the mere mention of the word she would jerk back from Buster and close up, rapidly changing the subject of conversation or suddenly remaining quiet all together. Buster tried to understand, but it was hard—especially where he came from, a metropolitan United States coastal city where the influx of people was so varied that marijuana and cocaine were commonplace. Even at the university, why it was, "No drugs—no bugs," meaning, if one did not do one form of drug or another, one just was not "Hip," not "Cool!" Even the campus police smoked on their beats—no big deal! So it was difficult for Buster to understand Barbara's explanation of the anti-drug campaign in Canada: "Drugs kill! One puff of marijuana and you're hooked for life. LSD is a trip to the insane asylum! And all that other "Reefer Madness."

But Buster did not push it. He felt that anybody so afraid of something should not be forced to do it. *What the fuck?* he thought. *Some people are afraid of taking elevators, or afraid of thirteenth floors, or stirring their coffee in the opposite direction. To each and to his own. Easy come, easy go, anyway!! I don't give a big flying fuck!*

It was time for senior teaching practice—the last week-and-a-half of February and the first week-and-a-half of March. This was when the second and third year college students left their own classrooms and went to other islands to put into practice their own teaching methods and knowledge that they were supposed to have obtained throughout the academic year. The group was divided up to go to three islands: Grand Bahama (Freeport), Andros and Eleuthera. The lecturers, overseers and coordinators of the groups were the Bachrans, John Dailey, the Rileys, the Collins, the Kentards, and of course, the almighty himself, Father Villeneuve. He was to be the roving preacher who would hop from island to island making sure the Spirit was with all students and that they were behaving themselves. A so-called "Skeleton" group of teachers were to remain on San Salvador to teach the remaining term to the first year students, of whose own teaching practice would take place on Great Abaco and Great Exuma Islands in the latter part of the spring.

Buster was a part of this skeleton corps along with Patrick Cramble and a few other lecturers. Because Buster's advanced students were leaving the island, his teaching hours were reduced to only nine hours a week; but of course, his pay stayed the same. Just what he needed, more free time! But this did not bother him very much now. He knew that in just two-and-a-half more weeks, it was spring vacation, and he would be totally liberated for two glorious weeks.

But these two-and-a-half weeks seemed to Buster more like two-and-a-half years. They just lingered on and on, and the minutes just trickled by like hours. The only grand thing that happened was his reading of the novel *Papillon* by Henri Charriere. For Buster, the book was so good, so filled with action-packed adventure on the high seas, that he could not put it down. He read the entire book twice. It filled his head with exciting ideas of escape on his own island. It gave him ideas of heading out on the mighty seas famished for any adventure that might come his own way.

He had to get off San Salvador. He needed new stimulation, new things to see and do, new places to go. He had to meet new people. He had to get away from that girl, Barbara: for although he never complained about her and was fully aware that he was very fortunate in having her while other men on the island were suffering, he needed a chance to get away. He needed a chance to establish a little distance between her and breathe freely once again for a change. With this vacation coming up, he would be able to do so, for Babs' vacation did not come until the latter part of March.

When final exams were at last administered, graded and the marks given out to the first year students (the Kentards not on his back this time), Buster gave a howl of relief and was ready to bust out of himself into freedom like a trapped miner seeing light at the end of a caved-in tunnel. Spring vacation had finally come.

Buster made his "Cavale" from the island on the mailboat, The *San Salvador Express*. "Cavale" was the French word that Papillon always used for "Escape." Papillon was always either trying to escape from prison or actually escaping from prison, and this was exactly what Buster felt like he was doing, escaping from a prison.

The young adventurer shot off San Salvador feeling like a race horse running out of the gates. On the three-day mailboat ride to Nassau, he thought of where he wanted to go for his two week vacation. He was stoned most of the time, high on marijuana amidst all the junk on the mailboat: crates, boxes, barrels, bath tubs, cars, boats, soda bottles, bags of cement, tires, lumber, paint cans, gas cylinders, plants, pigs, goats, people, spirals of rope, sewing machines, burlap bags, coconut trees. In other words, *The San Salvador Express* was a miniature Noah's Ark.

Of all the truly great literature in which Buster had buried himself, he was cast most heavily under the magical spell of the book *Papillon*. On the mailboat, he had visions of going down to Port of Spain Trinidad and getting a nice big tattoo. He had visions of going down to Columbia and chewing Coca leaves, and he wanted to meet the beautiful people of Venezuela that author Charriere talked so much about. Buster knew that the probability of his going to these places on this trip was slim, but the most important thing was that he was at least able to think on these terms. His mind was set loose, free from the fetters of his limited world on San Salvador Island.

Being out on the open sea did wonders for Buster's spirit. It gave him a complete cure to his island fever and it cleansed all of his bad thoughts. For him there was nothing more exciting, more exhilarating than to be totally surrounded by turquoise-colored water and engulfed in a three hundred and sixty degree horizon line. He felt young, free, independent and extremely high-spirited. He knew it was his time to fly, and fly he did indeed.

The young and free American went to the island of Jamaica for his "Cavale" trip. He had let all his inhibitions loose and went wild and wicked for these two weeks, leaving his mild, cooped-up English teacher mannerisms back on San Salvador. He was like a hunting dog, who, after being caged up for so long, had been finally let out, free to romp the fields chasing after anything live that moved.

In Montego Bay, Buster befriended two young, Italian, professional race car drivers who were on vacation. Snorting cocaine and smoking Ganja, the local word for marijuana, the trip was off and running, speeding around the island in a rented Ferrari as if they only had a short time left to live. They passed oceans of sugar cane fields and raced through the Blue Mountains taking every hairpin curve as if they were straightaways, several times almost not making them and landing in the coffee fields. They were so stoned that speed was no obstacle for them. They passed through Kingston only long enough to discover that they did not want to stay in a large city with such remarkable contrasts of wealth and squalor. They were on an island, and by God they were going to experience the West Indian flavor of island beauty—not city madness.

They quickly made a "Cavale" out of Kingston. They rested a few days at Negril, a medium size village on the northern tip of the island, mingling with the Rastafarians, smoking marijuana through the early hours of the morning, their philosophies on life contrasting sharply with the Rastafarians' more religious and tranquil, don't-worry-be-happy way of thought.

After six days of non-stop gallivanting around Jamaica with the Italians, it was time for Buster to start heading back to San Salvador. Taking Jamaica Airways from Montego Bay back to Nassau, the young American reflected on his stay on the largest West Indian island and wondered just how he managed to survive. He concluded that it was mere luck and that something or somebody, some force infinitely larger than he was, wanted him to continue on.

On the last leg of the three-day mailboat voyage back to San Salvador from Nassau, Buster sprawled on the top of the mailboat, nude, catching rays of the sun on the open sea. As the boat gently rocked from the swells, he had many thoughts. He reflected back on the "Cavales" he had made on his trip: some successful, some not so successful, some exciting, and none incredibly boring. His mind had been expanded greatly—new horizons opened for him and he was so glad that he had gotten off the island of San Sal for a while. But through all his "Cavales," like Papillon, Buster had to return—return to finish the year of school. It would be back to the little people with small minds, back to the intellectual prison and pseudo-sophistication, back to idle minds filled with contempt, and above all, the thing most confining, back to routine. But maybe someday, perhaps after eating enough corn meal and grits as did Papillon, and perhaps after suffering a great deal more than what he had already suffered, it would be Buster's turn to finally make his own coconut raft and drift not only to freedom, but also eventually drift to the knowledge of what he really, truly wanted in his brief, finite life in an infinitesimal, Papillonic world.

They say that Spring is the season for new love to blossom, and the Spring of 1974 on San Salvador was no exception. Love was in the air and all over the island. Or maybe it was not love, really, but just simply downright horniness. There was not much to do except swim, sail, dive and go to movies every once in a while—but after all that, what? So, the people who were fortunate enough to capture that magic energy of love, or whatever it is called, took full advantage of it. In short, couples, triples, quadruples and even more fornicated like rabbits. The weather certainly was conducive for it. Winter storms had ended and the climate was just right during the entire spring: not too cold, not too hot, and sunny skies every day.

And of course, Babs Oskalowski and Buster Murdock were no exception. Babs was there on the dock waiting for her man on the mailboat coming back from Jamaica. It is said that distance makes the heart grow fonder, and two weeks alone on San Salvador with Buster away on his "Cavale" gave Babs plenty of time to think about him and her and what she was really doing with this freak of an American. She thought of him as quite different and exciting—definitely not the old, run-of-the-mill Canadian insurance salesman. She was growing quite fond of him and remained faithful to him the whole two weeks: even though a couple of Coasties came over once, but she sent them on their drunken way. Also one night, the young, black customs man at the airport tried to seduce her, but she could not even bring herself to kiss his big, thick lips. He constantly kept saying, "Please, let me do it, please let me do it, why won't you let me do it?" This turned Babs completely off. Letters from Brad came pouring in as well, but Babs still thought that she was on her adventure and that Brad was up there and the man who was actually returning to the island and to her was that long haired, bearded, educated American freak, Buster Murdock.

As far as Buster was concerned, Babs really was not on his mind. He was so stoned out from Jamaica, in fact, so burned-out, weirded-out from all those days at sea, that he was not quite sure exactly where he was. He was not even horny. He knew that San Salvador was his destination, but he had seen so many islands that they all looked the same after a while. Plus, he had lost all concept of time and could not really tell how many days he had been gone or out to sea or anything. His clothes and Navy pea coat were dirty and oily from the boat. His hair was getting so long that it now started to part naturally down the middle of his head, and the length was now clearly on his shoulders. But with so many days at sea, the wind and salt air tied it up into knots and it looked like Rastafarian dreadlocks. His eyes were so glassy that they seemed to literally jet out of their sockets. He was truly "Spaced-out" in all senses of the word.

He got off the mailboat, and as the tradition was, he knelt and kissed the ground. Standing back up, his legs felt like rubber. He was giving them a massage when Barbara came up and flung herself on him, nearly knocking him off his weak legs.

"Jesus Christ!" he said, "What's this?"

Before he knew it, he was in the confines of his room, the four walls rocking with the motion of the boat, copulating away like a rabbit that hadn't had it in years.

The couple stayed in the room for three days solid, only leaving it to go into the kitchen every now and then to get some food that Barbara had bought beforehand at Jake Jones' dry goods store. For both lovers, the session was marvelous: three solid days of solid sex in every position imaginable and even unimaginable. There were two surprises, one on his part and one on hers. Buster was surprised because he did not even smoke anything the whole three days. He was so burned-out from Jamaica that he thought that with any more marijuana, his brain would turn into Swiss cheese. Barbara was surprised because she had never had sex like that before. She had indeed discovered something. She had

had sex with Brad—all the time, in fact, in his apartment in college, but it was usually a fifteen to twenty minute affair, then a cigarette and off to study or to sleep. But with Buster, "Good Lord" it was two hours, three hours in a row with high intensity orgasm after high intensity orgasm, doing it upside down, sideways and even standing on their heads.

"Oh my!" she thought. "He is just wonderful!"

And as for Buster: *Well, fuck*, he thought. *This welcome back to San Salvador isn't too bad—gets me in shape for tennis*!

During break periods of rest and relaxation, Barbara told Buster of the happenings and changes that had recently occurred on the island. It was all over San Salvador that John Dailey had been kicked out of the college for allegedly carrying on a love affair with one of his second year students on Eleuthra Island during teaching practice. Dailey had already moved back to Nassau to avoid more scandal. This news was hard for Buster to take, for Dailey was really the first guy he had really talked to on the island. He knew Dailey to a certain degree and knew that he was not the type of person to meddle with students, especially black ones, for Dailey was more racist than the Ku Klux Klan. But, as Buster thought, it was hard to pinpoint just exactly what island living could do to a man, and therefore was unable to say honestly, "Oh, but Dailey wouldn't do such a thing!" Also Buster thought that one day here, the next day gone seemed to be the general rule of this island. Babs also informed her lover that there was a new Coast Guard captain. Greg White was transferred. "Thank God" was the widely-accepted consensus, for nobody really liked him—a half a man, as everybody thought. He was replaced by a real leader among men, a young graduate from the United States Coast Guard Academy itself. But, according to Barbara, he seemed to hibernate in his quarters and nobody really knew him nor even saw him yet. The new group of Finger Lakers came, but they were busy being oriented to the island and kept pretty much to themselves—at least during this period of orientation. And finally, her letters from Brad were explained to Buster, but only during the least romantic times when he or she was in the bathroom taking care of necessities. As Buster was taking a royal dunk one time, Babs informed him that Brad had invested this year's annual savings in gold bricks and that he was hoping to gain a lot of money in this investment and that they could both live securely when she returned. After these statements, Buster gave a big "Heave—Ho" and produced a couple of kingly golden turds. He flushed like a cultured man. He could give a big "Flying fuck" what that "Asshole" did up there. And as she was sitting on the bowl once taking an imperial leak, she indirectly hinted that she did not write to Brad about her affair on the island—she was too unsure yet and wanted to keep her options open.

*Letters*! Buster thought. *You just can't trust 'em*!

And it was back to school for the final two-and-a-half months of the academic year—the home stretch. For Buster it was a full load, a fifteen-hour a week schedule. He hoped that it would not tax him too much and use up too many brain cells of his gray matter. In his first year Literature class, he decided to read orally Hemingway's masterpiece, *The Old Man and the Sea*. His Composition classes would mainly be expository writing themes and his Speech and Drama class would concentrate on debates, and most importantly, a one-act play written by a Bahamian female writer. He would use the video tape machine for assistance. At least he would try and make all of his classes credible for his students: something they could relate to and use in their everyday lives.

The first week back at school was not really a full week. It was Easter week and Good Friday was a holiday. *That was great*, Buster thought, *a full five-day workweek after a nice vacation would be too much.*

He was planning on spending another three-day weekend bash inside his room with Barbara. But, he was much more overjoyed when Mr. Ginnis diplomatically invited him to go on a fishing trip with him on Good Friday. They would leave early in the morning in Corporal Nightburn's boat, and stay out all day diving for conch and fishing for grouper. Buster was ecstatic. He had waited all winter for something like this and it finally came. "Sorry baby," he said to himself referring to Babs, "but love will have to wait!" So, it was back onto the high seas once again for Buster and another large dose of the Bahamian culture.

Corporal Nightburn was perhaps the most dynamic, unforgettable character that had come into Buster's life on San Salvador. He was the only official Bahamian policeman on the island. He was a huge man, standing around six feet four inches and weighing at least two hundred and fifty pounds. But the pounds were not fat—it was all solid muscle. He had this big, round head and most of the time a smile was on his face from ear to ear. When his lips were relaxed they still formed the shape of a smile. When he laughed, everyone knew it, for he threw his head back and his whole body shook out a thunderous roar of laughter. He was without a doubt one of the happiest men Buster had ever seen; however, interiorly speaking it was hard to tell if the man was the same as he showed on the outside. Having to slash goat robbers on his whipping post was certainly not what one would call a happy occasion. But nobody really saw him in this facet of his work. Most of the time people saw him drive around a small pick-up truck. When he came onto the college campus, everybody knew it. He would always honk his horn and yell and scream to let everyone know he had arrived. When he saw Buster he would let out a roar: "Hey, Murdunked! How ya doin', mann?"

"Hey Cop," Buster would reply, for everybody called him "Cop." "How are you, man?"

"Great mann, it's just great!" the Cop would reply almost every time. "Great" was his favorite word.

There were two other men who went fishing with the Cop and Buster: the mild mannered, quiet and pleasant Mr. Ginnis who had invited Buster along, and a first year student, Neville Grey. Mr. Ginnis had been a friend of Cop's for a long time and always liked to go out fishing with him in his fifteen-foot runabout boat with a one hundred and fifteen horsepower Evinrude motor. Ginnis was a rather plump man, not fat but plump, with a kind of baby face. He looked like the sort of man that could not withstand much discomfort and tried to avoid it whenever possible. But, he was quiet with a good sense of humor, and a very pleasant person to be around.

And of course there was poor Neville Grey on the boat trip as well. It was "Poor" Neville Grey because Corporal Nightborn was always yelling at the eighteen year old student throughout the entire day. "Do this and Do that!" Nightborn would say, "Don't do this!" and "Don't do that, boy!" As smiley as Nightborn was, he always seemed to need somebody to yell at. Neville, being the youngest of the lot and just a mere student, was a good target. But Neville was a good student, a delightful person, quiet in his own way, and just took the Cop's orders in stride, laughing at many of them because the orders, at times, seemed so ludicrous: for example, "Throw that line out boy, you're letting the fish get away!" the Cop would command.

So it was off to an early start that Good Friday. Cop's plans were to pick everybody up at seven o'clock sharp and be on the water by seven thirty. Being a typical Bahamian fishing trip, however, the group was picked up at nine o'clock and on the water at ten o'clock. Pre-water activities included a gas stop for the outboard motor tanks. The power was off on the pumps, so the inevitable had to happen: "Pick up the crank, boy, and crank!" Cop ordered Neville.

"Yes, Sir!" Neville said, realizing that somebody had to do it. And there he stood, cranking his heart out to fill the tanks.

Meanwhile, Mr. Ginnis was at the Jake Jones' grocery store speculating on the possibilities of hunger on the open sea. He was purchasing biscuits and cheese and sodas to curb the discomfort of hunger pangs as the day would wear on.

Finally reaching the dock, they all started loading the boat. After all the provisions were set, the men themselves piled into the boat and started their voyage out to a chain of small cays on the northwest side of the island called the Green Cay, White Cay area. The motor purred like a kitten and the boat, bouncing up and down, slapped the moderate seas like a hand splashing water in a bathtub.

"Wooooeeee!" Buster yelled, his heart feeling free and spirit flying high. "This is just fantastic!" He loved that exhilarating effect the open sea gave him.

The Cop threw back his head and laughed, his body vibrating like the outboard motor. "Just great, mann, just great!" he shouted along with Buster. "Isn't it great, Murdunked, mann?"

"Just great, man!" Buster replied, laughing and throwing his arms in the air. He felt great, too.

Mr. Ginnis was sitting in the front with a pleasant smile on his face, saying nothing but seeming to be enjoying every minute of the ride. Neville was in the back with Buster, his eyes bulging out of his head with a huge grin on his face, giggling at Cop's actions.

The first drop was to get conch. When they reached Collin' Cay, they anchored and Buster and Neville prepared to enter the water. Fins, goggles and snorkel were donned. They both looked like strange, amphibious beasts from the depths of King Neptune's realm. Buster splashed into the water first, sinking down and down. When the bubbles cleared from his vision, the vast, underwater world, clear as glass, appeared before him. This was his first time conch hunting. He had thought that the conch beds were found usually in four or five feet of water, but where they were, the bottom stretched down to at least twenty-five feet. Buster had his doubts about being able to swim all the way down to the bottom. Neville plopped into the water shortly after. Buster could see this black, bony, awkward figure of a young man trying to get adjusted to his new element. But as awkward as Neville seemed to be on land, he was a true Bahamian and knew what he was doing when it came to conch collecting. He peered down at the bottom. Buster did not see anything down there, but when Neville started making the descent, a small outline of a conch shell came into his view. Neville picked it up and scurried to the surface for air. He held up the conch to Mr. Ginnis in the boat, then started swimming down again.

*So that's how you do it!* Buster observed. *Well, if a measly student can do it, then I, a lecturer, can do it, By God!* He zeroed in on the outline of a conch shell down at the bottom. Taking a deep bite of air, he started the descent—going down, down, down. His eyes and ears started building up pressure and it felt like his whole head was going to burst. Breast-stroking down, deeper and deeper, he thought: *Lord Jesus, am I ever going to get to the fucking bottom?* He finally was almost within reach of the pink shell, just a few more feet, when suddenly a big black hand swooped down in front of him, covering the conch and then the shell disappearing right from under his nose. It was Neville. He looked right into Buster's eyes and had that look through his face mask as if to say, "Ha, ha! I beat you to it!" Buster was furious. *All that descending for nothing*, he thought. *Why you dirty, rotten student! I'm going to give you an "F" in Composition just on general principles. You've got the whole freaking ocean, man, and you steal my first conch. I'm going to have a word with you, boy, when I get this snorkel out of my mouth.* Buster's lungs were aching for new air and felt like they were going to explode. He hurried to the surface, blowing out the water in the snorkel and regaining that vital element that is so essential for human existence, air. The thought suddenly washed through his mind: *Water versus air, two totally different elements and yet so essential for all life on Earth. Fascinating!* Then he realized that he was not in a Science or Philosophy class, but hunting conch. So, it was back to the issue at hand. He saw another conch. Neville was by the boat so there would be no problem with him this time. He dove down into the depths, the conch shell getting bigger and bigger, his ears popping, sounding like somebody eating crackers in his ear lobe. He finally reached the conch shell, and with a quick swoop he picked it up. His lungs were tired already of the old air. He quickly scuttled back to the surface for air, then back to the boat to dump off his first conch. He finally did it and he felt proud of himself. After the first conch, diving got easier and easier. The American was getting so used to it, in fact, that after a while he was collecting as many as the old professional, Neville Grey. But after a few hours in the water, his ears were starting to hurt him badly. Every time he would go down to pick up a conch, an excruciating pain would shoot through his head from one ear to the other. He had had enough for the time being. He looked up at the boat. The Cop was standing up, all smiles, filled with glee at the treasure that they had found. He waved to Buster to get into the boat. It was time now to go elsewhere and catch a few fish.

"How'd you like dat, Murdunked?" Cop yelled, all smiles.

"Fantastic, fantastic!" Buster yelled back, trying to catch his breath.

Neville climbed into the boat and took his mask off. "That's deep water there, boy, deep water!" he said, taking a towel and drying his head.

"Isn't it though!" Buster said. "How are your ears?"

"They pop and don't hurt. I'm used to it, anyway."

"Yeah, mann," Cop said. "It takes a while to get used to the ears. We goin' to catch fish now, yes? OK, Brother Ginn," for Cop called Mr. Ginnis, Brother Ginn, "Up with the anchor!" Cop started the engine while Mr. Ginnis pulled up the anchor. He slipped once and nearly fell into the water. However, Brother Ginn managed to save himself from the trauma by falling down on his backside and grabbing onto the railing. Cop laughed uncontrollably. He laughed so thunderously loud that he almost fell into the water himself. Neville was in the back giggling, but Buster had an expression of concern on his face. *Was Mr. Ginnis hurt?*

he thought. He hurried to the bow of the boat. Mr. Ginnis, Buster found out, was laughing so hard himself that he let go of the anchor rope and the anchor kerplopped back into the sea. He was all right, to say the least. It was time now to catch some fish. Cop stuck the motor in forward gear, and with the anchor finally up, the seamen were off to the other side of White Cay.

The sea on the other side of White Cay was rather rough. The waves rocked the boat up and down, back and forth. Cop said that it was a moderate sea, though, and if it was rough, the waves would be coming inside the boat. They got their lines and poles out and baited the hooks with strips of filleted fish, throwing the whole works, hook, line, and sinker, overboard. Neville was rather slow at throwing his line over, and Cop got onto him about that.

"Throw you line overboard, boy!" the huge policeman said. "What are you waiting for, the fish to come hopping into the boat? Throw you line overboard—you too slow!"

"Yes, Sir!" Neville said, giggling a little. He then looked at Buster and said, "Wooooo, Lord!"

With the lines in the water the foursome waited for action. Buster began to sing: "Joy to the fishes in the deep blue sea / Joy to you and me!"

Cop let out a big laugh, "Ha! Murdunked, you all right, mann, you know dat? You all right!"

"Thanks, Cop!" Buster said. He began to sing another melody: "I'm all right / and so are you / Love your brothers / It's the thing to do / C'mon Cop, let's make a wish / Wish you'll catch the very first fish!"

"Ha, ha, Murdunked, you all right, mann!" And as soon as he said that, Cop yanked his line and up jumped a gigantic tarpon, the entire body of the fish coming clean out of the water. Cop's pole bent double; but the man was so strong, he had no problem with fighting the doomed fish.

A few minutes after Cop pulled his fish into the boat, Mr. Ginnis, sitting on the bow of the boat, caught hold of another tarpon, considerably smaller than Cop's, and hoisted it in with very little struggle. His face was one big teddy-bear grin.

Neville and Buster did not seem to be having much luck. Buster was never really a good fisherman. He always thought of fishing as being for the lucky ones. For him, fishing was all luck, and in this game, like many other games, one was either lucky or unlucky. As far as the fishing on this trip was concerned, Mr. Ginnis and Cop were having all the luck.

Because of the fish not biting on their lines, Neville and Buster became a little bored and disappointed. Neville laid down in the back seat of the boat and started singing the song, "Jesus Was A Capricorn" while Buster sat in the front seat becoming aware that he was not feeling very well. He was now conscious of the big swells that the boat was floating over. The small runabout began to bob up and down like a cork, rocking back and forth, up and down. He became dizzy and in a short time came to the stark realization that he might be getting seasick.

Mr. Ginnis looked at Buster: "Feeling bad, Mr. Murdock? You look a little pale."

"Yes, as a matter-of-fact, I am!" he answered queasily. "It's this motion going up and down and sideways, continually."

"Pass the biscuits and cheese!" Cop said, pulling his line taught from the bottom.

*God Almighty!* Buster thought. *Who could eat biscuits and cheese at a time like this?* But Buster happened to be the closest to the bag, so he prepared the snacks. The very sight of the food hurt so bad that he sat down and stuck his head between his knees. He tried desperately not to get sick, because he did not want to be the only one on board to lose his stomach. He had a strong will and momentarily felt a little better—it must have been the blood rushing to his head. He broke out the snacks once again and handed two biscuits to Cop and one to Neville.

"Ah, thank you, thank you—good for the belly!" Cop yelled, then laughed.

Buster turned to Mr. Ginnis at the bobbing bow going up and down. "No, thank you," Ginnis said, rather shakily.

"Uh, Mr. Ginnis, are you all right?" Buster asked.

"Feeling kind of bad myself," he said, licking his dried lips.

*Ah, saved!* Buster thought. *Now I won't feel so bad if I lose my guts. Jesus, seasickness is weird! There's nothing more embarrassing if you're the only one to get it, but nothing more comforting than to see someone else heaving over the side as well. Companionship, maybe- or maybe it has something to do with ego and strength.*

"Well, I know how you feel, Mr. Ginnis," Buster said. He pulled in on his line—no bites.

Cop wanted to go elsewhere—to a different drift. So they took up their lines and moved about a half mile further out to sea. The water was much deeper, bluer and the bottom looked a little more conducive to bigger fish. They dropped their lines in the water once again and waited for some nibbles.

Buster started singing, "Rocka my soul in the bosom of Abraham / Rocka my soul in the bosom of Abraham / Rocka my soul in the bosom of Abraham / Woooo—rocka my soul!"

"Alleluia brother mann!" Cop blurted out. As soon as he said that, he yanked his line and pulled up a nice big Jack fish. "Ha, ha, ha!" he laughed. "How do you like dat, Murdunked?"

"How do you do that?" Buster asked. "I've got the same bait, the same line and hook and everything! How come they're biting your line and not mine, Cop?"

"A good fisherman knows how to fish, Brother!"

"You're lucky is all!" Buster concluded.

Buster sat down in the seat and felt the motion of swells come over him once again. It was a perpetual up and down motion, rocking back and forth, side to side. "Oh Jesus, get me off this fucking boat," he said to himself. He thought that he was going to lose it anytime. He looked up from his seat to see if Mr. Ginnis was looking all right. However, he could not see him from where he was sitting. *Where in the hell did he go?* He thought. *What happened to him? Did he fall overboard?* Buster got up from his seat and peered over to the canvas-covered windshield. And there he was: Mr. Ginnis, the principal of the great San Salvador Teachers' College, flat on his back with his hands covering his face, in full contemplation as to whether he should lose his stomach or not. Buster let out a smirk and sank back into his chair, feeling somewhat relieved that he was not the only one; however, the rocking, bobbing, rolling sensation still punished him. Neville was in the back seat lying down singing the song, "Who Says God Is Dead?"

Suddenly, Cop yanked his line again and brought up another good size tarpon. Buster still had no bites, but really, at the time, catching a fish was the furthest thing from his mind. He thought: *Should I or shouldn't I throw up? Dammit if I'm gonna put my head over the side. I just don't want to get sick!*

He started to think of Disneyland and of Mickey Mouse and Donald Duck. Before he knew it, he was actually feeling a little better and more confident that he was going to conquer the seasickness.

Neville was still singing "Who Says God Is Dead." He had a rich spiritual voice and it sounded very good.

Cop started baiting his line again, when all of a sudden he let out a tremendous sounding, juicy fart that vibrated the whole boat. A few fish jumped out of the sea. Even Mr. Ginnis took his hands from his face and leaned upward—shocked at the thunderous sound of such an obscene act. "It ain't me, mann!" said Cop, shaking his head innocently. "It ain't me, mann!"

"Wow, Cop!" Buster exclaimed. "Gross me out, man! Are you wearing tight shoes or something?"

From that question, Cop threw his head back and roared with laughter. Mr. Ginnis, getting up now, began to whoop and holler, and Neville chuckled. Cop threw his line out, but it was a poor cast because he was laughing so hard. All crew members on the boat were in a frenzy, laughing so hard that they were falling all over the seats. Mr. Ginnis nearly fell off the bow again.

"Great, mann!" Cop said. "Just great! Ha, tight shoes, great!"

"Oh Lord, Oh Lord!" Ginnis blurted, holding his aching stomach from laughing so hard.

"Jesus was a Capricorn—He ate organic foods!" Neville began singing.

The laughter started to subside after about fifteen minutes, as well as did any thoughts of seasickness. Both Mr. Ginnis and Buster were feeling much better. They both had no idea that one giant, obscene remark, a word of wisdom coming from the voice of Cop, had so much cure for seasickness.

A few more booming, philosophical comments from Cop and several more fish later, the group brought in their lines and headed homeward. It was getting late and Neville was concerned about missing the students' party at the club. He wanted to get back, but Cop had one final thing on his mind: more conchs. They made a turn towards Green Cay and just off shore of the Cay, Neville and Buster took their second plunge into the sea for more conch. It was much more shallow than the last place and Buster's ears did not hurt nearly as bad. The area was literally infested with the shells. He and Neville were picking them up by the handfuls—four and five at a time. Both Mr. Ginnis and Cop were taking them from their hands as quickly as they could. It did not take long for the whole boat to fill up with conch.

"We better save some for the natives!" Buster said, wanting to get in the boat.

"That's enough for me!" Cop yelled, exuberant over the find. "Now go down and get a few for yourself! Ha, ha!" Buster dove down to get handfuls and handfuls more.

Finally, the boat just could not take any more shells. The two divers got out of the water.

"Good show, good show!" shouted Mr. Ginnis.

Neville and Buster were shivering: the air was getting chilly. Cop started the motor, stuck the gear in forward and jammed on the accelerator full speed. They headed towards the college to divide their booty.

When they reached the college beach, they pulled the boat up on shore next to the student union. They were greeted by many staff members and students as well. They rejoiced in the fishermen's catch. Many people were happy, jumping up and down, laughing, carrying on. Anne Villeneuve's eyes bulged out of her head and she screeched, "Ooooo, look at all da conch!" The students helped unload the shells and to clean and skin them. It was a matter of knocking the crown off of each large, pink shell, jamming a knife down into the top hole and cutting the muscle that clung to the shell. Then the white conch meat would slide out of the large opening, ready to be cut and diced, lemoned then gorged by a hungry human.

"Hmmm, very very good!" said Anne Villeneuve, already having half an entire piece of conch meat sliding around in her large mouth.

"Lovely, lovely!" said Osborne Stubbs. "Simply beautiful, beautiful."

Neville's girlfriend came running up to him, caressed him and said, "Oh Neville, we were so worried, mann. You took so long we thought something might have happened!"

"Oh, my sweet," Neville giggled, "No matter, we are safe!"

Buster helped Mr. Ginnis and Cop clean the boat. "Hey Cop," he said, "thanks for taking us all!"

"Murdunked," he said, "You all right, mann, you all right!"

"And so are you, Cop," Buster said. "It was great!"

"Yes, mann—great! Just great!"

After this great fishing episode, the only thing Buster could do was to slowly walk back to his room and flop down on his bed. He was dog tired after so much swimming, wind, surf and sea. He slept so profoundly that he did not even toss or turn. But when he woke up Saturday afternoon to the knock of Babs at the door, he got up but with great difficulty. He was so sore, every bone in his body ached.

Every step towards the door was a careful, meticulous, great-effort movement. Every muscle was so stiff in his entire body that he felt like he had been frozen in a deep freezer. He opened the door, bent over like an old man. His long hair sprung out in every direction.

"Oh, my God!" Babs said. "My poor dear, what happened to you?"

"Jesus, I fucking tripped on the sidewalk—whataya think?" he said, and limped back to bed.

Barbara spent the rest of the day giving her loved one massages and waiting on him like a mother waiting on her sick little boy. Except this sick little boy had such a foul mouth, saying, "Fucking bring me this, fucking bring me that, God-dammit take it easy on my fucking neck," that at one moment Barbara lost patience and nearly poured out the hot water bottle on him. But she refrained. He was too cute in his long underwear to do something like that.

Saturday night they slept together but did nothing physical. Buster's muscles were now more relaxed after Babs' treatments, but he was still tired. The sea really took it out of him—especially when he was not accustomed to so much swimming. And Babs was beat, too. Her fingers ached from so much massaging; besides, she had had it with Buster's orders for the day. So, she gave a big turn to the wall and fell fast asleep.

Easter morning was church service morning, and due to Barbara's request, the couple got up early for the eight o'clock, sunrise service. But Babs was Catholic and Buster was some species of an Episcopalian; therefore, they would have to go to different churches. They both got on Naomi in their Sunday best and sped off to their respective churches: hers, the Catholic church just on the outskirts of Cockburn Town, and his, Father Villeneuve's special, just down the road. Both churches looked pretty much the same, perhaps the Catholic one a bit more run down. The day was sunny—absolutely beautiful—and did not seem to be a good day to be in any one of the churches; but Buster would go for Barbara's sake. He let her off at her church and he continued towards his.

As he parked, he had to watch out for the flock of sheep that was occupying the small area in front of the church. As he walked towards the entrance, he kicked a group of chickens out of his way. They all rapidly dispersed and made such a screaming noise that the congregation turned their heads to see what was going on. When he entered the church, there in front of his eyes stood Father Villeneuve at the altar in all his divine glory, his Easter costume accentuating his tall figure. Buster entered a pew next to an open arched window with a goat peering in. He knelt and silently recited the Lord's prayer. His recitation was amazingly accurate for not having been to church since Thanksgiving. He finished the prayer with a Buster special: "And Dear Lord, may the spring be a good one—Thank you!"

After a surprisingly short sermon by the Father and an even more rapid communion with that energy-less wine and wafer, the congregation, dressed in all colors but mainly white and pink dresses for the ladies and dark blue or loud purple suits for the men, filtered out of the church to begin socializing. But Buster, after a few "Howdy, Ma'ams" and handshakes, sped off to the Catholic church to pick up Barbara. He pulled up to the entrance way. The service was still in session with the organ music flowing out of the door. Buster gave Naomi a big, huge rev. The engine screamed like bloody hell trying to enter the church. He gave another and then another. Finally, Babs came out with her head bowed down in utter disgrace at what this maniac of a motorcyclist was doing. But as the sun beamed on her face and the sea breeze swept her hair, she was glad to be out of that stuffy wooden building and free again—her spirit now being able to fly freely in the open air.

"Let's go home," she said, straddling Naomi and putting her arms around Buster's waist.

Buster looked at the love light in her transparent, blue eyes. He smiled, gave another screaming rev and peeled out down the road back to his apartment.

It seemed like they had no sooner opened the door of his room when they landed in bed, their beautiful Sunday school clothes strewn all over the floor. *This is a great way to celebrate Easter*, Buster thought. *There is absolutely no better way, really, than to express love for another human being. It's what Jesus would have wanted and what God wants always—World without end—Amen.*

About a half an hour later, when they were in some awkward, upside down position, they heard Patrick Cramble come in the front door. He had been to the Catholic mass as well and had sat next to Babs in the pew. But Cramble felt abandoned when she got up and left at the sounds of a two stroke Yamaha. He walked past their window, heard grunts and groans and walked right back out the door, slamming it and mumbling some obscenities to himself.

He walked over to the Troff's cottage. There they were, a typical, young, English couple out in their front garden, bordering off their yard with pink conch shells.

"Hey Patrick, old chap! What's up, mate?" David Troff greeted.

"Oh, I'm thoroughly disgusted!" Cramble said, effeminately pursing his lips.

"Yes, you do look rather pale and upset," Anne said. "Come, come, out with you! What is it?"

"Oh, that Barbara Oskalowski!" he said, waving his hand like a mongoloid homosexual. "Right after church, she went straight to bed with that repulsive Murdock fellow. What a big bully! And on Easter, even! That's downright blasphemous. They both better watch it, or they are going to go straight to hell!"

"Oh, c'mon now, mate," David Troff said. "Cheer up—tain't the end of the world, ya know! C'mon in for some tea!"

And the trio walked into the cottage for tea and biscuits.

# CHAPTER 9

## *Spiritual Incarnations*

Monday rolled around and it was back to school for Buster. He thought that maybe it would be a normal workweek with five entire days of work, fifteen hours of class altogether: it had been a long time. But Barbara's vacation just began and she had an entire ten days off from teaching. It was a pleasant relief for her. The children at the high school were getting rowdier and more difficult to control by the day. For her vacation she decided to stay on the island rather than spend money on a trip somewhere. Plus, she did not want to travel anywhere alone in the Caribbean. So she spent the first days of her vacation beachcombing and reading a couple of Polish books sent down from Canada by her younger sister.

But reading got old fast. When Thursday rolled around, she got the itch to at least get off the island for a few days—a change if nothing else. She was at the Riding Rock Bar

Thursday afternoon at three o'clock when the hotel pilot, a graying, distinguished looking middle-aged man, came up and sat on the bar stool next to her. They started conversing. Barbara, with those magical blue eyes of hers, dazzled the pilot with a couple mental zaps straight to his heart. After a few stiff drinks, the pilot invited her back to Fort Lauderdale on the hotel's twin engine Cessna airplane. There would be no passengers—strictly a cargo run—and she could come along free. Barbara, as scatter-brained as she was, immediately accepted the offer.

The pilot's eyes lit up suddenly like light bulbs. His mind started running a thousand miles per second. *Let's see*, he thought, *I'll put the plane on automatic pilot and screw the shit out of her in the back seat. Then we'll go to the finest restaurant in South Florida. Then it'll be to an obscure but swank hotel far away from the sick wife and kids for a couple of days—ah, Heaven!*

But after a few moments of mulling over the invitation, Barbara began to have second thoughts: *What would I do in Fort Lauderdale with a middle-aged man? Buster—Yes, that's it! Buster, dear!* She turned to the pilot: "Can my boyfriend come with me?" she asked suddenly.

The pilot's jaw dropped all the way down to the bar counter and the light in his eyes dimmed to a low glimmer. "Boyfriend? Well, uh…shah.. uh, fu …uh…"

"Oh, he won't take up much room, and we'll be real quiet on the way over—no bother."

To save face, the pilot could not back down. He faintly murmured: "Sure, I'd love to have him come along!" He broke a faint smile. "See you at the airstrip in an hour-and-a-half."

"Oh, thank you! You're wonderful!" She pecked him on the cheek and sped off looking for Buster.

Buster was in his room, right in the middle of smoking a joint, when Babs hurriedly burst into the room. He jumped clean out of his chair in complete paranoiac panic, not knowing who it was at first.

"Jesus Christ!" he yelled. "For crying out loud—knock next time, Babs. You scared the shit out of me!"

"Buster, dear, news! News!"

"What the hell? What's going on?"

"We've got a free ride to Fort Lauderdale on the Riding Rock airplane," she said, trying to catch her breath. "Can you come?"

"Jesus, I gotta work tomorrow!"

"Can't you get sick or something, love?"

"Well, Jesus, I dunno!"

"Yes, love, you can get sick!"

"Yeah, right, I suppose I could stick my finger down my throat and throw up in front of Mr. Ginnis!"

"Oh, you can think of something, can't you? C'mon Buster. It's my first trip to the States. It'd be just fantastic to see it with you."

"Well, I would be a first, then, wouldn't I?"

"Yes, dear! Oh hurry! We have to be at the strip in less than an hour-and-a-half."

"Are you sure it's OK if I go along?"

"Yes, love! The pilot said he would love to have you come along!"

"Yeah, I'll bet!"

"Well, come on!"

"OK, look—you go back to your place and … and get your stuff! And uh … meanwhile, uh … I'll go see Mr. Ginnis and throw up! I gotta get rid of this thing first." He mashed out the joint in his desk ashtray.

Within the hour-and-a-half, the two crazy kids met at the airstrip and waited alongside the twin engine Cessna.

"What did you tell Mr. Ginnis," Babs asked, cuddling up to her companion.

"Well, hell, I was going to heave away, but then I thought that would bring me physical pain—and I hate to suffer, ya know what I mean? So I just told him that I got a telegram from my Mom saying that she was sick and that I would have to go home for an emergency. The weekend would be a good opportunity to go."

"Did he believe you?" Babs asked.

"Oh man, of course!" Buster said. "We're really on good terms—especially after that fishing trip. He did not hesitate a second to say, 'By all means, Mr. Murdock.' Wow, he was so nice, I feel kinda guilty now about lying."

"It doesn't have to be a lie, ya know—we could go see your mother!"

Buster's eyes lit up. "Hey …. Hey … Well, you know, that's not a bad idea. Why didn't I think of that? It's just a short hop in another plane—fucking A! You got yourself a deal there, lady!" They both smiled and kissed.

And they waited, and they waited, and they waited. The pilot never showed up; the bird never flew. "Two is company and three's a crowd" never rang so true.

So Barbara, faintly realizing her naiveté, went back to the doldrums of beachcombing and reading more Polish books; and for Buster, whose mother miraculously got un-sick, returned to business as usual. The United States and Mom would have to wait for some other time.

Back to school it was. Back in the classroom, Buster received enormous vibrations of total apathy from the students. Students would come drifting into class, many times without books or even pens, and sit there for the whole period like bumps on logs, sleepy-eyed and limp. Spring Fever had finally hit and it hit hard. With all the surroundings of sea and sunshine, a four-walled classroom was just something super hard to believe in. Even a book, white pages with black printed symbols, had so little relevance to the surroundings, that Buster, as teacher, could hardly expect his students to go home and study.

The only thing, then, he decided was to put on reading shows of Hemingway's novel, *The Old Man and the Sea*. He stood on his desk many times, harpooning make-believe sharks, or exaggerating his rope burned hands—looking at the blood dripping over his callouses. The students did like the acting-out bit, for it circulated their own blood, watching a dramatic actor up in front doing his thing.

Another activity Buster created to help kill the boredom was a small play production for the students. It was a simple, one-act play called "Single Seven" written by a Bahamian writer, Susan Wallace. The play humorously depicted the corruption of the illegal lottery system. After selecting the cast, all students of course, Buster and his group of thespians held rehearsals three days a week for a few hours in the early afternoon. The debut would be later on, towards the end of the term.

At least this play passed the time, somewhat. Class hours were in the morning: then after class, what? Sports actually took the highlight this spring on campus. For the girls Austin Riley organized Volleyball games and John Collins refereed soccer matches for the boys. Buster mentioned his availability to supervise baseball games, but sour looks from the British quelled that idea fast. So Buster politely just said "Fuck you" to the British and decided to dedicate himself only to his own affairs after tedious, long and seemingly interminable classes.

One of his spring projects was to build a double-seated kayak from a kit that had been stored away in the campus utility room from years past. Austin Riley had ordered the kit years ago with Bahamian funds, but nobody had spent the time nor the energy to put it together. When Buster asked permission to assemble it, Riley gave a snicker and said, "It's all yours, mate!" He thought that the American would not have a chance to make the thing float.

Now probably any other person building the kayak would have taken one lousy weekend; but Buster was so determined to make this a good floating machine that he took his time. He followed the British directions precisely, using fiberglass that he had bought from Zebedee Jones to cover the balsam wood and seams. This was to make the craft much sturdier. After two solid weeks of working on it night and day on the side of his apartment, taking time out only for classes, Buster, the craftsman, finally finished it. He was right proud of himself for accomplishing something with his hands. It was a great feeling to print in white over the bright orange painted surface the letters, "The Bashka, eh?" It was quite a clever name, he had to admit to himself. Bashka was Polish for Barbara, and "eh?" was Barbara's Canadian slang word that she always tagged onto every other sentence she said. As Buster thought, though, contemplating on his new craft, it was one hell of a mixed-up vessel: the kit was made in England, assembled in the Bahamas by an American and it had a Polish name attributed to a Canadian woman. Ah, "The Bashka, eh?" he thought. "Not bad, not bad!" Come to think of it, he was right proud of it.

Christening day was the highlight of Buster's labors. Babs

bought a bottle of French Champagne, Veuve Calendrin. Instead of breaking such a beautiful bottle over the bow, they drank it first, and then they carried "The Bashka, eh?" down to the college beach for launching. Laughing and staggering under the influence of the grapes, Buster did somersaults in the sand. He hooped and hollered and stuck the long paddles in the sand, posing and showing all his muscles in front of Babs' Kodak Instamatic camera.

Then, shove off time and the craft slithered into the turquoise water. It was tippy at first, but the crew soon adjusted themselves and got used to the technique of balancing it. Babs took the front cockpit while Buster, in the back, steered between paddle strokes. They paddled out quite far, about one hundred yards offshore. Buster was apprehensive at first about the contraption floating. He was worried that maybe there might be a few leaks somewhere—especially up by the bow where the fiberglass resin was spread thinly. But to his surprise, the only water that came through was via the open cockpits—so all was "AOK."

They paddled awkwardly parallel to the shore for a while, Buster still being reluctant to go out any further. Poor Babs was definitely not in her element and was having a really difficult time with the paddle. Suddenly Austin Riley, his wife and John Collins appeared on the beach.

"Ha! Look at this Babs!" Buster yelled. "The British are coming! I bet those guys are green with envy! They didn't think I could do it, the assholes!" He yelled to them on the beach, flashing a peace sign, "Hey, Riley—Collins!"

"Ahoy, mate!" Riley yelled, cracking the first smile of his life to Buster.

"Hey, man, it works—it works!" Buster stood up and started jumping up and down. "It works—ya'll see?" The boat tipped, rocked, Babs let out a scream and Buster went right into the water, spinning around, back first. The Brits really got a charge out of this. They were all on shore in hysterics: Riley rolling in the sand, laughing, rolling, laughing, all the way into the water. While Buster was treading water, he took note of the sleek boat and prided himself in how well it sat in the water. It was a beautiful sight for him to see how perfect the orange deck was with its battleship gray siding. He was right proud of himself.

He climbed back on board and squeezed into his cockpit again. Babs was laughing too, but discomfort showed on her grimacing face. "Do you always have to put on a show, Mr. Murdock?" she said.

After the show was over, the two mariners decided to paddle around the tip of the college and down to the Riding Rock marina. Rounding the point, a few students stood on the rocks, watching, laughing, their huge white teeth glistening in the sun. The sailors' paddles, at times, clumsily hit one another and the craft nearly capsized several times. The students did not help matters any.

When they reached the marina there came into view a large, eighty-foot schooner anchored off the Cockburn Town point about a half-mile away. It looked fascinating, and Buster just had to go and see it. So instead of going into the Riding Rock marina like Babs had hoped to, because her arms were about to fall off and her head about to explode from half the bottle of champagne, they headed towards the ship.

The vessel was strikingly beautiful. The closer they got to it the more grandiose and magnificent the boat became. The hull was ivory-white with teakwood trimmings. The two huge masts stretched so high that they seemed to have command of the whole sky. A mass of lines webbed the entire riggings.

"Suppose there are nice people on board?" Babs asked.

"Sure," Buster said, digging his paddle deeper into the water. "They'll probably even ask us up for dinner and for dessert and even give us a suitcase full of dollars!"

The closer to the ship they got, strangely enough, the quieter the atmosphere around them became. The wind seemed to stop and waves calmed down. They only became aware of the synchronized paddles splashing the surface. Finally, they were within talking distance of a few figures seen on deck.

"Ahoy!" Buster yelled. "How are you?" He saw one young man about twenty-eight years old in a waiter's uniform up on the bow. The man gazed at the rather ludicrous looking couple in the kayak drifting towards the ship. He looked deadly serious, gave a sneer, and shook his head as if to warn the couple not to come closer. But they did not pay any attention to him. The kayak glided passed the bow of the ship and drifted to the mid-section. There were two middle-aged men, big, brawny, gray-haired with sharp, dark facial features, sitting at a table playing cards. They both gave a very austere look at Buster.

"Where are ya'll from?" the American yelled briskly. But there was no reply. The two mafia-looking card players sat ignoring the little boaters. They conversed in a language that Buster deciphered as being some form of Italian. "Where are ya'll from?" he asked once again.

This time one of the men looked up from his fan of cards in his hand and snapped a quick answer, "Deutschland!" He then went back to his cards.

"A friendly lot, eh?" Babs said quietly.

The boat drifted to the stern. A young black-haired, beautiful looking Latin woman came out from below deck. She was the only one that halfway smiled at the visitors. She leaned over the railing, her hands folded.

"It's a beautiful ship," Babs said.

"Thank you. It's forty years old," she said in a definite Italian accent. But then she whisked her hand as if to tell them to keep on moving.

"Hey, Babs," Buster said, "I think we better get outta here—this place stinks!" And they slowly paddled away from the ship, heading back towards the college.

Buster was right. The ship reeked of illegality. There was something about the boat, an air of hostility that sent out vibrations of Mafia dealings and smuggling. Buster had heard about these kinds of ships before, but had never come into actual contact with them. San Salvador was actually the stopping off island for boats coming from the East over to the New World and making it down to South America and other parts to make their drug runs, arms runs, or whatever.

It sure was a beautiful boat, thought Buster, but it sure was not the kind of atmosphere he would like to be in. "How'd you like that dinner, Bashka?" he asked.

"Yes—some banquet, eh? And I can't paddle another foot!"

So it was up to the builder of the kayak to paddle the rest of the mile-and-a-half back to the college beach and to see his own beauty of a woman safely back to shore. Babs behaved well. She did not let out one single complaint the entire return home, for she knew the boat was built for her. The maiden voyage of "The Bashka, eh?" was a success.

Throughout the entire month of May, love affairs, scandals and feuds seemed to festoon throughout the small microcosm on San Salvador and become the order of the day. The largest and most publicized love affair was, of course, that of Barbara Oskalowski and Buster Murdock. They could not keep it amongst themselves any longer—everybody knew. So the couple just let it ride and let people talk whatever they wanted about them—they did not care. They would stick to their frequenting Berry Silversmith's and his wife's place. Buster liked to go sailing with Berry in the afternoons and Babs always liked to chat with Ethlyn. In the evenings Babs and Buster would take in the Coast Guard movie and on occasion they would go to the Rip; but the rest of the time was theirs to themselves. They definitely would not pay any attention to small-minded people spreading rumors.

Their relationship was coming along real strong, getting more solid by the day—each giving and taking and compromising to satisfy the needs of the other. Babs especially was changing rapidly. After Buster building the boat for her (as he told it), and after Buster loving her the way he did, she was slowly becoming convinced that this American hippie was for her. She was slowly leaving Brad back in the depths of her Canadian past. She began to believe in everything Buster did, said and was. As a result, she began to trust him fully. Therefore, she gave in to her conservative upbringing and started smoking marijuana regularly. She did not think it had any effect on her at first. In the beginning she was somewhat lackadaisical about it. However, one night, seeing that her fear of it was disappearing, Buster shoved joint after joint down her. He then took her to bed, and she had some of the biggest orgasms of her entire life. She loved it!

Barbara was opening up so rapidly that she was willing to do anything with Buster. When he mentioned an LSD trip together, she did not even wince. So Buster, one Sunday morning at the Navy base, took two beautiful, square hits of Window Pane, one of the slang references for lysergic acid, from an envelope Brother Tom had sent down from Florida. He ceremoniously put one tiny, clear square on the tip of Babs' tongue and the other on his. They were off on a fifteen-hour journey into cosmic regions of the mind and body. They could not stop touching each other the entire trip. They did the sex number with their bodies actually melting into one another. That eternal, bottomless first acid kiss, mouths completely wide open—teeth hitting, tongues swirling, took them deep down inside their bodies to explore the burning innards of their human flesh. Then the orgasm of cosmic dimensions came. After hours of fondling, petting, soul-searching kisses, the final orgasmic explosion and sudden awareness of God's entire scheme of the birth-death process of life blessed them both. With all this emotional and physical energy zapping their very souls, the two spiritual incarnations became very much in love.

But as the true love energy beautifully captivated these two young human beings, other relationships that flowered on the island seemed much more animalistic and physical rather than anything spiritual. A new, hot number came to the island via the Finger Lakers named Maria Dolores. She was a beautiful, black-haired Puerto Rican girl with an hour-glass shaped body. It was not long before she discovered the Coast Guard station whereabouts. She made a direct beeline to the new captain's quarters—and possibly to the barracks, but that was unknown at the time.

It was also very strange to see the conservative English couple, David and Anne Troff, always walking around, not by themselves but with a male companion, Chief Bilgo of the Coast Guard. The Chief was that disgusting non-commissioned, thirty-five year old lifer of whom R.B. Baker despised because he always sucked his teeth after dinner and made such a repugnant, irritating noise. Both Buster and Babs thought that such a young, married couple as the Troffs would want to be alone and enjoy the company of themselves. They could not really figure out why this Coastie was always with them and always parking the Coast Guard van outside their cottage.

It was also well known throughout the island that the Finnans, part owners of the Riding Rock Inn, were having their own bashes, orgies and wife-swapping affairs with clients coming down from the North. Often they could be seen skinny dipping late at night in the pool and drunkenly gallivanting around the premises in total nudity.

Even the students at the college had their share of sexual activity on campus. Sex seemed to be much more important than studying ever would be. They took every advantage of attending a co-educational institution. However, they seemed to be going about it in the wrong way, the dumb way. The girls kept getting pregnant. At least six girls throughout the course of springtime got "Knocked Up," as the girls would say. They had to be sent off the island for either special gynecological attention or to avoid embarrassment amongst their peers.

Even within Anne Villeneuve's circle of friends there was a lot of hanky-panky going on. One weekend when Father Villeneuve was away conducting special religious ceremonies on Rum Cay, Anne decided to throw a going-away slumber party for a classmate of hers who was being kicked off the island by the priest himself for being seven months pregnant. She was a bad influence, the priest had said of the girl. But scandal became more scandal when the party got so intoxicatingly noisy and out-of-hand that Mr. Patrick Cramble, the infamous Assistant Warden, had to come to the rescue. In the interest and protection of all innocent students on campus, he busted up the bash, commanding everybody to quietly return to his or her respective dormitories and turn out the lights.

Poor Patrick Cramble! As dutifully minded as he was, he just did not realize how unpopular he was getting. He was just such a blind, unaware, naïve, stupid, Baby-Huey dimbulb, that he still could not understand why his motorbike tires were perpetually going flat and major working components on the machine perpetually disappearing daily.

The week of the play, "Single Seven," was really the last week of heavy student activity on campus. The play rehearsals had come along smoothly and the students all chipped in with full cooperation in constructing the set. After all, there was not much else to do after class. The participants went out and collected palm tree leaves and bushes to make the typical Bahamian house on stage look more authentic. The girls made all the costumes: police uniforms for the bust scene for the illegal lottery, large exaggerated suits for the men, and long, dangling Bahamian skirts for the women characters.

The night of the debut the whole campus showed up—except the British lecturers and company. Their absence was highly noted by the Bahamian officials. Buster found out that they were having a large feud with the white Englanders. The arguments were cottage feuds, so-to-speak, with differences in having to live alongside one another. The fact that the Brits knew very well that they were going to be kicked off the island after this academic year by their black administrators had a great deal to do with their absence from the play. Animosity and downright hatred was slowly building up. Not attending the play was one, subtle English way of protesting.

But Buster could not give a "Flying fuck" about this feud madness. He minded his own business. He was really proud of his students for having pulled off the play the way they did. In front of the capacity crowd, people even standing up along the walls and out the door, his actors recited all their lines perfectly and with good feeling and confidence. The spontaneity of humor in the play worked well, and the scenes had everybody in fits of laughter throughout much of the presentation.

After the play the students had a big bash of a party in the same recreation room—stage area. The party included a live student band, lots of rum-punch and plenty of conch fritters. Buster stayed for about forty-five minutes, wallowing in his glory, listening to student chants of "Murdock! Murdock! For he's a jolly good fellow!" It amazed him when it suddenly dawned on him that he was the creator of this happening, of this grand reunion of people. He felt an immense feeling of satisfaction melt over him.

Babs, too, was extremely proud of Buster for actually accomplishing such a tremendous feat with these people. She could not wait to drag him away from the punch bowl and back to the divinity of his room and show her affection and admiration towards him. He deserved it, she thought. And that's exactly what she did: she dragged him away from the punch bowl and back to his place to screw his eyes out before he could even finish reaping the full benefits of his ego-reaping harvest. But he did not complain. *Which is more important anyway*, he thought, *Ego building or making love?*

When it was time for Teaching Practice for the first

year students, the academic year was considered over for all practical purposes. After the freshman students took off for their three-week stint on Great Exuma island, the classrooms seemed empty. Campus activity slowed to a snail's pace. It was amazing how the freshman group of students contributed to the spark of campus life. They were younger with seemingly more energy than the others. After their stay on Exuma, the students were to continue on to Nassau for a few days of briefing and conference at the Ministry of Education, then return to their respective islands for the summer. With the addition of David Troff, the usual corps of lecturers went with the students to Exuma, including Father Villeneuve, of course. Patrick Cramble stayed behind to valiantly guard security and behavior on campus.

With a third of the students now gone, Buster's schedule dwindled to only six hours of teaching a week for the final three weeks on the island. As a result, the main battle was what to do with all that time. Loneliness was not a problem now, because he saw Babs every afternoon after she finished at the high school. Or he would go sailing with Berry Silversmith in his sixteen-foot day sailor. He could not complain about that. He loved sailing: the winds were perfect and the waters ideal. However, the idleness did give Buster time to think about himself—perhaps too much time.

Uncertainty crept into his life like a slow sea turtle on the beach. The uncertainty was mainly due to the fact that the end was slowly drawing nigh: he did not know what to do with himself after school finished. His dilemma was threefold, mainly: one, he did not know what to do with his three month summer vacation; two, he did not know what to do with Barbara; and three, he was not quite sure if he wanted to return to the island in September.

The summer vacation was extremely important to him. It would be the first summer that he would not have to work in years: actually, not only a few years, but ever since he was a little child. Under the jurisdiction of his parents, they always made him do some kind of menial work during summer vacation. Whether it was washing and waxing cars, mowing lawns or delivering newspapers, his parents always said, "It builds character!" If Buster was not working, his mother or father would get very angry and make him feel guilty. Even when he went away to the university, he always had to come back home for the summer and work. He would save money, but only for the university to devour it all up during the very first month of the Fall term. And during the university years, Buster's jobs were part-time "Gross" jobs in the summer: washing dishes, waiting on tables, pulling weeds, selling encyclopedias, stocking merchandise, peddling ice-cream, delivering pizzas, shoveling hamburgers—all for a measly one dollar and twenty-five cents an hour.

Now, for the first time since he could remember, he had an entire three months off and did not know what to do with it. But one thing was for certain, he was not going to work and that was that!

One of his desires that laid heavily on his mind was that of "Hitting the Globe," as he put it. Why the hell not? he thought. Such thoughts filled his mind: he was young, alive, single and ready for travel. He would have no ties, no parents to make him feel guilty for not working, and plenty of money, thanks to the Bahamian Ministry of Education. He could do what he wanted, go anywhere he wanted—anything! He was open and free. What a thought that was, too: *Really! How many people could ever put themselves into my situation? How about all those men with families and unending lists of responsibilities? What about all those poor people who have to work every hour of their awakened state just to make it through the night?* He was fortunate indeed, and he was the first one to realize that fact.

Then there was the dilemma of Bashka, that beautiful blonde, blue-eyed Polish dame from Kapaskasing, Canada. One afternoon when he was sitting in his bamboo chair smoking a joint from his diminishing supply of marijuana, Buster reflected back to the time he hitchhiked through Canada, passing through Sudbury and North Bay. He remembered he was in a youth hostel one night and overheard a conversation between two young travelers in their mid-twenties. The conversation echoed through his mind over and over again:

"What made you decide to hit the road?" one man asked.

"I broke up with my girlfriend," the other responded. "I just had to get away from the same town—too small, you know what I mean?"

"Yeah, I know what you mean! Traveling gets you away, that's for sure!"

"You know, it's funny, but now that I look back with an objective point of view, I was really tied down—routine—rut—you know what I mean?"

"I know what you mean—women tend to do things like that to a man. But didn't you feel bad, breaking up with her and all?"

"Bad? Fuck no! Girls come and go. Girls are like standing at a bus stop—wait ten minutes and another will be by."

Buster's thoughts continued with the smoke rising up from the joint. No, he was not in a rut or anything like that with Babs, and he did feel he loved her now. It took a little time, but he did discover that he was quite attached and had a lot of feeling for her. And even though Babs was not sure herself whether to go back to Canada or stay with Buster, the decision was his. It was Buster who was in control of the situation—or at least so he thought. She was waiting for him to ask her. She loved him deeply and he was the first to realize this.

However, he just was not sure—he just did not know what to do. He could not take her with him on his travels because he simply could not afford her. Well, he could, he thought, but that money was for him! Not only that, but he had never traveled extensively with a woman before, and he had that tremendous fear that she would slow him down. Not to mention the fact that if he just happened to meet a beautiful Spanish girl that he would like to get to know, why, he would not be able to because of … well, Babs would be there.

And yet Buster was the first to realize that if he left her behind, there would present the great possibility of losing her. He did not want that to happen because, well, he loved her. But, he thought: *Fuck! We are all under the control of the God force and whatever happens, happens. Qué será, será / Whatever will be, will be.*

The dilemma kept getting worse as the slow, sunny days dragged on. It was sort of like watching water trying to come to a boil but never does. The questions of what to do and where to go obsessed Buster every waking minute. He went to Peter Kentard's immaculate library in the old, converted radar shack and checked out all of the books in the *Time-Life* International Book series. He devoured these books in the confines of his room as if the world were going to come to an end as soon as school terminated. All kinds of countries sparked his interest: Germany, France,

Spain, Eastern Europe, Mexico, South America; but he just could not make up his mind. He changed ideas with every book he read. After reading the book on Turkey, he, along with some female companion, was all set to smuggle some heroin and opium back to the United States, sell it, get rich and then finally buy his yacht. It was highly possible. According to recent news flashes on the radio, the Turkish government had just resumed the cultivation of their poppy fields, contrary to the United States' wishes. Sticking opium up his rectum and heroin up the girl's vagina would be something to tell his grandchildren about. After that pipe dream faded away, thumbing through pictures in a book on Windjammers set his imagination a-sailing again. He was ready to hop on a sailboat and crew for three months. But when he came to the conclusion that he would just be bobbing up and down like a cork and wasting his talents for three months, he picked up another book. Somehow a book on American Jazz got mixed up in the pile. While looking at pictures of Louis Armstrong, the Preservation Hall Jazz Group and Billy Holiday, his mind swung over to the idea of going to New Orleans. He would form a music group with some friends of his who were living there and would record some of his songs he had written over the years. He would be able to push them onto major recording companies, have them nationally aired, including international exposure, become famous, rich, then buy his yacht. Nothing better, he thought! But then again the Andes sounded inviting. To see mountains again would do wonders for his head—just to see a deep, rich, green color again, real trees and breathe crisp mountain air. Or even just to rent a small shack in "La Boca," the Italian section of Buenos Aires, would be sufficient. Just to be in this artist colony and brush up on his university Spanish would be quite exciting. Possibly writing and just being with other artists like himself for three whole months would perhaps satisfy the dry, cultural thirst that San Salvador was giving him. Or hell, he thought, he could just stay at home in Daytona Beach in the good ol' United States and save money, work like a bastard one more year, then go on a world tour for five years. It would not be hard to do—the five-year world tour, that is; but that one year in Daytona would be a "Bitch!" Diving back into the lost, dry regions of American middle-class, Mickey Mouse mediocrity? He picked up a book on Nepal.

But Buster's thoughts on Babs seemed to go up and down with the comings and goings of the tides. Some nights he would be definitely decided that he would leave her behind; he just could not have a woman dragging him down on his travels. She would have to understand that. Plus she herself needed to go home for a period of time. This year being her first year away from her country she should be with her family. Maybe then she would be better able to decide what it was she really wanted.

But then again, he thought, why would it have to end just like that? Why couldn't they be away from each other for the summer, then reunite in September and continue where they left off? One evening at the Riding Rock Inn Restaurant under candlelight with French wine and blue marlin for dinner, they worked it out: at least for one week, anyway.

"Let's get married!" Babs suggested.

"What?" Buster said, shifting in his chair. "That's madness!"

"Well, Buster dear," she said, "I refuse to continue our relationship as it stands now! I can't stand people talking about us anymore; I can't stand these pre-arranged meetings anymore; I can't stand dating anymore; I can't stand it—I can't stand it!"

"Well, Jesus, woman, and I can't stand the thought of marriage—it makes me nervous! And besides, I'm too young for all that madness already. I don't want to get tied down!" He took a good swig of wine. The white juice was taking effect on both of them. Their speech was getting a little slurred.

"Tied down?" she said. "How on earth would you be tied down? You could do anything you wanted to do—I can take care of myself!"

"Right! That's what they all say!" He watched her as she twirled her shining blond hair with her index finger. *Could I really marry her?* He thought. *She's very intelligent—on my level now for sure—beautiful to look at and I love to talk to her. I can communicate with her. But she is already showing signs of flabbiness on her long, slender legs and a belly is starting to form. One thing I can't stand is a fat woman. Jesus, please keep me from a fat woman! Please! Hmm, this chick also doesn't like the outdoors like I do. She hates camping, and boats don't really turn her on. She likes to be comfortable and cries when she doesn't get her coffee, tea or occasional cigarette. Damn, those God-awful cigarettes that kill so many people; Christ, those God-awful cigarettes that pollute my atmosphere and give her foul, fucking halitosis. Fuck! No way I'm going to marry her.*

"No way!" he firmly said to her.

There was silence.

"Then let's just live together," she said after the pause.

"Right! That would really go over great with the natives!"

He shot back to thinking: *But yeah, I suppose I could get into living with her. Jesus, her long straight, blond hair accentuating her seemingly aristocratic Polish features would be a godsend to my eyes. Her long, slender body is the desire of every man on this God-forsaken island. And granted, those things she does for me help me make it through the night—those lovely mornings waking up and looking at sheer beauty. Jesus, she's always beautiful in the morning. Yeah, good ol' Dad always said that a true mark of beauty was if a woman looked pleasing to the eye in the morning and not looking like an old, wet mop. Yeah, man, Babs sure does look beautiful in the morning. I suppose I could get into living with her. But Christ, what would the fucking, narrow-minded natives think about that one on this God-forsaken island?*

"No way!" he said to her. "It just wouldn't work. The natives are too restless."

"Well, it's either that or we split up!"

*God-dammit!* he thought. *Why is it that a woman always has to push, push, push—push a man into something that he might later regret? Why are they always looking for that fucking false sense of security?*

"Look Babs," he said, taking another swig of wine, "this is absolutely insane! We've established the fact that we want to be together next year, right?"

"Right!"

"Now, you want to live together and I want to live together, but I'm just not going to get married over it, that's all!"

"OK, we won't have to get married, Buster," she said, determined to work this thing out. "We'll just say we're married—they won't have to know."

"Right! And how do we swing that, pray tell?"

"Easy! Just say we're married."

"Right! And what happens when the Ministry of Education asks for legal documents?"

"Say we just forgot them and that they are up at my house in Kapaskasing for safe keeping."

"Shhhh," Buster whispered, leaning across the table nearing her. "Not so loud for Christ's sakes!"

Their rather corpulent Bahamian waitress was nestled in the corner pretending to shine the silverware.

"Oh, you're right!" Babs said, lowering her voice. "That's all we need is more rumors flying around this place."

Some tourists came in the dining area to eat and made a little more noise, putting a welcomed muffle to their conversation.

""Hey, I've got a better idea!" Buster said. "We'll go to Mexico and get married for ten dollars and then get a divorce for five bucks the same day. That way we'll have the documents."

"Sounds too much of a dreadful complication to me."

"Well, at least we'd have the documents!"

"True! But it would be easier just to say it."

"But wait a minute—suppose we find out we don't get along and we don't want to live together anymore?"

"Simple, dear! I'll just leave—I promise. I'll leave! All you'll have to do is tell me and I'll go."

*Oh yeah?* Buster thought. *That's heavy! How many girls would say that to their man? This is gonna take some thinking, that's for sure!* He emptied his glass with a quick jerk.

The more they hashed it out the more credible it became. *Right!* he decided silently. *Telling the natives that they were married would create quite an exciting scandal: everybody on the whole island, the microcosm of life, thinking they were married and yet on the outside they would be simply living together grooving on each other's love—or hate—or whatever it would turn out to be. OK!* It was decided.

The wine bottle was empty—finished—and so was the conversation. They went to Zebedee's Harlem Square Bar and celebrated their decision. They drank Crème de Cacao— one right after the other and managed to get sufficiently smashed on their "Bums," as Babs put it. Their spirits were flying after making such a monumental decision. They felt they had accomplished something and the beginnings of new embarkations together floated freely in their drunken thoughts.

And as they sat on the bar stools listening to Bahamian songs on the juke box and old timers slapping down dominoes on the Formica tables, Babs kept repeating, "Isn't it wonderful, Buster dear? Whatever happens, it's all a part of the rich pageantry of life."

And Buster, puffing on a White Owl Diplomat cigar, bluntly responded, "Jesus! Qué será, será!!"

# CHAPTER 10

## *Tunas, Wild Dogs and Goodbyes*

Monotonous, sunny days were the rule rather than the exception: one sunny day right after the other. It seemed that everybody woke up to the sun, worked in the sun, played in the sun and went to bed in the sun. It was sun, sun, sun. The only exception was one day when a gigantic school of tuna fish slowly moved from one end of the island to another. There was a menacing, gray, overcast sky that hovered over San Salvador and its waters. Austin Riley, who had now started to open up and actually talk to Buster after his seamanship demonstration in the kayak, stood with Buster on the college point, simply gazing out at the school of tuna. It was a miraculous sight: a huge, underwater cloud with seemingly thousands of seagulls hovering over it.

"Fantastic, that!" Riley said in pure, British English. "Absolutely fantastic!"

"Sure is beautiful, no doubt about it!" Buster said.

Larry Young, a tall, strong, new addition to the Coast Guard group, drove up in the white Coast Guard van. "Hey, fellas," he said in a deep southern accent. "Whatcha'll lookin' at?"

"Hi, Larry!" Buster said, smiling. "Hey man, come and see this! There's an incredible school of tuna off-shore." Riley did not even acknowledge the new Coastie: his southern accent was atrociously offensive to the Brit.

Larry got out of the van, a tall lanky figure but muscular. He was relatively famous in his swimming circles in Fort Lauderdale and Palm Beach for being an excellent diver and fisherman. He had joined the Coast Guard to avoid being drafted into the army: he felt his talents could be used much better serving people in the Coast Guard rather than killing people in Viet Nam. He gazed out at the flock of sea gulls over the school of fish. "Shore is a honey all right!" he said. "What do ya'll say we take the boat out and catch a few of them Motherfuckers?"

Austin Riley cringed at this bastardization of the English language.

"Sounds great, Larry!" Buster replied. "Great idea! But we better hurry or we'll lose 'em!"

"Let's go for it!" Larry said.

"Riley, you comin'?" Buster asked.

Riley finally cracked a smile. Surrendering his mother country to two colonial fishermen, he finally said, "Well mates, would not miss it for the world, actually. Off we go!"

And they sped off like demons to prepare the Coast Guard boat. They certainly did not want to miss a chance like this. It was not often that tuna ran by this side of the Bahamas; but when they did, it was exciting for everybody.

The Coast Guard launch boat was a twenty-foot runabout with a seventy-five horsepower Johnson outboard motor. It was anchored off shore, just a few yards beyond the Coast Guard dock. The launch was always rigged for instantaneous dispatch for possible sea-rescues or any other incident that might occur. But because so very little happened on the island, the boat was mainly used only for practice drills once a week and the rest of the time for leisure fishing and diving trips.

The boat was perfect in the case of the tuna run. All the trio had to do was grab the life-jackets, gas tanks, a few poles and extra gaffs that were stored away in the aluminum Coast Guard shack on the dock, and they were on their way to a grand tuna-hunting extravaganza. With the smooth, glassy sea the way it was, the fiberglass boat seemed to glide over the surface. The seven miles from the Coast Guard station to the college point seemed like nothing. They were on the outskirts of the college only in a matter of minutes. A crowd of students had gathered on the rocks, watching the agitated water area of the tuna.

The tuna were now on the surface, feeding off millions of tiny fish that the sea gulls were also engulfing. The water was so stirred up where the tuna school was that it looked like whipped-cream topping. There were a few wooden Bahamian skiffs on the outskirts of the area as well, taking advantage of what was approximately a one hundred yard square mass of smooth, blue fish tails and fins slapping the water. The screams of the sea gulls added to the sound of these slaps, and the noise in its totality was so loud that the fishermen in the Coastie boat had to yell at one another to be heard.

Larry and Buster threw their lines with gigantic hooks

out into the outer circumference of the school The fish were so concentrated that the boys did not even need to bait the hooks. It was just a matter of throwing out the hooks, snagging any part of the fish, whether it be the tails, side of the body or gills, then reeling in for Riley to jam the gaff in the body and hoist it up into the boat. Each fish weighed at least twenty-five to thirty-five pounds. Their poles bent like rubber bands every time.

But this heyday did not continue for long, because after only a half an hour, the Coastie boat was filled to the brim. The boat was so loaded with tuna that the waterline almost reached the top of the railing. It was time to stop and head back to the Coast Guard beach and unload their booty. Each fish could be frozen and served as a feast for a family of four for several weeks.

But King Neptune was evidently not very fond of the way the three human beings had taken the treasure and run. The gray, menacing, overcast sky had converted into immense, black thunderclouds and rays of lightning started jutting down on all sides of the boat. Strong gusts of wind suddenly came out of nowhere.

The Johnson outboard motor screamed as the boat started racing towards the Coast Guard side of the island, trying to beat out the storm. Riley and Buster were in the back, trying to prevent some of the tuna from bouncing out of the boat. Larry tightly gripped the steering wheel, trying to keep the boat on a steady course in white-capped waves that had suddenly perked up like boiling water. The closer they came to the station the larger the waves became. The boat sometimes jumped clean out of the water, only to pounce back down in a large deafening "Bap" sound; the spray reaching up high over the boaters' heads and rushing down into the boat. The wind was so strong and the sounds of the water mixed in with the screaming motor were so loud, that with the men even yelling at the top of their lungs they could not hear each other. Hardly a word, then, was exchanged.

They were still a couple of miles from the base dock when it happened. The boat hit a large wave and went flying completely out of the water. When it finally landed, it hit the surface with such a tremendous impact that everything and everybody went bouncing almost completely out of the launch. Tuna fish went spilling out and the two sailors in the back almost went flying over the railing. The motor went out of the water and miraculously somehow locked in a tipped-up position, giving no forward motion to the boat.

Above the scream of the engine could be heard Larry's pained cry: "My arms—my arms! Oh my God, my arms!" His eyes were popping out of their sockets, looking in sheer horror at his broken forearms. At the impact, his hands had slipped inside the steering wheel and had gotten trapped in the middle. Somehow, in some God-inexplicable way, the part of his arms between his hands and elbows snapped in two, crisp, like a pretzel. The bones stuck out like smooth white ivory. Blood began spurting out immediately.

"Riley!" yelled Buster as hard as he could, "Larry's hurt up front!"

Larry gave a final, "Oh, my God, my arms!" and he fainted back into the driver's seat.

Buster pulled himself off the railing and grabbed the young Coastie, being careful not to touch his dangling arms. Riley, as well, instinctively acted immediately. Riley jammed the motor out of gear and then pushed it back down into the water. He then hurried to the broken steering wheel and started to maneuver it the best he could. Now back into a forward motion, he aimed the boat towards the Coast Guard beach. But it was very difficult. Riley intended to avoid bouncing out of the water, but the waves showed no mercy. Sometimes the waves came clear over the railing, washing tuna out of the boat and drenching the sailors.

They were so occupied with what they were doing, with surviving, that nothing was said. While Riley did the best he could to steer, Buster was in the back holding the unconscious Larry Young, his arms dangling, blood now streaming down into the mass of dead, slimy tuna. Buster kept pressing the vessels in Larry's armpits to try and prevent bleeding, but he was not sure that that was the right thing to do. The remaining two-mile destination now seemed like an eternity.

With the rain finally coming down in sheets, the boat finally reached the shore of the Coast Guard base. Fortunately, the Coast Guard captain and a few of the crew were on shore waiting and worrying, suspecting that some sort of trouble had arisen because of such a strong and sudden storm. Their suspicions were rightfully warranted, for the boat barely made it. Riley was so exhausted that he could hardly hold the half steering wheel any longer, and Buster's own arms were about to fall off from holding the unconscious Larry steady.

As the captain and the chief in the van whisked the three back to the station for first aid treatment, the three other Coasties took care of the boat in the hard rain and tumbling surf.

While both Austin Riley and Buster Murdock were being treated for mild shock, Larry, lying unconscious with a sheet-white color to his face, was being put in tourniquets by the base corpsman to keep him from bleeding to death. There was really nothing else they could do for him until a doctor came. The captain had immediately ordered one down from Fort Lauderdale.

It was amazing how fast the rumors and news flashed across the island. Even before the emergency military plane arrived two hours after calling, there was a large crowd of natives outside the station, wondering what was going on. Even Babs caught the news quickly and was by Buster's side worried sick.

But Buster was all right. He was sitting upright now, cracking jokes and drinking a cold can of Budweiser beer, supplied by the Coastie rescue. Riley had also recuperated somewhat and was content with his hot cup of tea. The Brits and their tea!

"Jesus Christ, man, you shoulda seen it!" Buster said. "More tuna than the stars in the Milky Way!"

"Bloody fantastic it 'twas, all right!" Riley added. "Bloody marvelous, that!"

Now that the island was with a good supply of tuna for several weeks, Larry Young was without hands the rest of his life. Gangrene had set in at the hospital stateside, and the doctors had to amputate both arms at the elbow. This news was just enough to jolt Buster right back into a depression for several days. *Jesus!* he thought. *I didn't mean it! After all, Lord, all we wanted was to have a little fucking fun. Why did you have to go and do this, for Christ's sakes?* It absolutely awed Buster how fast things could happen—especially something like this. Larry Young, almost a perfect specimen of a human being, a terrific athlete, was on the island one second, then the next second, gone—handicapped forever. Buster just could not believe it.

That was the last storm of the spring. It had come and gone in a flash—seemingly coming as if only to take away Larry's arms then going to let the incredibly monotonous, sunny days take its place. The routine was stifling Buster once again. He would get up in the morning and look out to see the same setting: administration building across the scrubby field, some bush, and a few goats. He would then make coffee, take a walk to the beach, return to the apartment, grade a few final student compositions, have lunch, try to think of something to do afterwards, and go see Babs at three o'clock. Then they would eat dinner together—tuna fish. They had decided to eat tuna fish the rest of their stay in remembrance of Larry. It was the very least they could do for him.

Buster wished his kingdom for a little variation in life. The only thing that was keeping him alive was his mind tripping. He was traveling to new places every day. His mind was taking him through dimensions he had never experienced before. One hour he would be in Yemen, another hour he would be walking through the labyrinths of obscure Arabian cities accompanied by lions, his newfound friends. He had been known amongst his peers at the university for being a world famous daydreamer, but this was getting ridiculous. At least it was keeping him alive.

The days were also getting incredibly hot and humid. He took a walk one morning around eight thirty and noticed that the thermometer on the recreation hall door read eighty-seven degrees, relative humidity, eighty-seven per cent. The sun came pouncing down as hard as a conch beater. But it was never fear—no sweat! For Buster Murdock's intelligence had come through again. The second-hand, office air-conditioner that he had bought in Nassau over the vacation was working fine and well. The only problem was that if the machine was not turned up all the way on full cool, it would stop altogether; therefore, there was only one speed, full cool. So day after day Buster would sit reading his travel books in a crisp, sixty-degree room temperature with two pairs of woolen socks on, Long-John, thermal underwear and two coats, still freezing his butt off. And just a doorknob away it would be ninety-five degrees—boiling.

There were only three weekends left for the couple on the island. Buster wanted to be alone with Babs as much a possible. "Ah, thank God it's Friday!" Buster said to himself. "Babs doesn't have to work tomorrow and she can spend the night. Ah, alone at last again with Babs. Hmmm, let's see. I'll pick her up at the Navy base and bring her back on Naomi—that way she won't have to park her car out front. Ah, it's going to be great to sleep in on Saturday again with her. With my air-conditioned room we'll cuddle up to each other and sleep as tight as two magnets. Then we'll go exploring to Watlings Castle, and then stay home Saturday night and be by ourselves. Then we'll sleep in again on Sunday—have a late breakfast and coffee—Sweet Jesus, life's fantastic!"

He hopped on Naomi and roared towards the Navy base going eighty miles an hour. He reached the base in record time, seven minutes. He was getting pretty good at making those curves now. He pulled into Babs' driveway, and with a final, screaming rev, he cut the engine.

Babs' head peered out the door. "Hmmm," she said with a mouthful of pound cake. "You're here! Come, I just made some Kool-Aid."

Buster entered her apartment. Babs started to pour a glass of Kool-Aid, but before she could put the container down, the two were hugging and kissing. Then they finally made it down to the floor, rolling around, laughing and giggling like two kids wrestling.

"Hold on, woman, let me drink my Kool-Aid, will you?" Buster said, standing up and brushing off his clothes. "All this rolling around is making me thirsty!" He took a big swig from his glass.

Babs moved to the dining room table. "Guess what, Buster?" she said.

"Can't guess!"

"I've got something to tell you!"

"Uh oh, it's one of those, eh?"

"Not really."

"Well, let's have it!"

"Mr. Garville, the chief Education officer from Nassau, wants to see me for an urgent meeting tomorrow at 9:00 A.M. sharp!"

"Well that son-of-a-bitch! There goes our sleeping in, eh?"

"It sounds important. It sounds like it could be about us, and I'm nervous."

"Oh, don't worry! It's probably a commendation or a transfer to a better island."

"No, I just have a feeling!"

"Damn, there goes our Saturday morning sleep- in!" He walked over from the refrigerator and gave her a kiss on the forehead. "Oh well, there'll be a few other Saturday mornings."

"Oh, well I hope so, certainly," she said. "But I have another confession to make."

"Uh oh, now what?"

"I just got a telegram from Brad an hour ago."

"Oh yeah? And?"

"It said that he had received the Dear John letter I had sent to him and that he was willing to take a chance." Babs had sent a negative sounding letter to her loved one in Canada a couple of weeks ago, stating the state of the union to him: "You can come down in July if you want, Brad, but after all this time, I'm not sure if I still love you or not," she wrote.

"Well, he's willing to take a chance, eh?" Buster said. He chuckled, for the news did not really bother him in the least. "Well, when do you want to go to Buenos Aires?"

"Anytime, Buster, anytime. I want to tell you right now that come hell or high water, I love you! You are the man that I want."

"Right! That's what they all say. You know, what is all this madness, anyway? I came here to have a good time starting from this afternoon onwards and already I've been slapped in the face and beat down twice!"

"Oh, Buster dear, don't feel bad!" she said stroking his cheek. They kissed hard and went into the bedroom, Buster carrying his glass of Kool-Aid.

After bouncing around on the bed for a "Quickie," Buster started getting dressed. He turned to Babs lying limply on the mattress. "Hey, Babs, I have a confession to make, Love."

"Eh?"

"Ha! Eh? you say. You Canadians and your 'Eh's'!"

"Eh?"

"There is a social tonight at the student union for those ministers from Nassau. My presence is required. Mr. Garville himself is going to be there!"

"Well Jesus Christ, those sons-of-bitches!" She sat upright. "There goes our Friday night together, eh?"

"Yeah, I suppose so—but there'll be a few more Friday nights together, don't worry!"

"Do you think I should go?"

"I don't know. What do you think?"

"It's up to you!"

"Hell, I dunno! What do you think?"

"If Mr. Garville is going to be there, maybe not, eh?"

"Maybe you're right'" Buster agreed.

"I could just go to the Rip at the United Estates Village with Maria Dolores while you go to the social—then you could pick me up afterwards."

"OK, that sounds OK. Jesus Christ, whatever happened to this Friday? Maybe we ought to start all over again!"

"It's a deal!" Babs said. "We'll start all over again tomorrow morning. It couldn't be worse than today, eh?"

"See you later on tonight then. And don't get picked up!"

"Right!"

Buster returned to his apartment.

So Friday evening, Buster went to the social at the student union and Babs went to the Rip at the bar in the United Estates Village. The social was horribly boring for Buster. Everybody asked him where Miss Barbara Oskalowski was: "Where's Barbara, where 's Barbara? At least you could have brought Barbara along—Where's the young lassie?" These people made Buster feel bad. *But*, he thought, *what the fuck? These are just little people anyway*!

The only person who did not ask where Babs was and the only person who supplied a somewhat hardy conversation was Mr. Ginnis. He was exceptionally nice to Buster this evening.

"How's the kayak, Mr. Murdock?" Mr. Ginnis said, keeping a diplomatic smile.

"Oh, it's just fine, thank you Mr. Ginnis," Buster said politely. "But now I think I know why you refused to take a ride in it last week."

"Why is that, Mr. Murdock?"

"It's not insured!"

"Ha, ha, ha, ha, ha!!!" Mr. Ginnis shrieked like a hyena.

"And your wife doesn't like boats that are not insured, right?"

"Ha, ha, ha. Right indeed, Mr. Murdock. Right indeed." He continued to laugh, his teddy-bear belly jiggling.

As boring as the party was, at least they all had a good meal: chicken, peas and rice, salad and lots of Cold Duck champagne. After the meal, Buster just had to go and see Babs. He could not stay with these "Little people" any longer. He hated to just eat and run; but, he ate and ran.

When he got to the Rip, Babs was sitting over in a corner all alone—the band blasting away.

"How come you're not dancing, Babs?" he asked.

"You know, I've been alone all night and no one has asked me to dance. I have been tagged as being owned by someone—sacred ground, eh? Now nobody will even talk to me!"

"The hazards of being in love, Babs!"

"And I love it! Let's go home!"

The two went back to her place and made love. Then Buster returned to his apartment to start all over again on Saturday, leaving Babs to contemplate the up-coming conference with the Education minister, Mr. Garville.

On Saturday morning, Buster slept late in his cool, air-conditioned, sixty-degree room. He woke up around nine o'clock, figured out where he was, realized that Babs' meeting did not even start until nine o 'clock and that she would not be in his room until at least another hour or so, so he rolled over and went back to sleep.

A horrible dream came upon him. He dreamed that Babs had gotten pregnant. Because of the mishap, she wanted to get married and have the baby; but because marriage and children made Buster nervous, especially at his young age, he wanted her to get an abortion. He believed in abortions. It was just one of those things. He believed that a human being was not a human being until after it was out and breathing, eating, urinating and defecating. In the womb the baby was just like any other organ, a growth, a tumor, and getting an abortion was like getting one's tonsils out. Certainly it would be better than bringing the thing into the world without one of the parents around. The woman especially would undergo a lot less emotional strain. Buster did not agree with the Japanese, who believed that a human being was a human being starting from the moment of conception, and that a baby was already nine months old at birth. Polish Canadians thought somewhat similarly; at least in the fact that an abortion was murder and "All that other madness," as he put it.

He woke up just at the time of the decision, so he really could not tell the outcome. He did wake up shaking, though. Maybe it was because the dream brought back bad memories of when he had to go through an abortion scene in Gainesville. The girl he was dating at the time somehow or another got pregnant. He could not understand how she did get pregnant, but she did. In any case, she did not want the baby and he did not want it either. So, they went through a nightmare of experiences to get rid of the bulging organ: pushing her down the stairs, which did not work; hauling off and slugging her in the belly as hard as he could, which did not work; throwing her some Judo moves, Ogoshiis and Tamoinagiis, which also did not work. She then threatened to throw Buster in jail and sue him and tell the police and "All that other madness," if he did not go to New York City with her for an illegal, but doctor performed, abortion and "All that other madness."

Barbara banged on the door, barged in the room and woke Buster up. "It's what I thought!" she said, her eyebrows crinkled.

"Well, God—damn!" he said, wiping the sleep from his eyes. "What happened?"

She started talking ninety miles an hour: "He was forced into talking to me—I know it, he was forced into it! We sat down in the office right at 9:00 and immediately he broke out in a cold sweat."

"Well, what did he say, for crying out loud?"

"It was Ginnis—Ginnis, I know it was Ginnis!"

"OK, OK, OK, but what did he say?"

"OK! He said first: 'Now Miss Oskalowski, there have been rumors going around that you have been staying overnight quite frequently at the college.' I tranquilly said yes. Then he said, 'Well, I have no idea of the validity of these rumors, but we must see to it that such things be curbed.' He started wringing his hands like he was washing them with a bar of soap."

"Well, go on, go on!" Buster demanded. "What did you say after that?"

"Well, all I said was, yes, Mr. Garville. What else could I say? I assured him that these rumors would not continue."

"And that was it?" Buster said, shrugging.

"Well, we talked about transfers. He was rather surprised as to why I would want to leave, especially after only one year here. But other than that, yes, that was it. But I swear to you that it was Mr. Ginnis who forced him to talk to me—I just know it!"

"The asshole! Really! This turns me right off!"

Just then Ethlyn Silversmith pulled up to Buster's front door in her Toyota and gave a honk. He walked outside to greet her, still grumpy at Babs' news.

"Hi, Buster!" Ethlyn said. "Get the news?"

"Yeah, fuck, I got the news!" he grunted. "What's up, Eth?"

"Message for Babs: Canadian telephone call for her between two and two thirty this afternoon at the telephone shack."

"What? You mean the thing's actually working?"

"Miracles can happen, Buster," she said. "Even on this island! See you later."

"Well, I'll be damned! Thanks Eth. See you!" He went inside. "Hey Babs—Telephone call for you between two and two thirty."

Big tears welled up in Babs' eyes. "Well, there goes our Saturday."

"Yes, Babs. There goes our Saturday! But there'll be other Saturdays."

And the phone call did ruin their Saturday afternoon, too, because the two lovers sat for three hours anxiously awaiting the call, expecting it to be of some importance. But it only turned out to be Brad in Canada. He was really "Fucked up," as Buster bluntly described him, over the Dear John letter Babs had sent. Over the phone Brad sounded like a lost puppy dog whining for its master. Babs was disgusted with his weakness. Buster just plainly explained to her that Brad was one confused guy whose college sweetheart was finally breaking away and that he was having one hell of a time trying to understand it all.

"Ah, yes," Buster explained, trying to perk up Babs' spirits. "To be young again and have that happen for the first time again. Well, I remember the first time when it happened to me. It came down on me like a big, fucking sledgehammer. But the first time was the hardest. Then the second time a chick shafted me, I was almost used to it. Then after the fifth time, I just started numbing out altogether. Now I'm at a point where I could give a flying fuck! Don't worry 'bout it baby doll. He'll get over it. Smile!"

She did not smile. After the phone call she cried on Buster's shoulders on the back of Naomi on the return stretch to the college. They entered the apartment, melancholically made love, then slept away the rest of the afternoon.

That evening, as much as they wanted to be alone and wallow in their sorrow, they had been invited to Anne Troff's place for dinner. They felt obligated to go. Spaghetti was on the menu with lots of Cold Duck champagne. Maria Dolores from the Finger Lakers, from San Juan Puerto Rico, was going to be there as well. Buster thought that it just might turn out to be a rather interesting evening.

Maria Dolores was strikingly good looking. She had that Latin American look: dark complexion, long, black hair and deep, penetrating eyes set back in her head. Her voice, not to mention her body, was smooth, suave and sexy. She was actually Buster's type of woman. However, he could not sit and really google-eye her because he was with Babs; but, the Puerto Rican did something to him just by looking into his eyes.

At the dinner table Buster had come to the realization that he was probably envied by every man on the island.

There he was, surrounded by three extremely beautiful women, having a great meal with all the wine he desired and listening to Beatles records. He really had it made. It felt fantastic to him. A certain air of contentment filled his heart. Inwardly he gave thanks to whomever, or whatever was responsible for all of this. He was happy.

Since he was surrounded by women, they did most of the talking. The conversation centered around fornicating, of course. It was quite interesting for Buster. He got a good insight on the female viewpoint of the birds and the bees. Through Anne Troff's gossipy mouth, he found out that Mr. Ginnis had two children on the island by two female students at the college—all of this occurring last year. Anne also mentioned that girl students were spotted coming out of Osborne Stubbs' cottage at all hours of the evening and early mornings. She also mentioned casually, and in passing, that while her husband, David, was on Great Exuma Island for Teaching Practice, she herself was balling one of the second year students on campus. Not only that, but she herself had never achieved orgasm by a man—only she herself could achieve such a feat. While she was telling all this, she was crying in her spaghetti.

Meanwhile, Maria Dolores was sitting next to Anne, comforting her and telling her that everything was "Cool," and that she had been faithful to her husband for seven whole years until she started "fucking around." Then the shocker came. Maria Dolores said that she could not understand why Ethlyn Silversmith had been so cold to her this whole week. Maybe it was because she had made love to Ethlyn and her husband, Berry, last week in their big king-size bed with an overhanging, sex-view mirror. "But that would be no real reason for being given the cold shoulder," she thought aloud.

Maria Dolores just could not understand this frigidity and "Snobby" treatment—especially after she loved everybody and everything. Then, she started crying in her plate of spaghetti.

Meanwhile, Barbara was sitting opposite Maria Dolores with her eyes bulging and her heart sinking down to the floor. She could hardly believe this story. She nervously smothered her spaghetti with garlic, salt and thyme. She then added a little bit of her own salt with a stream of tears falling from the bottom of her tomato-pasted chin, not understanding the actions of Berry and Ethlyn—especially after all the things these "Great friends" of hers had preached to her about being good and faithful and true. Her tears dropped into the entanglement of spaghetti on her plate.

Meanwhile, Buster was sitting at the head of the table, smoking a cigar and constantly refilling his glass with Cold Duck. His own tears welled up in his eyes. He just could not believe the lying, cheating, scheming, unfaithfulness and instability of womankind.

After dinner, Babs and Buster went back to the apartment and went to bed. Lying in the darkness Babs said, "Buster, why won't people let us love each other?"

"Perhaps it's not in the stars, Babs," he said.

"Oh, cut it out!" she snapped.

"Well, hell, what else can I say? What kind of an answer do you want me to give you?"

"Something with more wisdom than that!"

Buster sighed long and hard. "I'm too young for wisdom," he managed to blurt out softly. And he rolled over and drifted off to sleep, trying to dream of a Sunday alone with Babs— trying to dream of a perfect day together.

Strangely enough, that day came on Sunday. Everything

went right, contrary to all the wrongness that had happened to them in less than two days. Babs and Buster spent a beautiful day together, not caring that in three weeks time they would never see each other again. It was "Be here now, baby," day and "Big ice-cream cone in the sky, baby" day. And it was beautiful. They went to the East Beach, which stretched for miles. They were alone, just the two of them on a ten mile long beach. They took their clothes off, and for the whole day they enjoyed each other's love.

However, that night they went to the Coast Guard station to take in the movie. It happened to be a horror movie called, *Hitler, the Last Ten Days*. The movie was filled with violence, death and concentration camp miseries. What a contrast it was to the life and times the couple had experienced just hours before. But they erased the picture from their minds, refusing to let it ruin their day.

Buster went home alone for the evening. He needed time to himself, time to mentally prepare himself for the skepticism he knew he would confront in the last remaining days on San Salvador.

According to both Henri Charriere and Alexander Solzhenitsyn, it is in prison where a man does the most thinking. So Buster thought that, being on San Salvador, he could get some good thinking accomplished. But then again, he thought that maybe these two authors were wrong. Being in prison could work both ways, either extreme: thinking or non-thinking. Surely there must be a lot of dullards, listlessly, thoughtlessly rotting away in their cells—just as well as there are a lot of people listlessly and thoughtlessly rotting away on San Salvador. *God Almighty!* he thought. *The plethora of dull, narrow minds on this speck of land.*

People were so concerned with trivia: who did what,

where, when, how and to whom. And the problem was, every rumor was taken as the cardinal truth. Pregnancy was the biggest rumor, and gigantic preposterous rumors as to who made love to whom were flying all over the place. Rumor had it that Mrs. Ginnis already had five children on another island by a man other than her husband, and that Father Villeneuve's wife, Anne, had been pregnant now for two years.

And Austin Riley and his wife were not invited to the last Friday night Anglican Spiritual program—which caused a war. The Riley-Ginnis Feud had been carrying on for some time. The differences were mainly that Mr. Ginnis simply could not stand the white little, British physical education coach, and the coach still failed to recognize the reality that this roly-poly, teddy-bear of a black man could hold such a position as principal of the college.

The war reached new heights when one afternoon the Ginnis' Volkswagen was involved in a hit-and-run accident on the campus. Mrs. Ginnis had hit one of Riley's chickens, and the car, instead of stopping, high-tailed it up the hill, back to the Ginnis cottage to avoid confrontation. At the time, Buster was tuning up Naomi and taking her around the block for a spin. When he passed the Riley's apartment he noted chicken feathers strewn all across the road. "No shit!" he thought. "The chickens must be molting for the summer!" He took another spin around the block, and when he came back around, he saw the short, stocky coach carrying a dead chicken by the feet. Buster pulled up alongside Riley thinking that the coach had butchered the chicken for dinner, like he had done many times before.

He looked at Riley straight in the eyes. "Go tell Aunt Rhody!" he innocently said, revving the motorcycle.

"What?" Riley snapped, his eyes red with anger.

*Jesus*! Buster thought. *What's gotten into this guy?* "I said, Go tell Aunt Rhody—the old gray goose is dead!"

"What?"

"Go tell Aunt Rhody—the old gray goose is dead!"

"Hmmm, yes, very funny Murdock!" Riley stated with a stiff, upper lip. "Very funny—very funny indeed." He turned his back and walked home.

It was only later that Buster found out what happened. He felt truly like a "Donkey's ass," as he thought. But what could he do? It was not his war. And the war got even more complicated when Riley dragged the Assistant Warden in on it, demanding that he report the incident to Corporal Nightborn. But the Cop just happened to be Mr. Ginnis' best friend. The British ex-patriot did not have a chance.

The final days were dragging by so slowly that Buster just had to do something to occupy his time. But to do anything different was hard to do: there was absolutely no variety. He tried keeping a small diary to write some of his prison thoughts down, but the boredom kept distracting him from writing anything profound. However, the diary helped at times, even though the writing was spontaneous and very sporadic. Using yellow, legal pad paper, his writing sessions were short; mainly for cathartic reasons more than anything. The sessions were divided on the paper with thick lines. Half the time he was stoned and his thoughts seemed much more profound at the time than they really were.

Some of his first sessions produced various thought patterns:

"Trivia— trivia around this dump! Just trivia, trivia, trivia. My kingdom for a Guru! Somebody tell me about life! I mean, after all, I've seen some hard times in my young asshole life. Surely life can't end up to be something as simple as this."

---

"And now for the fucking complications. Yes, you guessed it: Barbara! I have just been informed by her that she is going back to her boyfriend in Canada. Oh, woe is me! Hurt my heart! And doesn't it figure that it must be in the stars for me? But I didn't want her anyway, remember, Buster ol' boy? She's not my type, anyway: fat when she gets older—chain-smoking, maybe—yuck! I had a dream the other night that I saw my true love side by side with Barbara. Boy, what a difference. I smiled with great joy and elation at my sweet smiling brunette-haired girl. Boy, was I relieved at the choice I made."

---

"So go away my fair-eyed lady of Polish descent from Canada land! And remember my love goes with you. And remember me in the morning when our kisses were deep and warm and your head was upon my shoulder like the sun upon the sea. And now I'm getting too sentimental and schmaltzy. Goodbye, Babs, my Barbara. Good luck and screw you!"

---

"I think the first thing I'm going to do when I get back to the United States is find a whore and spend a whole fucking day and fucking night with her—just for fucking's sake. Fuck all this romance bullshit!!!"

---

"I wonder how many more loves I am going to have in my life?

---

"Every man has got a life story—Wow!"

---

"Grass stash almost empty—gotta get back to the States!"

---

There were only seven days left on the island. Buster was still so confused as to where to go for the summer. But one thing was decided: he was pretty sure of coming back to the island in September. After three months of travelling, he would be broke and would need the money. He did not feel like looking for another job or having to move all his junk. So, it would be back to San Salvador for at least one more term in the fall. Perhaps then he would take the money and run. South America, Mexico, Spain? Anywhere, just off the island.

But he remembered that it was just a month ago that he was really enthusiastic about returning in September: especially making that nine thousand dollars a year. But these last several days gave him very serious doubts. The pettiness, the idle minds, the trivia was getting increasingly irritating. He began to realize that the people around him would stab their own mother for personal gain. A good example was when Buster talked to Patrick Cramble one morning in the kitchen. The conversation was halfway decent. Cramble was very polite and in unusually good spirits.

Then that afternoon, Buster found out that Cramble had talked to Barbara later on in the day and told her that that repulsive Murdock bully was greedy, inconsiderate, self-centered and did not have any marking to do on final exams because Peter Kentard did not trust Mr. Murdock with the papers.

Buster wrote in his diary: "What *an* asshole!! And this slovenly, bedraggled imbecile told that to my very own girlfriend? What a complete, utter, idiotic, mongoloid asshole!!!!"

---

Buster was beginning to think of Cramble as the lowest form of life on Earth—even lower than an amoeba. The day after this incident, Cramble came back from the airport telling Buster that his absence from the airstrip was quite conspicuous as well as the absence of Mr. Ginnis. Cramble, the fat, pudgy, baby-faced excuse of a man was almost in tears over this. He thought it was incredibly stupid for the principal to miss such an important event as the summer farewell to the students.

*Trivia*! Buster thought. *Such fucking trivia! What an asshole! The man is dead! Here he is, Patrick Cramble, a twenty-eight year old, supposedly educated man with a Master's degree, who thinks in this manner. His mind doesn't seem to be there but really back with the nuts in the institution that he taught in for five years. Fuck*!

All this did not make sense to Buster. He tried to see the good in all people, for every person had his story—as the writings of "Desiderata" proclaimed. But people like Cramble seemed to be dangerous—willing to stab anybody in the back. It just did not make sense to him. Buster knew everybody had a mind for some reason on Earth, but to try and see the purpose of Cramble's mind seemed hopeless. All Buster could see was waste, total waste. The man was dead.

Trivia upon trivia kept eating at Buster. The age-old war with the Ginnis family versus the Expatriates proved that apartheid would be the only solution. Plus, the students possessed their share of mindless trivia as well. The students seemed to be more concerned with being spoon-fed rather than actually wanting to learn something. He proctored a mathematics exam one day and could not believe the amount of cheating going on. The exam entailed solving simple algebraic equations that any American eighth grader could work out quite easily. Granted, Buster realized that these students were behind in the world and needed help, but at times they did not seem to want it. They had an arrogance about them that showed that they were "Cool, hip," and because they had been selected as the elite to attend the college, they did not have to study. But the hard fact was that the reality was quite the contrary: they were not "Cool" and they seemingly did not know anything.

The trivia that the administration also pulled off at times worried Buster.

Sometimes thoughts would flash through his mind that he would be kicked off the island— just like John Dailey had been in the early spring—unexpectedly and without warning. Out-and-out lies reported on Dailey to Mr. Ginnis, all the way from drug pushing to raping students, were just a way of getting a white, ex-patriot Brit kicked off the island. This worried Buster. What would prevent this from happening to him? He could not know this, however. But he did know for a fact that Dailey had absolutely nothing to do with either drugs or girl students. Dailey literally "Busted his ass" to help students develop their musical talents—and there were no thanks from the head man, either. Was Buster's turn coming up next? Columbia anyone? Venezuela, Argentina?

He wrote in his legal pad diary: "It's just incredible! Time drags on so much here. It just fucking drags, drags, drags, fucking drags, drags, fucking drags, and I gotta get outta here!"

---

"The love that I have for Babs is dying. I'm just tired of everything here right now. It has gotten to the point where I don't even like to ball her anymore. She comes over and smothers me with kisses and sprawls her body on *my* bed. But Jesus, I just can't get into it anymore. And I can't tell her that either, or she'll get all bent out of shape and cry and commit suicide and all that other good stuff. So I just go along with it hoping that the days will pass swiftly, which they don't, and hope that I can endure this last week and bid Babs a farewell that will be as pleasant as possible."

---

"Grass stash almost empty—gotta get back to the States!"

---

As for returning in September, probably if Buster had stayed another two weeks on the island he would have derived a definite negative conclusion. Things were getting so bad it was almost unbearable. Everybody he talked to said something derogatory about someone else—it could not be avoided. It was really disappointing to always have to be in contact with people containing no more intelligence than this. It was almost frightening to think about the narrow-minded, dangerous people coming back here to work next year: Mr. Ginnis, Osborne Stubbs, Father Villeneuve, Patrick Cramble and Lord knows who else new would come drifting in. These people were some of the most dangerous people in the world. They were dangerous because they forced their own ideas, values and lifestyles on others. It was fortunate, indeed, that such a collection of narrow-minded, fun-hating, un-loving creatures was concentrated on a small island with only a thirty-five mile circumference. Not much damage could be done on an island with nothing on it. It was like bailing water out of a boat with holes in it. But the holes in these people's heads were as hollow as empty conch shells, and fortunately the sea set a limitation as to how far their ideas, values and lifestyles could go.

Buster wrote in his diary: "Let me off this island!! I need intellectual stimulation very badly and contact with normal people (whatever that means). And I won't be able to eat tuna the rest of my life. I'm screaming. I'm drowning. I'm climbing the fucking walls. This is a prison, and I must escape! Fuck!"

---

"Grass stash empty—gotta get back to the States!"

---

And like most diaries, their writers losing interest and leaving unwritten thoughts to drift into the cosmic abyss, these words were the last that he wrote in his own diary.

And it was off the island at last—back to civilization at last: back to television, newspapers, real people, decent food and all that other American "Bullshit," as Buster described it. But the whole affair of getting out of the Bahamas was one big strain mentally, physically and emotionally.

The mailboat trip was the biggest strain. Typically Bahamian, the *San Salvador Express* reached its home island at eight in the morning. Buster asked the first mate how long the vessel was going to be docked before leaving: "Half an hour or so, mann!" the sailor replied. So with only a half an hour, Buster did a six hour packing and room-securing job in fifteen minutes. He jammed all his clothes in the closet and secured Naomi with chains inside the corridor. He was then off to the dock with only one suitcase and his guitar.

When he arrived, Babs was waiting for him. She was surrounded by all her worldly possessions. She had decided to definitely not return in the fall. The two knew that they were going to part shortly; however, this fact had still not registered in their minds. They both did not think it was possible that a separation was coming up. The two proceeded to jump on the boat, thinking that they had just made it on time. But, in reality they had to wait for four hours before the boat shoved off.

Meanwhile, on the other side of the protected harbor on the jetties, several native islanders were drowning a pack of wild dogs that they had captured earlier in the morning. The men mercilessly grabbed the poor, squirming mutts by the neck, the canines literally yelping for their lives, making a terrible, eerie sound of death. They then jammed the dogs' heads down in the water until their bodies stopped moving. Then the men let them go, leaving the limp, inanimate corpses to drift in the water. The current threw several of the corpses up on the jetty rocks to rot in the salt water and sun. This revolting scene made the four- hour wait seem like days for the couple. By the time the "Express" actually did shove off, Babs and Buster were already worn out from the wait and asphyxiated by the diesel fumes from the mailboat's engines. As they waved goodbye to San Salvador, the island slowly sinking below the horizon line, they gave a hearty toast of rum to the island and finally cracked smiles that were as wide as the beam of the boat itself. Austin Riley, who was also on board accompanying his blue Volkswagen back to Nassau, managed to crack a wide grin.

When the boat reached Rum Cay much later than scheduled due to the failure of one engine, the vessel anchored off shore so the crew would have a chance to fix the engine. While the men were working, mosquitoes were feeding: millions of mosquitoes feasted on skin and blood. Babs was sick. She hated suffering like this. She longed for a tea bar with dainty flowers and white tablecloths. This true-grit madness of the *San Salvador Express* was contrary to her entire way of being.

Finally after five hours of unscheduled anchorage, and with all the engines repaired, the boat was on its way on a steady cruise to Cat Island. But Babs and Buster could not sleep that night. Their stateroom, one of the very few, was filled with diesel fumes that gave them migraine headaches. The two, soon-to-be-parted lovers had wanted to make love on the high seas, but they were too sick and oily to even touch each other. In the middle of the night, Babs got seasick. She threw up out of the porthole, half-digested peas and rice splashing all over the side of the steel hull. It was a nightmare for her—how she suffered so!

The next day on Cat Island, the *San Salvador Express* had to wait another five hours at the dock because the man who was to bring the badly needed diesel fuel for the engines was at church. He refused to make a move until he was let go by the spirit.

After the long wait, the ship made a short hop to another part of Cat Island, to Smith's Bay, where goats, pigs, chickens, crabs, dogs, a car and a small, cabin-cruiser sailboat were all loaded on board. It was like Noah's Ark all over again. Following behind all of this came three distressed sailors and an eccentric old hermit—all white-Caucasian Americans.

The three distressed sailors were all bummed out with abysmally low spirits. Their twenty-four foot sailboat had gone down on a reef at three in the morning. They had rowed eight miles to shore and barely got out with their own lives. They had spent a week-and-a-half salvaging their things by going down in air tanks. Besides losing their boat, they lost a lot of cash as well.

The skipper of the lost boat, Jay, was a real character. He was tall, lean, long blond hair and with a deep southern accent. He told Buster that the wreck was a result of navigational problems: the charts were wrong and the beacon lights were out. As a result, they ended up behind the island rather than in front of it and ran right into a coral reef that came right out of nowhere. Skipper Jay lost his whole house—everything he owned—gone in five minutes. But he took it in stride. He said something divine was happening to him. He had been in nine accidents in the past nine months, and he wrecked his boat on the ninth of June: "Strange, very strange," he said to Buster. "But luck all anyway! Just a few months work in a boatyard and I'll have enough for a down-payment on another one."

For the rest of the trip, Noah's Ark made a straight shot to Nassau—non-stop. It was quite a pleasant voyage for Buster. But Babs was still in misery, not being able to eat the cook's peas, rice and pigs' feet in the galley. She also could not sleep with the diesel fumes bothering her, could not go to the stern because the people were packed in like the slave trading days and she could not make love to Buster because she felt so dirty, oily, salty and "Everything else."

But as she wallowed in her misery down in the stateroom, Buster, Riley, the three distressed sailors and the hermit, all sat around on the top deck, drinking dark Matusalem Rum and exchanging jokes and stories the rest of the night. "This is great!" Buster said, "Absolutely great!"

On the third day they rose again with Nassau finally in sight. When they docked, everybody was totally wiped out, feeling and looking like zombies: tired, sick, weary and windblown. Buster and Babs unloaded their possessions and immediately went looking for a hotel. The first one they went to turned them away because of Buster's long hair and knotted beard: also because of the foul aroma from the mailboat that they were emitting. But they finally landed a place at the Pilot House. They were so tired, that without even showering, they plopped in bed and passed out, totally dead to the world within five minutes.

After a few days of recuperating from the mailboat journey and running around Nassau getting bank accounts and paychecks straightened out, it was off the island of New Providence and back to the continent for the forlorn couple. On the plane back to Florida they hardly spoke a word, knowing that within a matter of hours they would never see each other again. Just the mere thought of this chilled both their spines and set them back into quiet depression.

Saying goodbye to Babs was much harder than Buster had anticipated. The Miami airport was too sterile for such things. They ate breakfast in one of the restaurants, but both could barely swallow their overly-buttered toast. *Fucking people*, he thought. The white, short-haired, clean-shaven suits sitting to the right of them were talking Life Insurance, the black businessmen on the left of them were engulfed in a Real Estate conversation, and the mixed-colored people in back were talking about selling "Fucking" encyclopedias. *Money, money, money*, Buster thought. *These people live it, breathe it and shit it –incredible!*

When the first call for flight 904 to Toronto came over the loudspeaker, Buster picked up his heart from the floor and mustered up enough nervous energy to try and explain to Babs just why he was sending her back to Canada. But his reasons just did not make sense to him anymore—they sounded so dumb and childish. He therefore stood stupefied in his own silence. He put his sunglasses down on his nose so that he would not look so ludicrous: a grown man with long hair and a beard, carrying a guitar and crying his eyes out.

Babs was swimming in tears, just looking at Buster with those blue eyes of hers. But this time they were not beaming with enthusiasm and zest like they had always shown. They were now more like a dog's sad eyes begging its master not to go away. "Buster, dear, are you really going to make me go?" she said in a low, soft, breaking voice.

"Well, uh, you see it's uh— well, ya know we loved each other well, and like uh… Well, ya know?"

Babs just stared at him. "Yes, I know. Maybe if we were a little older, say like if you were 32 and I was 28 or something like that—then maybe, right?"

"Yeah—uh, right!" His sunglasses fogged up.

"Then maybe we could've made it—but I understand! You want to see the world and be free. I just wish we could've been together a little while longer."

"Well, uh, Jesus, ya know, I…uh…, I was gonna uh…"

Babs was looking around at all the people rushing past them, then interrupted Buster's poetic farewell: "Buster, I don't want anybody to look at your body but me!"

"Well Jesus, Babs, I didn't know you felt…"

"I don't see anybody here I want—nobody! I want you!" Her voice had tones of desperation.

Then it was time to part: final call for flight 904.

"Good," choke, "Bye," choke, "Babs," choke. Buster could not say anything more.

Babs stood there looking so good to Buster, so sophisticatedly sad, so beautiful. She gave a little wave and walked to the boarding area.

Tears were flowing down her face as she sat in her seat, not believing it was possible that she was actually in the plane alone. Her one last hope was that Buster, full of surrender, would make a dramatic entrance into the cabin, drag her off the plane and carry her off to a new road of life.

But Buster, with his suitcase in one hand and guitar case in the other and hiding behind his sunglasses, walked out of the main concourse to try and avoid all the people. *But Jesus!* he thought. *People, people every-God-damn-where, and they all seem to be selling Life Insurance, Real Estate and fucking encyclopedias.*

He walked over to an overnight parking lot and sat down on the railing looking into another layer of cars down below. He noticed a bumper sticker that read, "We Pray Daily." "Oh Jesus!" he said aloud. He turned away, listened to the dry wind and the sound of a jet taking off. A car whizzed by. He then broke down and wept.

Back in Daytona Beach, Buster wandered around for several days, not quite sure where he was, and above all, not believing that the Barbara Oskalowski affair was over. He felt empty. Strolling down the wide beach of Daytona looking at all the bikinis meant nothing to him. This was truly a strange phenomenon for him because in the "good ol' days" he would always look at the girls. His wang would pop up like a bedspring and he would start to salivate like a panting, hungry dog. But this time? He felt nothing. It was truly strange.

Where to go for the summer mingled with his lovesick thoughts. He was almost obsessed by it. He had to go somewhere—now that he was free. But that somewhere was the problem: Mexico, Peru, Brazil, Columbia? But he could not go any place where there was a culture that beat on drums, danced in circles and played dominoes. He was sick of all that—he had had enough.

He woke up early one morning, swearing, disgusted at himself for not having decided anything in two whole weeks. He took his checkbook and walked to a travel agency. On his way there he made his decision: "I fucking need culture!" he said to himself. "Culture, culture, culture is what I need! I don't wanna see anymore beaches for a while—I'm sick!" And he bought a two-month Eurorail pass and a ticket on the next flight to Luxembourg.

# PART 3

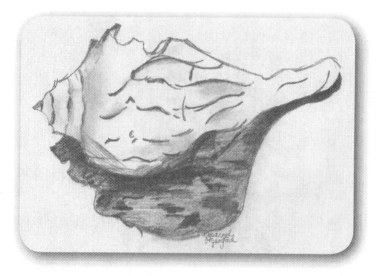

# CHAPTER 11

## *Wild Dog on the Loose*

For Buster Murdock, his hair cut reasonably short to clear customs easier, Europe was not anything spectacular—especially after all the things people had said about it. But his mental state contributed a great deal to this way of thought as well. He was not too receptive to new things at the moment. He did not much care about historical events and monuments nor the differences in culture.

The first several weeks in Europe were spent with an incredible loneliness and emptiness felt by the separation from Barbara. Spending time alone in drab, cheap European hotels magnified this loneliness tenfold. Of course, he had left her and not the other way around. However, from that very first day in Luxembourg, walking around those green parks with fairy-tale castles bordering them, he had caught a case of the "Blackass" and he had caught it bad. He kept thinking that maybe he had made a mistake after all and never should have left her like that. After all, she was really good to him: faithful, never treated him badly, and he always could do what he wanted. The emptiness was "A killer." He had never gotten used to separations from his girlfriends, no matter what side of the fence he was on: whether he had left them or they had left him, emptiness was emptiness—a large hole in the soul.

All he could remember during these first weeks were trite, little things that impressed on his mind when taking long walks around cities. Lausanne, Switzerland was clean—too clean for comfort. And all those "Stinking rich assholes" on their tiny, but un- believably expensive yachts down at Ouchy turned him completely off. Sailing on Lake Geneva just did not have the adventurousness that the Caribbean had. The whole thing was too "Asshole" artificial. And down in Florence, Italy, all he could remember was the bombardment of Florentine, marble busts of patriarchs, poets, painters, pontiffs, and philosophers raining down on his head all at one time, challenging his capability of fathoming any of it. When he walked around Rome, just about the only thing that stuck to his mind was the large, open market place and all the chickens with their heads being cut off and then being hung upside down for the blood to drip down into a large barrel.

But in Spain he started opening up. It was a combination of three things: one, he was getting tired of crying and thinking about the same thing all the time; two, it was almost a shame for him to let a woman, or the absence of one, bring him down like this; and three, he was beginning to become aware that he was on the European Continent.

Coming out of the Barcelona train station, he met a young American traveler like himself making the grand tour of Europe. His name was Steve Lechenstein from New York City. The two travelers decided to see the Catalan city together. Being the typical American tourists in Spain, as they were, they were not in the ancient metropolis even for two hours before they headed straight to the Sunday afternoon bullfights. Buster wanted to be with a lot of Spaniards, but discovered that the only real live Spaniards were the people actually handling and fighting the bulls. The rest of the people around him, and seemingly in the entire stadium, were English, French and German. The two got totally soused anyway on cheap *Spanish* wine and threw up in the middle of the third quarter of the game— that is to say, at least they thought it was a football game back in the States. Being so drunk, they could hardly see ten yards in front of them.

The following day, after they both had recovered, they walked the ancient labyrinth of Barcelona, a two thousand year old Catalan city. Buster poured out all of his pains, sorrows, and confusions to his newfound buddy. It was like mentally vomiting out everything he had kept inside of him for the entire year in the Bahamas. Buster talked to Lechenstein about things that he could not have communicated with to anybody on San Salvador: little things, cultural things that only another American could understand. They walked down by the port and saw the famous replica of Columbus' ship, the Santa Maria. Buster kept thinking all the time of the cross at the Columbus monument on San Sal. No matter how much Buster talked or even tried to forget, the small Bahamian island was still very much a part of his entire being.

Spending a week in Madrid was one of the highlights of Buster's entire trip. His first day there he met a pretty little

Spanish señorita named, of all original Spanish names, Maria Pilar Alolea. The two met at a hot dog stand in the Plaza del Sol. Pilar had stopped in for a quick Horchata de Chufa drink while Buster was gorging down some resemblance of a hamburger with mustard. Then he asked Pilar to pass the salt in his broken Spanish. She laughed at his accent, and it was all downhill after that. The young brunette with wide, black eyes and dark complexion instantly took to the cute looking Yankee with a "Barba Española," a Spanish beard. She took him all around Madrid, visiting the Prado Museum, La Plaza Mayor, the famous flea market called "El Rastro" and the Retiro Park. Pilar was so different, such a pleasant change from all the Caucasian women Buster had been with. She had such a nice disposition and mentality that she seemed to have cleansed his wounded heart and gave him a reason for becoming light hearted and level headed once again.

It was on the train back from an excursion to El Escorial, a large royal palace on the outskirts of Madrid, when she started to smother Buster with kisses and to crawl all over him, whispering occasionally in his ear, "Te quiero, te quiero," I love you, I love you, and repeating, "No te vayas mañana, no te vayas mañana," don't go tomorrow, don't go tomorrow. This almost convinced him of staying in Madrid the rest of the summer. But once back alone in the hotel and with a severe case of blue-balls wincing with pain (Pilar did not want to lose her virginity until she was absolutely sure), Buster decided to make a "Cavale" to Seville. That was all he needed— to get involved with another woman at the moment. Pilar had filled that hole, that vacancy in him, and he would always remember that. But that was as far as he wanted it to go. "Thank you, Pilar!" he said to himself on the train to Andalucia—"I love you too."

Seville was hell—one large burning furnace. Nobody told him it was so hot down there and he found out the hard way that late July, the first of August, was the hottest time of the year in Andalucia and nobody in his right mind would go down there then.

Rumor had it, whether it be true or not, that to drink from the fountain in the Seville train station brought good luck and that one would someday return to the enchanting city. So before Buster went looking for a cheap pension, he took a couple of nice big gulps from the blue tiled mosaic lion's head—the clear water steadily flowing beautifully from its pursed lips.

Buster paid for this dearly the rest of his European trip. The following day his stomach was in total chaos, in uproarious turmoil. His tongue changed colors: a sickly yellow with purple specks. It wasn't even mid-morning, just after breakfast, when he lost his entire innards, both frontwards and backwards. He vomited continuously the whole day and his number two was pure brown water. It came draining out so often that with the hard, crunchy Spanish toilet paper, his anus started to sting and bleed. And the room temperature was so hot. There was no breeze in his tiny cubicle and he lay for hours in bed in a pool of sweat, hallucinating nightmares of mosaic fountain lions spewing out brown water from their mouths: millions of lion heads menacingly coming at him, one right after another, spitting out diarrhea water, then drifting away leaving the sopped sheets as evidence that they were possibly really there.

The fourth day in Seville the sickened traveler managed to get up enough energy to drag himself out of bed and go to the city's cathedral, one of Europe's largest, where Christopher Columbus' tomb was. Buster was so determined to see this cathedral that he was going to get there if he had to crawl, and that's practically what he had to do. His body was emaciated. He had lost five whole kilos in four days. His rib cage stuck out like a Bangladesh refugee and his eyes were black and sunken back into his head. It was as if he had had a severe battle with death itself but had come out on top for the moment.

He walked slowly to the cathedral at midday, his clothes, soaked in sweat. He passed a bar with a thermometer hung in the shade outside: forty-two degrees Celsius. It was at least ten degrees more in the sun. Buster let out a quiet, whimpering, "Fuck Me," and limped onward.

Inside the dark cathedral it was much cooler. He sat down in a pew and prayed. In such pain, such total, energy-less submission to the divine, he muttered: "Dear Lord, please help me outta this place. I gotta get outta here! And I need your help—I'm in your hands now. Take me where you want me to be because I sure as hell can't get there by myself. Thank you, Amen!"

He got up and shuffled over to see Columbus' tomb. He was astounded by its size. It was a large white marble sepulcher with four giant male figures standing on top of it. The large figures, appearing to wear fifteenth century garb, carried a big chest on their shoulders, symbolizing the treasures that one of the world's greatest mariners of all time brought back from the Americas. Buster was deeply touched. He felt graced and thought it a high, divine honor just to be able to be where he was and see what he was seeing. Tears welled up in his eyes.

But suddenly he felt an excruciating bowel movement. He broke into a frantic search around the enormous cathedral looking for a toilette. But no! This was dysentery—not the ordinary Pepto Bismol cramp case, but the stomach disease that at times can get so bad that people die from it. And this case was so bad that it had no mercy on the sphincter muscles of Buster Murdock's anus. Nor did this disease care where Buster was. The warm liquid flowed out like water bursting through a broken dam and rushed into the lake bed of his sweaty Jockey underwear. He stopped short and felt the gooey substance ooze around his legs. He discovered himself by a small side chapel with a large, golden cross at the altar. A life-like wooden Jesus was nailed to it with a bigger than life expression of surprise and terror on its face. Buster looked at it shamefully and said: "Jesus, forgive me! I haven't done this since I was a baby—but I know you understand."

He fled quickly back to the pension—back to safety from the hot, cruel world. He cleaned himself and flopped onto his bed, grimacing in pain with every involuntary anal muscle spasm.

For the next two days all he could do was lie in bed and think of the cool sea breeze of the Bahamas and its transparent water and all the swimming and sailing. "Jesus!" he thought aloud, moaning and groaning to himself, "How I'd love to be sailing now—sitting back in Berry's boat, the sails snapped full of air, moving along at a reasonable clip, and with my fingers wrapped around a nice cold can of Heineken Beer—with twenty more in the ice chest. Oh Jesus, the sails, the sails, boats, boats! And after a nice day's sail, it's back to the warmth of Babs. Oh Jesus, Babs, Babs, Babs! Boats, Boats, Boats! That's it!! God-damn! That's it! I'11 go up to Canada and pick up Babs, and then we'll both go back down to San Salvador together and live just like we planned at the Riding Rock that night. Jesus, I love her.

Lord God give me Babs, give me sails, give me boats, boats, boats! I don't wanna hear another train whistle in all my life. Give me my own house, for Christ's sakes! I can't do anymore of these hotels—in my life—ever—again!"

Moan, groan and a long, gooey passing of wind—and he drifted off into sleep.

And that did it. That was his decision right then and there. It would be back to the Bahamas—away from all that European urban pandemonium and back to paradise once again. Enough of the European mid-summer bedlam, full of guidebook-toting tourists, arrogant polyglots, filthy, century-old train stations, car-honking street noise permeating un-breathable air pollution and stuffy, dank and dark art-cluttered cathedrals and museums. He needed turquoise water, sea breeze, sailboats and people speaking English again. He could not stand it any longer. Without stopping for a drink at the lion's head, he would catch the first train out of Seville the next day, even if he had to involuntarily defecate on every seat on the whole train. Europe was over.

# PART 4

# CHAPTER 12

## *High Tide—Low Tide*

After his European escapade, Buster Murdock went back home to Daytona Beach for a week-and-a-half. He needed to rest and recuperate and to collect some things to take back with him to San Salvador. It was once again a nice feeling to be back in the United States. It all looked so new in comparison with old Europe—it looked bigger, more expansive and somehow much cleaner. After several days of a steady diet of hamburgers, milk shakes and hot apple pies, his stomach was also getting back into shape.

But Buster's mind was still confused. He wanted Barbara more than anything else now. His mother said that Babs called just after he had left for Europe. He was glad to hear that. He called her several times every day, but there was no answer in Kapaskasing. He thought of even going up to see her, but both time and money were running a little short. Anyway, he would give a call once back down on San Salvador.

Going back down to San Salvador, he took the Monday Mackey Airline Special out of Fort Lauderdale. Mackey Airlines was going to go out of business shortly, and it was the last run to San Sal for the doomed airline. Because of this, there was only one other passenger on the plane back to the island; and of all passengers, it just had to be Buster's favorite human being, Patrick Cramble. *Jesus Christ*! he thought. *I've been halfway around the world this summer and I have to fucking end it all with this dope. If this is any sign of what it's going to be like this academic year, I have a feeling I'm not going to last very long.* They only exchanged simple courtesy greetings "Hello, how are you?" "Did you have a nice summer?" "Yes." "Good'" "Fine." Then Buster went into the cockpit and talked to the pilots the rest of the flight, while Cramble sat in the back of the passengers' cabin reading a book on Special Education theory.

When the plane landed and taxied to a halt, Buster went back to his seat to get a few things he had carried on the plane. Cramble had already stepped off the plane and disappeared. When Buster looked out the window, he saw a blue Yamaha one hundred cc with two Caucasians on it, waiting for mail. "Jesus Christ, it's Barbara!" he said loudly. "Jesus Christ, what the fuck is she doing down here already?" He walked down the plane ladder and stared at a surprised looking, blond-haired girl. She whispered something to the short, stocky male motorcyclist. She hurriedly got off the bike and stood planted on the airstrip while the motorcycle sped away.

Without saying a word, the two embraced, and they both started crying.

"Why did you leave me, Buster?" Babs said, finally breaking the silence.

"Babs, I'm sorry, baby—I'm sorry as hell! I missed you a lot and now I know that I want you. We can start again—this time it'll be much better!"

"Oh, Buster—why couldn't you have stayed in Europe or something? We've got to talk, eh?"

"Yeah, well let's go to my place!"

"OK, but Buster, we've got to talk, eh?"

"Of course—we've got all the time in the world now to talk. Baby, we're together again! By the way, who was that guy you were with on the motorcycle?"

"That was just Bub Sudner, the new British Physical Education coach at the high school."

"Oh!"

Buster went through the small customs trailer with his suitcase and guitar and then the two walked through a shrub field and behind the electric house to his apartment. He opened the door, and there was Naomi, just like he had left her. He gave her a kiss and a pat on the gas tank. They walked in the bedroom—musty with that smell of not being occupied for months. Buster immediately walked over and plugged in the air conditioner. All the time he was thinking that at last he had got Babs back again. At last he would get laid after a long, dry summer. He was so horny that he felt like a true Coastie. He was afraid that maybe he would prematurely ejaculate and make Babs think of Chris White again. He grabbed Babs and kissed her hard on the mouth. She resisted at first, but then they both slowly fell onto the double bed.

Suddenly, Babs turned strangely cold and stood up immediately. "Buster, before we do anything, I think you should know that Brad was down and we spent an entire week together here," she said in a rapid barrage of words.

"Oh yeah?" Buster's wang was as hard as a springboard now and his brain seemed to be in his penis.

"It wasn't the same as you and me, of course," she continued. "He did not like the island—no swimming, no sunning or anything, and he left last week. But I just thought you should know!"

"Well, that's OK—he's not here now. Come here!" He wanted to feel her body again. More than two long months without the comfort of a familiar female caress was driving him crazy. The past did not mean anything to him. What was done was done. It was the here and now that was important and he wanted her to sit on his face.

But Babs was cold and standoffish. She only lay down on the bed because of Buster's horny insistence. It was one of those flim-flam, thank you Ma'am sessions—a one sided orgasm on Buster's part. They flopped around on the mattress for only ten minutes and it was finished. Then came the time to talk.

"Buster, why did you come back? I was hoping you would stay in Europe!"

"Well, wait-a-minute! That's an awful thing to say. Baby, aren't you glad to see me?"

"If you want to know the truth, no! Especially after you left me like you did."

"Well Jesus, first of all you knew! We had it settled that we were going to separate —at least for the summer, right? And second of all, you were the one that wasn't coming back, remember? So the question, is, dear heart, what are you doing back here?"

"Well, Brad wanted to see the island. He had never been south of Toronto before."

"Oh, how romantic—and how you are concerned with the well-being of this dude, eh? Jesus Christ, now you're beginning to sound like Patty with that fucking hippie, Rick Ruft!"

"Well, what do you want me to do, Buster? You left me, remember? I was yours. I would have gone anywhere with you, done anything for you—but you abandoned me!"

"Well, I uh…"

"How terrible it was on that flight back to Canada. I didn't want to go, and the whole time I was crying, tears running down my face not believing you actually didn't come and take me off that horrible plane."

"Well Jesus, it wasn't exactly a happy occasion for me either, you know!"

"And when Brad picked me up, I just couldn't love him like he had hoped. My heart was with you all the time. And when we took a trip to Quebec together, the whole time he was crying because I did not love him, and I was crying because you left me, and it was absolutely dreadful!"

"Well Jesus, I told you I'm sorry, OK? I'm sorry, right? Look—I spent a lot of time thinking alone this summer. Travelling alone made me realize how much I missed you and how much I really care for you. I want you now—you are the one for me and we can live a happy life together."

"Oh no, that's not possible now!" She was getting colder and colder.

"What the fuck you mean, that's not possible?"

"It's just not possible now, that's all. Your own doubts showed me that you don't really love me. You were the one that doubted, not I."

"Well, now I'm not doubting and I want you!"

"It's too late, Buster—too much has happened now for

me to go back to you. I have decided to go back to my own ways. The things that you do frighten me now."

"Frighten you? What do you mean?"

"I mean that for example, if you smoked marijuana now, I would get up and leave. I'm totally against drugs now."

"Hey, speaking of that, I brought back some really good Peyote buttons that a friend of mine got in Colorado. We can do some, sometime."

"Buster, that's just what I'm talking about! I would never do drugs anymore. They scare me. And you scare me now, and I don't want any part of it."

He looked at her hard. "Jesus, you have changed, haven't you!"

"No, Buster. It's just that I had changed going with you. But now my year of adventure is over and I'm-going back to being myself again. I've made up my mind."

"Well fuck, what are you going to do now?"

"I was going to teach until December, but only under the hope that you would possibly not come back. But now that you're here, it's not possible for both of us to live on the island separately. It would cause too much of a scandal amongst the natives, and too many bad feelings between you and me."

"Jesus, fuck the natives," Buster said. But she had a point there. Plus, Buster thought, after having such a perfect island romance, it would not be the same seeing Babs every once in a while and not being able to touch her. Plus, the hard reality of her possibly starting another romance with some other man would be intolerable. Seeing them walking down the beaches embracing and kissing could do irreparable damage to his ego. He could not bare even the thought of it.

"So, I'll leave," she said almost without thinking.

"You'll leave?" he said without contesting.

"Yes. I'll go back to Canada. I'll catch the next plane out of here. I believe a plane leaves tomorrow for Nassau."

Buster thought quickly again about the possibilities or impossibilities of living separately. But she was right. It was best for at least one of them to leave. He did not argue. "OK, Babs. Perhaps it's the best thing to do. I don't think you should've come back down in the first place. You've probably already created a scandal bringing Brat down here."

"That's Brad—please!"

"Or whatever the fuck his name is!" His voice had a tone of sad surrender to it.

"I don't think we created much of a scandal. Poor Brad was inside most of the time. The first day on the beach he got cooked like a lobster. His skin was so red, so badly sunburned that he couldn't move for four days."

"Poor, little, delicate, Northern Canadian Bastard!"

"Please don't talk that way."

"Hey, let's get outta here!" Buster said. "Let's go for a ride on Naomi!"

They quietly got dressed. Without saying a word to each other, they prepared themselves for a ride on Naomi.

They rode to the white limestone cliffs near the Coast Guard station, Babs on the back gently squeezing Buster's stomach and lying her head on the back of his shoulder. When they reached the highest point on the cliffs, they got off Naomi and just gazed out to sea. The wind was blowing strongly, but there was a silence in the air that was almost deafening.

"You know, Babs," Buster said, contemplating, "It's amazing that after being in some of the most important cities in the world, I come back here and discover a certain peace, a silence that's just so marvelously incredible. All those cities are so fucking noisy, filled with mass confusion."

"Yes, I know. I noticed that when I was in Toronto."

"But this place—it's so silent—it's unbelievable what there is in nature. It just soothes the soul, you know what I mean?"

"Yes, I sure do. It is amazing, eh?"

They sat down on the edge of a cliff looking down into the breaking water over the rocks. The rest of the afternoon they both sat in quiet contemplation, reflecting on themselves, the summer apart, what they had and what they were losing, and their uncertain futures. This time it was definitely the last that they were together: true ships passing in the night.

The next day Barbara Oskalowski whizzed off the island with no words of parting, and leaving almost no signs whatsoever of ever even having returned to the island. Buster was only assured that she had left San Salvador when Corporal Nightburn came cruising on the campus and informed him in a most casual, modest way: "Your fun's gone now, Murdunked!" The Cop smiled maliciously.

Meanwhile, Buster was too busy for anymore crying over a "Fucking" woman. He was fed up and could not even think about Babs anymore: he refused to waste any more energy on something he could not do anything about. He was in the process of changing apartments— which represented the beginnings of a whole new world on the island. He had received permission from Mr. Ginnis to move into the new efficiency apartment that they had built over the summer. Actually, it was not a new apartment in itself. It was really the old video tape recording studio. They had just converted it into an apartment, petitioning it off into a bedroom, living room and dividing the living room and kitchen with a large bar. A small bathroom and shower was off to the side. It was a nice little place, even though it was further away from the beach than the other and was closer to the electric, station. But at least Buster was now away from Patrick Cramble's mongoloid idiosyncrasies and out of the room that haunted him with the past of Barbara memories.

The first couple of weeks back on the island was time for meeting new people and reacquainting himself with old timers. The old Bachrans, the retiring British ex-patriots, were back. They had never left; but as usual, they kept pretty much to themselves in the confines of their apartment close to their booze. The Troffs were back in all their hypertension, representing the only few remaining white people still living in the cottages. The rest of the old timers were black Bahamians in all their glory, enjoying the fruits of their newly attained independence. Mr. Ginnis and family were still in their cottage on the beach side, now accompanied by their neighbors, Osborne Stubbs, Father Villeneuve and his wife, Anne, and a new black American English department head, Mrs. Abernathy, who took the place of the Kentards. This woman later turned out to be for Buster a true black witch in disguise. The only other whites living in the cottage area, right next to the Troffs on the roadside, were a new American family called the Cowmans. Leonard Cowman, a tall, thickly bearded, balding man of thirty-eight, along with his attractive blonde wife, Joanne, and their three young children, seemed to add unwanted salt to the predominantly black, elite neighborhood.

Another new white man on San Salvador was the motorcyclist, Bub Sudner, a short, stocky, light-haired, shaggy-dog-cropped English divorcee with a face that looked like a thin-lipped boxer hound. He was the new Physical Education coach at the high school, but frequented the college campus often—he liked the black girl students.

And speaking of students, the college got off to a bad start. It was mass confusion from the very beginning. Nobody knew where to go, nor did they have student schedules worked out in the administration office. Plus having a shortage of teachers did not help matters. The Ministry of Education was fast in kicking the British out of the country, but extremely slow in hiring the Bahamians. But they could not hire Bahamians to teach because there were not any qualified teachers to be hired. However, because of their independence fervor, which included ego and national pride, they would rather do without.

This meant extra teaching hours for everybody. An island "Do Better" campaign set off by the vice principal, Mr. Osborne Stubbs, started all the classes at eight o'clock in the morning—something unheard of previously in the history of the college. But Mister Osborne Stubbs thought that laziness could be cured by getting up early in the morning and that a productive student would make for a productive Bahamas. Right! He even went as far as to organize a "Get up—Get up—Rise and Shine" Club. The members of this new organization would get up at six o'clock in the morning and take healthy jogs around the campus and down on the beach. A healthy student meant a healthy Bahamas. Right!

After two weeks when things started settling down and people started groping around to their respective classes, the first English department meeting was called. Mr. Bachran was ill and was unable to attend the meeting. So Patrick Cramble and Buster Murdock gathered around a table in the library to hear what Mrs. Abernathy had to say. She would have a tough act to follow after Peter Kentard's six years of building up the English department. However, after what Mrs. Abernathy saw, her first impression was that she could do much better as the boss.

She started the meeting off by giving her background: she was a fifty year old widow from Southern Indiana and presently doing field work for her Ph.D. at Fordham University in New York City. She considered herself a liberal black American and that even though it was her first time in the Bahamas, she told her subordinates that she knew these Bahamians well. They were her people, and she could understand them.

"I am absolutely appalled," she said, as the English teachers sat at the round table, politely listening, "with what the former head has done to this department. The library is in shambles. It is unorganized and incomplete. The English classes must be tightened up with more of a definition as to what is to be taught. These damn, white British have ruined this island and it's up to us to make it what it's supposed to be."

"Uh, excuse me, Mrs. Aberpanthy," Buster interrupted.

"Abernathy!" she corrected him with a stiff upper lip.

"Uh, yes, Abernathy, but I uh, think that uh, the library was in pretty good shape, considering what Mr. Kentard had available. He made this library. Why if it weren't for him, there would be no books here at all! And the books are, in fact, categorized and in alphabetical order. I see no…"

Taking her glasses off, she forcefully interrupted the young, bearded teacher, "Mr. Murdock, this library is a disgrace—thanks to the British. And I see now that I myself will have to rearrange it. I, plus my designated student helpers, will take all books from the shelf and categorize them according to the Dewey Decimal System."

Cramble just sat there with his hands folded, nodding his head and agreeing with everything she said.

"As for your classes," she continued authoritatively, "you all have your designated assignments. Now I want lesson plan outlines for each class showing me what you are planning on doing for the term. Is this clear?"

"Yes, Ma'am," Cramble said.

"Uh, just one thing, Mrs. Aber—Abernathy," Buster said sneering. "What do you have against the British?

"Mr. Murdock," she said matter-of-factly, "I find it very difficult to have a favorable side for a race of people who, first, invented racism, and second, tried to destroy countries. They tried to destroy ours, but we Americans would not let them. They tried to destroy the Bahamas, but fortunately these people, my people, refused to let them. And this is not to mention what they tried to do in India. Now if that's understood, we shall go now, for we have lots of work to do." She stood up and went to her office in the library.

Buster wanted to ask her how she could really know the Bahamians after being on the island for only three weeks, but her direct beeline to the office was too fast. He had a strong suspicion that she had been talking to Mr. Ginnis, Father Villeneuve and clan.

Buster walked out of the library with Cramble. "Well, Jesus, whataya think, Cramble?" he asked.

"Oh, I think she's very good—we'll get a lot done this year!"

"Yeah, you would think that way. Look, I'll catch you later!"

*Jesus Christ, what an Asshole*, he thought walking back

to his new apartment. *Cramble, I mean Abernathy, I mean the both of them! Jesus, what a fucked up woman! Absolutely fucked up! And I gotta work with this bitch? And poor ol' man Bachran, the only British English teacher—Jesus, if he were only there.*

Buster made it back to his apartment and cooked some scrambled eggs, but found it difficult to eat them. *How could anybody think that way?* he pondered. *And why is it that people with newly obtained positions with a little power in their hands always try to change things at the very beginning—try to change everything and reinvent the wheel in just a matter of a few weeks?* He could not understand it. He went to the Riding Rock Inn for the rest of the afternoon to try and forget the people he would have to work with for at least another term. It was enough to depress him for a long time.

The first month back on the island was the most difficult for Buster—mainly because it was such a world so distinct from the island life he was used to before. The hardest part was getting over Babs— doing things without her, going places where they used to go together, seeing familiar things. And answering questions from both the natives and students as to where she was and why they separated made it even worse to forget. Also, his job did not help much because it was hard enough for him to even look at such a sour—grape face as Mrs. Abernathy's every morning at eight o'clock on the way to class, let alone talk to her. He made up his mind to stay away from this woman and have as little to do with her as possible.

So he decided it would be best not to have any contact with the outside world for a while. He would "Monk- Out" and socialize not at all. He would hibernate in his new apartment, leaving it only for walks on the beach or to buy food. He would go straight in and out of class doing only what his profession demanded of him and nothing extra.

His classes seemed to be pretty much like last year's with compositions and Caribbean literature. But these were so boring. The students were so lethargic and uninterested, that it seemed that the only class with any life to it was his Speech and Drama class. Because of this life and enthusiasm, he decided to write a small play for the class and put it on as a late autumn, student project. Therefore, he used his "Monk-Out" sessions for writing the play. He enjoyed himself immensely, writing the play. Teaching was just plain work for him; however, writing served as a good diversion. It was healthy mental therapy. Many days Buster worked hours upon hours on it and sometimes way into the small hours of the morning. He would wind himself up into the actions of the characters, lose himself completely and forget the things of the past and the horrors of the present. He wanted his students to be able to identify with it. So he always kept in mind his particular students to be the actors and made the setting San Salvador with the plot centering around love affairs and student life at the Teachers' College. He even wrote songs for it—pounding out melodies on his guitar, knowing that with the black, soul touch to them, his singers would carry his new tunes to spiritual heights.

But monking-out at times got difficult, especially in his new apartment. The weather was suffocatingly hot and muggy. An afternoon sea breeze kicked up around four o'clock, but it stopped completely after seven. The air conditioner he moved over from his old apartment was too big for the electric current on the dormitory block, and after only five minutes of cool air, it would blow every fuse in the building. So with the air conditioner out, he had to keep the screened windows open and pray for any puff of air that might come off the sea.

Another problem was mosquitoes. Gigantic mosquitoes, literally the size of fists sometimes came in huge swarms off the shallow, salt-water, interior lakes, squeezing through the screens of the open windows and attacking the human occupant, seemingly taking big hunks of skin with every bite. There was really no remedy to the situation, because if he bombed the room with Baygon insect spray, he would have to go outside for at least a half an hour to breathe some air. But going outside was murder because of the millions of mosquitoes waiting in line trying to get inside. They would land on his arms, hundreds at a time, virtually covering his skin like a blanket and sucking up blood like lemonade through a straw. They certainly did not show these things in the Bahamian travel brochures. That was for sure!

But conquering mountains was easy for Buster on San Salvador. He was bound and determined to be a man and withstand all those "Fucking Asshole" mosquitoes and "God-damned" heat. The nearing of October brought on the near completion of his play and a feeling of contentment and satisfaction of having accomplished something. He started going out more at night and socializing with newfound friends. One of these friends was Chris Opurst, the new Coast Guard captain. Buster, at first, never believed he would associate with a straight society Academy man, but he soon found out that they both had a lot of things in common. And even though Opurst did not "Blow Dope," he was young, single and attracted to the Finger Lakers just like everybody else. He also knew a lot about the sea—something Buster liked so much he could talk about it for hours. There was something about the sea, Buster thought, which brought a kind of unity to men found nowhere else on Earth.

One night over a beer at the Riding Rock, Buster expressed his interest in learning navigation. Opurst suggested immediately that they ought to offer a celestial navigation class at the college. He would offer his services, free of charge, as a diplomatic gesture of Coast Guard goodwill to the civilians on the island. The very next day, after securing permission from Mr. Ginnis, Buster ran off several leaflets on the ditto machine announcing the class. It would be held every Thursday night at eight o'clock at Buster's apartment, with the official U.S. Coast Guard Captain Opurst as the honorable instructor. He tacked up the announcements all over the campus and Cockburn Town, hoping for a grand turnout.

After a week of advertising and talking up the class, the first night brought in a grand total of six people. Leonard and Joanne Cowman were the first to appear, for they had high hopes of one day living aboard a yacht. They thought that this navigation knowledge would be very useful to them. Then came stumbling in Bub Sudner with his beady eyes, wiry lips and puffy face, ready to listen to an American seaman. And wonders upon wonders, two college students actually came drifting in to see what this class was all about. With Buster rolling in a portable blackboard and using the bar as a pulpit, the captain, in full U.S. Coast Guard dress uniform, first went into a small, formal history of himself. The twenty-four year old officer looked like a true, military instructor. However, he did not really realize that his students were not academy cadets, but simply a motley group of civilian sailors sitting in a semi-circle on the sofa and chairs in front of him. After an hour-and-a-half of basic explanation and chart description, Buster broke out the rum and Cokes and popcorn. The party began and a Thursday night tradition was established.

The first holiday of the academic term was October twelfth, Columbus Day. Everybody on the island took the day off to go to the grand carnival near the Coast Guard dock. There was a makeshift straw market there with natives selling their goods. The smell of hot dogs and conch fritters filled the air and there was plenty of Coca Cola and red rum punch to go around. Local bands supplied the typical Bahamian beat, and everybody, including the white tourists, was decked out in straw hats, shorts, and dashikis.

The main event of the day was the sailboat race. There were fifteen Bahamian fishing skiffs all lined up on the beach near the dock ready to push off at the sound of the gun. The captains and crews of each boat were making last minute preparations on their riggings. Buster Murdock, who kept thinking he was Papillon, was also working on his borrowed skiff, loading it up with cement blocks to give it enough ballast so that it would sit right in the water and not tip over. It was an ancient, fourteen-foot craft that none of the islanders would go near; but when one of the local fisherman from the United Estates Village offered it to Buster for the race, the young sailor's mind went wild for another Papillon-style "Cavale" and he could not refuse.

"Hey, what are you doing Murdock?" asked Chris Opurst, just coming down from the base.

"Howdy, Captain, what's happenin'? I'm just loading this Baby up for ballast. Ya know what I mean?"

"You don't mean to tell me that you're going out in that thing, do you?"

"Sure man, why not? You wanna come with me?"

"Not on your life, Buddy!"

"Come on Skipper—give a fellow American a hand, eh? I need some help here, can't you see?"

"Boy, you're gonna be needing more than help—I'll tell you that!"

"You're an Academy man, aren't you?" Buster asked.

"Yeah."

"Well then hell, man, show your skill!"

"Sorry, Murdock, but not in that thing! Absolutely not!"

"Hey, look, Captain, you're not in uniform now and you don't gotta have one to be on my ship—c'mon man!"

"Christ! I know I shouldn't do this!" He thought for a moment more, "But... OK—I'll go with you!"

"Thanks, man, we'll have a good chance now—Great!"

"At least let me go get my officer's hat," the captain said, smiling. "I can sail better with it."

"Right!" Buster said, loading up more concrete blocks. "Hey, Captain, we'll show these 'Bohemians' what real sailing is like!"

"Right!"

The crowd gathered around on the dock to listen to the island commissioner give his annual speech, saying how great it was to be a San Salvadorian. He also reminded the crowd, as if it needed to be reminded, that it was only some four hundred odd years ago that Columbus made his first footprints in the New World. The crowd stood solemnly as the warm wind came stiffly down from the North, flapping their loose clothes against their bodies like flags against a mast.

When the old, political windbag finally finished rambling, he yelled to the seamen standing by their boats on shore: "And now, at the sound of the gun, contestants will commence!"

A loud twenty-two pistol shot sound mixed in with the brisk breeze and the yelling of the sailors; they were off and running. They pushed their skiffs off the white sand and into clear turquoise colored water. The skilled fishermen immediately hoisted their dirty white sails, and the fifteen skiffs went skimming across the water passing the starting line buoy and speeding towards the halfway marker-buoy two miles off shore. Every crew on each boat worked with such rapid skill that it was easy to tell that they had been doing this all their lives. They passed the starting buoy with such graceful ease that it seemed like the Master himself, Christopher Columbus, was helping them in some way or another.

But as for the white misfits, it seemed like Amerigo Vespucci was seeking revenge for the English conquest of the North American continent. Buster and the captain had pushed off all right, but the boat, instead of skimming smoothly across the water, only bobbed up and down, back and forth like a bath tub. With Buster at the tiller, he tried to keep the boat heading straight into the waves while the captain tried to raise the sail. But the halyard got stuck in the pulley at the top of the mast and the sail went up only half way. Opurst, therefore, climbed up the mast while Buster, tiller in one hand, started bailing out the boat with the other because the waves at times were spilling over the railings— not that there were that many waves; it's just that the boat sat so low in the water with all those concrete blocks for ballast.

Finally, setting the entire sail, they had to tack close to the dock, make a come-about and then tack back to the starting buoy. As Buster was making a successful turn dangerously close to the dock, he could see the whites of the eyes of the smiling black crowd, their white teeth glistening in the sun. The whole mass seemed to be laughing at the trouble the boys were having. Many men on the dock were pointing at them, their heads jerked back in hard laughter. Some of the Bahama Mamas were bent over double, slapping their legs and screeching at the boat that hadn't even crossed the starting line yet, while all the other boats were nearing the two-mile marker.

"Hey, Captain," Buster shouted, "Look at all those Bastards up there laughin' at us— Sons of Bitches! We'll show them!"

"Hey, Murdock," the young captain yelled, "What kind of boat did you get here? This has gotta be a joke—and the joke's on you for takin' it!"

"You mean the joke's on us, Brother. We're in on this together! Hey, shift you're body a little bit towards the middle more, will ya? This boat don't seem to be too seaworthy— ya know what I mean?'

"Christ, how did I let myself get involved in this? I'm the U.S. Coast Guard Captain and we can't even get across the fucking starting line!"

"Captain, watch your fucking language! Do you see the buoy up there close? Are we close?"

"Yeah, just keep going—you're all right. Pull in on the boom a little bit and we'll catch a little more speed. I'll start bailing out some of this fucking…"

He was cut off. Complying with the orders of the captain, Buster pulled in on the boom but much too rapidly. A gigantic white-capped wave hit the boat broadside. With the extra heel from pulling in on the boom, the wave went right over the railing and completely swamped the skiff, suddenly stopping its forward motion and slowly sinking it towards the bottom. There was nothing else the crew could do. They sat close to each other on the railing just looking at one another in complete disbelief as they slowly went down with the ship: the crowd on the dock in uncontrolled hysterics, going absolutely berserk.

The Coast Guard captain was not seen in public for several weeks after that. He even skipped navigation class and had nothing to do with Buster Murdock. He hibernated in his officer's quarters, making macramé nets for Portuguese fish balls. Buster really could not understand this reaction, but he really did not care that much either. *Win a few friends, lose a few friends*, he thought. Friends rapidly came into his life and disappeared just as fast—he had no control over this phenomenon.

Just as fast as Chris Opurst went out, George Bunson came in. Bunson was a thirty-five year old millionaire stockbroker from Falls Church, Virginia. He played around with the stock market for three months out of the year, then the rest of the year he just played around in the Bahamas, hopping from island to island in his little Piper Cub airplane. When he landed on San Salvador he stayed at his own private house in the United Estates Village. He was so fat and chubby that everybody called him Santa Claus. At Christmas time he was even known to go island hopping in a Santa Claus suit, giving out gifts as he pranced through each little village.

But George Bunson was also so fat and chubby that no amount of money would help him in obtaining the love of a woman. So to suffice for his sexual needs, he always lugged around with him in his airplane a Super Eight movie projector and a whole trunk filled with sex films—hard core pornography—downright motion picture smut.

When word got around that Santa Claus was on the

island, most of the single men, including Buster Murdock, swarmed around Santa's place every night to watch the action in living color on Bunson's gigantic screen. While drinking beer and rum, the audience's eyes feasted on life-size moving images of two-foot long penises penetrating Lincoln—Tunnel size vaginas, and gigantic boxer dogs foaming at the mouth and having violent contractions over nymphomaniacs with their tongues hanging out. It didn't take much to keep the boys happy. Santa made sure of that!

Watching all this sex was good, healthy stimulation for all these boys on the island. At least it showed them that there were women in the world and that a good, healthy sex life was possibly awaiting them off this God-awful, end-of-the-earth, seemingly womanless island. And anyway, it kept the men off the streets and away from the goats. When Bunson left for another island a few weeks later, he took the movies with him to share with others his joy and well being, leaving the lonely men on San Salvador high and dry—for a few days anyway.

But word got around fast that the young Troffs at the college were in heat and were doing strange things out of the norm: things like "Fucking around" to mention one of them. As a result of this rumor, the Coasties had their eyes and ears open, always abiding by their motto, "Be Prepared." When they realized what was in front of them, a woman by the name of Anne Troff, they took advantage of the situation and preyed on her like lions after a wounded antelope.

The fact was that Anne could not reach an orgasm easily with her husband, David. He would have to make love to her several times before she could even come close to having one; and most of the time when she was just about to climax, David would flake out with sheer exhaustion and leave his wife in mid air. They had tried everything in the book to get their "Jackies" together, but it just did not seem to work. This is where Chief Bilgo came in last spring. Buster later found out, through Anne's confession, that Bilgo would do all the work. He would fuck Anne a couple times, getting her very hot, and when she was just about to have an orgasm, David would mount and penetrate. The married couple would then terminate together in true, orgasmic love. So thanks to Chief Bilgo; even though he nauseatingly sucked his teeth after every meal, he was a marriage saver.

But because Chief Bilgo was transferred off the island in September, the Troffs went hunting for a new sex partner. They singled out Buster first, for he was young, single, available and attractive to Anne. They went over to his house one night, invited by Buster himself to play Scrabble; but before they even got passed the first word, which just happened to end up being the word "Fuck," David started to explain their little family problem. After only two more words, Fez and Feet, the proposition was made. However, Buster, being as pure as he was and really not interested in being used and abused like that, expressed disinterest. He said he would rather work on his play. The Troffs took offense to this and immediately left the American to play "Fucking Scrabble with himself," as Anne bluntly put it.

So the couple started working again on the Coast Guard: As David Troff's philosophy was, "Where there is one, there's more." And when there were two there were three, and when there were three there were a hundred. Pretty soon Anne was balling up to eight Coasties at a time, realizing very little that the more men she fornicated with right in front of the eyes of her onlooking husband, the harder it became for her to have an orgasm.

And nobody realized, above all the Coasties, that the more the Troffs frequented the Coast Guard barracks, the more the couple themselves were becoming mentally unstable. Anne would go into her elementary classroom at times in the morning and in the middle of a song, playing the piano, she would break down and cry right in front of her six and seven year old students. David, as well, did not know what was going on. Sometimes on those mornings after, he would trot into class, glassy eyed with that empty stare of the mentally insane, and belch out fragmented sentences and write indecipherable equations on the blackboard— his mind just not being in the classroom at all.

David started complaining of the conditions at the college and started broadcasting to the students that the administration was incompetent and a disgrace to the Bahamian government. Anne also began to complain to the island commissioner that the living conditions were deplorably intolerable and that if something was not done, they would have to leave.

And leave they finally did. Late one night in the early part of November, sailors were literally waiting in line for their turn to pounce on "Little Annie Fannie," as the Coasties had nicknamed Mrs. Troff. David calmly sat in the corner anxiously waiting to enjoy those few seconds of ecstasy that his wife took so long to reach. Suddenly the captain walked into the barracks and discovered the parade. He busted everybody. He ordered all his men back to their rooms immediately. Then, he not only banned the English couple from entering the military premises again, but also threatened island government disciplinary action.

But before it got too deep and to avoid further scandal, the couple wisely left the island the following day, disappearing forever, like a puff of smoke, from the eyes of the inhabitants of San Salvador.

The sudden departure of the Troffs marked the beginning of an epidemic of whites leaving the island. The Coast Guard captain was quickly losing popularity among his men and was having his problems. Being an Academy man, he was definitely not used to working with such a loose-knit outfit, and he was not quite sure how to handle it. Putting all of his men on probation except the new chief, Chris Jacobs, a forty-year old career boy, did not help his rapport. But when the chief took advantage of his liberty, this added oil to the fire. Chief Jacobs continually took the Coast Guard van back and forth to the Riding Rock Inn and carried on an intense love affair with Mrs. Finnan, the wife of one of the resident owners of the hotel. When the chief, at times, failed to report in to the station, even after several days at a time, Opurst really had no other alternative than to confront the career man with the possibility of disciplinary measures. When the time came for this confrontation, the chief, a bit drunk, blew up and lost all composure. He started yelling at his commanding officer, accusing him of being a little, spoon-fed military academy boy with no experience, trying to tell a career man with twenty years in the service what to do.

Opurst quietly listened the chief out, then sent him on the next plane back to Fort Lauderdale under military police surveillance and under a strong recommendation of Court Martial on grounds of disobedience, subversion and absence without leave. Opurst, though young and inexperienced, was no fool.

Shortly thereafter, Mrs. Finnan suddenly fled the island in the Riding Rock Cessna, barely escaping with her life the wrath of her husband's jealousy. At first, Mr. Finnan himself approved of the affair, rationalizing that all was fair in love and war, and that if she could do it he could do it and vice-versa, etcetera, etcetera. But watching his wife walk romantically hand in hand down the beach with that ugly non-commissioned officer and watching them skinny dip late at night in his own swimming pool, then seeing them return for the evening to one of the cottages that he himself helped to build got to be too much for him. He just could not bare the strain—especially when there were not any other women to go around on the island. Mr. Finnan got a little drunk one night and started smacking his wife around the cottage room, calling her a dirty, rotten whore and threatening to feed her to the sharks. But she jumped out the window and ran down to the airstrip, spending the night in the bushes and waiting for the plane to come in so she could get on board and return safely, but in disgrace, back to the continent.

Things at the college did not look too swift, either. Dr. Leonard Cowman's diligence and dedication to the field of Education was highly admirable amongst his peers. He was even one of Buster's idols, a great friend and counsel. But these qualities were what destroyed Cowman on San Salvador. He came to the island with great hopes of trying to improve the college —slowly and in his own professional way with no hurry. He was really the only teacher on campus that had exciting new ideas for change within the college. It was not change in the sense of Mrs. Abernathy's change, that of revamping the whole library, but that of slow change, using the mistakes of the past to build for the future. And, these ideas were merely ideas. Cowman merely made suggestions as to how to better the institution.

Suggestions like: "Maybe we could have group teachers' meetings where the teachers could all sit on the floor and get to know each other better;" or suggestions such as, "There ought to be a student counselor service informing students of opportunities in other parts of the world."

But Mr. Ginnis and clan saw this as a communist plot to overthrow his administration. It was a definite threat to the further advancement of Bahamian progress. Cowman, therefore, was placed on Ginnis' black list. He purposely spread rumors around that Cowman was a useless lecturer and was not needed on the San Salvador campus. And to complicate matters even worse, Ginnis forbade Cowman's children to play with his children because the little white boys were a bad influence on the pure race of the island.

Cowman was so upset upon hearing these far out rumors that he could not even talk for a couple days. He did not mind these people attacking him, but when the accusations hit directly at his children, they really hurt him. Cowman was a sensitive man and was not the type to blow up like the chief at the Coast Guard, for example. He was the type of man that withdrew inside himself to try and understand the why and wherefore of things. And that is exactly what he did upon receiving these bizarre attacks. Being new and not understanding island living nor Bahamian culture was very bewildering for him. He went over to Buster's place several times and talked about the problem for hours. Buster was the only American on campus—that is, the only American he could really talk to. According to Cowman, this guy Cramble was not any nationality— he was just a "Rat's Ass Zombie."

When the hour of truth came, Cowman 's confrontation with Ginnis was a mere energy-less absurdity. Cowman entered the office and just stood there looking down at a scared, little, pudgy man sitting behind a desk playing principal, accusing an American Doctor of Philosophy, the highest achievement in American education, of being useless and not needed. The only thing the bearded, Caucasian could do was to turn around and walk out, saying to himself, "Hang it up brother— what the fuck am I doing here?"

That very same day Dr. Leonard Cowman submitted his letter of resignation, effective in December, the end of the term.

Even Buster started to have his problems. Although at the time he did not know it, his problems really started when he finished writing his play. He had the cast of characters all set and the rehearsals had begun. It was a good play entitled *A Funny, Unexpected Way*. It was three entire Acts with five songs, written and composed by the master himself, Buster Murdock. It was about a student love affair on campus, complete with typical scenes of dormitory bull sessions and Harlem Square Rip scenes. The plot was simple—boy meets girl type of thing with the dialogue in the local Bahamian accent.

The students took to the play immediately and were highly enthusiastic. It was just as Buster had figured: as he played the tunes to the songs on his guitar, the students' inborn feeling for music picked up the rhythm and put such soul to them that it was like the Spirit itself singing away. Buster was awed, amazed and completely satisfied with what his students could do to his songs. It was such a great feeling for him. He experienced such a tremendous sense of accomplishment, that all those hours of slaving over the typewriter—all those hellish, hot nights with the mosquitoes and sweat, all seemed like a mere dream now. It was all worth every minute of it.

Then one morning after class, Mrs. Abernathy, alias Mrs. Sour Grapes, as Buster called her, approached the young playwright and demanded a copy of the play. Buster, with pride, presented her gently with a copy and politely said that he hoped she would like it.

The following morning Mrs. Abernathy, with glasses down on her nose, swiftly appeared at Buster's classroom door, interrupting a lecture. "Mr. Murdock, I would like to see you in my office immediately after class," she said dryly.

"Yes, Ma'am," he replied. And the rest of the lecture all he could think about was what this lady wanted from him.

After class he made a straight beeline to the library, overstepping books strewn all over the floor. These books were in the process of being re-classified and re-shelved —a process that had taken the whole term thus far, and would not be finished until late spring— a process which impeded Buster from giving any library assignments to his students. When he entered her office, Buster saw Mrs. Abernathy, in all her *Wizard of Oz*, Wicked Witch of the East demeanor, thumbing through his play.

"Mr. Murdock, have a seat please!"

"Yes, Ma'am."

"Mr. Murdock, first I would like to say that I am absolutely shocked at what you have written here."

"Shocked, Mrs. Abernathy?"

"Yes appalled is maybe the better word."

Buster let out a chuckle. "Huh, huh—in what way? What do you mean, Mrs. Abernathy?"

"I mean, Mr. Murdock, that this can hardly be considered to have any form of literary value whatsoever!"

"Well, I must admit that I'm no fuc…— uh, that is Shakespeare, but I do believe that it captivates the flavor of college life here on the island."

"Hardly so, Mr. Murdock. It is dirty, filthy, almost pornographic and it must be cleaned up at once!"

"Ha, ha, ha, ha! That's a good one, Mrs. Abernathy," he said. *Surely she was joking*, he thought. *Pornographic? Ha! There are a few kissing and romantic embracing scenes underneath the San Salvador moonlight— but pornographic? And there are a few swear words in the student bull sessions, but they would sound almost angelic to any sailor's ears.* "Ha, Mrs. Abernathy, did you like the part where the…?"

"Mr. Murdock, I am very busy," she interrupted. "All I want to say is that you must re-write this entire work and make it decent and respectable for the people on this island. And I want to see the revision before you continue with anymore rehearsals— is that clear?"

"Uh… wait a minute now— are you serious, Mrs. Abernathy?" Buster got a sudden sensation over his whole body that told him that maybe she was.

"That will be all, Mr. Murdock!"

Anger welled up inside him. He was not the kind to get angry, abused and beat up by old ladies, but there was always a first time. Thoughts rushed through his mind: *Who is she to be literary critic, a so-called Ph.D candidate in Elementary School Education? Who is she to be the judge of people's tastes— especially people of a different country with customs and traditions totally different from her upbringing?*

"Mrs. Abernathy, I don't know what you think these students are, but they are not little children, you know! They're grown up adults with adult, human feelings and attitudes. You can't go around treating them like five year old kids."

"Mr. Murdock, I know these people. They are my people— I feel close to them and I know what they are and know what they like. They are black and I know where they come from. That will be all!"

"How do you know these people? You may be black, but, Jesus, that has nothing to do with it! You are an American, not Bahamian! You've been on this island only for a few months. You don't know the culture, you don't know where these people come from, you don't know what they really think like. These are island people, not your Fordham, New York City madness race of people."

"Mr. Murdock, I said that will be all— you must go now!"

"No, I won't go!" he yelled and suddenly stood up. "I worked long and hard on this play and all my students like it. You just can't throw it back in our faces and tell us we can't put it on just because it doesn't fit your tastes."

"You heard me and my word is final. Clean it up or don't put it on!"

"Well you just lost a God- damn drama instructor then. Do a little kiddie play yourself!" He grabbed the copy of his play and stormed out of the office, tripping over a set of Encyclopedia Britannicas. But he nobly picked himself up off the floor and casually walked out of the old, converted radar center.

The only thing Buster could think of doing after that was to go over to Cowman's place and bitch. However, Cowman was having problems of his own. Joanne, his wife, had just accidently sprayed the Ginnis' flowers with water from a hose. Mrs. Ginnis had come running out of the house, yelling and screaming, telling Joanne to water her own damn flowers. Cowman was not very receptive to anybody.

Buster then went immediately to Father Villeneuve 's cottage and gave him the play to read. He asked Father to read it and if he found anything immoral, dirty or filthy with the play, then he would not put it on. Father, the next day, came over to Buster's apartment and returned the folder. He told Buster that he had thoroughly enjoyed the work. It indeed captured the mentality and actions of campus life, and that he found nothing whatsoever dirty, filthy or immoral with it. However, if that was the way Mrs. Abernathy felt about it, then Buster should heed to her way of thinking and not "Rock the boat!" Buster just looked at the lean man wearing a cross and said silently to himself that this man should just go directly to hell.

Buster was depressed for days. His first real work of art had been, according to

him, unjustifiably rejected. He felt crucified. What was worse was telling his students to forget it. To see their long drawn faces and hanging heads brought tears to his eyes.

He tried to forget what was happening to him. He tried to drink a bottle of rum like those pirates in the movies; but he only got halfway down the bottle and threw up. Getting stoned was no solution, either: the high just made him more depressed.

In a matter of only a few days, it seemed that Buster's whole Bahamian world came tumbling down on top of him. A few nights after his confrontation with the rum bottle, he met Bub Sudner at the Riding Bock bar and had a few drinks with him. Sudner started in on stories of his first few days on San Salvador and how he had met Barbara Oskalowski.

"But you didn't do anything with her, did you?" Buster asked.

"Well, yes, in fact I did," he said in his English accent.

"Like what?" Buster said, anxiously downing a gin and tonic.

"Well, let's see, we took a few trips around the island on my motorbike— and I must admit, we hopped about a bit in the sack."

"No you didn't, Bub, come on— you don't gotta brag!".

"I'm not braggin' mate. I'm just tellin' you we did, that's all!"

"Well, I knew Babs last year intimately— and she's not that kind of girl to be bed hopping like that— besides, her old boyfriend was with her." Buster ordered another drink.

"Oh, that bloke! Yeah, I remember him. Bloody useless fellow, he was. She got rid of him shortly, though, and was soon a free girl… until you came and blew it for me."

"Well, she was my girl, God-dammit! And I still don't believe you did anything with her. I just don't believe it!"

"And I'm telling you I did!" He laughed.

"OK, Sudner, if you did, then where is her mole?" They both broke out in laughter.

"I don't know that!" Sudner said.

"OK, then you didn't!"

"And I'm tellin' you I did!"

"Well fuck! At least I know where her fucking mole is!"

"Well, I must say, ol' chap—you got me beat on that one!" He gazed into his drink, then looked back at Buster. "By the way, ol' boy, where is her bloody mole?'

"It's on her left cheek, just to the side of her asshole."

Sudner went into a rugby song, "Rum, pum pum, five fingers up her bum!'

And the two proceeded to finish out the evening, drinking each other underneath the table. Buster went down first.

9 December, 1974

Permanent Secretary
UPS Head Teacher
Ministry of Education and Culture
Nassau, Bahamas

Dear Permanent Secretary:

Because of my disillusionment in small island living, and due to the fact that my talents have not been given sufficient opportunity to be utilized, I have been forced into a seemingly inevitable situation on the island of San Salvador. Therefore, after long, careful consideration and weighing of all factors involved, I feel in all fairness to myself, students, faculty and administrators alike that it would be best for me to resign my lecturing position at the San Salvador Teachers' Training College, San Salvador, Bahamas.

I have thoroughly enjoyed my stay in the Bahamas and leave the islands with only fond memories. As I leave for other parts of the globe, I would like to wish this country all the luck in the world as a free and independent nation.

Sincerely Yours,
Signed, Buster Murdock I

It was inevitable. Buster had thought about it and thought about it until he could not think about it anymore. Too many negative things were coming down to stick around on San Salvador. Everything seemed to be dissolving: The Rise and Shine Club had dwindled down to one member and that was Osborne Stubbs himself; all possibilities of the play had fizzled out; all possibilities of getting laid diminished to absolute zero; there were no more navigation classes; his dope supply was depleted; faith in Barbara Oskalowski and in womankind in general became virtually non-existent; and his spirits reached an all-time low. It was time to move on: there was really no other choice, no other decision to make.

# EPILOGUE

"Columbia, Venezuela, Saudi Arabia, India, anyone? Curse the thought of going back to the United States. *What would I do back there?* Buster thought. *Teach high school English to giddy adolescents? Teach junior college to pimple-faced know-it-alls? Lecture at a university to scraggly bearded intellectuals who live off the old man's dough? Fuck— I'd rather sell used cars. And what else? Jesus, I suppose I could meet some nice American chickadee whom I could marry and settle down with and have a nice little house, a station wagon, a few kiddies, social security and all that other madness. Oh my God—I'd rather sail off the edge of the earth."*

And these were the thoughts Buster was having on the *San Salvador Express* back to Nassau. He was thinking in terms of the future now rather than of the past. He would leave Cramble, Villeneuve, Abernathy and all the others like them to wallow in their ignorance forever. They would not have Buster Murdock to kick around anymore. And his future thinking was only immediate. Of course he would have to settle a few things on New Providence before he went home for Christmas: such as go to the Ministry and settle affairs, sell Naomi to the best offer, and go to the Bank of Canada to close his account. But then what? Then where?

But then again Buster thought that was the exciting thing about being abroad: being unstable, being unsure. Why was it that people sought out security, sought out some form of regularity and definitions for their lives? All that could be found in a jail cell. Why not be young, free, independent and adventurous? Why not move out, go to some place different, search the unknown? After all, wasn't that what Christopher Columbus did? If it were comfort and security he wanted, he never would have stepped onto the Santa Maria. Comfort and life assurance do not discover new horizons. So why not open the mind and learn wisdom from youthful folly rather than conform and drift into that sea of mediocre adult thinking that attracts so many unimaginative, non-creative souls?

Buster did not know where he was going to go or what he was going to do. He only knew one thing for sure: that he was not going back to the paradise found on San Salvador, Bahamas. Columbia, Venezuela, Saudi Arabia, India, anyone?